Prelude

THE NOCTURNE SYMPHONY

Prelude

LYRA R. SAENZ

4 Horsemen
Publications, Inc.

4 Horsemen Publications, Inc.
1497 Main St. Suite 169
Dunedin, FL 34698
4horsemenpublications.com
info@4horsemenpublications.com

Typeset by Sydney Wilder & Michelle Cline
Edited by JM Paquette
Triskele design by Sea Cat Art - Instagram @sea.cat.art

Paperback ISBN-13: 978-1-64450-256-3
Audiobook ISBN-13: 978-1-64450-254-9
Ebook ISBN-13: 978-1-64450-255-6

DEDICATION

To my parents, who have only ever supported my love of books, pens, and journals. To my loving partner, who puts up with my fancies. And to my dearest friends whose feedback helped make *Prelude* everything you will find in these pages.

TABLE OF CONTENTS

ACKNOWLEDGEMENTS

Thank you to Kinsey Britton of Sea Cat Art for her beautiful triskele design. And to my sensitivity readers Eiko Ito and Alan Sien Wei Hshieh.

The Wastes

Ser

Sekh

Aighneas

New
London

Orisvmi

Ebele

Deri

nim
Vatidomus
City
Shinka
Temple
Lorelei
City
Tokiseishu
Murasaki no Yama
Aureus
New
Chernobyl
The Tai Tai
tierra

Do you know why your blood sings in the night, witchling?

It's because there is magic in the moonlight. Our heavenly guardians. We are born under them. We die under them. We fall in love under them. And on those rare, starry nights when Deus's two moons dance in an eclipse, that, my child, is when soulmates come together.

"Koi and Dei–the Two Moons of Deus"
A Hexen myth passed down from mothers to
daughters for generations

1

PAGE OF SWORDS

Present Day–32nd Day in the Month of Fire 1877 A.P.–
Aventu Post

"NOCTURNE... WREN NOCTURNE..."
A voice calls her name, several voices... but the sound is muted, like she's underwater. Cradled by the ocean, she has been drifting here for a while. In the calm. In the quiet. How long has she been here, a buoy in the sea?

The voices drag her up, out of a pool of warm, comforting darkness to look into a searing sun.

"Songstress, please..."

"We have suffered."

"Make them pay...Make them all pay!"

The world is a portrait of black and gray, blurry at the edges, then sharpening into high definition, as though experienced through a camera lens. Then red. So much red. Red like blood. Blood red. And people, people standing around her in a circle— *it's so loud here*—girls and boys, mostly girls in dirty hospital gowns.

A thick shard of glass, a mirror, clenched in a fist at the other end of her consciousness.

PRELUDE

Too much stimuli.

A face not her own stares back at her—dark eyes, darker skin, dirty golden hair. This body is not her own. Its movements not her own. She is not in control.

"We found your ashes."

Another soul screams, trapped with her.

"We call you back!"

No, not trapped. In control.

Glass opens her veins, pushing into the tender flesh in which she resides.

What are you doing?

Three lines carved into each forearm—

Stop!

Blood pulses, hot and viscous, as archaic words echo back at her.

It hurts.

Sharp, ghostly pain felt intensely and yet dulled. Pain inflicted on someone else, but also her, but someone else, but still her.

The room vibrates, dark and angry.

Stop it!

And there's screaming. Deafening—*too much*—anguished wails...

Too much after nothing.

"They deserve to die."

Dark energy leeches off the bodies around her in waves as the flesh of each corpse sizzles.

"I demand...you ...you take... re-revenge for ussssss!"

A death rattle.

Let me out!

The energies collecting in the room collapse on her. The intention of each sacrifice forces its way into her subconscious, slicing through her psyche—*stop it*—and cries of pain slam into her. She writhes, agony coursing through her already mangled soul. For an eternity, their suffering is her own.

Enough!

Every abuse, every defilement, every humiliation. Their torment becomes a cage around her spirit, and with her trapped inside, the body dies.

She's been in a dying body before.

Let me out of here!

She screams and screams and screams and screams, but the souls of the dead are mute creatures and cannot be heard by the living. She reaches, grasping for the other soul housed in this body with her to save it to no avail. The contract is signed. The body of the dark-skinned girl is destroyed. Recycled. And redesigned. Bone, flesh, nerve-endings, skin, hair, nails, thoughts, her insides pulled to her outside. Her skin stretches and contracts, the hair ripped from her scalp and regrown, the body's limbs lengthen and shorten, the spine creaks and breaks, and her blood boils. Dying muscles seize and reanimate, and the convulsions begin. White hot and burning, her spirit is yanked out of the soothing waters of eternity, condensed to a fixed point, and shoved into a body too small and too large at once.

A body ripping itself apart. Changing itself to suit the needs of the new soul being jammed inside of it. Its new soul hooking into it like a parasite. The consciousness beside her own dissipates into the ether, and then...

...she's alone.

The seconds of rejection dissolve into whole-hearted acceptance, and her soul settles into the new skin. Awareness hits her like a hammer on an anvil. Real and kinesthetic in the worst possible way. Her pulse pounds erratically in her chest, and air forces its way into her lungs cold and unspeakably real. It's the first breath she's taken in a very long time, and she screams. Audibly, physically, screams.

She turns her head, and the acids of her stomach spill from her mouth.

She's naked, dressed in blood, bile thick in her throat and her head spinning. Her back aches against the cold of the floor, the stone hard and unyielding, like she has been lying on her back for hours, sticky and wet.

Her eyes flutter and then open.

She winces.

A single lightbulb flickers on and off above her. It sways gently. Her limbs feel heavy, but they are hers. She's in control. She moves gingerly onto her hands and knees.

The mirror shard lies on the floor beside her covered in gore. Her hand shakes as she picks up the piece of glass, but this time when she spies the reflection, Wren Nocturne stares back at her.

Wren's own face—sea-green irises, angular cheekbones, and dusty-pink lips with too much of a cupid's bow—stares back at her. Wren's hair—thick, blue-black tresses long enough to cascade over her breasts—falls in tangled waves around her face. Wren's fingertips come to her cheek to touch skin the color of sun-soaked wheat. The faint scar on her chin, earned from a nasty fall when she was a toddler, is missing, the skin smooth and untouched like a newborn babe's. This new skin is her old skin remade.

The bodies of those who resurrected her (*Other witches? Or just desperate people?*) are gone, dust in the wind. Runic sigils on the floor pulse with red luminesce. The symbols are familiar to her.

"Wren Nocturne... Please...Avenge us..."

The last whispered request echoes more in her head than in the room, and the blood-painted array quiets, turning black as the magic diminishes.

They have performed the *Ultimata Offret Kallar.*

A sacrificial resurrection: blood to make blood, flesh to make flesh, souls to call back a soul. A price to be paid in blood and life. A price she in turn will have to repay to those who brought her back whether she wants to or not. In the centuries since its creation, no one has ever performed it successfully. Wren researched it herself a long time ago. She vaguely remembers writing the array in her Book of Shadows, but goddess knows where that tattered thing ended up after she died. What could have made them so desperate to attempt such an unreliable means? How did they even manage it?

She notices with a hiss the lingering wounds on her arms, open and angry but no longer weeping blood. Three diagonal slashes on each forearm mark their dying wishes. Six total. Six souls upon which she's been asked to seek vengeance. She has no choice in the matter. It's part of the contract, and if she fails to fulfill the contract, a second death will be the least of her worries. Her very soul will be ripped to shreds, and there won't even be an afterlife for her to sleep through.

Merde! She didn't ask for this!

She didn't ask for this, but they did. They gave everything they had for it.

She doesn't even know their names...

Wren curls into herself and mourns the lost souls of the newly dead, and they are lost—souls torn asunder for the crime of pulling a soul back from the veil, their spirits destroyed as soundly as their bodies.

There should be sad music playing. Something like Mozart's Lacrimosa. Something in a minor key that makes you want to cry or scream or both. Something Monet would have painted lily pads to or something that could have been the overture for a tragic ballet where the fairy princess loses her wings, and the willies have to keep her from opening her wrists. That would be mournful enough. The notes drift around her, a slow adagio, beautiful and graceful, accented by the chiming of ascending and descending notes and sets of notes. Hopeless but lovely. Like something she herself might once have sang. Wren shivers, chilled to the bone on the cold floor, and the music suddenly stops.

Oh, she was the one singing...

When she opens her eyes, the wild script on her hands greets her, swirling patterns of leaves and runes in a vibrant emerald green. Geometric shapes and spirals trail along her skin, familiar but strange at once. Has her wild script grown? It didn't use to trail all the way to her hands before, and oh... she has two of them. Wow! Wren hasn't had a left hand since she was ten years old. Not a flesh one anyway.

Odin's eyepatch *y la máscara de Tlaloc!*

PRELUDE

She feels like she's just woken up as the main character of a video game. Welcome back! Here's a mysterious quest for you to deal with, and it's an open world RPG with no navigation pins. Good luck! Oh, and by the way, the punishment for failing is total and complete obliteration.

She sighs, frustrated and sad, angry and destitute.

At least she still has her magic. It echoes around the room, glittery cascades of viridian brought to life by the call of her voice. Her own brand of chaos, necrotic in nature and achingly beautiful. A spell meant to calm the dead, even if the dead in this room will never hear it. It's strange, this pulchritude of the kinder aspect of her magic. It dances in her elegy's notes, in sweet sparkling swirls of emerald and viridian. The sight reminds her of watching thousands of tiny fairies flitting about like children, innocent and carefree, as they light up the forest.

"*Repose en paz, lamentable muertos*," she prays, knowing there is no peace for lost souls, but at least they won't be trapped here. Wherever "here" is, of course?

She pulls on one of the dirty hospital gowns while she investigates her surroundings.

The room appears to be a hospital room. The walls are decorated with cheap striped wallpaper, yellowing and torn in places, molding in others. There are scratch marks and bloodstains everywhere, evidence that pain and death are not newcomers here. Lining the edges of the room are four small cots. The meager number wouldn't be able to sleep all of the innocents who had been involved in the ritual, the remains of which lie scattered about the floor.

Various knickknacks lay around the circle as part of the resurrection: an old pocket watch, a locket, the torn-up photograph of a small child, a very dirty piece of jewelry, a weathered deck of tarot cards—much loved, well read, old and wise—at least that's what her empathy reads. An exploratory shuffle and she draws the Ten of Pentacles. A coming of...

Interesting...

Page Of Swords

On the periphery of the array, charred remnants mark each unfortunate's passing. These remnants are the synthetic materials left behind after the rest of the participants' bodies have disintegrated in the heat of æther flame. Eight tarnished and bloodstained hospital gowns (similar to what she is wearing, more nylon than cotton and uncomfortable against the skin) remain where each person once stood, all of them coated with the emotional residue of hatred and despair. There is not much more left beside this.

Wren finds this odd.

Why is there not a scrap of tech lying about? Whatever this place is, it's clearly housing a multitude of patients/inmates. There should have been microchips and cybernetic implants—at least the mandatory, state-issued ID chips should have been left behind, one for each body. If these patients were indeed witches, they would most assuredly have had suppression technology affixed to them, yet there isn't a scrap of charred metal, plastic, or microtechnology anywhere to be found.

Additionally, if they weren't witches or hexen, then at least a few of them should have been augmented. There should be clockwork tech and prosthetics, muscular and neural enhancements, birth control implants and visual aids, computational devices, and maybe even electrical nodes for full-system implants. Surely, one of them had to have some sort of transplant either internally or externally. Limb replacements had been all the rage in many parts of the world before her first death for both practical and aesthetic purposes. Wren herself had a mechanical left hand in her past life. The device was knit and graphed to her arm as a permanent fixture after losing her hand to a sea monster as a child, the clockwork prosthetics a trademark of her family. Looking at the limb now, it's surreal to see unmarred flesh and skin staring back at her.

After becoming a technomancer, she had undergone integration, the surgical graphing of total-body technomancer specific augmentations designed to hone her already superior physical abilities. Of course, the tech had all been ripped from her body in the process that made her a witch however many years ago. The scarring left behind that once marred her arms, legs, and torso is gone as well. No evidence anywhere on her body that she was once a technomancer.

Wren picks the locket up off the floor and opens it. Inside are two small photos of a pair of women. They don't have any familial resemblances, and on the back of the square panel, an endearment is written in calligraphy.

"To my dearest Lulu. Forever yours, Desiree."

Wren feels the adoration seeping from the necklace. It hums with shared feelings and experiences between two souls. It reminds her achingly of someone she used to know.

Jessabelle...

Wren closes her eyes and concentrates within. She can feel it still, the hum of chaos in her blood. It takes some concentration, but as the seconds stretch, an old arcane muscle flexes. Three interlocking spirals at her brow alight with a faint blue-green glow.

Clearing her throat, she begins to hum, looking for a melody to match the locket's ethereal signature. The locket starts to shimmer as the first notes resonate with a mere ripple of Wren's magic. She urges a bit more of her power into it, and the locket progresses in its song. She follows its tune until a crisp melody in A minor takes shape, and its secrets are laid bare. Her magic draws the tiniest of arrays on the back.

The other scattered objects about the room rise from the floor at her will. Still humming the sad, sweet tune of the locket, she places it open on the floor. Carefully maintaining the rhythm, she ushers each prize into the locket's new dimensional pocket until every one is safely stowed away. The locket continues to glow as she brings the melody to a close. She floats it up to settle around her neck, and the light fades. The wild script on her hands glows a soothing viridian in the dim light of the room.

Well, that worked nicely. What else can her shiny new body do?

She walks over to the steel door. Hn, there's no doorknob. Must be system-operated. Okay, well this might take a little more magic than toying with a locket, but she'll manage.

Page Of Swords

She takes a deep breath and digs deep.

Her indicia—the interlocking spirals at her brow that form the triskelion—blazes to life, a full emerald luminescence, and she pushes.

Telekinesis:

Root word—Kinetic—Of or relating to the motion of material bodies and the force and energy associated therewith.

Prefix—Tele—Originating in the Greek language of the old world, 'tele' refers to distance or at a distance.

Therefore, telekinesis implies an ability to move physical objects at or from a distance. Psychic witches have been seen to accomplish this in a variety of ways: some of them can make objects levitate, while others are capable of calling things to and away from them or, more still, capable of locking and unlocking doors without touching them.

Beware the witch with telekinetic abilities, for they are capable of far more than simply throwing a ball across the room or flicking the lights on and off.

An Excerpt from *Hunting and Identifying Hexen*
by Finnick Lockecraft, 1852 A.P.

2

THE MAGICIAN

THE DOOR SMASHES AGAINST THE OPPOSITE
wall with a deafening bang, and Wren winces.

Oops...She definitely overdid it, but it's nice to stretch her muscles, magical or otherwise.

The hallway is well-lit, much brighter than the darkened cell, stretching in either direction to end in a stairwell on both sides. Edison bulbs line the walls, and overhead lights cast a glaring white light down onto her head. This place would be rather quaint with its checkered flooring and gilded wallpaper were it not for the steel doors lining the walls. There are comm screens embedded in the paneling beside each door. She moves to the one adjacent to her door and presses the power button, but it doesn't respond, not even to request an access code.

"Hey! How did you get out of your room?"

An orderly, a rather large one at that, with several mechanical prostheses, marches her direction, red-faced and noisy. His augmentations spark yellow, and a coil of electricity rushes down the hall toward her from a stun gun grafted to his left forearm. She dodges, and the probe hits a Mona Lisa knock-off on the wall. He barrels her direction, readying another charge. She lets him reach approximately five feet in front of her before holding up her hand with a flourish. The stun gun squeaks pathetically as she psychically yanks it from his arm, and the orderly finds himself lifted off the floor, held midair by tendrils of Wren's emerald green magic.

"What the hell!"

He struggles as Wren closes the distance between them, carefully looking him up and down. The orderly has replaced both of his arms with mech. The design is crude, war-like and reminiscent of the large tanks used by the Aighnean military and inlaid with various weapons that can be used to subdue someone: the stun gun, a tranq cache, and chloroform chemical storage. The engineering alone would provide him inhuman strength and speed in the fashion of many championship boxers and martial artists. To further support her theory, the entirety of his scalp has been fortified with a steel exo-cap. Maybe he had dreams of stardom in the ring once upon a time. It isn't unheard of for gambling sponsors to pay good money to get their fighters modified. He certainly looks more like a speakeasy bouncer than a hospital orderly, unless of course this place sanctions roughing up the patients. Well, whoever paid for his augmentations didn't give a rat's ass about the longevity of the modifications.

The work is shoddy.

Certainly not technomancer grade. It's barely passable even for an adept. She can see the screws embedding the mech into his skin. Some are beginning to loosen. There's scar tissue everywhere and the metal finish is tarnishing. There are also several visible neural cables connecting his arms to his torso and his torso to his brain. Whatever hack modified him did a cheap job, choosing to save time and money by not laying the cables beneath the skin to connect the mech directly into the man's nervous system. Were he to fight anyone with even half a brain, he would be downed in 30 seconds. Just one good tug on the right cable and lights out. Dei help him if someone yanks the wrong one.

"How do you turn on these comms?" she asks, sweetly.

"What the fuck! How are you lucid? Put me down or I'll—"

She pulls one of the neural cables. Its head disconnects from his shoulder with a sputter of electricity. Boxer-man screams from the shock.

"You crazy bitch!!"

"Answer my question before I unscrew your skull cap."

She finds one of the loosened screws, holds it between her index finger and thumb, and twists.

"Okay, okay. There is a stylus in my pointer finger."

She glances at his mechanical hands, contemplatively clicking her tongue. She scratches her head, looking just a tad sheepish as she asks her next question.

"See, that wasn't so hard. Now, what year is it?"

"What year is it? What the hell are you going on about, you lunatic! Let me go!"

Figures... *Pendejo.*

She flings him face first into a wall and lets him crumple to the floor. Disconnecting his neural cables, she deftly removes the pointer finger from his right hand. Someone will have to plug him back in later.

When she presses the mechanical digit to the comm tablet, it lights up happily (like for real...there's a dancing bunny on the screen): "Stonehearst Hospital for the Mentally Infirm."

Great! She's been brought back to life in an insane asylum. How appropriate. They always did call her mad in her last life.

Wren died in the Month of Soil, 1865. According to the homescreen, today is the 32nd day of the Month of Fire 1877. She's been dead for twelve years and two months. How ironic her rebirth should be on this day.

"Happy birthday to me, I guess. Finally 21? Or is it technically 33? Do dead years count?"

Who cares?

It's not like she's celebrating. She has to admit though—Some party! Resurrected on her birthday by a group of vengeful misfits. Not to say they don't deserve to be avenged but... Did they have to choose her? And how did they get her ashes in the first place? Was she just lying around in a pill bottle somewhere? *Enfer!* How did they even find the means to accomplish such a complex ritual in the middle of an insane asylum anyway?

She swipes the screen to display several file folders. These must be the patient files of the inmates who were locked up together. She peruses the profiles one by one: Katrina, LuQin, Atalia, Sarah, Emilio, Hoshi, Amani, and Nadia. She opens each inmate's file, and what a bunch of bullshit diagnoses! Hysteria, gender identity disorder, homosexuality, neurasthenia, dysaesthesia aethiopica. All of them have been obsolete diagnoses for centuries! At least among respectable circles. From what she can tell, most of them were victims of abuse, runaways and outcasts who suffered from depression and prejudice.

Each file has a picture of the patient next to the name. The only one who looks vaguely familiar is Atalia, the face that looked at her through the mirror during the resurrection. If Atalia ingested Wren's ashes before the ritual, then that would've made Atalia the central sacrifice and therefore the body Wren woke up in. The ritual itself destroyed Atalia's body as readily as all the others to remake Wren's original body, a body whole sacrificed to remake a body burned.

Loki's mistletoe! What were you thinking, Atalia?

It's an aspect of the resurrection summoning she never even thought about. She'll need to write it down.

Atalia Vaishi had been a Firefly-in-training in the Ebelean court. Expelled after being found pregnant, her family had her committed after she aborted her own pregnancy, claiming the child a product of assault. She was considered a lunatic and madwoman for "crying rape" against an apparently distinct political figure, though the file doesn't specify who she accused. Also, in her file is a running treatment schedule. It's a miracle the girl survived such aggressive 'treatments': electro-shock therapy, leeches, hydrotherapy, blood transfusions, etcetera... the usual madhouse excursions, but the file seems incomplete, and she can't quite put her finger on why.

As she goes to look at the other files again, voices carry down the hall. *Gears!* If only she had her old hard drive so she could save all this information for later.

Wren ducks back into the holding cell, fixing the door as she goes. She uses the piece of mirror-glass from earlier and slices into the heel of her left palm. Blood gushes forth, and she uses it to paint a glamour over her face. A few sung notes later, and Atalia's face replaces Wren Nocturne's. Don't worry. She asked permission, or at the very least, the girl gave it when she choked down her ashes. Bonds of blood and decay and all that.

"Welp! Brought back to life in a loony bin. Might as well fit in."

So, she starts to scream.

She cries murder and rape and fire and Loki's dottir! There's a giant spider in here!!! She screams and beats her fists into the walls. She tears around the room like a tornado, and when the pounding of feet finally makes it to her door, she throws herself into a corner, a madwoman thrown into hysterics.

"They're dead. They're all dead. He killed them. He zapped them all, and they're all dead!"

But the people who enter are not wearing the same uniform as Boxer-man. They aren't even wearing medical dress. The pair, two teenagers, one boy and one girl, are wearing adept battlegear common to the northeastern region of Murasaki no Yama, the largest country of Deus: mid-length yukata-style tunics over thick trousers and braced with leather belts, vests, and bracers. While their dress is not terribly unique in this regard, the patterns and symbols on their robes, accented in deep reds and purples, speak volumes for their identity and their purpose here. Even more telling is the gleaming silver tech of their headpieces, the power nodes on their hands and temples, and the telltale glint of visual mods, called sights, in their eyes. Such augmentations were the trademark of only one house of technomancers.

Miyazaki—the royal family of Murasaki no Yama.

Merde... If they're here, if *he* is here, it'll prove more than a problem for her.

At first, the pair don't know what to do as they take in the bloodied mess of the room, but eventually, the boy runs to the corner she's shoved herself into.

"Miss, please, calm down."

"You calm down!"

"Akari, go fetch the doctor," he says to his female counterpart.

"No!" Wren screams. "They did it! I saw them!"

But the girl is already gone, sprinting down the hall as fast as she can. The boy, a sweet-faced fifteen- or sixteen-year-old, smiles, reassuringly offering his hand. She stares at it like one would a venomous snake.

"It's alright. I'm not going to hurt you."

She pouts at him, huddling further into herself.

"Go away."

"My name is Renki. What's yours?"

Wow! What a polite young man? He should really learn not to talk to mad people.

"That's none of your business!"

She shrieks and lunges forward. The adept finds himself bodily thrown backward as she pushes him, making a mad dash for the door. She ignores him as he calls for her to wait, but she is through the door and racing down the hall in moments. Or at least she would be if the doctor didn't intercept her.

"Vaishi! Goddamn it. Causing trouble again! Madame Favreau, I told you to make sure all of the inmates were sedated before the representatives from Miyazaki arrived."

A harried nurse runs up, a syringe in hand.

"We did, Dr. Faust. She shouldn't be running around like this now. I'll give her another dosage."

"No, it's poison! They're trying to kill us." She ducks behind Renki who followed her out of the room. "Don't let them hurt me."

"Miss, please. They are trying to help you."

"They've been killing us!" she shouts, shielding herself with the lavender sash hanging from his belt.

"Beg pardon, highness. Some of our inmates suffer from hysteria and are prone to fits. This poor girl is one of our worst cases."

Highness, eh? She stands in the presence of a prince.

"Dr. Faust, I am concerned about the state of this room. It seems a great violence has occurred within."

The nurse by his side speaks up.

"Yes, sir. This room is commonly in disarray as it is the quiet place we keep especially self-destructive patients. As much as we try to keep them from harming themselves, they still somehow manage it. Forgive the mess. I'm sure all of the inmates who were last kept here are just fine."

"Liar!" cries Wren from behind the gentleman.

"You would do well to confirm for us. I'm sure your local government would be happy to hear of the fair treatment of their most vulnerable population, the sick and infirm."

"Of course, young lord. We will see to it."

Renki turns back to Wren, a soft expression on his face. "I'm sure this is just a misunderstanding."

"But—!"

A needle stabs into her thigh from behind and the syringe plunges.

"I hate needles..."

Within moments, she finds herself woozy and tumbling sideways into the young man. Favreau fishes her out of his hold, though he seems reluctant to hand her over.

"I would like to check on this young lady before we depart."

Dr. Faust's mouth opens in surprise. "Of course. We will treat her with the utmost care."

He gestures widely, bowing his head to the young man who smiles kindly in return. "We appreciate your righteousness."

She is hoisted off the floor by two orderlies. Renki looks on in concern even as Faust assures him they will take good care of her while they tote her away. She listens blearily as the world around her shifts from dingy hallways to more refined décor.

"Doctor?"

PRELUDE

"Take her to the changing rooms. We are entertaining today, and this one is always a patron favorite." The doctor looks sidelong at Boxer-man on the floor. "And plug Malcolm back in, will you? I want to know what happened in that cell."

Before the first Hexen took refuge in Deus, an old bard by the name of Bill wrote of a woman who took her own life by drowning herself in the river. Why? Who knows? But it cannot be argued there is something unspeakably provocative to be found in the visage of a pretty young thing sacrificing herself for love.

The Illustrious Eugene Winnifred's
expose on "The Ophelia Tours"
New London, Aighneas, 1867 A.P.

3

SIX OF SWORDS

WREN REGAINS LUCIDITY WHEN FREEZING water is dumped over her head.

"Did Winnifred really need to arrange a soirée today?"

"That peacock is always worried about finances. You think it's cheap to bring in plusies. Dang adepts are expensive."

Soirée? A soirée in a mental hospital? What? She sputters as the nurses scrub her down—Ow! *¡Se pica!* Did they shave her legs and...? Oh Goddess, who gave them permission to go down there!?—douse her again, then throw her into an air dryer.

"Thought the council covered their fees."

"Where do you think your taxes go?"

"As though Winnifred has paid a quarter of what this place owes in taxes. Why do you think we keep so many inmates? The poor bugs sleep on the floor with the rats for lack of beds."

Wren shivers and chokes in the circulating air until they judge her sufficiently dry. She lets them move her like a doll, the drug still clogging her reactions.

"Alright, dearie, here we are," says one, promptly shoving her into a corset which the woman tightens with a merciless vengeance before manhandling her into a cheap lace dress with far too much beading and too little cloth. Goddess above, her cleavage!

"I can't believe the boss invited those Murasaki adepts here," one of the nurses says to another as she tugs a brush through Wren's hair. "He's always going on about how he can't stand 'borgs."

"Not like he chose them. You put in a request, and the council decides who should help you. Look up, dearie," says the first, armed with a make-up palette and tugging 'Atalia's' chin up with finely manicured fingers. "And Primarch Thames told Faust he would only send the best. Besides how else are you supposed to get rid of a ghost in the machine?"

Ghost in the machine? Is this asylum haunted? Well, this just gets better and better. She winces as a make-up brush jabs her in the eye.

"The damn thing has been unlocking cells, making equipment malfunction, and wreaking all manner of havoc ever since it got on our servers. One of the nutters nearly ripped out Malcolm's throat during treatment when the restraints unlocked themselves."

Interesting... That's not typical ghostly behavior.

"No wonder he's desperate. Think they'll be able to get rid of it?"

"Who knows? We don't even know how many ghosts there are. Could be forty for all we know. Do you realize how many patients have expired over the last year? The crematorium has been on overdrive since midsummer."

Well, that certainly explains the desperation of her resurrectionists... They probably thought they were going to die here anyway.

"Do you think the doc told them that number?"

"Hell no! Do you want to still have a job tomorrow?" says the other as she slaps some playdough-tasting lipstick on Wren's face.

"Of course!"

"Then keep your mouth shut about the inmates, alright? If it got out to the families how many inmates have died... Stop moving, girl, and give me your feet!"

Heels two sizes too big are shoved onto her feet. They expect her to walk in these? A glance in a nearby mirror confirms she looks the part of a cabaret showgirl—not that there's anything wrong with that—but could they at least do it correctly? Atalia's blonde hair has been piled on top of her head in a messy updo and decorated with brightly colored feathers. The make-up on her face is too thick, too dark, and too gaudy, and they didn't blend the shadows properly. They tried to make Atalia's lips bigger with a lipstick shade that is entirely uncomplimentary to her creamy coffee skin tone, and the foundation they've caked on her is too pale, making her look patchy and ill.

It feels like a rubber mask has been painted onto her face.

"Take this, dearie," says her hairstylist, shoving a pill between her lips. She protests, about to spit it out, but the woman slaps her palm over Wren's mouth. Wren at least has enough sense to tuck the pill behind her back teeth and pretend to swallow before water gets poured down her throat.

"Good girl," the woman praises her when Wren opens her mouth to show the pill is gone.

"Look, just keep your mouth shut about the inmates until the plusies are gone. Murasaki is the best for exorcisms, but they're also the worst when it comes to human rights protocols. If they find out what's really going on here, it'll be curtains for all of us. I'll take this one to the courtyard."

And her trek through the facility continues, the nurse whisking her into the courtyard.

There are several buildings, old in aesthetic but young in the foundations: a place built on a lie and haunted by secrets. Several tables are laid out on the lawn for finely dressed ladies and gentlemen. Other men and women, dressed equally suggestive as Wren, are scattered throughout the festivities. Some serve drinks and hors d'oeuvres, a few of them play instruments about the tables. A few are posed in gilded cages—a girl here, a boy there— one such cage even holds a couple locked in a coital embrace. Each and every inmate bears the dilated pupils and red rimmed eyes of drug usage. Their emotions are palatable on her senses: numbness cased in synthetic euphoria and peppered with stale reassurances. Drugged. The lot of them. Probably with the same pill currently tucked behind her teeth.

Additionally, drifting around the festivities, much to the ignorance of the living, are a few spirits wearing similar attire to the inmates dancing and entertaining. The only stark difference between the drifting dead and their living brethren are the varied markings of their deaths. Black veins decorate the necks and faces of a few of them, indicating an injection cycle treatment gone terribly wrong. One of them has electrical burns around his temple. Another spews water whenever she opens her mouth, and two more have chemical burns along their faces and forearms. The nameless dead, visible only to her in this manicured circle of hell on earth.

Wren is ushered into a cage and told to sing.

She obeys, avoiding anything more than a common folk song lest she attract unwanted attention, but she pours a little bit of her empathetic magic into it to lull the restless spirits into something resembling peace. The flex of power is meek, but it will help burn the rest of the injection from her system.

She notes, dully—what the fuck did they give her? Diazepam?—that Koi and Dei, Deus's two moons, rise together for a rare waltz across the sky this evening: a double-moon eclipse: Koi, majestic and lavender against the dark of the coming dusk, and Dei, smaller, glowing pink as she dances before her lover.

In the meantime, the adepts are now in conference with a man wearing a rather extravagantly curled wig atop his head. He carries himself with all the pomp and circumstance of a circus ringmaster. He even looks the part in red coat tails and a matching top hat. He must be the asylum director, in charge of the façade and the patronage but knowing next to nothing about even the most surface-level psychological theory—a show puppet pulling strings in a flowery accent while his master sits in the shadows.

"'Tiz a pity zhat His Royal Highness could not stay to enjoy zhe festivities." He is speaking to the same girl who ran off earlier at the young Renki's instruction. Akari, was it?

"Prince Kaito prefers to let us try to solve missions ourselves. It's how we gain field experience as his students. And since yours is a low-level case, it's a good opportunity for us to test our skills."

"Will you be able to manage on your own?"

"His Highness is a call away if we run into trouble, but we should manage just fine, Director Winnifred. The missive details a ghoul infestation in your mainframe. These types of fiends are relatively easy to handle and can be removed within a few hours."

"A few hours! Mademoiselle, we have patrons who are visiting zheir... um, zheir loved ones."

"I'm afraid it might be best if you cancel the present festivities, Director. We wouldn't want anyone unnecessarily placed in harm's way."

"But zhese events account for more zhan fifty percent of the asylum's funding, and our next revue isn't scheduled for another zhree weeks!"

"I am sorry, Director, but I cannot guarantee the safety of your patrons unless you send them away, and I would certainly hate to imagine the damage it would do to your facility should one of your honored guests meet with harm while we work."

"Zis is ridiculous. Summon your mentor zis instant!"

At this point, Renki arrives, walking up to stand next to his friend. The boy, tall for his age, stares down at the director, brow set and shoulders squared with indignation at the treatment of his mission partner.

"Director Winnifred, we have been instructed not to summon Prince Kaito unless the need arises. Now, if you please, we ask you to clear the courtyard and ensure all of your patients are accounted for."

The director, for all his bluster, looks a bit stunned by the youth's appearance. He seems flustered at the idea of taking orders from a teenager, but at the determined shine in the young man's blue-green eyes, he relents with a sputtered apology. He offers a clumsy bow to the pair before calling over several members of the staff to begin ushering people out of the courtyard. As he passes Wren, she slips the pill into his champagne flute.

Wren, for her part, continues singing airily, not quite on key, but not quite off key either. Thank heavens! Kaito, more properly known as Prince Kaito Miyazaki, is not currently on the premises.

She isn't quite certain she's ready to meet that particular ghost from the past. Or maybe she's the ghost, more frightened of the living than the dead? She certainly meets one of the prerequisites. Present heartbeat notwithstanding.

Several nurses usher the various show-inmates back to their rooms, and Wren finds herself readily accosted by a burly looking warden. There are bruises around his temple, and he's missing an index finger. Oh, hey, it's Boxer-man, though she guesses his name is Malcolm. His finger is tucked away in her locket. He doesn't look happy at all. How fortunate her glamour is still active despite the sedative. He would probably love to punch a hole in her real face right about now.

"Come on."

She allows him to move her like a ragdoll, feigning the same dazed expression and disassociation every other patient in this hellhole exhumes. Akari sets up boundary beacons around the perimeter of the courtyard while Renki hardwires himself to several of the comms in the main lobby. His sights are on, glowing golden as he works. He's probably installing much more sophisticated systems to the mainframe to phish out whatever is haunting the asylum servers.

She takes in their array formation. It looks like they'll be summoning the ghouls into their reinforced servers. If she wants to take care of business fast, she'll need to beat them to it and shackle one or two to her will first. As Malcolm leads her past a piece of the array, she pretends to trip over the skirt of her dress, flailing her arms so wildly Boxer-man lets her fall.

Her shout echoes around the courtyard, "Ouch, you ape!" drawing the attention of most everyone in the vicinity.

"Come on, you useless wretch." He grabs her bicep, and she screeches like a banshee.

"Let go! That hurts!" It doesn't. Not really. She's tougher than that, and he's still missing a finger.

Akari looks over as Malcolm picks her up and slings her over his shoulder like a fucking caveman.

"Put me down! Put me down! Put me down!"

She kicks and rants and pounds on his back. She is pretty sure one of her pretty high heels goes flying into a rosebush. When she bites him, he throws her back into the grass, right next to one of the array beacons. Her head knocks into a rock.

"Help!! Fire! Abuse! My hair hurts!!"

Boxer-man raises a fist to pummel her further into the ground, but there's a clang of metal as another body steps between her and the mechanical fist. Akari stands tall in front of her, a chisa katana, shorter than the regular katana, in her hand. The blade glows with ultraviolet light. Saibāki—Cyber energy. Unique to the Miyazaki family, this life energy, or 'ki' as Murasakans call it, is capable of bending reality into a virtual-scape. Mixed with their advanced neural networks, this allows Miyazaki technomancers and adepts to hack into foreign systems, map an area of effect, increase the potency and resilience of their weapons, and affect change in their environment via their virtual signatures—a data generated mirror of themselves that can travel through cyberscape to touch, alter, and attack anything mapped into their field. Its most advanced users can even attack an enemy virtually and vitally at the same time, though Wren only knows of one person capable of that.

"What do you think you're doing?"

"Outta my way, brat!"

Boxer-man's fist aims to hit Akari, but someone hacks into the limb, and the hand freezes mid swing. Renki rushes over from the opposite side of the courtyard. His sights spin, traces of saibāki lingering around his hand augmentations as well.

"Akari, what's going on?"

While their attention is diverted, Wren grabs the small beacon and tucks it into her bodice. It's a tight squeeze. And yikes! It looks like she's gained an extra cup size.

"I saw this staff member about to hit a patient!"

"That's not your place, girl!"

"Sir, please," says Renki as he gently nudges Akari out of the man's direct path. "This manner of treatment is unorthodox toward a mentally incapacitated individual."

Boxer-man huffs at being admonished by someone who is clearly years his junior. The hum of saibāki disperses as both teens release their influence, Akari sheathing her sword and Renki releasing Boxer-man's tech. Boxer-man jerks his fist back to his side as he regains control over the augmentation. Well, now she knows for sure, these teenagers are not just Miyazaki pupils, they're members of the royal family—which really does not bode well for Wren. It's one thing for Murasaki to send people under the supervision of one of their highest ranked technomancers. It's another for members of the royal family to deal with the problem themselves.

"Careful not to turn your back on the patients, your highness. Many of these inmates bite. They need a firm hand."

"I understand, sir, but an excess of punishment is unacceptable."

She startles when a hand appears in her line of sight. She didn't even hear him approach. He must be wearing some good boots. Way better than heels. She accepts the offer and grasps his hand. The hand itself is nothing spectacular, but the circular node on the back reminds her of Kaito—though it glows gold rather than purple.

"Are you alright, Miss?"

The cut at her temple throbs, but it's a small price to pay for the device she slipped into her bodice. She looks down as though embarrassed, humming in affirmation.

"I'm glad. What is your name?"

"Umm... Atalia. Atalia Vaishi."

"Miss Vaishi then. We're going to take care of the supernaturals who have been hurting people here. Wouldn't that be a good thing?"

She nods quickly, keeping her gaze pointedly down.

"Alright. Akari, why don't you help this good gentleman escort Miss Vaishi to her room?"

"Renki," the girl protests.

The boy gives her an insistent look, and the female adept frowns but nods.

The warden growls under his breath but takes her by the arm and resumes corralling her toward the main building, Akari following behind. Boxer-man pushes her into the room she woke up in and shuts the door. The lock clicks into place, and the guard's heavy footfalls diminish down the hallway.

Wren waits for a few moments more before fishing the beacon out of her bodice. About the size of her palm, the device's casing is comprised of sleek steel and dark black glass. She sets the small disk on the floor and passes her index finger over the central button. A lavender glow blooms from the center, and the contraption opens. It locks itself to the floor as a holograph unfolds. Lines of code drift across the holo, spiraling systems of numbers speeding by in rapid ascension.

She learned about VR coding systems during her technomancer summit, and while she can tell where people are stationed and where a wall or door might be standing, trained decoders could read all the way to the smallest birthmark underneath a person's clothing if they so desired. It's scary how intimately coders can read into a person's private life based solely on their number series, but she guesses people would say much the same about her empathic abilities which allow her to read the surface emotions of any unguarded psyche around her, and Koi help the poor soul should she try to dive deeper. It doesn't usually work out well for them...

But she isn't looking for anything nearly so specific here.

Beings are coded in a virtual reality code by a series of 0's and 1's with ones indicating the presence, or positive value, of something: i.e. pulse, a lifeforce, various vital signs, and cognizance in living creatures. Supernatural or undead beings, ghosts and ghouls in this case, are always indicated by a 0 at the 23rd, 47th, and 2nd to last numeral in the series, indicating a lack of pulse, vital signs, and lifeforce while the placeholder for cognizance was still positive. Beacon arrays, like what Renki and Akari have set up around the courtyard and the building interiors, are designed to map and translate the vital world into a virtual landscape where ghosts could be lured to be exorcised by individuals capable of seeing and interacting with the virtual plane.

While anyone can don a VR headset, Murasakan adepts are augmented with visual and sensory systems which allow them to connect directly into a computer system just by looking at the monitor. So long as they have access to a connection point or network, they can use their tech for various tasks, including exorcisms.

Looking through the coding for a little more than an hour, she finds a few possible candidates rushing about the facility. They might be supernatural entities, but none of them feel malevolent—just your average run-of-the-mill spirits. Okay, maybe just reading the code is giving her a headache. She blinks to clear the artificial light from her eyes before standing up and shaking out her stiff muscles.

"Okay. What do we know about our situation?"

She knows the asylum is haunted. She saw the ghosts herself. The teenagers seem to think it's a ghoul causing all the commotion in this place, and that might be true, but she's not finding anything in the code to indicate a ghoul. Neither has she sensed one, and she's fairly well attuned to dead things, but it's early yet, Òr, Deus's sun, just dipping below the horizon. Such creatures don't usually present themselves until true nightfall even in VR coding.

So, what could it be? Locked up as she is, she has no way to find out, and she's not sure she wants to be caught roaming the hospital again. Maybe... She looks down at the beacon as though it has personally offended her. Renki and Akari have probably mapped the whole hospital into their servers by now. She could take advantage of that. She hasn't ventured into cyberspace since she was a technomancer, and she doesn't exactly have the equipment or the set up to do so the traditional way, but creativity and astral projection can take a witch a long way.

She paces a circle around the room before using her nail to cut into the flesh of her thumb. The blood comes readily enough, and she hastily draws a projection array around the holo-display. She calls the deck of tarot cards from the locket and pulls The Chariot from its depths. She places the card face down in the array before drawing another card at random.

The Eight of Pentacles Reversed: Misdirection. Not a bad idea.

She sits in the center of the blood-drawn circle. Placing her hands into the light of the holograph, she hums. Anyone watching from outside would see a dull green glow slowly emanate from under the door jamb before extinguishing with a flash.

When Wren opens her eyes, the world is tinged in lavender and the walls cascade with code. Virtual Reality, Cyberspace, the Matrix... call it what you will. It all amounts to the same thing. A coded world that exists between the wires. A vast network of connections and integrations that blanket all of Deus, its own organism. Just like magic exists everywhere in Deus, so too does the network: two sides of the same coin, as opposing as light and darkness without all of the mysticism and morally attributed baggage but just as intertwined.

She steps out of the room, cautious of being seen by the adepts running amok. They would be the only ones able to recognize her in VR space lest someone else is wearing a headset, but she doubts it. Wren walks along the corridors, keeping a lookout for any ghouls or spirits.

The main offices of the asylum are located on the first floor of the compound's central building, and she makes her way there fairly quickly, despite having to duck behind a wall for five minutes to avoid being seen by Akari. The teen keeps moving back and forth along the same hallway with an EMP device in hand. Thankfully, the teen doesn't realize the electromagnetic waves she's picking up are Wren.

"What do you mean, you can't find those patients!"

The head nurse, the same one who stuck her with the sedative earlier, Madame Favreau sits in the office going over files. Merely a coded mirror of the real thing, this Favreau is basically a 3D outline of the actual woman, moving around and gesticulating like an animation that hasn't been given color or texture or, really, anything more than a graphed outline. She is speaking into a comm unit rather angrily.

"Like I said. Seven inmates are currently unaccounted for. We have searched the entire compound and nothing."

"Six months' worth of research lost! Do you really expect this facility to survive that kind of setback? Our benefactor is expecting at least three prepared subjects by fall."

"The only one accounted for is Atalia Vaishi. She's unruly as ever and nearly broke my nose earlier. You get a control chip for that one, or I'm not handling her again."

Control chip?

"Hmm," says Favreau. "We can schedule an installation later. While we're at it, a lobotomy might be in order. We can't risk losing the last of the experiment group. What of your attacker?"

"I told you. It was a damned ghoul!"

Excuse her? Does she look like a ghoul!

"In the daylight."

"Well, what else could it be? It used magic and looked like a walking corpse."

Hmphf! It's not her fault she was reborn covered in gore.

"Fine. I'll check the security cams myself."

Favreau shuts down Malcolm's protests, deactivating the comm with a click of a button, and shuffles over to a computer hub sitting to her right. She unlocks the screen and begins scanning files, a master list labeled "Batch Y7K." Atalia Vaishi's name flashes across the screen. The woman tracks through at least twenty more files, more than half of which are labeled in red with the word "EXPIRED" written underneath. Barely a handful are labeled "ACTIVE" in blue. She goes through seven of these and highlights them red as well, leaving Atalia's file the only active case in the grouping.

She clicks the file database closed to access camera footage from earlier in the day. It's Wren's room. Eight inmates sit in a circle in the center of the floor. Atalia sits at the center as they all huddle in close. One of the women gets up from the huddle, and the camera is covered with a piece of cloth as one of them breaks a mirror and another begins to draw the array. Lights play through the fabric—an aurora of colors, reds, then blues, yellows, then purples, and ending, finally, in the glow of Wren's viridian green.

Favreau reactivates her comm.

"Malcolm, bring Atalia Vaishi to Examination Room C now, and bring a dispel node."

"But the adepts said no one should be walking about while they're working."

"I don't care what they said. Get her to me now!"

"Fine."

Ah. That would be her cue to return to her body. Before though, she draws a lure talisman on the underside of the woman's desk and activates it with a short hum. She knows it's set when she hears the faint hum echo back to her, the array shimmering green in contrast to the lavender sheen of cyberscape.

She settles back into her physical form with a shudder.

Her muscles ache from sitting on her knees. She stretches before deactivating the beacon, sliding it back into her bodice for safekeeping. She lays back and waits, watching the sky darken through the pathetic excuse for a window, night stretching across the asylum like a cat rising for a hunt. She wonders what the moons look like now the sun has set and the stars are out.

The door to her room bursts open.

"Get up!"

"But the ceiling is pretty."

A loud crash rattles the building, followed by a woman's scream. Malcolm jerks to look for the sound. Wren kicks him in the balls with her heel. The man goes down like a ton of bricks.

"Argh!! You bi—!"

She disconnects him again, powering him down manually like a computer stuck on the blue screen of death. The shouting comes from the direction of the courtyard, and Wren follows.

Glass and wood shatter as Favreau is thrown into the courtyard. Her scream cuts short when her head hits the cobblestone with a squelch. After her, shrieks a dark mass of contorted energy. Drawn into corporeal visibility by the sigil Wren left under the desk, the mass shapes and reshapes itself, first into a man, then a woman, then a child, constant and unending. Wren's eyes widen. This is not a ghoul or even a pack of ghouls. No, this is something far more sinister; already, blood has been spilled by the dark conglomeration of souls who died painful, tormented deaths.

Welp! Guess she's not the only vengeful entity in town.

It's a fucking poltergeist.

"They say the Songstress of Lorelei keeps corpses as pets. Collared carcasses for her personal amusement."

"My cousin is a military op. He told me she's amassing an army of hexen alive and dead to take down The League."

"She lures men and women into her bed with glamours and love spells and then tears out their hearts. My sister barely survived an encounter with her."

-*Rumours* as published by The League Tribunal

4

THE KNIGHT OF PENTACLES

A PAIR OF ÆTHER PISTOLS FIRE ON THE poltergeist as the two adepts fly into action.

Renki and Akari draw their swords, a full-length katana for Renki, the shorter chisa for Akari. Their blades, hardwired into their forearms, glimmer with saibāki, and their eyes shine with the glow of their sights. Their cerebral tech is active.

Black tentacles, blurred and misty, lash at them.

"Akari!" calls Renki.

"On it!"

The two trainees throw their swords. The weapons, attached via extending and contracting cables, fly through the air to flank the undead. Unfortunately, their control is not quite perfect, and the poltergeist evades their attacks, ensnaring the blades in its ghostly tentacles. The two teens are ripped off their feet and thrown across the courtyard.

Before they hit the pavement, Wren flexes her magic and catches them lest the impact break something. Their blades clatter to the asphalt, and the cable attachments begin reeling the weapons back to their respective owners. Wren turns to the poltergeist and wrangles her own necrotic magic around the undead forcing it into stillness. A note of vanquishing on her tongue, she starts an exorcism aria. The poltergeist waffles at her music, a few spirits escaping into the ether. It balks, then vanishes back into the virtual realm through one of the beacon arrays.

"What 'az happened? Why have all of zhe systems gone out?"

Director Winnifred runs into the courtyard yelling at the top of his lungs. Several staff members follow behind with Dr. Faust in the lead. Before the director can make it farther into the dark courtyard, a wave of necrotic energy crashes into him and his body goes completely limp, levitating into the air like a damp towel. The dark tendrils disappear under his skin, and when he is placed back on the ground, his body is stiff as a cadaver, menacing and filled with killing intent.

Faust barks orders at the screaming staff, going so far as to slap one woman for going into hysterics. The malice drips off the director in near tangible, syrupy globs of ooze. Black blood seeps from his eyes and mouth, and he attacks Akari. The girl deflects the blow with her sword before diving back out of the way to shoot him with her pistol. A single beam hits the walking corpse, and the creature shrieks, an explosion of rage that shakes the very foundations of the building.

Dr. Faust is shouting.

"Save the database! Terminate the files!" and he dives for the back office, a gun in hand. Wren gives chase. Right as she gets ahold of his coat, the lights go out.

Every light in the courtyard, every light in the building, everything save for the violet glow of the beacons and the various computer systems blinks out completely. The doctor knocks her knees out from under her but trips on the way, the gun flying from his grip. She grabs it, but he lunges for her, wrestling her for the weapon. They scuffle on the floor while the adepts outside try to subdue the possessed director. A charge goes off just past her ear, and she punches Faust in the face as another wail falls from the newly possessed corpse's mouth.

It races into the building heading directly for Wren. Wren's eyes glow green as she pulls kinetic force into her hand. She shoves the doctor off and aims the pistol at the dead man's body.

The shot hits, and the poltergeist releases its host with a screech before whirling away into the darkness of the building.

When she turns back, Faust is gone, and she has no idea where he's run off to. She stands and shakes debris from her clothing, glowering at having lost the doctor. Her right arm tingles, and she pulls up her sleeve to see three of the cuts on her wrist have disappeared. One for the head nurse, one for the director, and who the last one was for, she is unsure, but one of the remaining cuts is bound to be for the wretched doctor.

Renki and Akari run up to her. Renki scans her, checking for injuries.

"Renki, should we call Miyazaki-sama?"

"I think it would be wise. We don't know how long it will take him to get here."

Oh, goddess above and below, no!!

"Ohh, there's no need to do that. I can take care of it."

They ignore her. Akari activates her sights, no doubt already composing the message as Renki dictates it to her.

"Let him know it's a poltergeist. A lot of malignant energy has built up here."

"Look," she calls again. "I think I have a better grasp of what may have caused this to happen, so why don't you just let me take care of it, okay? There are at least 20 tortured souls powering that thing."

The pair actually stop and look at her this time, shocked by number of people who have died so recently in this place.

"Send the message, Akari."

Akari nods, and the teen's sights begin to swirl ultraviolet. Wren holds her hands together in a pleading gesture.

"It really would be best not to bother his highness with this. Let me take care of it, okay? Besides these were my friends. I'd like to see them put to rest."

And she needs to get her hands on that bastard doctor to do it. She won't be killing anyone if Kaito comes snooping around.

Akari shakes her head and continues relaying the message, and Wren lunges forward to grab the comm from her hand, but, spry youth she is, she dodges her and clicks the send button, sending the message spiraling through cyberspace directly into the prince's ocular comms to be seen in microseconds. Wren nearly weeps from the thought of it.

Great! This is great! Kaito Miyazaki, in all his self-righteous glory, is on his way here right now. *¡Pinche puta!*

"Miss Vaishi, did you see which way it went?"

She purses her lips, hand on her hips. "Oh? Now you care about what I have to say..."

"Ma'am, please. We are doing our best," says the girl.

"I haven't a clue where it went, but I'm going this way."

"But it's pitch dark in here," protests Akari.

"Well, it's not like the lights will be coming back on their own any time soon. Our poltergeist has likely dismantled the entire lighting system."

She hears a scraping sound, like a match against its box. There is a smoky smell, and a small patch of light blooms from Renki's fingertips. When Wren sees the tiny flame, she shrieks, jumping back and away from the now lit candle in the boy's hand.

"What are you doing?" she sputters and blows it out, much to the pair's aghast faces.

"Lighting a candle, Miss. So you can see?"

"Don't you know that's a fire hazard?! Do you want this whole place to go up in flames! Machines! Has no one taught you common sense!"

"Miss Vaishi, it was just a candle," says the female adept, confused and a bit taken aback.

"Yeah, well little candles become burning buildings if you're not careful. Be sensible! Don't you kids have night vision settings in those prodigious eyes of yours?"

She storms away, muttering to herself about senseless teenagers and their stupidity eventually burning the world down. Besides, it's not like she's a blind billy in the dark.

There are scratching sounds coming from inside the walls. Rats, maybe... or something more sinister. She begins to hum softly, an obscure rhythm surely neither of the adepts behind her can recognize. They still have their weapons drawn, their vision accoutrements swirling steadily in their pupils as they scan their surroundings. Wren shuffles her way through the dark easily, the glow of their weapons providing plenty of light for her. The scratching persists, and something skates across Wren's perception.

"Well, that isn't good..."

Renki comes up beside her. "What is it?"

Bloodlust. That's what it is: a steaming heap of it.

She pushes Renki aside as a metal fist punches through the space right where his head used to be. The teen lifts his sword to deflect another blow, but Wren grabs the arm as it is pulled fast backward. Her head spins as the world goes topsy turvy. She sings a high-pitched series of skipping notes and arpeggios, and the now possessed Malcolm yells as pain wrecks through his head at her siren's song. He shakes his arm, violently trying to dislodge her, but she holds fast as the two adepts round on the walking corpse.

Alarms wail through the building, red lights flashing bright enough to peel the skin off Wren's teeth. She lets go and is flung through a nearby window and back into the courtyard. 'Malcolm' follows as she tucks and rolls across the grass, but the adepts intervene, engaging the undead in combat. She watches them parry around the possessed corpse. They're good, well trained and capable, but still young and inexperienced. They won't be able to hold it without reinforcements. She rolls her way over to Favreau's dead body.

"*Rís upp og þjóna mér.*"

The words spill from her lips in a half-song as she cuts the meat of her thumb open to paint the appropriate runes on the corpse. The discordant melody resonates in the atmosphere like a curse before folding into the woman's cooling corpse. The body rises from the ground. Blackened eyes focus on her as Wren pushes more of her will into the enchantment. The familiar curl of her energy shimmers green around her fingertips.

"*Ráðast á!*"

The nurse's corpse, Wren's new poppet, flies forward at Wren's command. Its fingers clench into claws as it lashes at the possessed Malcolm's throat. The adepts draw back in confusion as the two undead begin to rip at each other like animals.

The alarm continues to blare as Wren ducks back into the building just in time to see the doctor run past with a briefcase in hand.

"Hey!" she shouts, and he fires two shots at her in response as he bolts.

She ducks under the desk, a bullet ricocheting off the metal of the chair. The dead eyes of the nurse who nearly broke a comb in her hair stare up at her. She swallows and takes a moment to close the woman's eyelids before pulling the beacon from her bodice and scanning the code for Faust's signature. He's heading for the parking lot. She dashes after him.

"Give me back that beacon!" Akari orders.

Ah, she has a pursuer. Wren runs, using the holo to navigate her way, unconcerned with the girl chasing her.

"Stop, thief!" She is so loud.

Wren rolls her eyes. "Back off, kid. You'll just be in the way."

She isn't entirely sure she can outrun the teen, though. The girl is training to be a technomancer, after all. Wren herself was a fully-fledged technomancer in her past life; she knows how rigorous the training is, but unfortunately her new body is quite green, unaccustomed to physical activity. Not to mention while the teenager may not have technomancer-grade augmentations, she's definitely got some physical enhancements whereas Wren has none. So, like an angry ghost, she throws gurneys and tables and lamps in the girl's path much to the child's astonishment.

"Stop it, you—"

And she takes a pillow to the face instead. Telekinesis for the win.

Akari stumbles, and Wren makes it out to the lot just as the doctor revs up his car. She aims the pistol and fires. A bullet ricochets off the hood, and the car backpedals. She keeps firing as the car's headlights burn in her direction. Her next shot goes through the windshield, and a shout of pain comes from the driver. The accelerator growls.

8...7...6...

She fires off the rest of the clip and throws it to the side, lifting a hand to her teeth. She bites into the soft flesh at the heel of her palm and blood flows.

5...4...

"Get out of the street, you lunatic!" Ah, Akari's finally caught up.

3...

She holds her bleeding hand out, a dark green mist steaming from the wound. A discordant melody falls from her lips in a language both old and new, corporeal and ethereal, opaque and translucent.

2...

Pressure builds inside her head.

"Miyazaki-sama!"

1.

Her eyes close and she releases a furious swirl of psychic power. Two things happen at once:

First, the doctor's car flips back over front mere meters from where she stands. There's a terrible screeching sound as the metal grinds against the gravel. She covers her face, prepared for a world of hurt, but there's the second thing. Something barrels into her side, and she is pulled off her feet by a very solid body. Her vision goes black, and there is an explosion as the car lands on its hood.

When her vision clears, the first thing she sees is a fine silk sleeve in the lightest shade of grey embroidered with lavender and black peonies attached to a torso covered in a smooth leather vest, bracers, and belts over black work leathers protecting his legs.

Wren's throat clogs, and her eyes travel up the corded length of his neck to a face which might have been mistaken for a woman's were it not for the strong line of his jaw and the prominent Adam's apple. She takes in the steely facial features of the man carrying her. Clean-shaven with a pointed chin that somehow softens into a razor-sharp jawline, the smooth planes of his cheeks descending from high cheekbones, the aristocratic line of his nose, full lips presently drawn thin into a serious line of calculation, and silver almond-shaped eyes, glinting violet with active tech. The ever-so familiar mole at the outer corner of his left eye is the singular imperfection on his clean complexion, if one could call it an imperfection.

The dark line of his brow, deadly serious, is crowned by the violet glow of inlaid tech which decorates his temple.

His hair is longer than she remembers, a few stray chestnut-colored strands falling into his face while the rest is pulled back into a knot. The hair at the sides around his ears and temples is shorter, shaved close to the skin, more tech nodes visible along the curve of his skull. It's a rugged look for a man who is the crown prince of his country but appropriate for someone who spends far more time on the hunt than in the throne room.

He is crouched over her and dead focused on the overturned vehicle. Twin sword hilts decorate his back. They glint, menacing in the moonlight.

Prince Kaito Miyazaki. The highest ranking technomancer of Murasaki no Yama holds Wren Nocturne in his arms for the first time in twelve years.

Not that he knows, of course.

Technomancers, human+ who stand above the laws of their nations, dedicate their lives to the task of bringing justice against Hexen, but not just anyone with a sense of righteousness and an automated hand can be a technomancer. Adepts seeking advancement to claim the title of technomancer may only do so by completing The Technomancer Trials. Held annually, young adepts, combat—augmented youths from the ages of 15 to 21 from across the world, face the gauntlet for a chance to ascend and join the ranks of the highest class of human+ warrior in the League.

They do this, of course, at great personal risk to themselves.

An Excerpt from *On Technomancers and Adepts: A History on Human+ Soldiers*
By E.X. Icarus, 1812 A.P.

5

THE APPRENTICE PART 1

16 Years Ago–The Month of Songs 1861–**The** 247th
Technomancer Trials

KAI IS SIXTEEN YEARS OLD WHEN HE CHOOSES
to undergo the Technomancer Trials. His mother and aunt
offered him the option to attend the year previous, fifteen being the
minimum age requirement for attendance, but he refused, stating
since the summit would be held in Shinka the following year, he
might as well wait the additional year before attending. He could
use the extra year to better prepare for the examinations. While
he would certainly try his best to pass the trials his first year of
attendance, he was in no way impatient to ascend. His elder brother,
Hikaru, who he looked up to and respected above all others, had
waited until he was seventeen to attend his first summit. He failed
the first time but passed his second year at the age of eighteen.

In many ways, his mother had been relieved.

Murasaki no Yama has long been known to garner the fewest
deaths whenever they host the trials due to the strict process of
elimination leading up to the final trials. As such, trial attendance

is usually quite high when they host. This year, the summit would host the heirs of nearly every major royal family on the continent.

Kaito would be representing Murasaki as the younger son of Empress Mirai Miyazaki. Prince Chike Nagi, the heir apparent of the southernmost country of Ebele is in attendance for his third attempt. From Aighneas, the western democracy, came Rihannon Gewalt, younger sister to the country's first president, for her first try at the trials. From the desert country of Sekhmeti came Jamar Sahra, the crown prince and son of Pharaoh Rameses, to try for the completion of his certification after taking a year of study between his last failed attempt and this one.

From the northerly urbanized, religiously zealot country of Seraphim hailed two candidates: Oswald Llywelyn, trying for the last time to pass the trials at the age of 21, and Donarick Johnson Thames, the only recognized son of Seraphim's spiritual leader, Pontiflex Catalan. Llywelyn, hot-headed and arrogant, is the son of the League's technomancer general, Archibald Llywelyn, while Thames, often considered kind and soft-spoken, will be attempting to pass for the first time this year to meet his father's inflated expectations.

Lastly, from the island country of Deriva would come two children of the court: Prince Xipilli Moctezuma, heir apparent to the Coral Throne, and his younger half-sister, the Lady Wren Nocturne, daughter of Vulcan Tlanextli and his second wife, Firefly Freya Nocturne.

Of course, it is not just the peerage who send their teenagers to vie for the title of Technomancer. Children of wealthy business owners and military powers and teenagers from the commonwealth will attend. There will even be several teens from poor, impoverished, possibly even subservient families looking to make a better future for themselves and their loved ones. Art Lionheart, a farmer's boy from Aighneas, is a name Kaito has heard uttered during discussions. Another well-whispered name is Irene, a girl from a smaller nation who would be returning for her fifth chance to earn a title and free her mother from slavery.

While Kaito is not particularly excited about strangers entering his quiet home of Shinka Temple, he understands the significance of their familial land acting as the host site for the summit. In the months leading up to the event, he and his brother, in addition to their usual duties, oversaw the preparation of the candidates' guest quarters and the hiring of additional staff to account for the caretaking of the facilities. His brother, Hikaru, as a summit graduate, would be sitting on the panel of faculty this year alongside Kaito's aunt, Fumiko. This responsibility assigned his brother the additional task of summit preparation meetings and evaluation organization. Since Kai would be participating this year, he was not allowed to be privy to any of these conversations.

The first day of the summit, Kaito's mother, Empress Mirai Miyazaki, and his brother, Hikaru, as the crown prince, stand on the raised dais of the throne room where the opening ceremonies of the summit are to be held.

To either side of her stand the leaders of the League's various nations: President Gewalt, mocha-skinned and powerful, looking severe in her military uniform, Earth Shaker, the cannon hand, resting at her side ready to be brought to life at a moment's notice. Pharaoh Rameses Sahra, dressed in the golds and linens of Sekhmeti's trademark industry, stands tall and hulking over many of the others, his long goatee tapered at the end. Vulcana Elisabeta, present in her husband, Vulcan Tlanextli's stead, wears the traditional island garb of Deriva, layers of silk cloth dyed in an array of watery colors drape elegantly about her frame in billowy folds to mask the various accoutrements molded to her form for underwater combat. From Ebele, Orisha Absko sits wearing the bright colors of his home and its collective tribes. His mechanical eye glows red as it scans the assembled crowd for threats. Lastly, Pontiflex Catalan, born Howard P. Thames, the religious and spiritual leader of Seraphim sits beside General Llywelyn, a man who ascended to his station from humble common roots. While not a technomancer, the pontiflex wears the traditional decorations of his station, an oversized hat and garments of a deep divine red, while the general stands in stoic observance, dressed in immaculate military blues, his technomancer badge shining at his breast.

The empress of Murasaki no Yama stands proud at the podium as she looks out at the assembly.

"Welcome all. Leaders of the world, members of the peerage, honored technomancers, and young hopefuls undertaking the challenge of the Technomancer Trials. For decades Murasaki no Yama has been honored to stand beside Seraphim, Aighneas, Ebele, Deriva, and Sekhmeti as an ally and friend. In the establishment of the League, we have better served our peoples, protecting them from the forces of this world that would do them harm. It is Murasaki's honor this year to host the 247th Technomancer Trials."

His mother continues her speech with decorum and elegance, delivering unto the group the expectations of all attendees as well as a brief overview of the Miyazaki principles and temple etiquette all of them are expected to adhere to during their stay. Kaito sits, dutifully listening, with the rest of the trainees who will be attending the lessons and trials with him, but somewhere to his right, he hears hushed voices.

Three students, two girls and a boy, huddle their heads together; granted, the boy seems to be rather off-put about being the middleman between the two girls who are whispering to each other about the gods know what. One of them, he recognizes as wearing the same military garb as President Gewalt; she must be the younger sister. The other girl he cannot see very clearly, turned away from him as she is. He glares in their direction for their disrespect, and the Gewalt girl catches on rather quickly, pink rising into her cheeks as she quickly rights herself in her seat, pointing in his direction to the other girl. Long dark waves of hair bounce as she turns to look at him curiously.

Her eyes are quite possibly the clearest shade of aquatic blue-green he has ever seen, and they sparkle as she grins his direction, one of her hands coming up to wave at him good-naturedly. He sees rather than hears her laughter, and his eyes narrow at her impudence.

When he doesn't acknowledge the greeting, she almost pouts, turning back to give attention to Kaito's mother only when the boy next to her elbows her in the side. She huffs dramatically but returns her attention forward.

"As customary, we begin the summit with opening presentations as our candidates demonstrate and perform their talents for their peers. Then we will depart, leaving our perspectives to the Apprentices' Dance."

Behind him, a pair of boys whisper excitedly.

"Do you think any of the girls will be looking for prospects?"

"There usually are. Boys, too, looking to attract someone's attention, no doubt. What, you looking for a wife?"

"Goodness no, just a fun time, but my father asked me to keep an eye out for any promising ones."

Kai tunes out the remainder of the conversation. It is true enough. Many of the wealthier candidates attend the summit for the sole purpose of scouting out possible matrimonial matches for themselves and their families. With so many members of the peerage and world leadership in attendance, it is a great opportunity for advancement if a son or daughter from a less prominent family, should they capture the attention of a higher-class student or their family. Kai has no such inclination for such behavior, and the Miyazaki family has never once arranged a marriage between trial trainees based on such displays. Nor would he be participating in the social interaction reserved for trainees after the ceremonies. Games, dancing, drinking, unsupervised indulgence. It is a bit of a sham but a tradition, one his aunt had fought tooth and nail to dismantle for the year, but his mother felt it was necessary to uphold as a means to give any youth who might pay the ultimate price for attending the trials a last taste of life in an evening of carefree dalliance.

At this point, Mirai takes her seat at the center of the dais. One of their vassals steps forward with a tablet in hand and begins to read off the names of first-year potentials. The first name called is one Heather Ables. A rather tall girl wearing Gewalt blues steps forward. She salutes her president and turns to take her place by the microphone. First years could present any such display of talent they would like: music, dancing, physical fitness demonstrations, theater presentations; a few students even take the time to create a visual work of art to present to the crowd.

The girl is exceptionally nervous as she takes her place on the stage before the entire congregation, a piano accompanist joining her at the nearby grand. Kaito's heart goes out to her. It is not easy being first, and it most certainly isn't easy standing in front of such a crowd if one is unused to performing, but there is a certain level of charisma expected of technomancers. In fact, it is not uncommon for a student to be held back due to a lack in quality of their performance. One could almost think of it as an entrance exam to the trial itself, the first test they would all need to pass before continuing their paths.

It is not unusual for an adept to study music. In fact, there are many who choose a musical instrument as their weapon of choice, manipulating soundwaves to attack and defend, such is the prerogative of the Sahra family who favor their stringed sitars and portable drums as conduits for controlling and commanding their robotic companions rather than serial commands, a measure to prevent hacking.

The girl does not do a bad job. The song she sings is classical and recognizable but unremarkable. Her voice shakes a bit, and she stumbles through one of the passages, but overall, she does well. Polite applause rises for her as she bows and steps down from the platform. Several of her second-year compatriots congratulate her as she returns to her seat. The girl in Aighnean blues claps for her as she goes to sit, and she shakes her head and blushes. The raven-haired girl also cheers loudly, happy to support her friend.

The next few candidates perform their talents in a steady stream that neither captivates nor entirely bores him. There is a blooming painter in 2nd Lt. Rhiannon Gewalt, the girl he assumed to be The Morrigan's younger sister; Colton Huntmeiser demonstrates his skill with a bow and arrow; one of the boys who had been sitting behind him sings and plays a decent jig on his lute; Donarick Thames of Seraphim performs a stage monologue while

Anika Kashtri decides to both entrance and horrify with a stunning display of sword swallowing; and pair of twins from Murasaki, a boy and a girl, perform a duet of juggling and acrobatics. They are nearing an hour into the ceremony when his name is called.

"Prince Kaito Miyazaki of Murasaki no Yama."

Kai rises as his name is called. He has been rehearsing for this presentation. It would not do for him to embarrass his family when they play host to the summit. He walks, holding his head high, to the grand piano, and he takes a seat after bowing to his mother and brother at their places on the dais. The piece he plays is old and classical, difficult and technical. He plays it from memory. The notes flow from his fingertips easily, and he loses himself in the music he coaxes from the instrument. Into the piano, Kai pours the parts of himself he would never share with anyone other than his family.

The piece is in a minor key, and while it rises and falls as any properly composed piece of music should, there is a lilt of sadness in it, and when it concludes, there is an air of anticipation as the listeners wait for a resolution that will never come. He rises and bows as the room applauds, but they matter naught to him. He sees the looks of pride in his mother, aunt, and brother's eyes, and that's enough for him. And if he happens to notice the raven-haired girl's smile, unreasonably bright in the dimmed light over the assembly seating, it is of no consequence to him.

Surprisingly enough, the bright-eyed girl is summoned next.

"Lady Wren Nocturne of the Derivan Royal Family."

It is a peculiar introduction. A few whispers flit about the room as the girl rises and makes her way to the front of the room.

"I heard the Vulcan of Deriva had a lovechild with his Firefly, but I thought it was just a rumor. To think he would allow her to attend the trials alongside the Crown Prince?"

"I heard her mother was an unparalleled beauty who seduced the vulcan into marrying her as a second wife, but she died several years ago."

PRELUDE

"They say he favors his lovechild over his heirs. Vulcana Elisabeta threatened divorce if he even thought about giving her the Moctezumo name."

"No wonder Vulcana Elisabeta came instead this year. She must be looking to marry her ward off to get her out of her hair."

"Silence!"

Hikaru's command of the hall successfully shushes the gossip. Wren makes her way up to the dais deaf to their whispers, a light expression on her face. Vulcana Elisabeta rises as the girl bows in salute to her stepmother. With a stern expression on her face, she curls a hand under the girl's chin and lifts it as though for inspection. She gives her husband's daughter a scathing word before dismissing her to take her place on the stage.

Wren removes her boots from her feet and takes the stage, moving the microphone away from where she decides to sit on the edge of the stage, her feet dangling off the lip while her accompanist, a violin player, takes her place farther upstage. Kai expects the violinist to begin playing first, but it is Wren who begins, a gentle hum falling clear from her throat without the aid of a mic.

Misty light on the water
The moon lights the night for my lover's soul.
And the sea lulls with whispers of hope.
Fire burns with ardor's touch.

The strength of the mountain
Tall in the storm.
The north wind desperate,
Cold it blows,
Screaming out, "Let go" and "Bend low,"
But stone tumbles down for no one, least not to thee.

The Apprentice Part I

Hear now the siren's song,
For she calls for her mistress,
Ocean heart singing long into the night.
Breathe deep and water crashes over.
I am pulled to the deep.
Drowned by time's first love, I am but lost.

Pulled under the ocean blue,
I catch my breath, singing her call.
Smoke and fire, war's cruelest lovers,
Surrender to the deep; heal the woe.
My heart, a willing slave to the sea.

As her voice fades, the violin begins to play, and Wren dances around the stage. He notices the dress she wears is less formal than would typically be expected at an event like this. It clings to her form in carefully designed layers of material that fly away from her body as she twists and turns in a display of grace and acrobatics. She dances and her movements cast a spell over her audience. Her movements pause as she sings a second part of the verse. She doesn't even sound out of breath.

Even the might of mountains is but sand to the sea.
The heat of wrath, most violent, quenched by Danu's waters.
And if the sky falls, the surf be my weapon,
Mountain's shadow looming down, my blood is the ocean.

Pulled under the ocean blue,
I catch my breath, singing her call.
Smoke and fire, war's cruelest lovers,
Surrender to the deep; heal the woe.

My heart, a willing slave to the sea.

The duet ends with a small refrain from the violin as Wren descends to the floor in a full split, humming the final few notes of her song to the ready applause that engulfs the hall. Wren rises from the floor and bows, thanking her accompanist before descending the stage. The boy in the seat next to hers, who must be Prince Xipilli and therefore her half-brother, rises to help her return to her seat. She nudges him away with her shoulder before pulling the seat out herself.

How uncouth.

The remaining trainees perform their prepared arts, but none of them compare to Lady Wren's stunning display, and soon enough, the congregation is dismissed save for participating adepts who wish to take part in the Apprentices' Ball which will begin once the peerage have left. They are reminded classes begin promptly at 800 hours, and once the trials begin, a strict curfew will be observed.

Kai makes his way to stand with his mother and brother on the dais. Hikaru speaks first.

"Well done, Brother. You should be proud of your presentation."

"Thank you. It was a passable performance," he says. Mirai steps forward and places a hand on his shoulder.

"So humble, my youngest. Clearly your aunt has taught you well."

"As is proper."

Fumiko, Kaito's aunt, steps forward to join them from where she was previously seated with the other evaluators and faculty members. His aunt wears a traditional yukata in the men's style, her long dark hair done up in an impeccable topknot which only sharpens the severe expression on her face. Any outsider might look at the two sisters and think the younger of the two to be years older than the elder, even though they are, in actuality, twins born mere minutes apart. Kai's mother is too self-aware to allow her exasperation with her younger sister to show on her face, but it comes through plenty in her next statement.

"Ah, my sister is ever the wisest in the matters of our familial honor."

Fumiko Miyazaki, or Miyazaki-sensei as she would become known to many of the trainees present in the coming weeks, does not rise to the bait, choosing instead to address Kaito.

"Kaito, you have done well today. Do you intend to participate in the evening's frivolities?"

"I have no reason to."

"Good. You should return to your rooms and rest before the morrow. These next weeks will be a test of your knowledge, strength, and perseverance."

Another voice from behind them calls out. "Oh, Fumiko, ever so stringent. Allow the lad to socialize with his peers. I've encouraged my own Derivan attendees to live without boundaries this evening."

Elisabeta approaches the Miyazaki family with a rather cunning smile on her face. Mirai turns to greet her with a gentle expression on her face.

"Elisabeta, you must be proud of your stepdaughter. A great show of skill and an enchanting performance from Lady Wren, one I only remember as having been matched by your eldest daughter, Princess Atzi, during her presentation ball."

The vulcana scoffs.

"You are too kind, Your Excellency, but I'm afraid my stepdaughter far surpasses her elder sister in both talent and grace. If I were a lesser woman, I would have thrown such a child out long ago, but she is quite dear to her half-siblings, and Atzi has secured a promising marriage with young Chike of Ebele. I can only hope my ward will somehow manage the same during her time here."

"Is Lady Wren not a bit young for marriage prospects, Vulcana?" inquires Fumiko.

"No younger than your fine boy here, Miyazaki-sensei. Marvelous playing by the way, young prince," she says to him offhandedly. "My beloved stepdaughter is far too much like her mother. The sooner I marry her off, the better."

Mirai hums in understanding.

"But if Lady Wren passes her trials, you will have no such say in Wren's affairs."

Elisabeta all but laughs.

"As if that girl could pass these trials! I have full confidence Fumiko will do her due diligence and frighten her off. She'll fold under the pressure and come running home after the first week. But, if you'll excuse me, I wish to see my son before I depart."

Kai bows his head as the vulcana bids the Miyazaki family adieu, calls over her charges, and makes her way out of the grand hall, her son and stepdaughter on her heels. And if the girl glances back in his direction and mouths "good job" to him, he pretends not to notice.

Later that evening, with the Apprentice's Ball in full fling in the main hall, Kaito walks the grounds of his home in solitude.

The courtyard is empty. The stone walkways which start at the temple's arches and twine in circular patterns all the way to the central zen garden are vacant save for the stray wildlife that have ventured from the forest to roam the quiet but lit grounds. A few rabbits graze in the grasses at the edge of the courtyard, an owl hoots somewhere up in the rafters of the dormitory porches, and in the raked sand of the rock garden, he can see where a deer has set foot in the last hour or so.

Shinka Temple is not just a singular building. It is an entire compound taking up acres upon acres of land. Land which does not end at the forest line but reaches well into the snow-capped mountain peaks that glow lavender in the moonlight from the rich levels of magnesium in the rock and soil.

Leading away from the infinity bands of stone and grass that frame the gardens, wooden ramps lead visitors up to the elevated walkways designed to preserve the grasses and gardens below various parts of the temple compound: the adept/devotee dormitories to the east and west of the courtyard where many of the trial participants will live for the next two months. Between them lies the central hall where the opening ceremonies took place. Beyond the main hall clockwise is a spiraling tower where most of their lecture halls and laboratories are, and past that is the library pagoda, the main banquet hall, and training fields. Farther back from the entrance, the royal family apartments are tucked away on the far easterly side of the compound—where Kaito normally resides with his brother were he not a participant in the trials this year. All of these surround and lead to the shrine for which these grounds even exist.

Shinka Temple, his family's pride: three stories stacked high enough that Kaito can see the topmost level from where he stands, a rooftop comprised of swooped raking that ends in a skyward pointed arch, lit by strings of amber twinkle lights in the night. Older even than Murasaki, Shinka Temple was built centuries ago as a safe haven for non-magical people seeking refuge from witches in a time when scientific study was illegal.

The first technomancer was born here. The man would learn how to use science and technology against hexen oppression and give normal people a chance for freedom. The temple still stands today as a reminder for perseverance and dedication to the technologic arts, the central hub of Murasaki no Yama.

He can just hear the pulsing music coming from the main hall. A few girls stumble out laughing and clearly intoxicated; a male he recognizes as Oswald comes out after them, but they laugh him off and continue to their dorms. He watches as the older boy returns to the hall, no doubt in search of someone else to spend the evening with. Kai shakes his head and thinks maybe he should just go to his room as his aunt mentioned, but just as he is about to head back inside, he hears a series of loud blasts fire off in the direction of one of the temple training ranges—a training range which is certainly not open for anyone at this time of night.

His eyes narrow as he scans the virtual coding around the grounds to find the gate unlocked and someone in the firing range. He does not recognize the signature as one of the faculty or Murasakan adepts, which can only mean one of the visiting candidates somehow found a way into the grounds without permission. The training grounds are security warded against unauthorized entry and for whoever it is to be firing a ranged weapon unsupervised at this time is both unsafe and irresponsible.

He goes to investigate.

As suspected, the person standing in the center of the range is not anyone with authorization to be there. It's the girl from Deriva: Wren Nocturne. She wears a dark corseted dress, cut and strapped to her form for combat mobility, a glove on her left hand. Her skin glows under the moonlight, and her dark hair is tied messily at the top of her head. She hasn't noticed him yet. He is too far away, his approach too quiet. Her head is tilted down as she recharges the weapon in her hand. She takes a wide stance and aims another shot that is sure to make enough noise to disturb those already asleep.

His sights whirl as he remote hacks into its mainframe, and the pistol deactivates in her grip at his behest. Confusion laces her features as she looks around, turning finally to see him standing there. Surprise decorates her face before she waves at him far more exuberantly than she has any right to be, having been caught breaking and entering a secured area her first day in Shinka.

"Oh, your highness! Sorry, did my shooting disturb you?"

"Shouldn't you be at the dance?"

She shrugs.

"Eh, didn't feel like sticking around. I grabbed myself a bottle of rum and left."

That's when he sees the bottle of alcohol at her feet, half drained of its contents. She is shooting a weapon under the influence of alcohol!

"How did you get in here?"

She drops her firearm to the side. She laughs seemingly abashed, while the fingers of her other hand twirl a lock of her hair.

"Ehehe, I kind of just let myself in. It isn't too big of a deal, right? I mean, I just needed to blow off some steam, and it seemed like a better idea to do so away from the main building. Wouldn't you agree?"

"You are practicing with a firearm without supervision in a restricted area after ingesting alcohol. Does that seem like a big enough deal to you?"

"I mean, it isn't hurting anybody, is it?"

"It is a violation of the temple rules to which you apparently paid no attention."

She smiles brightly at him. Her green eyes glitter in the moonlight.

"I was too paying attention. I just think rules are superfluous, but alright." She holds up her hands in a peace-giving gesture. "I'll go back. Let me just finish up this last round."

She powers the weapon back up and turns back to her target. Anger curls in his stomach, and before he knows it, he has flickered across the distance between them until he is right beside her. His hands deftly steal the weapon from her hands.

"Report to your quarters, Lady Nocturne. This is your last warning."

"Warning for what?"

"Return now, and I will request the Grandmaster pass you a lenient punishment."

She laughs aloud at that, shaking her head in disbelief. "Wow, your family really is stringent, aren't they? I heard rumors but didn't think they could possibly be true." She grins at him like a cat. "Don't worry, Kaito-san, I'm happy to accept any penalty your aunt can think up."

She winks at him. That in junction with the use of his first name jars him so much she steals the pistol back from him and dances away, aiming another shot at the target. Her aim is true, hitting the target dead center.

She turns back to him, a tilted smirk on her lips. Fury burns through him. This girl is actually mocking him.

He doesn't think. He moves, aiming a kick at her hand to disarm her once again. She drops the pistol to the ground and ducks to evade him while aiming a fist into his abdomen. He deflects her attack and delivers his own. Her left hand blocks his swing, and he is only somewhat surprised the flesh doesn't give beneath the hit. A prosthetic.

He whirls a roundhouse kick at her, but she jumps back and away from him in a back tuck. He presses her, and she evades, twisting and turning in her retreat. Occasionally, she swipes at him in turn, her laughter ringing like bells on the wind. She matches him, blow for blow, and it's frustrating and startling. Exciting... He's never sparred with someone this capable. It's... it's exhilarating.

There is a dock and lake at the far side of the grounds used for training water-based skills. It also serves as an access point to the port, an underground river flowing from its bottom straight to the sea. He's herded her straight to the edge of it. Or was it she who led him? Either way, by the time he realizes it, it's too late.

She rams her shoulder into his chest, and he goes careening toward the water as a result. He catches her upper arm in his right hand and pulls her right along with him into the water. Ice cold water. The winter frosts have only recently melted, and the mountain springs could be considered chilly even at the height of summer.

They hit the icy water with a loud splash.

He releases her and swims, breaking the surface with little more than a long inhale. She stays under just a touch longer before she breeches with a spew of curses, sputtering, and general uncoordinated splashing as she hurriedly climbs out of the water. She pulls herself from the lake like a drowned cat and flops on the ground, hissing and spitting.

"*¡Pinche mierda!* That's cold! Did you have to pull me in with you?"

He ignores the so-called lady swearing up a storm on the shore.

Used to the temperate waters of his home, Kai pulls himself from the water with much more decorum though the formal kimono he wears is now drenched, hanging heavy from his body in layers of soaked fabric. His bangs hang limp and sopping wet in front of his eyes. Thankfully, his hair is an easy short length, so he simply combs his fingers through it to get it out of his face while doing his best to wring the water out of his clothing. He hears her doing much the same with far less success as she continues her tirade, cursing in her native tongue. When he hears teeth chattering, he looks up. She is shivering violently, and her lips are beginning to turn blue, clearly more accustomed to the tropical humidity of her home. A quick thermal analysis of her signature confirms her body temperature has dropped below the recommended range. She is guaranteed to be ill come morning.

With a huff, he marches past her, only tilting his head back to deliver a brisk, "Come on."

She is thoroughly unhappy with him, but she can either follow him or catch her death out here in the cold, and while she grumbles the whole way, she follows him as he leads her to the infirmary. He pulls two towels out of the cabinet and passes one to her which she accepts quizzically. The second item he reaches for is a heated blanket. When he turns back to her, she is looking between her damp clothing and the towel as though both have personally offended her. He clears his throat, and she looks at him.

"There's a privacy screen in the corner."

"You mean you don't want to watch?" she teases him. He scowls.

"Your temperature is low. You'll need a tonic if you don't want to end up right back here come morning. Go and dry off, and I will make it for you."

She smiles, a whispered thank you under her breath before she shuffles across the room. He begins to boil water, making a point to tune out the sound of rustling fabric as he works. It's a simple enough concoction, one his mother and aunt made for him countless times as a child to prevent him catching a cold after playing outside in the frost.

"Aren't you cold?"

He grinds several medicinal herbs down using the mortar and pestle.

"I am well acclimated to the temperatures of my home, Lady Nocturne. Though you should be grateful I don't just let you become ill for your foolish behavior."

She laughs, and it rings around the room like bells.

"Ah, I heard Prince Kaito is as chilly as the harsh winters of Shinka. I didn't realize they meant in his constitution as well. Unyielding as ice. This unruly one hasn't a chance at melting him, does she?"

The way she says it makes his ears burn.

"The lady should mind her language lest she bring a worse punishment upon herself for improper conduct."

"Improper? It's the Apprentice's Ball. Words like that have no meaning tonight."

"Then Lady Wren should have stayed in the main hall rather than sneaking into a restricted area."

What inspired her to seek out weapons practice of all things when there was a loud rambunctious party happening right next door? Surely such trivial things are right up her alley.

"You're probably right, but I can handle whatever punishment your aunt sees fit to give."

She sounds indignant. He adds the herbs to the boiling water and lowers the heat. Into the mix, he adds two measures of apple cider vinegar and lemon rinds. He leaves it to reduce for the next five minutes.

"How troublesome..."

He hears her exhale in relief.

"His Highness is too kind. He needn't trouble himself for a hopeless deviant."

She steps around the privacy screen, the heated blanket now wrapped around her like a cocoon and takes a seat in a nearby chair.

"Why did you go to the training grounds?"

"I told you: I needed to blow off some steam."

"Why not 'blow off steam' at the dance?"

"Shooting targets is better. More cathartic, less touchy, and better yet—actually useful."

Intriguingly enough, her words make a strange sort of sense, but...

"You were reckless."

"Productive more like."

"You consider breaking rules productive?"

"Not at all, prince. That's just an entertaining bonus."

"Is there nothing you take seriously?"

"Sure, there is."

"Like?"

"Like teasing the handsome stranger who insists on making me some god-awful tonic after pushing me into a freezing lake."

She smiles.

Never mind the fact that it was she who pushed him into the lake. He just dragged her in with him. He turns away to pour the tonic into a pair of mugs. He keeps one for himself and passes her the other.

"I'm impressed, by the way. Your combat skills match your playing."

"Drink."

Her face drops now that he is once again ignoring her. But she does take a sip of the drink only to immediately gag at the taste of it.

"Are you trying to poison me?"

He takes a calm draught of his own. His face doesn't so much as twitch as the bitterness washes across his palette.

"There's not much that is medicinal that tastes good."

Her face screws up. She pinches her nose shut and downs the rest of the tonic in one long drink. When she finishes, she looks very much like she is seriously considering spitting it back up, but she holds it down and sets the mug on a nearby table.

She stands carefully, the color already returning to her face.

"Thank you, Prince Kaito, for your care, and I do apologize for causing you difficulty. If his highness is unopposed, I shall return to my own rooms."

She offers him a slight bow of her head along with a shaky curtsy. It is the most proper she has behaved all evening.

"Perhaps the lady will see fit not to break rules in the future."

"The lady will do her best, your highness."

It is the most sugary assurance he's ever received in his life, and he doesn't believe her for a second.

"It's rather unbecoming for a lady to lie."

"As opposed to a prince, whose charm is clearly limited to his gift with music and does not extend to social interaction."

Were he a lesser person, he would have rolled his eyes. Instead, a completely different sense overtakes him that he really can't describe. He shakes his head at her antics, brushes the thought to the back of his mind, and finishes his own tonic as she gathers her things. He relays a comm message to his aunt and brother on the girl's rule-breaking. His brother answers quickly with what her punishment will be and asks Kaito to relay the message.

"You can return the blanket in the morning. My brother would like you to report to the lecture hall at 6AM sharp."

"Training doesn't start until 8."

"You'll need to begin writing lines before classes start."

"You already reported me!"

His sights whirl as he looks at her.

"Damn, Miyazaki tech is scary. Fine. I'll see you in the morning."

"Do not be late."

Judging by the way she absentmindedly waves her hand at him on her way out, he fully expects she has no intention of reporting to the library on time. He makes a mental note to have one of the temple's non-participant adepts wake her up well before sunrise to ensure she makes her appointment with his brother.

In the morning, she doesn't thank him for it and glares at him all through morning training. Not that he pays her any mind whatsoever.

6

FIVE OF CUPS

Present–32nd Day in the Month of Fire

KAITO LOOKS DOWN AT "ATALIA" WITH THE same steely indifference he always gives those with whom he is unfamiliar. Wren recognizes the whirl of his sights and knows his internal hardware and data systems are scanning her, probably circuiting through facial recognition software to identify her or checking her over for injury.

She shudders. And what's frustrating is she doesn't know if her body's traitorous response is out of fear or something else entirely.

She feels something wet on her lip and winces. Her nose is bleeding. Probably from the massive wave of power she just exerted to flip the car. She holds the back of her hand to the flow.

He stares down at her for so long she recoils, nearly forgetting that she is wearing a mad woman's face, and while his tech— some of the most advanced in Deus—is good enough to detect the sheen of her magic, it could never see through one of her spells.

"Well, can't say I've ever been swept off my feet by a plusie, but there's a first time for everything."

His eyes narrow at her.

"I guess your kind don't like 'plusie' very much. Would you prefer cyborg? I could say postie as well. Ya know, posthuman."

He does not look at all amused by her. *That's not surprising...*

The sharp sound of glass hitting pavement rings high-pitched across the lot, and Wren sees the doctor sputter his way out the shattered window of his car. He coughs and pulls a compact pulse pistol out of his pocket. He aims for Kai's back.

"Behind you!"

In one seamless motion, Kaito shifts her to the ground and turns, drawing his katana, Tsukuyomi. The blade hilt unlocks, wires slither up his arm to hook into his wrist, and a pulse of saibāki coats the weapon. The blast dissipates against the charged blade. Kai lifts his free hand, sights spinning wildly, the nodule on back of his palm glowing violet in the dark, and the weapon in Faust's hand deactivates, and sparks with an electrical surge. The man topples backward from the electric shock, unconscious on impact with the car.

Wren whistles low under her breath.

"Shocking."

No acknowledgement. Tough crowd. Clearly her jokes are rusty.

"Akari, take Miss Vaishi somewhere where she will not come to harm, and see to it Dr. Faust does not disappear."

"Yes, Miyazaki-sama."

And just like that, he's gone, his second sword, the tanto blade, Amatsu, drawn to his hand as he moves to the fight in the courtyard between her poppet and the poltergeist.

¡Maldicion!

Her poppet. She needs to release it before Kai can analyze it, or it'll be a dead giveaway of the kind of magic she's infamous for.

Akari is just coming to check on her after tying Faust down when she jumps up and races back inside.

"Wait!"

"Sorry, kid. Gotta go!"

She hears a rather nasty curse escape the girl's mouth.

Oh! Fumiko-sensei would never condone such language!

She wants to laugh with pride at the girl's creativity despite her upbringing. High and mighty Miyazaki, her culo! They're mere mortals like the rest of them. They just play the decorum game better than any other royal family around.

The lights are flickering now as she rushes through the hallways. She doesn't even really need to remember the way. The noise of the battle is riotous, easy to follow. When she rounds the corner into the courtyard, Kai is already there. He strikes twice, once to each corpse, and the force of the attack knocks both undead to the ground. Her poppet flops greasily onto the brick, its right arm dangling off its shoulder. It tries to rise again, but Wren whistles to release the casting. Kai's eyes catch the now lifeless poppet's fall. He turns his head, following the energy release, and his eyes narrow on her place against the doorway.

"Renki!" Kai calls, returning his attention to the poltergeist.

"Hai!"

The teen's call comes from somewhere to her left, and she makes an embarrassing squeaking sound as she finds herself bodily lifted off her feet and hauled backward. She kicks and thrashes—the poor teen is going to have bruises on his shins tomorrow—but his grip stays gentle as he pulls her away from the fight.

He doesn't pull her terribly far. He finds the nurse's office and deposits her inside before closing and locking the door. She hears him set something on the door with a click, and when she reaches for the doorknob, she finds the door unsurprisingly warded against her escape.

She kicks the door anyway and promptly regrets the decision. Imagine kicking a steel, electrically guarded door in naught but stockings. Speaking of, her feet are absolutely filthy, but she can rectify that situation later. She needs to get out of here. She wanders toward the back of the office to a walk-in cabinet and meets a dead end. While there is a grate on the floor, it's nowhere near big enough for her to squeeze through.

Prelude

It isn't a complete wash. There are medical supplies, food stores, water canteens, and even a few empty knapsacks she can sweep supplies into. Oh, and look at that! There's a key rack as well. She nabs the first pair of keys that look like they could belong to a reasonable mode of transportation and pilfers one of the knapsacks. She stuffs a few days' worth of supplies into it before swinging it over her back.

She does a quick once over of the room before noticing a safe tucked under a nearby shelf. She smiles to herself before pulling out the beacon still in her possession and attaching it to the safe's façade. She's never called herself a hacker, but she's picked up a trick or two as a teenager. Just a bit of coding, followed by a telekinetic nudge, and the safe swings open for her to reveal stacks of currency inside, but the credit chips aren't all. There is paraphernalia of all sorts in the safe: a box full of ID chips, memory beads, and other small micro-augmentations, a bag of comm units and cells, a rather expensive looking pair of earrings, a wristwatch, and several pairs of gloves both for men and women. She pauses at the last item, a well-loved stuffed animal, probably brought in by a young patient. She sets the bag on the floor and pulls the little creature out of the safe. The teddy bear is fraying in places, and one of its eye sockets has come loose. There's a mismatched stitch where someone repaired a tear, maybe a mother or father. Maybe a grandparent.

A toy loved near to death, ripped from its child.

She catches a shallow emotional residue off the toy: feelings of love and warmth, sadness and comfort, visions of childhood nightmares being chased away by a mighty plush defender and tears being dried by soft synthetic fur. Memories from another life threaten a sob from her chest. Little Fae had a stuffed cat, and she carried the little toy with her everywhere. Wren could never get her to part with it. Not even at the very end.

She had been too young...

A tear slides down her cheek as she sets the teddy on the floor. She prays to any god, goddess, or devil who might be listening for the teddy to be reunited with its charge. Prays they were not one of the unlucky ones who met their death in this hellhole. And if they had, well, was she not a demon of vengeance summoned for that very purpose?

She clears the heartache from her throat and continues looking through the safe. Tucked behind the bear is an instrument case. Curious to the contents, she pulls it out and opens it. A classical violin rests inside the bedding. The bow is old, and the strings are probably completely out of tune, but when she touches the neck, another feeling washes over her. The nudge urges her to take it, so she does, closing the case back up and willing the instrument into the dimensional locket for safekeeping.

Done with the safe, she rises to her feet and returns to the room proper, taking the beacon with her and stowing it away in her bodice once again. The wound on her hand, while it has mostly stopped bleeding, only requires a little bit of coaxing before the blood flows afresh. She draws an array on the floor. This particular casting will cost her a lot of energy, but it will get her out and away from the Miyazaki. After all, the teen warded the door, not the walls. Lucky her. He should've used an anti-magic ward. No way is she going to be arrested her first day back among the living. Not a chance.

After all, it is her birthday. Time to make a wish.

Outside, Kaito Miyazaki subdues the poltergeist quickly and efficiently via a mixture of VR-scaping and swordsmanship. The augmented warden it was possessing lies cooling on the ground while the undead's shadows collectively buzz inside a cage of saibāki generated beams. It almost seems to be crying.

Malignant though they may be, poltergeists are naught but a collection of restless spirits. People who died too young and in too much pain gathered together to form an energy mass capable of wreaking extreme levels of havoc. This one is responsible for the deaths of several staff members at the facility they are now standing in, and with the information provided to him by Akari and Renki, he can imagine why it formed.

When Akari arrives with the unconscious doctor in hand, the poltergeist tries desperately to escape the bonds holding it, no doubt in an effort to attack the man. Kaito pushes his will into it and assures the convoluted mass of lost souls their aggressor will be brought to justice and penalized for the pain he has caused. This satisfies the creature enough for the younger adepts to trap it in a housing port for transit back to Tokiseishu. But there is far more to do before they can clear out.

Kai doesn't have to sit himself at a computer hub to hack into a database. He can do it right inside the confines of his own mind. Sights whirling, he connects himself into the network, and before his eyes, rows of datafiles crop up. Shifting through, he finds, mysteriously enough, there are hardly any files on the drives when the system should be relatively full and in need of an update, having been in use for six years.

For this much drive space to be free... Someone must have wiped the system clean.

He opens the programming files on the system's maintenance history and sees a system clean-up was performed less than 30 minutes ago along with a disk defragmentation which would in theory destroy any evidence of files even being deleted. What is strange, though, is it looks as though the tasks were executed remotely. From a server labelled Br4nchH0us3_24756. When he attempts to trace the origin of the server, a firewall impedes him.

Kaito's eyes narrow, sights spinning faster.

After Kai sets his A.I. to dismantle the firewall, he walks over to examine the previously animated corpse. The state of the woman's body is disconcerting. Her death by the poltergeist had not been kind, and her body is mangled to near unidentifiable from the treatment. Harriet Favreau. Aighnean Citizen. ID# 1268451274. Occupation: Nurse Practitioner currently employed as the head of nursing at Stonehearst Asylum. Red Flags: Previously dismissed by a past employer due to accusations of patient mistreatment. Suspected of organ thief but flew the coop before trial. It would seem this woman failed to uphold her vow to do no harm.

No wonder her death at the hands of a vengeful spirit was so violent.

Upon further inspection, he finds trails of magical residue lining her throat and eyes. The markings, visible only under his sights, are faint, lines of neon green under his necrotic magic scanners. Only someone who knew what they were looking for could identify such markings, and Kaito has spent a very long time looking for just such markings despite the sheer impossibility of them ever appearing again, and yet, here they are on a seemingly random corpse, amidst the debris of a seemingly benign case.

But it couldn't be... Not unless...

The woman who was run over by the car. He heard her whistle just before the corpse dropped back dead and inanimate, had seen the burst of power overturn the car right before it nearly crushed her, saw the magical aura blanketing her form during his scans.

"*Tousan?*"

"Yes, Renki?"

"The patients have all been accounted for, and Akari is contacting the local authorities to notify them of the situation."

"Excellent."

As they speak, his eyes never leave the body before him. His scanners are functioning at a thousand MB/s to solve the puzzle in front of him. An analysis of the markings matches them perfectly to markings discovered on poppets used during the war over fourteen years ago.

"Renki, have you performed an analysis on this body yet?"

The teen takes a moment. Kai watches as he performs his own scans, and while Kai's own face had remained impassive at the results, Renki's expression shifts to one of shock and perhaps a bit of wonder.

"The marks on this corpse match that of the poppets made by the Songstress of Lorelei. But how's that possible?"

"Where is the woman I had you secure?"

"I had to lock her in the main nurse's office. She caused quite a bit of havoc before you arrived."

He follows as Renki leads him back to the offices, watching as Renki dismantles the ward he placed on the door. It is solid work. Renki has improved his warding abilities to impeccable standard. Fumiko will be proud to hear of it.

"She is not well. She is one of the patients here, and while she certainly seemed to cause a lot of trouble for the staff, her treatment made me question the legitimacy of this place. I'm afraid her ailment is due to mistreatment here."

Renki unlocks and opens the door, stepping into the room carefully as though a wild animal is inside waiting to pounce.

"Miss?" he calls into the space. When there is no answer, he commands the lights on to reveal a very empty space. An empty space saturated with magic. "Impossible. How could she have gotten out?"

Kai steps into the room as Renki searches for the girl, but Kaito doesn't need to enter farther than the entryway to trace the magical residue to the bloody array on the floor and immediately knows what it is. He's seen it before. He turns back around and heads to the parking lot. Renki follows him, but Kai pays the teenager no mind, his footsteps carrying him with one sole purpose. If this is who he thinks it is, she'll be looking for an escape.

As he reaches the lot, a motorcycle pulls out onto the street, the helmeted biker obstructed from view, then disappears entirely as the bike curves into city traffic.

"Should we follow?"

"No," he says simply, despite already mapping the roads, virtually tracking as the bike weaves through the streets heading toward the northeastern city limit until it rips through the edge of his area of effect.

"But—"

"It is more important to ensure the safety of our charges here."

FIVE OF CUPS

Renki seems surprised at being cut off mid-sentence, but he is quick to recover, offering a small bow of his head.

"I understand. I'll organize with Akari."

He disappears back into the facility. Kai's sights replay the few seconds in which she was in sight. According to the interface he had pulled from his facial recognition software, her name is Atalia Vaishi. Ebele Citizen. ID# 30548T76. Previously a Firefly-in-training within the Ebelean court. Dismissed. This was the person whose face he had seen, but his intuition tells him not all things are as they seem.

After all, when it comes to magic, illusions are the rule—not the exception.

Cross-Continental Transportation in Deus: The Light Rail

Used primarily by technomancers and their personnel, the light rails of Deus are highly efficient, high-speed, electro-solar powered trains capable of transporting people and goods from country to country. They were established by the League in 1667 in secret as a countermeasure against the hexens' ability to communicate and transport goods via pocket dimension portals and catoptromancy (mirror divination). The light rails of Deus allow technomancers to transport vehicles and large weapons over thousands of kilometers in a vastly decreased timeframe.

They are also the only legal way to enter and exit highly restricted countries like Sekhmeti and Aighneas via land transportation.

An Excerpt from *Modes of Transportation in Deus*
by Heather Ables, 1873 A.P.

7

PAGE OF WANDS
(REVERSED)

WREN IS FORCED TO ABANDON THE motorcycle after leaving the city. Well, not so much forced, but for some reason she can't bring herself to stop at a gas station to fill the tank. She tried. Really, she did, but the smell of gasoline hit her nose, and suddenly she felt like she was suffocating, and if she stayed any longer, surely she would die a second time. It took all of two seconds before she turned right back around and fled the station, much to the entertainment of a charred spirit who had waved at her from the station window. She's seen her share of spirits who met fiery ends, but she's never had such a visceral reaction to one.

So, she finds herself on foot, making her way to the nearby light rail station. It's not the smartest idea, she knows, venturing into technomancer territory, but it's the closest transit to where she resurrected—at least she hopes the station she is thinking of is still there. Not to mention the added plus that there will be no lingering spirits for her to deal with on the premises, adept wards firmly keeping lost souls out of their territory and lost elsewhere, thank you very much. The Humanity+ Light Rail System™ is the fastest mode of ground transportation in the world, and it is used exclusively by technomancers and their adept underlings to get from place to place during cases that require them to leave their home borders.

You might be thinking, "Why doesn't she just teleport?"

Suffice to say, Wren isn't that kind of witch. The details to her new body are still a bit iffy, but as far she can tell her triskele indicia gave her dominion over the mental, physical, and spiritual realms: empathy, telekinesis, and you know, the dead/necrotic stuff. She can't fly on a broomstick, turn water into wine, or shapeshift. She can't control minds or time travel, not that she's ever met anyone who can, and she doesn't even want to try summoning fire.

Could she cast a spell outside of her natural dominion? Maybe? It would depend on the cost. There's only so much blood she can spill and magic she can push out before she either kills herself or drives herself insane. Considering how drained she is after getting through a single wall, long distance teleportation is not in the cards, not without help anyway. Silje, her long-dead familiar, used to displace her long distances, but Silje was a dimension traveler.

So, no, Wren can't teleport miles and miles at a time without activating a huge-ass array that would knock her on her ass the moment she got anywhere. She certainly will not unless the circumstances are dire.

Approaching the rail station is like walking into the past.

Nothing has changed. The floors are the same, the same solar energy panels patterned with purified stone. The walls are the same, the same hanging sculptures and paintings; the advertising holos may have been updated, but they're the same, still flickering with the latest celebrity product endorsement. The graffiti has been updated, and maybe someone repainted the varnish on the benches, but other than that, everything is same, same, same.

It is early in the morning. She hasn't slept, having travelled through the night, but the platform is empty save for the on-deck sentries and a few station live-ins sleeping in the corners. She approaches one of uniformed guards. The platform itself is open to the public, allowing family and friends to bid farewell to their loved ones before leaving on a case, so getting onto the platform is not the hard part. The hard part will be getting on the rail itself.

She greets the guard with a flash of the beacon she is still carrying. He nods to her, accepting the beacon as confirmation she is, at least, associated with a technomancer in some way, shape, or form despite the quizzical look he gives her attire, and she really can't blame him for that. Aside from the travel cloak, she's still dressed like a two-bit whore from the asylum, not typical travel attire. Perhaps she should have tried to wash off the makeup smeared all over her face before addressing him.

Oh, well. She'll do it after.

"What's the schedule for the day, good sir?"

"Miss," he greets, passing her an information card. She swipes it through the beacon's input port, and a holo appears with a detailed schedule for the day's trains. The next light rail does not arrive for another hour and a half.

"Thank you."

She goes to the bathroom and tries to clean her face. It doesn't do much good. The lipstick just smears in a faint line across her chin and cheek, and the eyeliner now halos her eyes like a racoon, but she at least feels a little cleaner and more human than doll. She scrubs her feet while she's at it and fixes her hair, despite a lack of brush or comb. Out of the locket, she draws out the tarot deck, drawing the page of wands. A young girl sits with goggles drawn over her face, a satchel at her side, mischief in her eyes as she plucks a piece of fruit from a merchant's cart.

The thief's card.

She hums an incantation under her breath, and when the card lights up, she tucks it away into her bodice. Anyone who catches her here will need to look twice before noticing her fully. With it, she should be able to pass the guard by without much of a trace when the train arrives.

She pulls the cloak hood over her head and leaves the bathroom to settle on one of the benches. Pulling a ration bar out of her pack, she settles the bag under her head, laying long on the seat.

Wren closes her eyes.

She doesn't realize she's drifted off until she's jolted awake by a purse landing on her face. She sits up with an "Ow!" and a teenage girl looks down, surprised to find her sitting there. Ah, right... Cloaking spells. Now that she's spoken, the girl can focus on her just fine. Wren holds the purse in hand, pulling it out of reach as the girl grabs for it.

"Give that back!"

"Perhaps you shouldn't have thrown it on top of me then."

Wren makes a face at the teen before pulling the bag away again, holding it behind her playfully. The girl's mouth drops open like a dead fish before she lunges forward again, a little more insistent, a lot more angry.

"I order you to give it back!"

Wren laughs.

"And who are you to order me around?"

Her face turns purple, and Wren tosses the bag back to her without another thought.

"Watch where you throw things," says Wren, rubbing her nose and cheek where the bag smacked her.

Expecting the girl to stutter an apology, she turns back around to curl back up and steal a few more z's before the rail arrives, but instead the teenager scoffs.

"What the hell are you doing sleeping on a public bench, anyway?"

Wren opens her eyes again to give the kid a onceover, pointedly not answering the question.

Dark, ebony skin and hair, elegant with clear blue eyes and a short-braided hairstyle, the girl looks Ebelean, possibly Derivan if the aquatic color scheme of her attire is anything to go by. She is too young for battle gear, a smattering of pubescent acne along her cheeks and chin, wearing instead simple cut sundress in a deep blue with green embroidery. A brown leather jacket protects her arms and back, and her combat boots reach up to her knee. She already has a few augmentations. Never too young for those in Deus. An exoskeleton around her left ear, a scanner lens rests over her left eye. Wren can also make out the telltale lines of leg augmentations on the exposed skin of her knees, which are pretty indicative of Derivan swimming augmentations. Such augments are a fairly common safety accoutrement for Derivan children just learning to swim. Wren herself had them in her last body from as young as four years old to help her swim faster and avoid drowning in stronger currents. There is a rifle strapped to her back, different from military rifles, more distinguished as though made custom to its user. Odd. This girl looks far too young to have attended a summit, therefore she can't have already made a customized weapon. Though there's a familiarity to it that Wren can't quite put her finger on, déjà vu tickling at the back of her mind.

At her prolonged silence, the girl gets irritated, fidgeting under Wren's scrutiny. She gets angrier.

"Are you going to answer me or not?"

Wren rolls her eyes. The temper on this one.

"I've been travelling all night. I can lay down and rest if I want."

"Then do it on the floor. You're taking up the whole space."

Wren's left eyebrow lifts at that.

"There are plenty of other benches."

"I always wait at this one."

What a pretentious little brat.

"Ah, forgive me then. My mistake."

Wren makes a show of scooting as far to one side of the bench as she can, curling her knees up so there is enough space for the young girl to sit. She frowns at Wren suspiciously before moving to sit. As she does, however, Wren slides her feet back down so the girl ends up jamming her arse cheeks on Wren's boots. Wren laughs as the girl bolts back up.

"How dare you!"

Oh! The girl is positively fuming now.

"Bratty teenagers who leave themselves open to offense deserve to be offended," Wren declares, crossing her hands behind her head and closing her eyes again.

The girl reaches for the rifle at her back.

"I ought to have you reprimanded for insulting me like this."

Wren pays her words little mind, choosing instead to sit up and give her a sidelong look.

"Aren't you a bit young to be travelling alone? So ready to sit next to a stranger just because they are at your usual bench. Haven't your parents taught you anything about self-preservation?"

The girl huffs, crossing her arms across her barely-there chest.

"My uncle's taught me plenty."

"Ah...Women are better teachers."

As the girl chokes and sputters at whatever new insult Wren has apparently handed her, the light rail arrives with a deafening shudder. An announcement is made that the rail will take the next 30 minutes to load and unload its travelers.

"Whelp, catch you later, kid. Hope you find your uncle."

She gets up quickly to get on one of the carriages closer to the rear where technomancers without specific country loyalty are most likely to travel. She flashes the ID she swiped out of the girl's purse to the sentry, and he lets her by with barely a glance. She chuckles to herself. Oldest trick in the book: flash an ID with enough confidence, and no one thinks to question it.

It's too early in the morning for anyone to really be riding. The train is so empty it almost gives her the creeps, but better for her. The fewer plusies around, the better. She chooses her seat and opens the window, preferring to feel the wind's touch for a while longer before they embark. She almost dozes off again as the girl whose ID she commandeered pleads with an attendant to let her on the tram.

"Come on! You know who I am. If my uncle finds out I lost my ID, he'll never let me go out on my own again."

"I'm sorry, Princess. I have been strictly instructed not to allow you on unless you have your ID. Unless I can verify who you are, I am not supposed to allow you aboard."

Something about the way the man says "princess" catches her attention. Wren isn't entirely sure he's just being domineering toward her.

Princess? Who is this girl?

The answer comes just a moment later.

"Zenza, hurry up and get in here."

"Tio Xipilli!"

Wren's eyes widen as Xipilli, her big brother, the Vulcan of Deriva, comes into view, taller and even more imposing than he was the last she saw him. She quickly takes out the ID in her pocket and sure enough, it reads: Zenza Nagi, ID#715863Y1, Crown Princess of Deriva.

Her heart stops.

"Did you forget your ID again?" Xipilli's tone is scolding and firm, dark brow drawn low over hazel eyes. He has a goatee now, which makes his face look even more pointed, and...Is he graying at his temples? She always told him he would stress himself gray by the time he was forty.

"I had it! I know I had it. I just used it at the checkpoint this morning. I wouldn't have been able to get here if I'd forgotten it again."

"Be more careful! One day someone is going to steal your identity, and I will not help you get it back."

"¡Tio!"

The pair disappear into the carriage, and Wren wants nothing more than to throw herself from the train the moment it starts moving. Zenza, her niece, her all-but orphaned niece, and whose fault was that exactly? Wren's. Wren and her cursed psychic powers!

She shuts the window with a snap and pulls the hood of her cloak down over her head breathing hard, her pulse in her throat. And isn't that a laugh! Wren has a pulse when she should be nothing but ash in the wind. Why did those inmates think bringing her back from the dead was a good idea?

She looks down at the bandages tinted red on her arm. She'll need to change them again soon. With three slashes left, she hasn't any idea who could possibly be left for her to take vengeance against other than the doctor, which leaves two unknowns, and she only has so much time left to figure it out before the summoning expires and she is cast back to whatever netherworld she was in before all this. And even if she does figure it out, will she even be able to kill them? The nurse, the brawler, and the asylum director all died purely by happenstance; she hadn't actually killed any of them. The doctor most definitely deserves to die, and she could probably get away with that murder, but what about the two unknowns?

For all she knew, one of them could be for her own brother! Or her niece! Or the primarch's pet turtle!

The PA system warns the train will be departing soon. Should she be more worried about Xipilli? Probably...

But she's too tired to care. So, so tired. Her head aches, and her eyes throb. Less than 24 hours back on the mortal plane, and she's burned herself pretty low.

The carriage door opens, and two adepts make their way in. Between them is Faust, still unconscious and bound to a hovering cot. She ducks her head down farther as they wheel him through the aisle and to the caboose, probably being used as a storage car.

"Forgive our tardiness. We ran into a bit of trouble on the way." It's the boy, Renki, who was leading the investigation last night.

"Your guest?" asks the attendant.

"A suspect taken into custody for questioning in Snowfall."

"Of course, your highness."

Who is he calling "highness?" Was the boy Hikaru's son or something? She doesn't remember Hikaru ever getting married, let alone having a kid, and Kaito... Well, Kaito walks right into the car, and Wren nearly chokes on her own spit.

The sentry must have been addressing the prince.

Renki follows behind him along with Akari. Wren slouches deeper into her seat to avoid drawing their attention, but Kai's eyes find her anyway. They trace over her, lingering despite the displacement charm, and she pulls the hood down lower over her face.

Kai speaks to his two charges in their native tongue before moving along the aisle. She sighs in relief when he exits for a car farther forward even as the two teens make their way to where the station attendants have secured the good doctor. They pay her no mind.

The minute the two disappear through the compartment door, she is up and on her feet, heading for the exit. She'll take a train that is Miyazaki-free, thank you very much, but just as she gets there, the doors close in her face, and the light rail lurches forward.

She goes sprawling to the floor.

¡Pinché tren! Great! This is great!

She is now stuck on the same rail with probably the two people who most hate her in the whole world. Angry-probably-vengeful half-brother: Check! Far-too-astute ex-lover: Check!

She's fine! Just peachy. Now what?

"Miss, do you need assistance?"

She whirls around to find Renki staring down at her. The moment he sees her face, he recognizes her as Atalia Vaishi.

"Wait, You're— Akar—!"

She slaps a hand over his mouth and stifles him from calling out to his friend.

"Shush now, dearie. No need to ring the alarm."

"Ngh!"

He tries to talk regardless of her hand over his mouth. She holds a little firmer.

"I'm just trying to find my way to...to, ah, Aighneas. That's right! Aighneas. I'm not here to cause any trouble whatsoever."

He doesn't believe her, not for one second. She can see it in his eyes. So, she does the next best thing and hums a lullaby.

His eyes round to the size of saucers.

What a well-trained boy! Recognizing magic so easily. No matter. She keeps singing, and steadily his eyes slide shut as she lulls him into a nice deep slumber before gently setting him in one of the seats. She breathes in relief, lightly brushing the boy's hair out of his face. She briefly wonders how old he is. Maybe

15 or 16, but he's so mature for his age. Must be the Miyazaki mentoring, like a mini Kaito. How cute!

"Hey, what are you doing!"

She bolts away from the sleeping teen to find the girl, Akari. She has a pistol drawn, and it shakes in her hands as she aims it at Wren.

Wren lifts her hands up to show she isn't armed.

"He's fine, just asleep. You, however, will not be fine if you shoot that at me."

"I fail to see the logic in that."

"We are on a train travelling at roughly 90 km/hr. You really think you want to fire off a laser into a space as compact as this?"

"It's only a problem if I miss."

She smirks at the teen and winks when her expression shifts to something more puzzled.

"You're going to miss, kid."

"You wanna bet? I'm the best shot in my age group. Step away from him."

"Alright, kid, alright. You're in charge." Wren backs up, hands still in the air.

"And don't call me 'kid'!"

"Yes, ma'am."

She bows her head. The teen frowns before turning to speak into her comm unit.

The windows darken as the train travels through an underground pass. The interior lights flicking on for them.

"Miyazaki-sama, there's a woman back here..."

Wren tunes out the rest of the girl's report as a dark shadow begins to form toward the back of the car. It hovers in the air, wispy tendrils curling and winding around the drapery near the windows before inching near the transit doorway leading to the storage room where Faust is being held.

The next moment, Wren pushes past Akari and flings a pulse of necrosis at the entity. Akari's protest as Wren shoves past her morphs into a full-on shriek as it rushes for her.

Akari lifts her firearm back up in a panic.

"Don't shoot!" shouts Wren, moving to slap the weapon from her hand.

She isn't fast enough. The shot fires and goes straight through the translucent shroud to reflect off of the steel-paneled wall behind it.

The laser ricochets around the car. Wren smacks the gun out of the youth's hand and pushes the girl into a nearby seat while she herself ducks down until the beam breaks through a glass window. The train's alarm system blasts on. The black mist solidifies into a horrendous beast. It stands upright with a raven's head, a grizzly crimson-stained feathered body, and razor-sharp talons.

Those talons slash for Akari.

Wren sings another high-pitched note as she lifts a hand to stall it in place, and the abomination shrieks, caught just millimeters from running Akari through, and Wren realizes what she's looking at. It's a Kenku, but this one has been modified. Bat-like wings stitched onto its back and blackened human faces are sewn into its torso like a macabre quilt. It screeches in her face, forcefully pulling itself out of her telekinetic hold as she falters.

She's expended too much energy.

The electric whine of a rifle charging up buzzes from the front of the car, and the next second, a blast hurtles through the narrow space. The kenku mystifies before the shot can hit, and instead of meeting its target, the energy barrels past, powerful enough to rip the entire back end of the train off.

"¡Mierde!" Zenza curses, the princess standing at the head of the car.

Wren redirects her intention, redirecting the bullet through a window and into the mountain before it can hit the back of the car and blow them all sky high. The kenku solidifies. Its beak shears through her upper arm.

"Ah!"

Renki jolts awake from the sleep spell. For a split-second, confusion laces his features, but then he sees the kenku, sees its beak in Wren's arm, and with wide-eyed horror, draws his sword and stabs it in the head. It releases Wren and dematerializes once more, and the witch collapses, sweat beading on her brow.

"What the—!"

Akari next to him is about to completely lose it.

"Soul-sucking dingleberries! It disappeared! Renki, what do we do!!!"

Oh, does Fumiko need to wash this girl's mouth!

The creature solidifies behind Zenza, raising its talons against the would-be markswoman who freezes at the sight of the thing.

"*¿Qué demonios es eso?*"

"*¡Bajarse!*" shouts Wren.

The girl drops to the ground, and viridian energy winds around the beast's form locking it in place before its talons can pass through Zenza's head.

Another furious presence enters the car as Wren psychically wrangles the kenku.

"Zenza!" Her half-brother's shout is deafening.

The high-pitched activation charge of Xipilli's trident, Opochtli, follows as it lights up in its master's grip. The weapon flies forward and embeds itself into the kenku's back. Vulcan Xipilli takes two long strides forward, yanks the trident out, and slashes, opening the beast's side. He pivots to take a second swipe, but as the strike falls, daylight trickles back in through the windows, and the beast vanishes in a cloud of mist, the vapors snaking their way into the ventilation system where darkness still pervades.

Wren ducks under the seats as the man rounds on their niece.

"*¡Idiota!* What were you thinking running back here?"

Zenza sputters at her enraged uncle while Wren sneaks her way along the floor of the car toward the caboose. Now is not the time for her to be in the same room as her estranged brother. Not now, not tomorrow, not ever! *¡No Gracias!*

"I heard the alarm. I thought I should check what was going on."

"You nearly destroyed half of the train. *¡Podrías haberte matado!*"

"I'm sorry, Tio."

Xipilli leaves his niece with a parting glare before kneeling down to examine the space the kenku occupied before the sunlight banished it.

"That was magic holding the creature still."

He rounds on the two Miyazaki teenagers. Renki and Akari stand at attention as the monarch addresses them, fury boiling in his obsidian gaze.

"Vulcan Moctezumo," offers Renki as both Murasaki adepts bow to the man.

"Which one of you is responsible for this?"

"Sir, Akari and I are both adepts. Neither of us are capable of—"

"Then explain to me why there are traces of magic all over this car. I know telekinesis when I see it!" His voice is rising, and he still hasn't released the electric energy pulsing over Opochtli's prongs. A new voice enters the conversation, and Wren tries to move faster, wincing at the wound on her arm.

"Moctezumo, if you have questions for my students, you can direct them toward me."

"Prince Kaito. How kind of you to make an appearance."

"Why are you interrogating my students?"

"One of your brats seems to be dabbling in witchcraft, your highness," sneers Xipilli.

Kaito's eyes flash, and Renki bows again.

"Your majesty, we study no such subjects in our training."

"Then who is responsible for it? I come back here and practically choke on magic as two Murasakan adepts stand unharmed while my niece is nearly cleaved in two."

Zenza pipes up at that. "Tio, there was another girl back here. She was singing."

"Singing?"

Akari chooses this moment to chime in. "That's right! I was just calling Kaito-sensei about her. She knocked Renki out just before the beast struck."

"Where is she now?" demands Xipilli.

Curses! She's almost to the door too. She clamps her hand over the gash in her arm and belly crawls forward, leaving a smear of blood in her wake.

"Well, she..." Akari trails off as she sees her missing from the last place he last saw her. "She was just there."

There is a rustle of fabric, and suddenly Zenza's clear blue eyes find hers. *Odin's beard! She has her mother's eyes!*

"She's on the floor."

Heavy boots march forward along the aisle. Wren is about two meters from the door. Xipilli's steel grip closes around her ankle and pulls her out from under the seats. Her hip pops in protest at the rough handling, though it honestly feels kind of good...She is hauled upward by her biceps and shoved harshly into the waiting hands of a man dressed in the uniform blues of the royal guard of Deriva. He's older than her brother and vaguely familiar. A technomancer's badge shines from his breast, and the wash of admiration the man feels for her brother might have been at once disturbing and sweet, but Xipilli's fury rolls over her empathy in volatile waves that make her stomach lurch.

"Identify yourself before I have you arrested."

Instead of answering the question, she bites out a retort worthy of a deranged lunatic. "Who picks up a lady by her ankles? At least pop the other hip. Worst chiropractor I've ever seen."

She sticks her tongue out at Xipilli, and the man at her back twists her arm, her injured arm. She laughs through a yelp.

"Ooo! Careful! I'm not into burly types. Really! Holding a defenseless girl down. Do I get to choose a safe word at least?"

"Quetzal!"

The captain, Quetzal, knocks her knees out from under her, and her kneecaps screech as they hit the floor. Xipilli's upper lip curls, Opochtli sparking in response to his disgust.

"Please, no," she whines shielding her face. "I really am not into this kind of thing."

"Answer the question, witch, or face the consequences."

Wren chooses instead to make a lewd gesture with a fist and her mouth. Xipilli's unarmed hand rises to slap her.

"You disrespectful wretch!"

"Vulcan Moctezumo," Renki's voice cuts through her brother's yelling, and suddenly another pair of boots wedge themselves between her and her brother, cutting off the man's strike. "Please, her name is Atalia Vaishi. We encountered her last evening at the sanatorium. She was one of the patients. She is not well."

"So, she's a lunatic," says Zenza.

"Says the brat who just fired an energy blast in a train moving at over 90 km/hr," Akari throws back.

"Who're you calling a brat? You aren't much older than I am."

"*¡Cállate!*" Xipilli shouts for them to shut up which they promptly do. "Quetzal, arrest her for witchcraft and the willful endangerment of the princess. We'll deal with her when we get back to Deriva."

Well, this is exactly what she was trying to avoid. When she finds the person who actually did summon the kenku, she is going to murder them. Assuming of course she still has the means to do so.

"Wait!"

The Miyazaki boy in front of her topples sideways as he is shoved out of the way.

Quetzal's boot shoves between her shoulder blades, and her face hits the floor. Stars dance in her vision as he pulls a device from his back pocket she's never seen before. A thick technolyzed bracelet, metallic and heavy. When he activates it, a murderous whirring sound floods her ears, so loud her head feels like it's going to split open. Her teeth grind together, though no one else is affected. She does not want that thing touching her and forcefully sews energy into her fingertips despite the pain ripping through her head.

This'll probably hurt her as much as it hurts them, but desperate times...

But the whirring device deactivates just as the manacle is about to come down on her wrist. She sags, the relief heavenly.

"Unhand her."

Kaito stands, sights activated, tall and imposing. His face remains impassive, but his voice crackles with warning. Xipilli turns, a sour grin on his face.

"Ah, Kaito-san. Are we going to really have this discussion again? A witch has stowed away in our midst, summoned some hellspawn to kill our young charges, and you wish to grant mercy."

"That isn't true," says Renki.

"Yeah," says Akari indignantly. "Even if she was using magic, she was clearly using it to protect us."

They think too highly of her.

"I don't care what she was using it for. Witchcraft is a scourge on the natural world. Murasaki no Yama may have softened in their attitude toward hexen, but Deriva will not tolerate it."

Kaito steps forward.

"The Vulcan will remember his jurisdiction. We are within the borders of Murasaki, therefore any arrests are my prerogative. In light of such, perhaps your captain will exhibit more gentlemanly behavior and allow the lady to stand, considering she has done nothing wrong."

The captain's hand on her forearm tightens, but he looks to Xipilli in askance. The Vulcan glares at the Murasaki prince with murderous intent.

"Quetzal, release her."

Quetzal does so, backing away as Kaito steps forward. A hand appears in Wren's line of vision, and she looks from it to its owner's face. Kai's silver stare greets her.

"Are you hurt?"

She averts her focus back to the floor, her hood falling back her head.

e train goes underground again, and darkness engulfs nce again. She senses it a moment before any of the cers do, head swinging toward the vents.

r goes out.

s, and the two young adepts in his charge attune of their sights spin at once.

authorized person in the conductor's cabin."

Page Of Wands (reversed)

A shroud of black ozone zings through the car. It hits Xipilli and Quetzal, sending them sideways into opposite walls. A shudder goes through the whole train. A shrill shriek sounds, and Wren reaches for the nearest piece of nailed down furniture as the train comes to a screaming halt.

If you find yourself facing a witch and have no clue what their abilities are, look to their indicia.

Every witch has a witch's indicia—a singular sigil that decorates their skin. While usually found on the arms or torso, the indicia can be found anywhere on a witch's body. The sigil or symbol hints at what the witch is capable of. For instance, a firestarter may have a simple upright triangle on their body somewhere. Someone able to heal others may have three stacked circles with a line going through the center. These are simple examples. They could easily be more complex and more difficult to figure out. For example, someone with a waxing crescent moon symbol on their body might be a telekinetic or a healer, or they may be talented with protection and love spells.

An Excerpt from *Hunting and Identifying Hexen*
by Finnick Lockecraft, 1852 A.P.

8

SEVEN OF WANDS
(REVERSED)

CHAOS ERUPTS.

Wren, having missed the seat, tumbles head-over-heels toward the back of the car. When her back slams into the metal of the door, the air is knocked from her lungs, and she falls forward, coughing to regain her breath.

The kenku towers over them all.

The glass windows shatter as a high-pitched shriek bursts from the creature's throat. Tsukuyomi, in Kai's grip, swings forward, its blade flashing ultraviolet in the darkness. The creature's talons glint as it clashes against the finely-forged steel.

"Renki, Akari. Establish a formation."

The two teens jump to attention, standing back-to-back as they cast an area of effect on the train, hands holding the Ahamkara and Apan mudras to channel concentration and energy.

"Boundary set."

"Capture!"

A pulse of violet light extends from the two adepts, cloaking everything along its path, Wren, Kaito, Xipilli, Zenza, Quetzal, and the kenku. Looks like the Miyazaki clan has made updates to their systems. They weren't capable of mapping eldritch beings into their VRscape in the past. Wren recognizes the transfusion of magic into technology she dabbled with before she died. Someone has perfected her work. Akari grasps Renki's shoulders and lowers him to the floor as he enters cyberscape.

Xipilli moves to attack the creature in the corporeal world, but his captain stops him, the space too compact for more than one person to engage at a time. At his side, Zenza levels her rifle, but Xipilli knocks it out of her hand with a scolding look. Kai and the beast are still locked sword to claw, its black gaze simmering with bloodlust. It surges forward to attack Kaito with its beak, and Kai breaks away from it, rotating to its flank. He gets a slash along its spine before it goes incorporeal again. Only this time, an unseen attack drives it back to the floor of the train. A new slash opens along its face. Renki, in virtual reality, has struck the creature.

The beast, now aware of the teen's method of attack, strikes at the space where Renki's virtual form is, naught but a ghost of golden coding. A talon strikes him across the face and sends his virtual form into the code wall. In the vital realm, Renki's head is flung to the side, three horizontal gashes opening across his cheek. Combat in the virtual realm may not involve physical muscles, but the body experiences what the mind experiences. Injuries taken become very real phantoms as nerve endings die and internal organs fail. Technicians killed in cyberscape will die in the real world.

Akari reacts, shutting off their territory and shaking Renki. The boy wakes with a gasp, sights spinning wildly, a peculiar gold rather than the typical violet.

Kai's katana stabs into the kenku's ribcage. The creature dissolves around the blade. The swirling mass rockets toward Xipilli, Zenza, and Quetzal. Xipilli pushes Zenza out of the way, his trident blocking the creature's attack as it solidifies, its injuries from Kaito and Renki recovered. Quetzal attacks and the beast dodges taking a swipe at the man's stomach. Blood blooms darkly against the sky blue of his uniform.

"It's held here by an array," Wren hears Renki tell Kaito and Akari.

"Where is the array?" asks Kaito.

"I'm not sure."

Wren stands up and climbs over the seating.

"Did you map the entire train?" asks Wren.

The teen looks to her in surprise but answers, "All of the interior."

That's all the information Wren needs.

She snatches Akari's laser gun, much to the girl's protest, before moving to the front of the car. The Miyazaki mapping system is capable of locating arcane objects within a set parameter, therefore the array would need to be outside of the boundary the teens set. They mapped the entire interior which means the array is not inside the train. And if the array isn't in the train, the next logical place is the roof. Launching herself up, she catches a ceiling bar next to an overhead emergency exit and flips up to kick the hatch open, pulling herself up and onto the roof. There is another crash in the car below followed by a high-pitched screech as she begins running down the line of train cars looking for the array.

She finds it atop the center car, very much active.

The circle is open, and as she watches, a small gust of mist emerges, taking shape in front of her. Another kenku begins to solidify, and she fires on it before it can fully enter this realm. It sinks back into the array with a shriek. She kneels down to examine the glyphs.

The sigils don't glow so much as absorb light. Darkness drips from them like an oil stain. The energy signature is familiar, like a lost memory. The markings are cold, like a void under her fingertips.

"Oh! I knew I should have drawn the array under the train."

Wren turns to find a petite girl with red hair, pale skin, and a freckled face in a pretty polka-dotted sundress. She would look the picture of sweet and innocent were it not for the set of curled horns graphed to her temple, blood still dripping from her fingertips, athame still in hand. She recognizes this girl!

"Summer?"

"Why, hello! And who are you supposed to be?"

Summer Helsdottir is supposed to be locked up in a dungeon for life, yet here she stands before Wren, once again conjuring beasts and wreaking havoc. Apparently, she is here for the doctor if Wren's intuition is anything to go on. Wren rises and smiles, close-lipped, at the other witch, Atalia's blonde hair whipping around her face and head.

"No one important, really, but if you want to walk out of here alive, I recommend you call off your kenku and turn yourself in to one of the fine technomancers below. I hear the Vulcan is rather hospitable."

"Oh! No, thank you. I have no interest in being arrested."

Wren shrugs.

"Then, I guess, I'll just have to bleed you to death, since I'm assuming it is your blood I'll need to reverse this summoning array into a banishing seal."

Summer laughs.

"Sorry, I'm afraid I'm terribly busy right now. You can play with my friend instead."

There's a squeal of tearing metal sounds as another kenku rises from the shrapnel. Summer pulls a corked vial of liquid from her pocket and throws it to the roof. Out of the shatter glass sweeps up a curse which folds around Summer in a black cocoon. Summer's visage begins to flicker in and out of this reality. Wren fires a shot at her, and the blast goes through the other woman's shoulder. The woman gives a pained shout, blood splashes onto the rooftop, and a moment later, the other witch disappears in a shattering of void magic. A teleportation spell! In bottled form?

The kenku charges, and she dodges around the beast, catching its ankles as she rolls to the edge of the roof. The sound of a sword whistles through the air. She unlocks the electrical charge chamber on the pistol and drives it into the creature's foot. The surge of electricity through its body shocks it into paralysis.

Seven Of Wands (reversed)

The blade of a katana slices through the kenku's throat. Black blood spills, and the creature falls in a heap of raven feathers and grit right on top of her, squishing the air out of her lungs.

She coughs and rolls out from under the creature, turning to look backward. Kaito stands there, blood dripping from his blade. Her eyes widen when she sees another kenku has risen from the depths of the array.

"6 o'clock!"

Kaito turns and blocks the kenku's swipe. Blades locked, Kai swings himself and the kenku off the roof onto the ground. Wren takes her chance, crawling over to the array on the floor. She pulls telekinetically on the splattered blood on the ground, drawing the fluid into a small globe. Hopefully, it's enough. She dips her fingertips into the globe of blood and begins painting over the array with Summer's blood, turning the runes and flipping their meanings in just a few brusque strokes. She digs her hands into the center of it, wincing as it scalds the skin of her hands. She pushes her own magic into the array, fighting to wrestle control over it. She cuts open her right palm and draws over the already existing sigils.

She hums first, finding the resonance just as she did with the locket in the asylum, but this time her goal is not to enhance the melody. It is to change it. She hums louder, fervently guiding it to change keys. Altering the dissonant tones and making them consonant, and then, once she has the tune under her baton, her lips part and an old wordless song spills forth. Something to calm and collect, to quiet and soothe. Something not quite written for the voice but for piano a lifetime ago.

Wren sings, pressing hard into the blood array. The circle's etchings, dark and hollow, shift and change as it is taken over by Wren's viridian energy signature, her song now resonating through the glyphs as she dominates it. Through it, she can feel the beings called forth. She sings until the creatures are completely vanquished, probably to some alternative plane that hasn't any chance of being their actual home. The beasts' wailed laments vibrate through her before abruptly disappearing, evaporating like mist in the sun.

The creatures gone, she begins to close the portal, her voice going into a decrescendo as she brings the song to a close.

"Wren?"

Her name whispered in shock, so quiet Wren wonders if she actually heard anything, but then she hears the zing of a weapon powering down and freezes. She turns her head, still wearing Atalia Vaishi's face, to see Kaito standing at the head of the car having jumped back onto the roof once the kenku disappeared, swords drawn, brow furrowed. Wren meets Kaito's steady gaze, panic already coursing through her system.

How long has he been standing there? Did she see her cast the banishment spell? Did he hear her singing? Does he know? There is no way he could know! She's wearing someone else's face!

The array closes, and a blinding flash of light bursts forth, the force of the blast punting her backward. Steel-corded hands catch her shoulders, and she breathes heavily, dizzy and disoriented as the array deteriorates. There's a shudder beneath her. She is shuffled around and feels herself free falling through an exit hatch as Kai returns them to the carriage before they can be thrown from the roof as the train resumes its forward track with a jolt. She nearly falls trying to get her feet back under her, her hands catching Kai's wrists. 'Atalia's' brown eyes are wide as they meet the prince's silver gaze. Kai's sights whirl to life, and she knows he is actively recording the stretch of time between them. The world is spinning, despite the firmness of the floor beneath her feet. It's a frightening feeling, irrational as it is. There is a noise above their heads as the hatch slams shut again, and Wren snaps herself out of it, moving backward and away from that penetrating gaze.

"It is you," he says.

She thinks she's going to be sick.

"I don't know what you're talking about," she hisses, shuffling backward even more. His swords, though no longer powered with saibāki, are still drawn, and Wren keeps a keen eye on them even as she reaches back for the pistol she shoved into her skirt, but she trips over herself in her panic to get away. "Stay back!"

Kai's eyes narrow, sliding from Atalia's face to something behind her. A familiar furious presence enters her field of perception, and an electrical shing makes the hair at the nape of her neck stand on end. She throws herself to the side as Opochtli zings past her head to embed itself in the middle of the floor before its master summons it back to his hand. Xipilli stands at the rear of the car, practically breathing fire.

"Explain yourself!"

Wren bolts upright, blood still freely dripping down her arm. To their eyes, Atalia looks from Wren's half-brother to Wren's ex-lover and back. Kai's neural guards prevent her from getting any kind of read on his emotions, but his gaze is steady, and when he looks at Xipilli, the intensity in his gaze tightens. Xipilli, on the other hand... Xipilli's emotions are all over the map: rage, hatred, and fury at the forefront mixed with disbelief, bloodlust...

What is that last emotion—hope? No...can't be.

In his hand, Opochtli buzzes for her blood.

She needs an out. Anything!

"Answer me, witch!"

"Moctezumo, I'm warning you. Back off," says Kai, calm but for the threat lurking in his voice.

"Screw you, Miyazaki!"

Lightning streaks out from the trident, and Wren lifts her arm in defense, ready to take a world of pain. The bolt hits her hand, and surges through her body, but there is no pain. She looks down in wonder at her palm, the energy still crackling around her fingertips. Xipilli and Kaito both look at her in wonder.

"Xipilli!"

Quetzal enters the car behind Xipilli, and the Vulcan moves. "I knew it!"

Wren flinches, and the power she caught surges out of her, a siphon of uncontrollable lightning. It shoves her into the wall and her head meets hard, unyielding metal. Kaito lifts his swords to block the blast, but Xipilli is not so prepared. Surprise passes over her brother's face as he is yanked back by his man. The lightning hits the younger technomancer square in the chest. The already wounded man goes flying violently into the wall with a sickening crack. Wren, arm still outstretched, withdraws into herself, lightheaded, dizzy, and confused.

She's never done anything like that before. Her indicia is visible through her glamour. It's spread to her hands?

Xipilli shakes off his daze and storms in Wren's direction, trident raised to impale her.

"Let's see what other magics you've been hiding, witch!"

Wren drags herself backward and away. The blood from her arm smears all over the floor, the back of her neck slick with it. She's bleeding from the head injury, may very well have a concussion. She's empty, her magic depleted. Her vision goes out, then in, then out, then in. Xipilli is shouting, but it feels like cotton has been stuffed in her ears. The last she sees before darkness engulfs her are Tsukuyomi and Amatsu' s shimmering blades.

9

THE APPRENTICE PART 2

ATRUE MONARCH RULES WITH GRACE AND elegance, a firm hand dipped in righteousness and a proper sense of justice.

All his life, Kaito knew, that while he would not inherit the throne as the younger of the two princes of Murasaki no Yama, it was his duty to better himself as a figurehead of his people. By the time he was sixteen, he had already established himself a learned prodigy, one of the most talented prospective technomancers of his generation, untouchable in his mastery of VR manipulation, marksmanship, and kenjutsu. He knew who he was body, mind, and soul, and his reputation for steely indifference suited him just fine. There was potency in silence, elegance in tradition and decorum, and honor in reticence.

So firmly set in those beliefs he was, questioning them never even occurred to him in his first sixteen years of existence.

And then Wren Nocturne crashed into his life like an atomic bomb.

Standing across the aisle from Xipilli, Kaito protects the witch from the witch hunter. Renki and Akari are in the doorway hugging each other in terror at his actions. Kaito is not normally one for conflict, content to remain impassive to such squabbles, but today Tsukuyomi and Amatsu glimmer in his hands, ready to spill blood should Xipilli continue to press his dominion over the unconscious girl on the floor.

Today, Kaito fights for a hope long extinguished, resurrected in the notes of a witch's song.

16 Years Ago–The Month of Songs, 1861**–The** 247th **Technomancer Trials**

During the first week of the summit, the candidates are put through tests of physical endurance and ability, submitted to some of the worst conditions any of them have ever experienced—a boot camp on steroids, if you will.

Initial cuts are made based on physical skill and fitness: physical wellness, timed obstacle courses, marksmanship, strength testing, and survival exercises. Trainees have to prove themselves capable of surviving the very worst that could be thrown at them. Extreme cold and heat, exposure, dehydration, near starvation. They must demonstrate their ability to track their way through wilderness, through cyberspace, through urban undergrounds. Individuals prove themselves capable of functioning without access to wireless servers, comm devices, and mainframe access.

In years past, many candidates died during these trials, but several years ago, Murasaki decided such needless death was unfounded, and Shinka is determined to minimize loss of life as much as possible during this stage of the summit, dismissing students who need rescuing or medical attention without a second opportunity. To this effect, each trainee is assigned a yield beacon which, when triggered, will disqualify a candidate from further trials. In addition, aerial scouting and health monitors keep a close eye on each candidate, and anyone who presses the beacon is promptly rescued and given medical attention. This doesn't save everyone. At the start of the second week, a noble's son dies of exposure after he couldn't track his way back during a wilds trial and refused to trigger his beacon until it was too late.

Kaito has no problems during the opening weeks of the summit. He is physically fit and trained to handle these trials while others are not so prepared, younger students mostly. The 15- to 17-year-olds who are not properly prepared face dismissal after failing to meet a time limit or after their health monitors drop too low. A few candidates bow out by initiating their beacons, lacking the determination, desire, or constitution to undergo anymore. It's for the best.

Being a technomancer is no walk in the park.

Of course, in the face of such grueling conditions, tempers flare among the candidates. Fights break out. Hikaru interferes in a dispute between Xipilli Moctezumo and Oswald Llywelyn that nearly devolves into violence. The argument began after Oswald said something lewd about Xipilli's sister. There had been no one present to witness the comment, but Wren had quickly pulled her brother away from the Seraphim plusie lest he open himself to some penalty or another. As it was, Oswald and Xipilli both serve a punishment of several hours kneeling on hard stone for interrupting training. In another incident, Wren breaks another girl's wrist when she accosts Wren during a training break. Wren performs the penalty of extra calisthenic exercises and laps around the compound while the other girl whines and complains it was Wren's fault. Her punishment is dismissal. The two incidents one after the other inspire more of the hushed whispers he first heard at the opening ceremonies.

Rumors float around surrounding the reason for Wren's presence at the trials. Some say she was sent to seduce as many young lords/ladies as she could to bring a decent bride price for Deriva. Others talk long and at length about the girl's mother and how the Firefly Freya imparted all of her knowledge on her daughter. A few of them, the more slimy boys/girls in attendance, claim to have made a conquest of her already.

Wren doesn't heed any of it, though her brother is quick to anger in defense of his sister. The instructors quiet any unseemly conversation, most notably Fumiko, who asks Kai to put a stop to any gossip he may come across.

Kaito, however, while he doesn't necessarily believe the gossip, has witnessed firsthand the girl's lack of decorum. Surely a person like this would have failed out during the first week of physical tests, but herein lies the conundrum. Wren, in spite of her unruly and openly friendly, sometimes flirtatious nature, actually seems wholly committed to making it through the trials.

In fact, her scores rival his own in many of their tests, and Kai finds himself unexpectedly intrigued by the Derivan girl, subconsciously competing against her as the trials progress, a thing which does not go unnoticed by her. Apparently, she even relishes the rivalry they've developed. She is overly affectionate with her friends and brother, and she has, much to his chagrin, deemed him a friend, and no action he takes will convince her otherwise.

She annoys him so much with her constant pestering he begins to expect it from her. Over lunch one day, Hikaru, traitor that he is, says he is glad to see Kaito making friends and asking Kai what he thinks of Lady Wren. Kai openly scoffs at his brother while his mother coos, asking for details from Hikaru about this apparently talented trainee.

The third week of the summit, after the chaff has been weeded out, continues with lectures and lessons for all participants. These lessons begin with a mind-numbing intensity that has all of them stressed and sleepless, resulting in more than a few nervous breakdowns. Their coursework includes lessons in music, combat, computer hacking, robotics, and energy manipulation. Alchemy and magical theory are covered as well through the careful filter of restriction and conduit manipulation. These arts are taught clinically through the scientific lens of mind over matter and energy transfer/manipulation, never to be attempted without technology acting as a buffer between the user and the casting.

For many of the first years, it's their first experience with technomancy.

Failure is not an option here. Low marks on tests or reports lead to dismissal, and there are indeed several students who leave at this point, unable to juggle the information given to them.

Kaito is nothing if not a dutiful student, taking it all in stride while others crumble under the pressure. Studious, attentive, a prodigy in the realm of the various adept arts. As a Miyazaki and the prince of Murasaki no Yama, he is well versed in bio-mechanical engineering and computer sciences. He doesn't favor robotics, but he understands enough to hack into a system and convert it to his needs. Energy manipulation is different, and he prefers his family's specific genre of such a craft.

Courses on witchcraft are strictly theoretical, meant to aid their ability to capture and vanquish the darkly malevolent creatures that inhabit this world: Hexen, Fae, Monsters, Netherbeasts, and Undead. These topics on hexen and forbidden magics, he embraces knowing such knowledge may one day save his life against any one of his foes: how to identify a hexen ritual, how to recognize and subdue supernatural beings like werewolves, vampyres, ghouls, and ghosts, how to deal with various magical abilities, how to hunt down a witch. These are the primary subjects which they cover under the tutelage of his Aunt Fumiko, who specializes in witch-hunting.

"Witchcraft is not to be trifled with. Learn about it, know its uses, and never forget these untamed arts are evil and unrighteous. The very foundation for the existence of technomancers is to combat and defeat them so that our people may feel safe in their beds in the darkest hours of the night."

A hand goes into the air as his aunt starts her first lecture of the day, even though she did not call for questions.

"Fumiko-sensei, I have a question."

It is Wren, interrupting class again. Since the first day of lectures, she has proven herself to be a most persistent irritant.

She is too inquisitive, always asking questions in class while at the same time being the first to give some cheeky answer whenever their instructors see fit to ask the students a question. Her boldness irks him. Not that his aunt minds. Fumiko positively beams at the prospect of having a girl in her lectures who is as thirsty for knowledge as Wren.

"Lady Nocturne, your question?"

"So far, we have discussed various monsters, faeries, and spirits and how to defeat them, but I was curious about something concerning witches."

"Go on."

"I was just thinking. Oftentimes technomancers and witches are put in conflict with one another when both sides are attempting to eradicate a common enemy. Traditionally, it is encouraged to take the opportunity to terminate said witch, even though they are attempting to reach the same goal as we are. Killing two birds with one stone as it were."

"That's right." Fumiko gives Wren a curious look. "I'm still not sure what your question is."

"Yes, ma'am. Sorry. It's just... wouldn't it be more conducive to partner with them when we share a common enemy?"

Fumiko shakes her head.

"That is not possible."

"Why not? Not all of their abilities are innately evil. Healing spells, for example, would be as useful to an adept as much as a witch."

"Why would we need healing spells when we have superior medical technology such as regenerative stims and wound sealants?"

"But it isn't quite superior, is it? A healing spell can turn a life-threatening injury into a papercut at a mere whim, and you don't have to carry around supplies."

"Miss Nocturne—"

"And what about more mundane abilities such as being able to speak to plants or animals, or purely psychic abilities such as telepathy, or imagine how helpful telekinesis could prove during a difficult case? Surely, these things do not make a person innately evil?"

Fumiko glares at Wren from her place at the head of the room.

"The lady's question, while innocent enough in intention, forgets a fact of witchcraft that nullifies any good intentions for which it may be used."

"What is that?"

"A person with the ability to heal would naturally also have the ability to harm. A person who can communicate mentally can also extract secrets out of someone's head. While telekinesis may seem like a purely wonderous thing to employ, imagine a person who can break bones from a distance, shatter a person's skull, or even tear a person's heart from their chest with nothing but a thought. The potential for vile acts far outweighs any help they might provide."

"But technomancers receive modifications that would allow them to crush a person's skull with a flick of their—"

"That is why," stresses Fumiko, cutting off Wren's statement, "technomancers are vetted by the very trials you are presently attending, Lady Wren. To ensure untrustworthy individuals do not receive such abilities. There is no such process among hexen."

"Yes, but just because they can do something harmful, doesn't mean they will."

Fumiko heaves a sigh.

"The League has tried many times to end the violence between hexen and human+ peacefully, and each time, the mad frenzy their abilities inspire has toppled any such hope for a lasting peace. Witches and their abominations are nothing if not steadfast in their lust for power and destruction. The practice of witchcraft is, by nature, barbaric: ritual sacrifice, bloodletting, eldritch worship. Can you imagine doing such things? These heathens worship demons and devils and would slaughter their own children to quench their bloodlust. They are driven mad by their own power, and every time we were foolish enough to extend an olive branch, many lives were lost in the crossfire because they cannot control their own natures."

Wren seems to chew on this information for a while, and Fumiko prepares to continue with the lecture, but just as she turns back to the holo screen, Wren speaks up again.

"But what if we could help them control it?"

Fumiko flinches back around so violently, Kaito worries her topknot will somehow escape its confines.

"Excuse me!"

"A partnership. We have so much knowledge at our disposal, couldn't we find a way to help them maintain their sanity? A balance between magic and science, one that doesn't immediately cancel the other out."

Kai's eyes widen as his aunt actually begins to sputter, face turning purple.

"It can't be done!"

"But they are just as human as we are. Can't we—"

"You would call something like this human!" Fumiko slams her hand down onto the projection and a chorus of horror rises around the room.

On the holo screen flashes a photograph of a male witch, larger than life and dressed in gnarled and knotted furs and fabrics. He towers over the two adepts in the photo with him, fearsome to behold. Dark, blue-grey skin, a witch's indicia (the runic symbol Mannez centered on the right side of his skull with various geometric symbols trailing away from it) glows a poisonous red over half of his face, throat, and chest. The witch's face is gruesome to behold, a pointed nose and crooked chin covered in braided white facial hair. Tusk-like teeth protrude from his lower jaw to split the flesh of his upper lip, fang-like surface piercings along his cheekbone and jaw, long pointed ears, and skin that seems more amphibious than mammalian. A mohawk of dreadlocks curls whip-like around his head, tipped with sharpened arrowheads. His eyes glow red in the picture.

"This is the Goblin King, Yggfret Bloodfang, the most dangerous living witch of this generation. He is responsible for the deaths of countless adepts and seven technomancers. Tell me, Lady Nocturne, could you establish a partnership with a creature like this? You think he would treat you with even an iota of human decency? And what about others like him?"

The screen flashes through several more images of witches, each one more horrific than the last. There is a woman who stands naked save for the discolored ridges along her skin caught mid-transformation into what seems to be a serpent, and a man who might have been considered kind-looking were it not for the webbed bat wings sprouting from his back and the blood dripping down his chin. Another woman's eyes glitter gold, Brigit's cross shimmering on her cheek, her hair windswept over her face, only just covering the insects crawling along her forehead, and one last witch, androgynous and as handsome as they are beautiful on one half of their face while the other side is withered and gray, skin so translucent Kai can see the white of bones beneath.

"Magic and Technology cannot coexist. It is an impossibility! We, of respectable society, will harbor no such whimsies, and you would be best served to forget any possible notion of forming any kind of bond with one of these heathens."

Wren looks as though she is ready to press the discussion further, but next to her, Prince Xipilli elbows her in the ribcage. Her brother glares at her hard, and she falls silent. Fumiko closes her eyes and takes three deep breaths before looking back at her.

"You are a bright young woman, Lady Nocturne, but you will cut yourself on your own wit if you do not temper it with good sense, so ready you are to act contrary to the most common-sense laws of the League."

"I just meant—"

"I can forgive your ignorance. This is your first summit after all, and Deriva has never been one to organize witch hunts. I can imagine your Derivan tutors largely focused on sea monsters and merfolk. You'll need to make up for that gap in your education. As such, I expect a one-thousand-word report on all of the negative effects of witchcraft on the body and mind. Deliver to me anything less than exemplary, and you'll be out of here faster than you can blink."

Wren sighs, slumping back down into her seat.

"Yes, sensei."

"Kaito will grant you access to the library outside of lecture hours. I want it in my servers at dawn, and you will not be getting a start on it until after morning lessons are over, and don't you dare think about skipping assessments this afternoon to work on it."

Fumiko powers down the holo, turns her back on Wren, and moves right along with the next part of the lecture. Kaito looks back at Wren, who doesn't look nearly as cowed as she should. If anything, she looks pensive, if not saddened by the result of the conversation.

Wren notices him looking her way and has the gall to smile at Kaito without even a hint of shame in her expression. He glares at her, and she sends Kai a wink in retaliation. Prince Xipilli shakes his head, and Rhiannon and Heather chuckle under their breath at the other girl's antics. The rest of the lecture passes by uneventfully.

Upon their dismissal, Wren approaches to ask if he wouldn't mind letting her into the library during the lunch break. Kai's aunt calls for him, so he tells her briskly to wait for him there. She rolls her eyes good-naturedly before exiting the room after her brother. Fumiko holds him back for a few minutes to discuss how his studies have progressed thus far. Their conversation is short and polite, and Kai is happy to report he is learning well and has already made good headway on the final task. Fumiko nods sagely before unhurriedly asking Kai to make sure the Derivan girl doesn't make a total mess of the library. He bows in deference and leaves, sorely tempted to leave the girl hanging, but that would be petty, though he certainly wonders, not for the first time, how much she actually wants to be here.

Most of his classmates go to lunch, but he heads in the opposite direction of the dining hall toward the library. When he gets there, he is surprised to find Wren is not alone. He hears her voice before he sees her.

"I'm not interested."

The words are airy and carefree as though a half-thought in response to whatever is being asked of her.

"Oh, come on," a male voice drifts over to him. "Don't play coy. I saw you wink at me this morning. What else could you possibly have meant by that?"

"I don't recall even glancing at you, Llywelyn."

Oswald was sitting on the far side of Kai this morning. He must think Wren's wink at Kai was aimed at him. Wren's voice is calm and questioning, the kind of voice one uses when the life of a hostage is at stake, but also mocking, trying to anger him into leaving her alone. He hears Oswald chuckle.

"Your mother trained you well, didn't she?" The sneer is audible in his voice. "So headstrong all the time, you make a blatant show of your ability, but I bet you are just waiting for someone to push you onto your back."

"Leave me alone."

Kai sees them as he rounds the corner. Wren steps away from Oswald Llywelyn who continues advancing into her personal space, going so far as to place a hand on the wall behind her, cutting off one of her exits.

"Come on. Your brother isn't around. I can be quick. Perhaps if you're good enough, I'll put in a proposal request to your stepmother. That is, after all, the only reason she sent you here, isn't it? Hoping her darling stepdaughter will catch a big enough fish."

Wren laughs in the man's face, and then speaks a little firmer than she has yet.

"I told you, I'm not interested. Now leave me alone before I—"

Oswald raises a hand up to touch Wren, now trapped with her back against the wall, but Kai interrupts before the boy's fingers can come within an inch of her face.

"I believe the lady has requested you leave her alone."

Llywelyn's eyes roll in Kai's direction, but he does not back away from Wren who stands with her back straight and her hands clenched at something in her skirts.

"Miyazaki-sama. I didn't know you were one to eavesdrop on the conversations of others."

"A proper gentleman would hardly call that a conversation, and this location is off limits to trainees who have not received permission to be here. Now leave."

Llywelyn laughs at some unspoken joke, but he steps away from Wren.

"Very well then, your highness." He throws one last glance at Wren. "See you around, my lady."

He is not expecting the other boy to pat him on the shoulder and hiss in his ear loud enough for Wren to hear. "I'll leave you to her, young prince. They're better when they've been broken in, anyway."

Kai's fist connects with the side of his face. Oswald goes careening sideways all the way to the ground. Kai reaches down and lifts him off the floor by his collar.

"If I catch you pestering anyone again, I don't care who your father is. You'll be dismissed from this summit indefinitely, a dismissal which I am certain would behoove you considering this is your final year of eligibility, Lieutenant Llywelyn."

Oswald's face reddens with rage. He shoves himself out of Kai's hold. He is smart enough not to retort directly though. Casting a glare back at Wren, he storms away with his wounded ego. Wren's gloved fist unclenches, and she exhales, her attention burning into the floor. Kai waits until the military brat exits completely before addressing Wren.

"Are you alright?"

She raises her head. There is something very much fake about her smile.

"I'm fine. He wouldn't have been though if he'd actually touched me. I was about to slug him across the face before you dropped in."

"I can see that."

She looks down, a bit of pink rising to her cheeks.

"Did you still wish to enter the library? You could always use your personal computer."

"What and miss the opportunity to utilize the Miyazaki family's near infinite database? Not a chance!"

She certainly shows enthusiasm for research.

He shakes his head with an amused exhale before turning to the code scanner. His sights spin as he releases the lock, access code scanned directly into the mainframe. The heavy door unlatches, and he pushes it open. He gestures forward, allowing her entry before following himself. Her eyes glitter with excitement, and she hurries past him with an eager expression on her face.

Shinka's library is vast but not in terms of books. There are physical books of course, older volumes of text published before paper printing became obsolete and entirely out of fashion. A few familial tomes stand alongside documents preserved more for their historical value than any informational preservation. Most of the books along the wall are, in a manner of speaking, for decoration or, on the odd occasion of someone preferring a physical book over a handheld tablet, computer, or neural mainframe, for in-house perusal.

No, what makes the Miyazaki family's library legendary is the central access terminal located at its center. Sleek and packed with information, the database is exalted as a triumph of information retention and delivery servers, and not only for the amount of knowledge stored on its home hard drive, but also for its ability to hack into and find information outside its own servers. Filled with enough energy to power a nuclear warhead, the database can search for, collect, and distribute information from all over the globe in a manner of seconds. It far surpasses any web search engine in the world. If knowledge is power, then Murasaki is the most powerful country on Deus simply because of this machine.

Of course, power like this could only be tempered by extreme restraint, grace, and a firm sense of righteousness. A knowledge of the law, a pious disposition, pacifism, and most of all neutrality. Murasaki no Yama, for all its military might and fortitude, has not entered into political conflict in over a century, a stance which requires complete autonomy, strictly observed by the royal family and peerage of the country, and the Miyazaki are secular to a fault.

Such is the reason Murasaki is so revered and respected by the other countries. So too is the reason their attention is so sought after. Murasaki may not be the wealthiest nation in the world, but they most certainly are one of the most formidable.

Wren's face lights up in pure wonder at the sleek silvers of the data server and its various access hubs, but she also takes in the deep mahogany of the bookshelves and the few desks in the room. Surprisingly, she does not head straight for the terminal, instead walking over to the bookshelf. She takes a few minutes to peruse the aisle before finding a section that seems to draw her fancy. Reaching her flesh hand up, she brushes her fingertips along the spines of the books And looks back at him.

"May I?"

Never could he recall anyone ever being brought here who would divert their attention away from the mainframe first in favor of searching the bookshelves. It's... perplexing.

He nods in the affirmative, and she gently draws the book from its seat and opens the cover.

"I heard Shinka's library held some of the oldest books in existence. I never thought you would have books like this."

He walks over to see what she is looking through. She has found the arcane arts section, books on divination, spellcasting, and runic craft. There are a few books on musical casting and tarot, as well as an old almanac on the comings and goings of the moons and how they affect spell potency. All above ground readings, of course, safe for adepts to learn from, hence their presence in this part of the library. Anything truly dangerous would be locked away in the vaults, which even Kaito will not have free access to until after he graduates with his certification.

"Here, let me show you how to access the database."

She tucks the text she was looking at under her arm and follows him to a terminal.

"Do you have a portable drive?"

"Um, yes. Give me a second."

She puts her things down on a nearby desk and pulls the glove from her left hand to reveal, as he suspected, a mechanical prosthesis rather than flesh. It looks state of the art as far as Derivan tech goes. Coated in bronze alloy, the various circuits and plates are designed for maximum maneuverability and strength. Her flesh hand reaches around to unhook a panel and press a hidden key into the augmentation. A moment later, a data drive is ejected right into her palm from where her augmentation connects with the organic part of her arm.

"Here."

He takes the offered USB drive and inserts it into the hub. He then activates a holograph screen.

"The system is fairly easy to navigate. Is your tech compatible with holographic interfaces?"

"I have a stylus inset in my hand," she replies and steps forward to watch as he adjusts the server settings for her with his sights. While he doesn't physically move, the monitor displays each function he inputs, reacting to his commands too quickly for her to follow the coding. Once he's adapted the settings for manual manipulation, he activates a keyboard and finishes the coding digitally, every so often reaching up to touch the holo with a fingertip. He steps out of the way when he finishes.

"I've set the system so you can manage the mainframe like you would a regular computer. You'll have access for the next hour and a half before the system resets to defaults. Any data you need to save for later, you can upload onto your drive."

She nods, sitting down at the hub while he heads to the opposite side of the database to conduct his own research. He keeps an eye on her as she works. She doesn't ask for his assistance, not even when the monitor warns her she is attempting to access restricted information.

Of the five great countries of Deus, Deriva is probably the least sophisticated as far as their approach to technological integration. Neural implants, while not unheard of in the isles, were uncommon among Derivans. Almost as a rule, most Derivan adepts opt out on neural implants. They had no need for them since the vast majority of their cases take them on ventures where the interface is inaccessible. Dead zones where having a network in your head was more of a hindrance than an advantage. Most Derivan tech consists of mechanical prosthesis, muscular and organ enhancements, and naval and underwater mining technologies.

Their wealth, and Deriva is a wealthy nation, comes from the valuable metals, precious gems, and natural resources mined from their oceans. It's what places them as one of the five great nations of the world. Metals could be perfected and used to manufacture anything from robot exoskeletons to wired circuitry. Gems could be crushed and inlaid into tech for technomancy. Derivan sand could be melted down and molded into the clearest of glass. As such, Derivan adepts and technicians were often skilled mechanical engineers and inventors. Most if not all of them understood very well how to operate a computer, and could even troubleshoot minor problems, but they knew little of coding or hacking.

Their other claim to might was their superb navy, a small fleet of the world's most advanced ocean vessels including submarines, nauticals, searunners, and a short roster of trained technomancers skilled in underwater combat.

Forty-five minutes into their work, Prince Xipilli's voice drifts from the library doors in Derivan, calling Wren out to eat something before the next lecture. She calls back, something ridiculous and utterly inappropriate even for a sibling. She rises from her hub and begins collecting her things as her brother curses at her in Derivan. She offers Kai a small bow of her head and a smile.

"Thank you, your highness. I'm going to hurry for some lunch before the next lecture. Would it be alright if I returned after?"

He nods, rising to reset her terminal before he locks back up as she flutters her way out of the room to the call of her brother outside the door. When he goes to reset the hub, he is surprised to find she's already reset it.

After their last lecture for the day, she returns with him to the library. He pays her little mind even as she works furiously to finish the report that will be due his aunt come morning. He winces whenever he glances over. It's like a hurricane has hit the opposite side of the library from him. There are whole pages of handwritten notes laid out around her that she shuffles through every so often. Her personal laptop is open, and she types furiously. She holds a pen between her teeth for the occasional moment she stops typing to write down a note or circle a passage with the stylus end of it.

Several more chaotic minutes of this pass while he scans through study materials and lecture notes, formulating a thought experiment about how historical battle plans could be adapted to modern day technologies in the event of war. So immersed is he in his own thoughts, he doesn't notice Wren approach him until she is already seated next to him.

"Miyazaki-sama," she sing-songs his name, and he makes a point not to look at her even as she sets her computer right on top of his notes. "Would you mind reading through my draft?"

So, she's already written a thousand words in the short two hours they've been here. He doubts any of it will be sound research analysis. He does not grace her with any answer, merely pulling his notes out from under her computer.

"Kaito."

He still does not look at her.

"Kai!"

Hearing the shortened version of his name, a nickname she has no right to use, sharp and irritated from her mouth, his eyes slide over to glare at her.

"Finally got you to look at me. Will you, please, read my draft? I need to know if it makes sense."

"I'm sure my aunt would prefer you manage this task on your own merit."

"I am working on my own merit. It's not like I want you to rewrite it for me. I just need another eye. Please!"

"No."

She pouts.

"So cruel, highness. What if your aunt fails me because of some stupid grammatical error?"

"Perhaps then you'll learn not to disrespect your elders."

"I wasn't being disrespectful. I was asking an honest question."

"A question you very well knew the answer to. The ways of the League have been perfectly effective for centuries for good reason."

"That doesn't make them indomitable. Is it not our responsibility to challenge the status quo? Just because a computer works just fine doesn't mean it can't be updated and advanced. We wouldn't be halfway to where we are if we did."

"There's a difference between reprogramming a computer and rerouting a way of thinking."

"But both start with the question of 'can this be improved?' and 'if so, how do we do it?'"

And there is that bull-headed attitude he's come to associate with her.

"That is the League's prerogative. Not yours."

"But every technomancer has a voice of equal weight to any noble or monarch or elected official within the League Nations."

"You are not a technomancer."

"Not yet."

"Not ever if you don't pass the trials."

"Fair point," she says. "That's why you should do me this one teensy, little favor."

"Do your own work."

"*¡Hay! ¡Ni modo! Que Burro...*" she says as she turns away from. He does not speak her language, but he has the distinct sense she is insulting him.

"Excuse me?"

"Miyazaki-sama is so stubborn. I'll have to just wither away under the weight of this report on my own. Oh well. You'll never know my brilliant thoughts, then."

She dances back to collect her things, leaving after throwing a half-hearted "thank you, highness" on her way out.

"*Urusai.*"

What an annoying girl!

He assumes when she is not dismissed the next day that her work proves satisfactory to his aunt, but he doesn't ask, and he most certainly is not glad to see her remain.

The witches hunt us down like dogs. We have no magic, so they seek to exterminate us as though we were not once their kin. There is a place to the east, nestled in the mountains just a few leagues from the sea. A refuge of sorts where they talk of science and technology and advancement. I take my family there. Perhaps they can protect us from these heathens. We only ask for our right to live. Why should magic have any say in that?

Excerpt from a refugee's journal kept
in the library of Shinka Temple
Circa 804 A.P.

10

THE APPRENTICE PART 3

A S THE MONTH OF SONGS COMES TO A QUIET
close and the Month of Storms rolls in with rain and
thunder, they are presented with a crystal conduit and an
assignment to begin the construction of their personalized
weapons. They must sit with the stone and feed it their spiritual
energy and intention for as long as they can before attempting
to integrate it into weapons they will each be responsible for
designing and constructing themselves. To successfully integrate
their energy sources into one stone requires hours and hours of
carefully centered, focused meditation.

Kai requests two crystals.

"Pistols, rifles, swords, maces, tritons... Any tool of war is a
tool a technomancer can utilize in battle. In your training, you
have probably found a preference in your choice of weapon. It is
now time to design and obtain resonance with a weapon of your
making and personalization."

Fumiko-sensei briefs them on the final task, her hands folded
gracefully behind her back as her robes trail behind her.

"This is your final task. Weapon construction that involves the
integration of your very soul. Each weapon and master pairing
is unique, but such dedication to your craft is expected of you

before you can fully step into the world as technomancers. For many of you, this will be your first time endeavoring in such a task, but in order to progress to the combat evaluations, you must have your weapons presentable for examination in two weeks. Most of you will fail to meet the deadline." She pauses to let her words sink in. "You have been granted full usage of technomancer-grade equipment as well as resources that have been prepared for you by Shinka Temple and Murasaki no Yama. If you fail to accomplish this task by the deadline, all of your materials will be destroyed, including your resonance stones. If you wish to try again next year, you will have to start from scratch."

With that, Fumiko dismisses the group. They have two weeks to complete their weapons before the combat trials. Trials that would pair them up 1v1 against one another.

Kai is the only one in the weapon's shop nearly a week after they are assigned the task. He is working on the hilt of his katana when the Moctezumo heir walks into the workshop, his unruly younger sister at his heels chattering on about something or other.

They go back and forth in Derivan, and Kai isn't familiar enough with the language to follow it, not that he is even remotely interested in the conversation, but he hears something about Fireflies and Elisabeta. Wren laughs ironically at something her brother says about marriage which she counters with something about getting her technomancer certification. Then his own name come up, curiously enough.

Kai looks up from his work, and he finds green eyes twinkling straight at him. She winks at him, and he glares at her. Xipilli also glances his direction, but determined to ignore her, Kaito returns to his work, modifying his father's blades to integrate with his tech more efficiently. Constructing a new hilt for them took nearly three days of work, but inlaid in the new skeleton, they already look entirely different from his father's weapons. If he can link his saibāki and his pair of soul conduits directly with the blades, he will have accomplished the assigned task of creating not one but two weapons unique to him.

Xipilli shouts a question at his sister, and she laughs him off getting up and leaving her brother's table. To say Kai is surprised when she sets her materials down on the workbench opposite him is an understatement. Wren's eyes sparkle brightly with excitement. Excitement at what, he hasn't the slightest clue, but he can practically hear Xipilli roll his eyes at her, and he does catch the other boy mouthing something along the lines of "behave" at his sister.

"Good afternoon, Miyazaki-kun," she says, brightly, putting emphasis on the less formal honorific. One she is using incorrectly, mind you. He's older than her, after all. Not that he corrects her.

Xipilli's palm meets his forehead, and he quickly leaves the table he previously claimed to go as far away from the inevitable conflict about to unfold.

"Lady Nocturne."

Kaito turns his attention back to his work. The small welding needle in his hand sparks as he holds it to the new hilt of what will soon be his katana. The wiring is complex at this stage, but it has to be finetuned perfectly into his spiritual crystal; otherwise it won't take, and he won't be able to properly imbue his energy into the weapon. When he turns off the needle and lifts his safety glasses from his face, he notices Wren has sidled around the side of the table to stand adjacent to him and is now leaning her hands against the surface of the wood.

"So, you're integrating your crystal into the hilt, too? A lot of other people seem to think it's better to embed them in our physical mods, but I feel like we should be able to train ourselves to run our spiritual power through our augmentations without the extra aid."

He ignores her, continuing with his work even as she sits adjacent to him. The supplies she pulls out of her bag are much more akin to the type of parts Moctezumo is known for using. Gear locks and spring traps. Brass casings and seaglass. The last thing she pulls outs looks kind of like a double-sided torch or flashlight. There are what seem to be two activation points on it, but he can't tell what they are supposed to do. The item looks largely incomplete.

She notices him looking and holds it up for him to see.

"Neat, huh? I just finished the skeleton yesterday. I still need to figure out the internal structure if I'm going to get it to work."

"What is it?"

"A hilt for a double-bladed weapon."

He doesn't ask what kind exactly since it doesn't mimic the appearance of any style hilt he's ever seen.

"Are not double-bladed weapons rather impractical? You run a greater risk of accidentally injuring yourself."

"True, but I'm hoping if I can pull this off, it won't matter too much. Which is actually the reason I came over here. I have a question for you."

She looks at him out of the corner of her eye as though she is afraid he'll ignore her, but he is not so petty. Now if her question is ridiculous, that will be another matter entirely.

"Then ask."

She beams at him so openly he is almost embarrassed.

"The Miyazaki family is able to channel energy into handheld weapons, right?"

"That is correct," he answers warily. Family specific techniques are secret by nature among all adept families and monarchies, and the sharing of such knowledge is strictly forbidden, not just in the Miyazaki family either. He cannot divulge any information to her that would enable her to mimic the ability in any way, shape, or form, but the next question she asks is not what he is expecting.

"What is the energy called?"

He mulls it over, wondering if the answer would compromise his family. He doesn't believe so.

"It is called Saibāki. Cyber Energy if you will. It is an energy type unique to my family's bloodline. None of our guest adepts and technomancers are able to utilize the technique."

"I see."

She sits thoughtfully for a moment.

"So, it is kind of similar to how the Moctezumo family is able to channel spiritual energy directly through the glass made from seasalt. It is just something we can innately do."

"You wish to channel energy directly into a weapon."

She hums, sitting back away from him.

"It seems the most efficient way to do anything if you ask me, and it can't be that much different from creating projectiles with spiritual power either."

"But you have no blades. And the shape of your hilt does not lend well to any weapon I've ever seen."

She laughs, scratching the back of her head as she moves backward.

"Ah, Prince Kaito is astute as ever. Yes. The shape of my hilt is not very traditional, but why carry around a sword when you can make one yourself?"

"You cannot pull a blade out of thin air."

The smile on her face is positively impish, and her eyes shine with determination.

"Not yet, no."

"You are utterly preposterous, you know that."

"Go big or go home, right?"

Kai shakes his head slowly, returning to his work lest he get even more distracted by her strange chatter. If she is bothered at all by his criticism of her, then she certainly doesn't show it, lapsing into silence, in favor of setting to work on her construct. For once, the atmosphere between them is calm. She isn't trying to edge him on. She isn't teasing him. She isn't even paying him any attention whatsoever.

He should count his blessings really.

"Are you serious about passing?"

Sea-green eyes rise from her work to meet his silver gaze. She quirks one eyebrow up at him. The left side of her mouth is twisted in a smirk.

"Why? Worried I'll pass and you won't?"

He shakes his head, not sure why he expected an actual response from her. She is infuriating in every possible way. He returns to his work.

"Don't be absurd."

"Me absurd?" Wren lifts a hand to her chest feigning offense. "Never!"

Right...

"Hey, Kai?"

His eyes slide to her. There she goes again, using the shortened version of his name. Too familiar...too intimate...not even his mom calls him 'Kai.'

"Fumiko-sensei didn't say how they decided the matches for the adjudication. But I think I would really like to be paired up against you."

He is surprised by the sincerity of her statement, not to mention the absolute lack of teasing in her words. She wants to fight him in a real match then, and he finds himself strangely intrigued by the prospect. He watches her a moment. There is an earnest determination in her expression, an open honesty he is unused to seeing in others, and he realizes he might very well desire the same thing.

He looks back down at his work.

"I wouldn't mind going against you either, Wren."

He can feel her beaming at him. His chest tightens and his cheeks feel unusually warm, but they both return to their work, and no more words are shared between them for the rest of the afternoon.

The final trial begins with as much fanfare as you can imagine. A fired-up audience of national leaders (royalty, politicians, wealthy members of the peerage, and anyone who managed to score a ticket to the event) all eagerly await the chance to get their first glimpses of the adepts who may be joining the tightknit ranks of technomancers before the first moonrise. Betting pools are cast, the broadcasting cameras station themselves around the venue, and the 247th Annual Machina Deus Adjudication commences. Every prospective will enter the arena to fight against another prospective for a chance to showcase their skills and abilities for the assessment panel.

While the fights are not meant to end in bloodshed, accidents happen. With so many hopeful youths putting on display both their skills in combat and their newly made weapons, deaths are not uncommon. Weapons that were passed during private demo showcases sometimes prove faulty in actual combat, lashing out against their wielders or proving too powerful for a friendly duel, killing the opponent.

The Miyazaki are doing their due diligence to ensure there is no loss of life today. Medics stand by, prepared to jump in at the slightest indication of a life-threatening injury. Veteran technomancers stand on lookout around the parameter in case any student should attempt anything untoward.

Kaito sits on the far side of the contestants' pavilion, cross-legged on the floor. A monitor is mounted across the room, several participants hovering around it excitedly watching the matches. The crowd cheers as Xipilli and Chike, both heir apparent to their respective nations, stand opposite each other in the arena—a highly anticipated match. He pays it no mind, choosing instead to meditate.

"Hey!"

His peace is disturbed as an almost electric energy makes itself known to his left. Wren slides next to him on the floor. He can tell it's her without opening his eyes. No one else feels so much like a tempest when they're sitting still. She must have decided to come over after her brother left for his match.

"Kai," she singsongs his name, and he turns his head only minutely in her direction. "Aww, come on. Won't you look at me?"

He hums at her but keeps his eyes closed. He imagines she is pouting. He hears the metallic chime as she places her now finished hilt down on the floor beside her. A short moment of silence stretches between them, disturbed only by the rise and fall of cheering.

"Ouch. That had to hurt," she says.

When he opens his eyes to look at her, she is smiling, green eyes glittering with mirth even though her brother has just landed on his back in the ring, Chike having tripped him.

"Would you not prefer a closer view for your brother's fight?"

"I can see fine from back here."

And so she stays, quietly—or not quite so quietly—giving him a commentary on the match as he continues his meditation.

Her brother walks away the victor of the match, his trident, newly christened Opochtli, pulsing with electricity in his hand. Chike, for his part, rises as from the ground, having conceded before he could be seriously injured and retrieves his specially designed rifle, Agni, thick-barreled and painted with the golds and reds of his country. The bell of victory sounds as they trade a companionable fist bump. Kaito's own match will be starting in a few short minutes. He rises from his seat, picking his blades up off the floor.

"What did you name your swords?"

"You'll find out."

"Aww, come on!"

When he answers her, after he is finished strapping his katana and his tanto to his back, it most certainly is not because she is pouting at him.

"Tsukuyomi and Amatsu," he says, gesturing to each sword as he recites their names. He doesn't expect her to catch any meaning from their names, but once again, he finds himself surprised by her, something she has proven herself quite good at since their first meeting.

"Hmm, the moons and stars. Poetic."

Poetic indeed. Companions who'll never leave him no matter how dark the night gets. He moves to leave as his name is called to report to the arena.

"Hey, Kai!"

He looks over his shoulder at her.

"Light 'em up!"

He acknowledges her encouragement with a short nod, passing Xipilli and Chike as they re-enter the pavilion.

Kaito faces off against a candidate named Titania Ruliff from Ebele.

His katana and his tanto blades pass demonstration. At the go, Kai draws each blade in unison, their hilts open up and plug themselves into the installation points in his forearms. This gives him the ability to manipulate the blades without actually holding them in hand. Kaito activates his sights and reaches to resonate with the conduit crystals embedded in each blade. They alight with the ultraviolet glow of his ki to the audience's roaring applause. He meets his opponent head on, and she returns the sentiment gladly with a fearsome assault. He dodges and parries her attacks, delivering his own with the intent to disarm. Halfway through their fight, his opponent's weapon, a battle axe, proves itself an unsuccessful integration, failing to maintain the additional elemental integration. But she puts on a good display. There's no doubt she will be welcomed to try again next year. After her weapon fails, the match doesn't last long. He disarms her with a pulse of energy from his blades, and the axe clatters to the floor, a declaration of Kaito's victory.

His family applauds, his mother beaming with pride as he walks from the arena. He himself is a bit disappointed by the shortness of the match, but when he reaches the participants' pavilion, Wren greets him with a "congratulations!" and a dazzling smile while her half-brother rolls his eyes at her before offering Kaito a nod. He knows his victory will not automatically grant him certification, but he is confident he showcased enough of his ability to warrant a passing score.

The next few matchups go by without much spectacle. There are a few more candidates who fail integration but still put on a good showing. A few candidates do well and are kept in mind for licensing even if they suffer the losing side of the match. He doesn't pay much attention to the matches, but when the next names called are Wren Nocturne and Oswald Llywelyn, he turns his attention to her. The girl bounces to her feet and stretches before grabbing the now finished hilt off the floor. She twirls her wrist, her hilt in hand, and she smiles at him. The weapon spins in the sunlight, sparkling and reflecting coppery prisms along the tent wall. She notices him looking at the weapon in her hand.

"Mångata."

When he doesn't ask outright, she elaborates.

"It's a word from my mother's natural tongue. It describes the reflection of the moons on water."

Before he can respond, her brother shouts at her from across the tent.

"Hey, don't screw around!" calls Xipilli as she leaves for the arena. She graces him with a wink framed by a cutesy twisting of her fingers, her index and middle finger framing her right eye.

Wren and Llywelyn face off at the center of the arena. Wren grips her hilt in her right hand while he aims at her with an oddly shaped laser pistol. At the sound of the starting buzzer, Wren lifts the hilt in front of her in both hands and activates the weapon. The crowd holds its breath as either end of the hilt sparks. At first, nothing happens, and Kaito worries she's failed to accomplish the task. But then she closes her eyes, and the sparks ignite, twin beams of golden energy taking shape on either end. A double-bladed kalis forms from Wren's very essence, focused and concentrated beyond anything he has ever seen and shaped by the conduit crystals.

The presentation of it is impressive enough to draw an uproar of applause from the crowd.

Kaito watches as Wren fights, graceful and light on her feet, easily dodging around the pistol shots as she closes the distance between her and her opponent. Llywelyn is a worthy marksman, grazing her shoulder and hip with his shots, and he keeps himself out of Wren's reach with a physical demonstration of his abilities.

His weapon, however, fails him.

Llywelyn's pistol activates easily enough, but it is unstable, the blasts released at infrequent rates and sizes. When Wren moves to disarm him, her ætherblade clips the barrel of the weapon. He maintains his grip, but Wren backs away as the weapon sparks and sputters before the pent-up energy in the pistol backfires, detonating in the Seraphim adept's hand.

Wren shields her face as the shrapnel goes flying, but Llywelyn is not so lucky. Bits of metal pierce his face and chest, blood spilling everywhere. Murasaki medics collect him from the arena as quickly as they can manage, his face and arming hand a mess of blood and torn flesh.

When Wren returns to the pavilion, she is covered in blood, lips cheerless as her brother gathers her into his arms. Oswald Llywelyn's death goes down in the record books as an accident due to weapon malfunction.

20th Day in the Month of Storms–1861

The following evening, a black-tie celebration is held in the honor of the candidates who passed the trials, each new graduate presented to society as newly accomplished technomancers, the peerless heroes of the League. Kaito is among them, the second youngest of his classmates to pass and holding the honor of topmost score. The Derivan prince, Xipilli, is also licensed along with his sister, Lady Wren, whose scores were second highest. Prince Chike from Ebele passes, to his father's pride, ranking third despite having conceded defeat to Xipilli during weapons demonstrations—or perhaps it is because he conceded that his scores were so high. Sekhmeti has much to be proud of as their crown prince Jamar passes, this year having been his final chance to graduate. Art Lionheart, the farmer's boy from Aighneas, passes. So too does the surname-less girl, Irene. There are a few others from smaller countries: Xiao Yixuan, Selene Fitzroy, Anika Kashtri, and Bakura Ganem.

PRELUDE

Eleven total graduates. Eleven shiny new technomancers qualified to undergo integration.

The only country without a graduate this year is Seraphim. Archibald Llywelyn does not attend the festivities, the general preferring instead to see to the burial of his son, and the pontiflex is only in attendance for the first portion of the evening. The Pontiflex's son, Donarick Thames, had been dismissed for failed written examinations, so he attends only out of obligation.

The formal banquet thrown for them is not overly extravagant, but it is certainly much more than would normally ever grace Shinka's sacred grounds with the families of the passing technomancers milling about the room. For the majority of the peerage, it is any other event, but for the families of the graduates that came from nearly nothing, this is a special occasion indeed. Farmers, merchants, and journeymen families are in attendance, their status elevated now that a son or daughter has become a technomancer. Hikaru even arranges for Irene's mother, newly freed from slavery, to be escorted to the dinner as an honored guest.

Kaito learns from speaking with the woman that she had been a slave to a plantation owner in one of the smaller nations where slavery was still legal. Not anymore, though. Her daughter's promotion serves not only to guarantee Irene's new elevated position in life but also her mother's emancipation from the harsh hand life dealt them. Naturally, however, they will not be able to obtain citizenship within said nation, but under the invitation of Vulcan Tlanextli, in attendance to celebrate the ascensions of his children, Irene and her mother have been offered a home in Deriva should they choose to move, an offer which Irene accepts for herself and her mother with grace and gratitude.

Kaito stays for a while, speaking with his brother and mother. A few of the other graduates and already instated technomancers offer him congratulations which he returns. Eventually, the musicians shift from providing general ambiance for the banquet to more lively music for dancing and entertainment.

When Kai's mother and aunt decide to dance, Hikaru comes to sit next to him, having just left the dancefloor after finishing a song with one of the many ladies in attendance. He slides into the seat next to Kaito and drinks from the glass of water he left there earlier, casually adjusting the burgundy lapels of his tuxedo jacket.

"Otōto, are you going to dance?"

"I do not wish to dance, Aniki."

"Oh? Is there no one you wish to dance with?"

"Hikaru," he says in warning, not wanting to endure his brother's lighthearted pestering. He doesn't hate dancing per se. He has, in fact, danced many times at social gatherings, the expectation being he dance with at least one or two girls during such events. The problem is it's usually more frustrating dancing with a complete stranger than it is enjoyable. Girls these days like to back-lead, or they lean too heavily on his arm, or they try and press themselves too close for his liking. A dance with a partner is as much a conversation as it is movement, and it is tiresome to try communicating with someone who isn't listening.

His older brother just hums at him. Just as he is about to speak, a small ruckus drifts to them from a nearby table as Elisabeta storms from the room, Tlanextli on her heels as she goes, a storm of blue and purple silk. In their wake, Xipilli turns to Wren, seemingly livid about whatever just occurred. He can hear only snippets of what they are saying, and they are speaking Derivan, so what he does catch is indiscernible, but the tone of Xipilli's words to Wren is unmistakably scathing. Kai's eyes narrow as Wren tries to placate him, but the boy physically pushes her away.

Rather than being cowed, Wren wraps him in a hug, speaking into his ear something which seems to subdue his anger for the moment. Their older sister, Atzi, who was just dancing with Chike, wanders over, splitting the two apart and soothing the tension from the table. Xipilli makes one more biting remark at Wren, and the girl laughs loud enough that Kaito can hear her over the pulse of the music.

"Lady Wren is indeed bright and talented. A few months younger than you and already a technomancer. Quite impressive. Wouldn't you agree, Kaito?"

Kai doesn't respond as he watches Wren rise from the table where her brother and sister sit.

"I heard she was able to match you when you caught her breaking and entering the first night of the trials."

"She is a nuisance."

Hikaru chuckles. "Hopefully, her new responsibilities will temper her."

"Doubtful."

Wren's spirit is boundless and untamed and so wildly unfaltering she need not look before she leaps because she knows she'll catch herself if she falls. A stark contrast to Kaito who is calm, calculating, and careful in all things.

"Her scores rival even yours. Were she not so unruly, she may very well have beaten you."

That's not right either. Unlike Kai, who is motivated by accomplishing the duties that come with his rank and birth, Wren's drive to succeed stems largely from her need to overcome the restrictions placed on her by society and, it would seem, her own family.

"It is her unruliness that drives her to challenge herself. She would not be here at all if she were the type to accept the hand dealt to her."

It is an attitude he recognizes now, despite how irritating her headstrong nature may prove, as one worthy of respect. Something he would even describe as admirable.

Hikaru's eyes glint with mischief.

"Perhaps you'll find yourself on assignment with her some time."

"I fail to understand why that seems so pleasing a possibility to you."

"I'm interested to see what you two may accomplish."

Kai's eyes flash in warning to his brother, who merely smiles warmly at him, before looking back in front of him as Wren walks past their table, offering a small bow to them in respect as she passes. She then walks swiftly out of the room, and even though she wears one of her usual quirked smiles, there is a note of sadness hidden in her expression.

"Don't worry, brother. You'll be paired together. I'm sure of it," Hikaru says, mirth dancing in his eyes.

Kai has never entertained the idea of hitting his aniki, but he is sorely tempted to right now. Instead, he gets up and leaves the bustling room in favor of some peace and quiet. Kaito takes one last look at where Atzi is still gently conversing with Xipilli, who is just starting to calm down. Perhaps he'll go to the rooftop.

It's a nice night, and Deus' moons are in eclipse, a rare occurrence considering such happenings only occur once every fifteen to twenty years, not that he needs their light to see, but something about the world being engulfed in their cool purple texture can charm even the gruffest individuals.

There is a skygazing gazebo atop the central building. It is a place he has gone since he was old enough to venture up here alone to find comfort in the quiet of solitude.

He finds Wren instead.

She is not in the gazebo, sitting on the roof's incline instead. She sits at the edge of the racked tiles, one leg dangling toward the ground, leaning back onto her forearms while her face lifts toward the moonlight. Her skin glows a cool bronze in the light of the moons, her dark hair curling around her neck and shoulders in a carefully designed updo for the occasion. Her dress, a floor-length two-piece ballgown in a dark emerald shade that looks almost black in the nightlight, rustles in the calm northerly wind drifting through, the fabrics pooling around her petite form. The line of her midriff shows ever so slightly, a crystal naval ring sparkling between the folds of the fabric.

It strikes him suddenly that he has never seen her so calm. Pensive and thoughtful. Up until this very moment, he hasn't thought her capable of such quietude, and his pulse jumps.

She looks ethereal.

It is not long before she notices him. He is rather conspicuous, wearing a red tuxedo jacket as he is. She turns, and the quiet is broken by the lilt of her voice.

"Oh! Kaito-san! What brings you out here? Come to admire the moons? My mother once told me a double moon eclipse can reveal a person's fate if they know how to appreciate them: one moon for the past and one for the future. Imagine that! A celestial event that can guide a person toward their destiny. Did your family plan that on purpose for commencement day this year? A way to help us all choose the right path."

"Only hexen place so much weight on the cycles of the moons."

"Ah, the prince has no time for poetry then."

"Lady Wren shouldn't sit on the edge of the racking. She could fall."

"Will you catch me if I do?"

He gives her the severest look he can muster.

"Okay, okay. I'll come back up."

She rises easily, shaking her skirts of any dirt before carefully picking her way over to where he is standing. It's a miracle she doesn't trip over her skirts or high heels as she goes, but she jumps backward up onto the railing. He looks away as she swings over one leg and then the other. She is about to slide her feet to the floor when he hears her gasp. Her skirt has caught in the guardrail high enough to prevent her feet from reaching the floor. He moves, catching her before she can fall to the ground or tear the dress.

His arms wrap around her waist. Her hands come down on his shoulders, her face buried into his chest. She twists to pull the skirt from the nail holding it hostage. She smiles, embarrassed about her near fall as she turns back to him, and he sets her on her feet, the dress settling back around her.

"Thanks," she whispers.

Their faces are very close together, and for the length of a pulse, he stands in awe at how the moonlight punctuates the blues in her seagreen gaze.

"Your eyes are really pretty," she says after a long moment.

Kai pulls back, nearly flinching at the compliment. No one outside his family has ever said anything positive about his eyes.

He has his father's eyes. The rest of his family have warm, chocolatey brown eyes, and while his aunt could be reticent at times, at least her appearance doesn't deter people from approaching her. His father had silver eyes, but he had been tender rather than cold...at least from what Kai remembers. He'd been killed by a witch when Kai was just a toddler, so there's not much memory there other than the stories his mother, brother, and aunt have told him.

He learned to hate his eye color as a child. Between their pale, seemingly unnatural silver color and his quiet nature, he was often called creepy by the other children his age. As Kai grew older, he started to hear more often how cold they made him seem. Eyes the color of steel, a disinclination toward much outward expression, and an introverted nature that didn't lend well to making friends... of course, he would seem glacial to his peers.

Yet here is this girl standing far too close to him and looking far too intently at him with a smile on her face like he isn't the most inhospitable person she has probably ever met.

"Don't be ridiculous."

She laughs at him.

Music drifts up to them from the ballroom, a slower swing number, and he remembers himself enough to remove his hands from her waist. Her hands don't leave his shoulders, but she doesn't try to hold him there either as he pulls back. Her gloved hands slide to his forearms.

"Dance with me."

"Nonsense."

She pouts prettily at him as he moves entirely out of her reach and turns away to look out at the moonlit courtyard.

"Must you always be so serious? Come on. Dance with me. I'll show you if you don't know how."

"I know how to dance."

"Oh? Prove it!"

He turns to her, a look of exasperation on his face.

"If you want to dance, go back to the ballroom."

"I don't want to dance with anyone in the ballroom."

"Yet you want to dance with me?"

"Why not?" She shrugs. When he doesn't answer her, she continues. "Come on. I promise I won't tease you if you're bad at it. Just one song."

Never mind that she is teasing him already.

"I will have you know I am actually quite good at dancing."

"Then show me," she says, a playful challenge in her voice. His eyes narrow at her. Fine then. He'll accept her challenge, if only to shut her up for one second.

"You are a menace," he concedes.

She sighs airily, not understanding the assent in his jibe until his left hand takes her right, and he pulls her into a classical hold, his right hand secure in the curve of her waist. He waits, expecting her to begin backleading any moment. Someone as headstrong as Wren surely wouldn't understand the push and pull of this type of conversation. But she settles into his hold, her weight balanced neutrally in her feet as she watches and waits for him to decide which direction they are going. She doesn't even look expectant of him, her expression open if only a little curious. There is no impatience or annoyance as he would have expected from her. She is just listening.

She's listening...

She's listening to him, so he allows himself to speak.

There isn't much room to really move in the gazebo, but he leads them in circles, his footwork easy and light in deference to the music playing, and she follows.

There are missteps, of course. Her heel catches the edge of a plank once or twice. His lead doesn't read as strongly as it should the first time he goes to spin her, so when she second guesses, he corrects her with a gentle firmness. The first time he dips her, she laughs a little, but bends happily in his hold, letting him maneuver her down and then back up as the song comes to an end. Before long, he realizes they've been dancing for more than just a single song, more than even just two or three songs. He's lost count.

The night is too cool for them to sweat, but his body feels warm. He brings them to a sway. At some point, he doesn't have any idea when, his right hand joined his left at her waist and her hands have laced themselves behind his neck. They stand too close yet too far at once, their feet hardly leaving the floor anymore as their hips shift from side to side. The song playing now has lyrics to it, and Wren sings along softly until she decides to speak.

"You are a good dancer."

"I wasn't lying."

She chuckles softly.

"No, you weren't. Top score of our class, a skilled musician, and to top it all off, he can dance. Is there anything you aren't good at, your highness?"

He turns his head away from her. He is not good at holding conversations like this, for one. She must sense his unease because when she next speaks, her voice is softer.

"My apologies. I shouldn't have teased you. Thank you for dancing with me." She looks down and away from his face. "To be honest, I wasn't feeling up for company when I came up here," she says.

"Your family?"

She winces.

"You saw that, did you?"

"Hm."

"I wasn't supposed to pass. Now, Elisabeta and Xipilli are both upset with me."

"They should be proud of you."

"If only..."

The wind picks up all of the sudden, Wren's hair tousling at the assault, and he angles them into a rotation to shield her from the brunt of it.

"Their anger is not a reflection on you. You have proven yourself their equal in the only way that matters."

"Yeah...I also managed to kill someone along the way," she says, her eyes drifting down and to the left. Guilt. This is the first time he has spoken to her since the arena, and he remembers vividly the shine of tears in her eyes after Oswald had been pronounced dead.

"It is not your fault Llywelyn's weapon backfired."

"But I was his opponent. If he'd been up against someone else, it may not have happened."

"It would have happened eventually. His weapon should never have passed the approval process."

She seems unconvinced, so he voices an opinion that may or may not be true but is his own nonetheless.

"If there is anyone who should take responsibility for his death, it is the adjudication panel and his own father for insisting he be let through to the arena. He may not have become a technomancer, but he would still be alive were it not for that."

"Do you really believe that?"

Kai thinks back to the time he interfered on Llywelyn accosting Wren. He wonders, if Wren were a weaker person or if he had not come along, just how far the man would have gone to get that which he seemed to think himself entitled to.

A character like that doesn't deserve her grief, he thinks but does not say aloud. Instead, he nudges her chin so she is once again looking him in the eye.

"You are not a killer, Wren."

She smiles at him, and it strikes him how rewarding it feels to have brought the expression back to her face as he continues to move them.

In her heels, she is about four inches shorter than him, he doesn't need to lean down to see her, but he does anyway. Her chin tilts up as the song ends, and for the first time since they began dancing, they still. The air nearly sparks with electricity as they breathe, slowly but deeply. He looks from her eyes to her lips and back again. They are too close, less than a hair's breadth between them. The distance hangs between them, heavy and volatile. Then Wren's eyes slide closed, and he moves until there is nothing in between. Her lips are warm on his, more of a gentle pressing of mouths than a kiss. His hands wrap fully around her back and draw her closer. The fourth and fifth fingers of each of his hands rest against the bare skin of her midriff. She is warm to the touch, and he wants...

Once again, she follows his lead and in turn pulls his head down to deepen the kiss.

"Wren, are you up here?" a shout reaches them from the stairs.

They break apart as though whipped as Xipilli storms the stairs.

"I'm here!"

"Where the hell have you been?!"

"Xipilli, watch your language."

Xipilli, when he finally makes it onto the landing, looks positively livid. He becomes even more so when he spots Kai before turning on Wren in their home language.

"*¿Qué estás haciendo aquí?*"

"*Solo bailamos.*"

"*¡Solamente! ¿No has creado muchos problemas ya? ¡Que vergonzosa!*"

"*Es nada para eso.*"

"*¡¿Y 'el?! Es nada por 'el también.*"

"*¡Basta!* Kai is a gentleman. He wouldn't—"

When Wren begins to speak back and forth between common and Derivan, Kai recognizes she is doing so for his benefit, keeping him privy enough to the conversation to understand what is going on. Xipilli becomes even more irritated by this.

"A gentleman would have escorted an unaccompanied lady back downstairs."

"*¡Cállate lo sico!*"

"*No me digas* 'shut up!' We've been looking for you for over an hour. *¡Una ora!* I had to ask Lionheart if he saw you anywhere, and he said he saw you head to the roof."

"I've been up here that long."

"Yes, Father is looking for you. *Nos vamos a Deriva esta noche.*"

"We're leaving tonight? But closing ceremonies are tomorrow."

"Father says we're leaving tonight, so we're leaving tonight. *Muevete.*"

"Okay, can I get a second?"

"Now, Wren!"

Wren sighs before bowing to Kaito. She gathers her skirts, walking past her brother to get to the stairs. As she disappears down the steps, she hesitates just a moment to send Kai an apologetic smile before her brother blocks his line of sight. Xipilli's eyes never leave Kai's face. He doesn't speak until Wren is out of earshot.

"If you know what's good for you, you'll stay away from my sister."

Kai keeps his hands firmly behind his back, even though his fists have been clenched, itching to punch the other boy for how he had been addressing his own sister.

"I have no ill intentions toward Lady Wren."

"You'll have no intentions at all if you know what's good for you," he spits out before turning on his heel to return downstairs.

"You should show better respect for your sister."

The older teen's eyes narrow.

"She is my sister, and I will protect her the way I see fit."

Kaito does not dignify that with a response, holding Xipilli's gaze steadily until the older teen breaks. The Derivan prince looks away and back, his frown deeper than before.

"Stay away from her, Miyazaki. I'm warning you."

And he storms off.

Kaito closes his eyes and shoves his hands into his pockets in frustration only to startle when he finds something there he most assuredly did not put there. He pulls it out. In the center of his palm rests a small cylindrical box wrapped in a handkerchief. He eyes it curiously as he unwraps the coral-embroidered cloth.

Inside is a simple, seemingly hand-woven leather necklace beaded with three beads of what looks to be malachite and two seashells. The loop of it is long enough he can just tuck it beneath his collar, and it sits light and soft against the skin of his collarbones. It hums with Wren's familiar energy.

Did she make this herself?

Inside the lid of the box, written in flowery cursive:

The Apprentice Part 3
Congratulations, 海斗
and
Happy Birthday!

Wren

Something tightens in his throat, and he's not sure if it's the fact that she wrote his name in the characters of his native language or that she somehow discovered today was his birthday and saw fit to give him a gift. Or maybe it's because he no longer has the opportunity to thank her himself?

Kai does not see Wren again that night, and sure enough, the Derivan entourage is long gone come morning.

He has been warned, in no uncertain terms, to stay far away from Wren regardless of what her thoughts on the subject may be. While he does not appreciate being threatened by the Derivan heir, now, fingering the band of leather around his throat, he can't help but feel a touch of shame. He doesn't know what possessed him, what brand of madness came over him in that moment, but he knows very well he had no right to kiss Wren Nocturne.

As far as indicia go, most witches will not have much more than a single symbol on their body. The most notable places to look for an indicia include the hands, feet, neck, and back. With reasonable suspicion, technomancers have the full right to demand a strip search of a person suspected of witchcraft. But don't waste your time with such trifles. A witch with a single symbol on their skin is not much of a threat. Worry instead about witches who bear Wild Script, additional markings that trail away from the root symbol of the witch's indicia. The most extensive indicia ever documented was found in 1794 on a witch who claimed to be a descendant of the Hexen Throne, Cascadia Polaris, an elemental master capable of manipulating earth, air, fire, and water who could influence the very spirits of others. Her indicia was rooted in the pentagram and trailed down her arms and across her neck.

The more wild script in a witch's indicia, the more powerful the witch.

An Excerpt from *Hunting and Identifying Hexen*
by Finnick Lockecraft, 1852 A.P.

11

FOUR OF PENTACLES

Present–The 2nd Day in the Month of Falling 1877–Jade Apartments–Snowfall Palace

THE SUNLIGHT FILTERING IN THROUGH THE window is warm on her skin. There are EKG patches on her temples as well as under each of her clavicles. Her eyebrows twitch before her eyes flutter open.

The world around her is blurry at first as she pulls the patches from her skin, but the space comes into focus as she blinks the sleep out of her eyes and wills her brain to start working again.

Refined and elegant. Those are probably the best words to describe the room. A cool breeze weaves through the space from the open windows. Decorated tassels rustle at its touch. The furniture is stylized in accordance with the Eastern most region of Murasaki no Yama: low tables, sliding doors, tatami mats, arched windows, and fine tapestries done in delicate calligraphy. Deep mahogany and wine red walls are accented by the deep greens of indoor plants and the silver sheens of various equipment. Through the open door, she can see a holo screen the room over, glowing faintly in slumber, and various other clean white and silver computational A.I. hubs are visible on the workspace. Sparse, neat, and thrumming with cyber energy.

The bed she is in is low to the floor, similar to a futon but still elevated by an elegant dark wood frame. As she sits up, an A.I. hub next to her flicks on, and a mechanical voice greets her.

"Good morning, guest. The time is now 10:27AM on the 2nd day in the Month of Falling. My name is AYA, and I have been authorized to answer your questions while my master is out."

And who is this master exactly?

Wren rises, noticing she is dressed in a light sleeping gown, the asylum clothes missing and hopefully burned.

"My master has requested I direct your attention to the wardrobe so you may dress. Several garments have been procured for you during your recovery."

The wardrobe doors slide open with a shing, and Wren realizes that, of course, there are cameras throughout the house. How else would AYA be able to monitor her? A moment of panic engulfs her as she searches fervently for a reflective surface. The black mirror of a monitor across the room answers, and she is relieved to find her glamour didn't dissipate while she was out.

By its nature, the spell should hold through sleep, but if someone saw fit to dispel her of any enchantments...well, let's just say game over.

Breathing a little easier, she lowers her feet to the floor. The rug at the edge of the bed is plush and fluffy, but the hardwood beyond its boundaries is cold, and she hisses a bit at the sensation.

"Forgive me, Miss. The master does not often use the floor heating feature. Allow me to turn it on for you."

Within seconds, the floor beneath her feet warms to a toasty temperature as she makes her way into the wardrobe. The first thing she notices is the battlegarb that comprises most of the space: men's trousers, vests, and coats, worn black leathers that have seen more than a few fights. And next to them pale gray and lavender robes, kimono-style tunics. It's these that give her pause.

"AYA, where am I?"

"Miss is presently a guest at Snowfall Palace, in the living quarters of His Imperial Highness, Kaito Miyazaki. I have notified him of your waking. He should return shortly."

Merde!

"Oh, did you have to?"

"Yes, miss. Such was my directive. I reported your waking the moment you regained consciousness. You would do well to dress before his arrival."

Wren scowls at a black ceiling node, no doubt one of the A.I.'s monitoring cams, before turning back to the wardrobe. On the far side, separate from the menswear, are several dresses, and she is surprised to find none of them are in the traditional kimono or hakama styles typical of this region of Murasaki. Instead, she finds a leather, tailed bodice hanging beside several dresses very similar to those she commonly wore toward the end of her first life. A fashion popular among the peoples of the wilds, practical cotton without any overly invasive materials which might impede their abilities. She chooses a soft, black, long-sleeved chemise, the length of which reaches just below her buttocks, and short, laced knickers as her undergarments before pulling one of the lighter dresses, in a rich green and black, over her head which she bustles in the front. Over the top, she pulls on the leather bodice. She covers her legs with long stockings and slips on a pair of leather boots tucked into the side of the wardrobe. She finds a pair of fingerless gloves to slip over her hands and arms as well before picking a belt from the wardrobe, one with various pouches for tucking away casting ingredients, and enough room to hang various talismans or vials should she feel the need.

Someone braided her hair in her senseless state, but she has since roughed it up, so as a final measure to make herself more presentable, she unravels the braid and sweeps her curls back and up into a messy bun which she ties off with a green ribbon. Several curled strands escape the updo and frame her face, and she wishes the glamour could do more than simply change the color of her hair. Atalia's straight hair would have been much preferable to her wavy bird's nest. She pulls on the travel cloak she commandeered from the facility and makes her way to the adjacent sitting room and the front door. The handle doesn't so much as budge when she tugs on it. AYA chooses that moment to pipe up again.

"Apologies, Miss, but Miyazaki-sama requested you remain here until his return."

"Is that supposed to be surprising?"

No matter, she'll just force the door.

She gathers energy into the tips of her fingers and points at the lock. However, as she is about to release the spell, a spark of energy shoots back at her, powerful enough to send her reeling to the tatami mats on the floor.

"Miss, I highly advise you not to force the lock. I have my instructions."

She collects herself with a huff.

"You certainly do."

Content not to aggravate the A.I., she settles herself at the table where a stack of plain paper has been neatly set aside. There is a woman's handkerchief beneath the glass covering of the table, pale blue with seashells and coral designs crocheted into it, very similar to something she used to carry around with her when she was a teenager and still bothered with decorum. This one, however, looks far too clean and cared for to be anything she left behind. A gift perhaps from the woman in his life? Kaito is most certainly of an age where marriage would be an expectation.

Oh! Perhaps he even has a prim and proper wife stowed away somewhere.

Poor girl, whoever she is, gets to enjoy Wren's leftovers for the rest of her marital life. Maybe Wren should start thinking of herself as a proper Firefly like her mother had been, training boys to become good husbands with practiced hands in the art of lovemaking.

She shakes her head with a chuckle. Good to know she had some lasting effect on the present. Taking up a sheet and pen, she begins to scribble arrays into the page before returning her attention to the A.I.

"How long have I been here?"

"The Master brought you here yestereve sick with fever and a head wound. You had a brief moment of waking during which you attempted to climb out a window, but his highness restrained you. You have been comatose since. Our doctors were worried your injury would incapacitate you entirely. Your waking will put them at ease."

"Prognosis?"

"You sustained a minor concussion, a deep abrasion on your bicep has been repaired, but several wounds on your forearm are not healing. Madame Nakano assumes they are from your mistreatment in the facility in which you were being housed. They have been bandaged and treated with a clotting factor."

Hmm... Yes, but not quite, though she doesn't feel the need to correct the misconception right now.

"You know about the asylum."

"Yes, Miss. Miyazaki-sama uploaded the data on Stonehearst Asylum into my database. His highness's retinue is overseeing the sentencing of all individuals involved. The surviving patients are currently being treated in proper hospitals in their respective countries of origin."

"Were any children found?"

"Yes, ma'am. Their teddy bear was returned to them."

It's more than a little creepy how the A.I. can almost read her mind, though she is glad the survivors will be properly taken care of now that they are out of that hellhole.

"Why have I been brought here?"

"The answer to your question is beyond the parameters of my authorization, Miss."

"Oh, come on. If Kaito thinks he can just—"

The door to the sitting room opens, and Prince Kaito Miyazaki steps in. Speak of the devil...

His swords are still strapped to his back but the leathers of his mission attire are missing. He's as regal as ever, wearing layers of cloth robes in a traditional hakama fashion all in shades of grey and lavender. *Mourning clothes*, Wren notes silently. He was wearing lavender during the case as well under his battle leathers, not a typical color to wear on a case. Someone important must have died recently for him to wear such colors on a mission, but the two teen adepts with him hadn't been wearing lavender.... Unless she counts Renki's sash, but Akari had not been wearing the same.

AYA is quick to greet him.

"Welcome home, your highness."

"So, who died?"

If an A.I. could stutter! AYA's attempts to scold Wren for her blatantly rude question are laughable, her poor processor probably on the fritz. Ha ha!

She isn't expecting an answer, not really, and she doesn't get one. Kai's eyes alight on Wren, and the violet spheres of his sights activate in his eyes. He's scanning her again.

Doing an analysis on her magic? Maybe.

The haze of it would be more than apparent to him which begs the question: why hasn't he dispelled her glamour himself?

"You're awake."

"Excellent observational skills. You clearly are the highest grade of technomancer, highness."

"Hn." He hums in what is almost exasperation but not quite, closing his eyes briefly. She is certain were it not for his upright upbringing, he would have happily rolled his eyes at her.

The door shuts behind Kai as he removes his boots and steps into the room. In his hand is a tray filled with a variety of dishes.

"Care to explain why you're keeping me prisoner? I had no idea royal families were making it a habit to keep prisoners in their personal rooms. Or is house arrest more in style these days? Keeping me tucked away like a dirty, little secret, Miyazaki-kun?"

"These are indeed my quarters, your presence here is known to my family, and you are not a prisoner."

"Your quarters beg to differ. Do you often instruct your A.I. to lock your guests in on pain of electric shock?"

"The voltage you received was inconsequential at worst. Had you continued to try and magically force the door, however, I could not guarantee you would still be awake."

He sets the tray on the table across the room before turning back to her.

"I wish to speak with you."

"Oh, what on earth could you want to speak with little ole me about? Is it not unseemly to be alone with a defenseless young woman?"

"You are hardly defenseless."

Wren chuckles at his cool composure, tapping her nail firmly against the glass of the table where the handkerchief sits beneath.

"Even so, what would your wife think?"

Other than the pressed handkerchief, she sees no evidence of a potential spouse about the place, but these are royals after all. Spouses are expected to sleep in different quarters, and if they dislike each other enough, separate homes entirely.

"Surely, such behavior from a member of the royal family would be unsightly. Aren't you supposed to exhibit at least a mild amount of discretion when conducting extra-marital affairs? I'd hardly count bringing a harlot into your rooms as discreet."

"I am unmarried, nor am I engaged."

Wren chokes on her laughter. For an aristocrat of Kai's age and merit (ehem, not to mention handsome visage) to be unmarried is, well, it's unheard of.

Kai seems unbothered by her inquiries, and he lifts the cover from the tray, arranging the food he's brought her.

"You must be hungry. Come. Eat."

His commanding tone irritates her, but the savory smell of teriyaki sauce and steamed rice wafts over her, and she realizes just how hungry she actually is. She rises from her place after tucking away the few sigils she's finished and approaches him cautiously. By the gods, there is sushi on the tray! Her mouth waters. She takes the proffered chopsticks in hand and tucks in. Kai does not eat with her, and the way he watches her, holographic irises slowly rotating, is unsettling. Such a penetrating stare... It's unnerving. She is fully dressed, magically disguised even, and still she feels like she's been stripped naked, but who is she kidding? Kai's always had that effect on her, the only person who didn't put up with her nonsense and met her blow for blow in intellect and combat. He had known her inside and out in a time when reality seemed more like a fairy tale before their world went up in flames. And after the flames left her charred beyond recognition, his gaze had the power to pry her open and drag all her dirty, unwashed truths into the sun despite her best efforts to hide them.

"Perhaps you should commission a portrait?"

He looks away, triggering a handheld to open in his left palm. The small holographic screen glows purple as he manipulates the screen. He addresses her as he opens several files for review.

"Forgive me. I did not mean to cause you discomfort, Miss Vaishi."

The way he says the name of her cover identity carries a hint of something that could be sarcasm were it not entirely out of character for him to speak in such a way. She narrows her eyes at him while taking a bite of the chicken he's brought to her. She chews slowly before swallowing with a drink of water.

"Why did you bring me here?"

"As I said, I wish to speak with you."

"Not sure what there is to speak with a madwoman about."

Kai's gaze slides to her from the holo-pad.

"How long do you intend to maintain this charade?"

"I never liked that game."

He does not respond to her quip, choosing instead to continue going through his work. She eats quietly, trying to formulate some plan or angle she can implement to get herself thrown out of this place and back on her merry way to finding who the last three slashes on her arm are meant to address.

"I always did fantasize about being wined and dined by an aristocrat. You've forgotten the wine though."

"Next time then."

"Next time! Next time with a 'lil strumpet like myself. How could I hope to be so blessed! To think I would find myself a prince who also happens to be a whoremonger."

Such an insult would not go unpunished. Especially in this place. The faster he throws her out, the better. She doesn't need him sniffing around. AYA whirrs to life so angry the A.I. would probably try to throw her out of the compound itself if it had a physical body, but Kai holds a hand up, and the bot quiets.

"I doubt you have ever willingly dealt in the flesh trade, Atalia."

She stares at him wide-eyed before recalling her bearings. Who is this person before her?

"Humph, you don't know the first thing about me."

"Atalia Vaishi. Personal Identification Number: 6408721594. Date of Birth: 13/27/1859. You were once a ward of the Nagi family, undergoing Firefly training, but you were dismissed from their service after you were found to be pregnant. You reported sexual assault, but who you accused has been redacted from your file, and no formal investigation was made. Several weeks later, you decided to abort the child yourself via an illegal potion you procured from a medicine woman who has since been executed. Rather than going to prison, you were committed to the Stonehearst Asylum for recovery four years ago."

Wren blinks. Well, that's useful information she didn't have.

Oh, great! He's looking at her again.

"Tell me, how does a person of questionable mental stability manage to successfully escape a locked and warded room with a complex teleportation array?"

"Haha, you don't honestly think me capable of—"

"And how, pray tell, were you able to trap and redirect lightning?"

"I don't know what you're talking about."

"I have little reason to believe that."

"What do you want from me? I said I don't know what you're talking about. I am not a witch, just a torn up invalid."

In response, he plays his memory recall of the event. Wren experiences a bit of vertigo watching it unfold from Kai's point of view: Atalia backing away only to be cut off by Xipilli's attack. Then the lightning explosion, Xipilli's man being thrown against the wall, and Xipilli himself going on the offensive. Kai's vision never shifted from Atalia even as he drew Tsukuyomi from her sheath to block the rebounded attack. When the bright flash clears, it is clear as day Atalia was responsible.

Kai allows the memory to play through an incredibly hostile conversation between himself and Xipilli that is barely kept from physical blows by their corresponding charges. Wren flinches when Xipilli moves to hit her prone form with Opochtli only to meet an aggressive undercut from Tsukuyomi.

When Kai takes jurisdiction of Atalia, to Renki and Akari's apparent surprise, Kai cuts the recall.

"Miss Vaishi probably does not realize this because she has been out of touch with League happenings over the years, but Vulcan Moctezumo does not take well to hexen of any kind, least of all witches."

"Oh? I hadn't noticed."

Kai keeps speaking as though she hadn't just interrupted him.

"The witch hunts in Deriva are notorious for the heinous abhorrence with which they are conducted. Once arrested, individuals suspected of witchcraft are rarely, if ever, seen again, and public executions were the norm for several years after the Songstress's suicide."

Wait, wait, wait. Witch hunts in Deriva? The Songstress's what...?

"I-I thought she was killed in battle."

Kai's silver eyes flash with barely veiled surprise, but the shock is gone so quickly she wonders if she imagined it.

"No," he says, withdrawing a bit. "The Songstress of Lorelei killed herself twelve years ago according to the technomancer council."

"No...That...That can't be right," she hushes, her voice so quiet, she's surprised he even hears her. He closes his eyes, tension lining his shoulders and neck, but he answers.

"That is the official statement that was given. If you want to know the details, you'll have to ask the Vulcan of Deriva.

According to his report, his sister was driven so mad by her own power, she killed herself right in front of him. It is the reason he so despises witchcraft. He had her body burned without an autopsy. The reports and rumors are easy enough to search on the internet."

"Well, sorry I've been a little too cooped up to play around on a computer."

"It is also taught widely in schools. You should have learned of it during your time in Ebele."

"Yeah, well, my memory sucks."

"Does it?"

"I never liked history," she snips at him, and silence envelops them. She continues to pick at the food in front of her, while Kai returns his attention to the report he is going through.

She is shaken to her very core. She killed herself? But that's preposterous! Wren would never have killed herself. She would have had to be completely mad. She had been completely mad though, hadn't she? No, that couldn't be.

Memories tumble through her mind at once.

Losing Control.

Someone yelling. Some pig-faced aristocrat who thinks he knows better than her and keeps shoving a disgusting cigarette in her face. If he does it again, she swears she is going to...

"Wren stop!" Kai is yelling at her again.

Sea green eyes snap open, and Farqaad is on the ground gasping for air that will never make it into his lungs because of the e-cigarette shoved down his windpipe and kept there via her telekinesis. She looks down in horror before she summons the object out of the man's throat.

Old confessions.

"...I've been losing time. Sometimes I'll wake up, get dressed, and the next thing I know, the whole day is gone, like a book that's had whole chapters torn from it. I'll go to sleep and find myself waking up with mud all over my night dress and my boots back on my feet, like I've been sleepwalking...

"Gods, my head hurts all the time. I can't think straight anymore."

Panicked conversations.

"I-I don't know what happened. I went to bed, and when I woke up, he was dead."

"Stay back... I don't want to hurt you."

Kaito's pinched and worried face.

"You aren't going to hurt me."

"You don't know that."

"Yes, I do."

"Well, I don't!"

Betrayal of Trust.

The letter from her lover. A plea she listened to. An ambush. The destruction of everything she cared about. A sham of a trial. Another massacre. A bloodstained cat plushie. More blood on her hands. Nowhere to run. No desire to hide. Only blood and death and vengeance...

She hasn't really had a chance to think about it since her resurrection. She knows she died; that much is obvious. She has a vague idea about how and why it happened, but now as she searches through her memories, there is nothing there. Just like before she defected from Deriva. Gaps in her memory. Migraines. Lost time. She remembers stepping into a packed arena for her trial by combat, one last mockery of an olive branch from the technomancer council to her, and then nothing. She assumed she simply lost the match, but that doesn't make sense either because she remembers Kai being there. She'd attacked him. She knows that much. The memory blurs again after that. Had he taken her somewhere? He disappears later. She remembers being alone. And then agony. Fire. Burning. The taste of gasoline in her mouth mixed with the smell of scorched hair and melting skin. How much time had she lost between her last recollection and her own death?

But suicide! It doesn't make any sense!

"Wren, stop this madness!"

"...mama..."

"Wren, stop it!"

"Wren."

"Wren!"

"Miss Vaishi?"

FOUR OF PENTACLES

The chopstick she had been unknowingly levitating in slow circles flies across the room to embed itself in the wall. It frightens even her, and she flinches backward, one hand over her own mouth to stanch the scream bubbling up from her throat.

Atalia Vaishi's dark eyes snap to the prince's face. How long has he been steadily watching her? He doesn't even glance at the chopstick now sticking out of his wall; his focus is solely centered on her.

How long has she been in her own head?

Kaito unfolds himself from his seat. He moves toward her, and she bursts out in laughter, standing up and backing away from his advance.

"Sorry, sorry. I get a little in my head sometimes. No need to look so intense. What were we talking about again? Oh right! You think I'm a witch, and I get it. Yeah, weird things happen around me every so often, but I'm not a witch. I'm crazy, but I'm not that crazy. Actually! You know what? I'm probably possessed. You people are good at dealing with that, right?"

She rambles on, a close-eyed smile on her face as she tries to make light of what just happened. Kai's stare is unnerving. She doesn't remember ever being so unsettled by him. Has he gotten more ascetic over the years? Must be.

He's probably already relaying a message to his brother or aunt or the whole damn palace that there's a dangerous witch on the premises, and he is about to take her down. She's flailing about in a riptide and can't figure out which way is up and which way is down.

"Forgive me," Kai's voice is gentle as he addresses her. "I've pushed you too far."

Her jaw drops. She blinks at him a couple of times. Surely, she misheard him.

"I'll take my leave for the moment. In the meantime, I hope you can clear your head. AYA?"

"Yes, your highness?"

"Grant my guest access to the grounds. Perhaps some fresh air will aid her recovery."

"Yes, sir."

He turns back to her.

"You are free to roam at your leisure. You might enjoy the gardens or the forest. However, I highly recommend you not try anything drastic. The staff and palace guards are not known for turning a blind eye to troublemakers."

"Me! A troublemaker? Never, your highness."

She twists her eyebrows up and pouts, wondering if she's actually gotten away with it. Kai pulls the chopstick out of the wall and returns it to the table beside its twin.

Ah, so that's a no.

"When you are finished eating, AYA will call for someone to clean up."

"Uh..."

She opens her mouth to say something, but he leaves without a second glance toward her. Wren practically sags to the floor, the stress threatening to boil over quieting like a teapot taken off the heat.

Well, that went swimmingly...

"Miss Vaishi, your vitals are reading as 'in distress.' Do you require medical attention?" asks AYA.

No, she does not need any attention from anyone or anything in this godforsaken place.

What she needs is to get the hell out of here before his royal pain-in-the-ass comes back.

Cavalry Units in Deus:

You can tell a lot about a country based on the vehicles their technomancers use to get around.

Because of their advanced understanding of naval and subaquatic engineering, Derivan adepts prefer their amphibious searunners, jet ski-like vehicles capable of converting into hydro-electric powered steamcycles for ground travel. In contrast, Murasaki no Yama, a country that has always been concerned with minimizing environmental impact, mandates the use of the lightcycle, electro-solar power hybrids with the added functionality of acting as connection hubs for their neural networks.

An Excerpt from *Modes of Transportation in Deus*
by Heather Ables, 1873 A.P.

12

THE TOWER

I N KAI'S ABSENCE, WREN COLLECTS HER things and gets the hell out of the man's quarters, much to the protests of the A.I. who, no doubt, is recording her every move.

She has no plan really. She can't get past the outermost barrier without a permit pass, the sensors powerful enough to sound an alarm if even touched by an unapproved person, but maybe she'll be lucky enough to find one. She's never been above picking pockets, especially when it comes to carefree guards. However, she finds no one. The walkways of the compound are mysteriously quiet, and for a palace centered in the midst of a city as vast at Tokiseishu, the city where time stops, that is saying something.

So, she wanders instead.

Tokiseishu is a booming metropolis that blooms along the cold northern coast of Murasaki no Yama, cradled on one side by the mountain peaks that comprise the rest of the country's northernmost latitudes. If she remembers her geography correctly, on the most coastal side of those same mountains hides Shinka Temple from outsiders. The Miyazaki family home, Yuki Ga Furu or Snowfall Palace, sits in the heart of the city surrounded by a vast undoctored forest of bamboo, magnolias, sakura, pines, and evergreens.

Acres upon acres of untouched forest surround the compound. How odd it is to see trees and forest only to look a little farther out and see skyscrapers rising into the clouds, metal titans looming above the forested gardens and floral lawns. She watches the animal life frolic at the very edge of one of the gardens. A few deer meander by, and birds sing in the treetops. She could feel at home in a place like this, her magical blood craving the wilderness while at the same time enjoying the strong walls and electricity she grew up with.

She closes her eyes and lets the forest guide her steps, singing along the way to its song until she reaches the subtly glowing barrier. Her body hums to the tune and ardor races through her system. A spell just beneath her skin, an enchantment coded at the tip of her tongue, magic in her blood. Her indicia and the wild script decorating her face, neck, and arms blearily wake at her walking meditation, but they remain faint in the light of day. Pooling her power will not activate them entirely. Only during spellcasting do they really light up with her personal brand of bio-magical-luminescence. Not that she'll be casting anything here, certain any flex of her power will trigger the magical detection nodes hidden around the grounds.

"Miss Vaishi, what are you doing out here?"

Wren jumps. Young Renki seems to have snuck up on her. These damn Miyazaki adepts. She can't sense them when they approach, and they are so damn quiet, she can't hear them either. The teenager is dressed for patrol, wearing light combat attire appropriate for both battle and interaction with higher ranking members of the family.

"My apologies. I didn't mean to startle you. I only heard you singing and couldn't stay away. Your voice is so familiar to me."

"Familiar?"

"I lost my mother when I was young. She used to sing me to sleep."

She winces a little at that.

"I'm so sorry."

"It's okay. I have my father."

Around his neck is a signet crest, denoting him as direct lineage to the crown, making him a prince of Murasaki, granted he is too young to hold any titles at this point. She wonders who his parents are and how they are related to Kai and Hikaru.

"Sometimes I wish I had a better memory of her."

"How old were you when she died?"

"I think I was three."

Wren hums in understanding, her heart aching a little bit.

"My mother was the most beautiful woman I've ever seen."

Wren turns her head to look directly at the teen.

"It's silly to say, I know," he continues. "Especially since I don't actually remember anything of what she looked like, but I know she was beautiful."

"Most children keep that impression of their mothers. It isn't unusual. My mother died when I was a child as well, but I was old enough to keep my memories of her."

"I know, but I think she really truly was. I can't explain it."

"Does your father not speak of her?"

The silence she receives is a resounding 'no.' She turns away from the teen's downcast expression, reaching to dance her fingertips over a nearby flower bed. Unfortunately, this late in the summer, most of the flowers are on their way to preparing for the autumn, their petals no longer as vibrant. Some of them are already dying as the temperatures fluctuate, but there are still a few standing strong. She strokes her finger along the petals of a still-blooming chrysanthemum. The bud wiggles a little as she touches it, and a bumblebee pops out of the pollen to alight on her finger.

She lifts her hand to her face as the little insect perches there, its feelers tickling her skin.

"Miss Vaishi, how do you know Miyazaki-sama?"

"What makes you think I know your Prince Kaito?"

"He insisted on housing you in his personal quarters."

She shrugs. "Perhaps his noble highness is just a pervert who was hoping to scratch an itch."

Renki's jaw drops, and he looks at her as though she has just personally offended his ancestors.

"Miyazaki-sama is the most honorable, distinguished gentleman in Deus. To accuse him of such debasing behavior... It's unthinkable!"

She wants to laugh. She does laugh, and the bumblebee flits away. She knows just how much of a gentleman Kaito Miyazaki is and can be. He'd always been so diligent in the past in addressing her desires. Of course, that side of him only belonged to her. At least back then.

Dance with me.

Kai. I think I really like you.

Do whatever you want to me. I can take it.

I couldn't fall asleep... I miss you.

"Renki, right?"

He nods. "Renki Miyazaki. Yes."

"Ah, so you are a direct descendant. I suspected as much. Well, Renki, your prince is indeed a gentleman, but even the most noble men have needs, and he is so handsome I doubt anyone would reject his attention."

The teen looks as though he wishes to argue further, but she cuts him off.

"You may be a bit young to understand this, but it is not a bad thing, Renki. It is healthy to indulge in pleasures of the flesh, and despite anything old lady Fumiko may tell you, there is no shame in this."

"Are you going to answer my question?"

"There is nothing to answer. I have no such acquaintance with him."

"But he brought you to the Jade Wing. Had you treated by our best physician!"

"Not anything to do with me, I assure you."

"But he never—"

"It doesn't matter to me what your prince's motivations are. The moment I can get out of here, I am gone."

She reaches her hand forward and gently strokes the forcefield. It thrums under her fingers, then stutters and disappears.

"Huh?"

She blinks confused as it reconstitutes.

Renki fidgets behind her, and the barrier around Snowfall Palace blinks out of existence entirely. As it is disabled, a cold feeling runs down Wren's spine. That should not happen. Ever.

Renki bolts upright, immediately cutting off Wren's directionality of escape should she decide to make a run for it.

"Did you do that?"

"No," she answers, turning to look back in the direction of the main compound. Something ominous lurks there. The ozone around Snowfall thickens like a spell about to be unleashed. It's so thick, she can taste it in the air. She gets up and begins to make her way back toward the palace, completely ignoring the fretful teenager who clearly doesn't believe her and looks like he is about to tackle her to the ground if the freshly drawn katana in his hand is any indication of his intentions. He's hesitating though, of course, because she is not going the direction she very well should be going.

"What are you doing?"

That's a very good question. Didn't she say she would be gone the moment she had the opportunity? Well, here is her opportunity, yet rather than bee-lining it out of there, here she is moving back toward the palace.

"Something isn't right."

The screams begin as they reach the edge of the forest. The heavy feeling of dark magic being used thrums through her senses. Renki's eyes go wide, and Wren races toward the sound and the confirmation of what it means. Someone is attacking Snowfall Palace.

Renki keeps pace with her as she runs. They find several bodies as they go. Guards and adepts bloody and still on the ground to Renki's horror. Wren only pauses long enough to check one of them. The adept's tech has been deactivated remotely, and she knows from personal experience that the resulting loss of consciousness stemming from the unauthorized system shutdown is quite painful if not downright agonizing-edging-on-fatal depending on the method of shutdown. As they near the heart of the power she senses, Renki falters. His knees buckle beneath him, and a hand goes to his head. She stops to check him over.

"What's wrong?"

"I'm not sure. I can't focus my eyes. It's like my processors are being scrambled." He gasps as another wave of pain washes over him. "It hurts!"

"Stay here. Don't move any closer until I can figure out what is going on."

She leaves him a safe distance from the building to climb the walls.

Entering the throne room through an upstairs window, she quietly makes her way to the banister overlooking the room proper. The scene that greets her on the lower floor of the meeting hall makes her stomach clench. Adepts litter the floor, all of them bleeding from their eyes and ears. A few of them flail about in the throes of seizures and others are still as death. Fumiko-sensei is on the ground unconscious, blood pouring from her mouth. Hikaru Miyazaki, Kai's elder brother and the Emperor of Murasaki no Yama, crouches on the floor next to his aunt, though he himself looks to be in little better shape with blood dripping from his ears and nose, teeth clenched in pain as though something were pressing heavily on his temples. His sword lies across the room, quiet and powerless.

On the floor in front of Hikaru is a metal case. A pandora's box used for capturing restless spirits and demonic entities. It shudders and quakes with the force of the rage of whatever is inside.

Kai is across the room, still standing but barely as blood trails fall from his eyes like the others. His katana crackles with shock power, but it fizzles and dies before he can properly harness his saibāki through his tech. Across from him is a large, feral-looking man who laughs at the state of things. Even from this far away,

THE TOWER

Wren can feel the extent of his sadism, more than a lust for blood. It's a lust for torture.

She's known men like this. Sick, demented fucks who probably played with their food as toddlers and never got scolded for it. Toddlers who ripped the wings off of butterflies and burned ants under a magnifying glass. Adolescents who shoved their pet hamster in the microwave and purposely drove their car over the stray dogs. Men who rape for sport and torture for art.

Her blood boils as bile rises in her throat. She leans forward, knuckles white on the banister, biding her time before she grinds this scum beneath the heel of her boot.

Kai lunges at him once more, but he dodges his attack and kicks him in the gut. Kai rolls across the floor to where his brother and aunt lay before shakily lifting himself back up to glare at his opponent. Unlike everyone else in the room, Kaito's sights are still active, his tech not entirely subdued by whatever force has crippled every other cyborg in the room. He pulls himself up from the floor, coughing, blood spilling from his mouth to splash on the floor.

The man laughs.

"It's a pity how easy it was to neutralize your entire compound. Where is the fun in staging a prison break if everyone just rolls over for you?"

"Proper planning, Zero. Proper planning and an excuse to make good on an old promise."

A woman, tall and long-limbed with severe features, enters from the far side of the hall. In her hand is a strangely shaped glass phylactery, its top pointed and curved like a bird's beak. Inside is a viscous liquid, blood red, almost black in color, and floating within the liquid are several pieces of glowing tech; however, they don't glow with the usual electrical charge of an activated mechanism. There is a staticky quality to the light, a shutter stop glow, like the power is coming from the outside of the phylactery. It pulses with red light as the mechanism absorbs the power of the surrounding tech.

"Did our friend find the doctor yet?"

"He is fishing him out of the dungeons as we speak."

"Wonderful. Now on to our secondary objective."

This woman's psyche is not as easy to read, coated in some sort of block, but the glee that dances at the surface level is smug, rotten, and tinged with iron.

The woman begins chanting in eldritch as Kai comes to standing. The phylactery in her hands begins to glow in harsh shades of red. The radar-like pulse it emits is almost tangible on the air, and it makes the hairs on her arms stand at attention with static. As another wave reaches her position, the comm unit in her hand goes dark before it implodes on itself. The small explosion singes her fingertips as she drops it.

Did the phylactery neutralize the tech of the entire sect? How is Kai still standing?

Kai drops to his knees from the new blast; his sights shut off, having finally given out. His teeth grit, and blood drips from his eyes.

"Why don't you stay down, your highness? This can only end one way."

The woman smiles to reveal razor sharp fangs.

"You'll have to do better than that if you want me to stay down," he says, supporting himself on his blade.

"I suppose you'll just have to be the first to die."

The color of the phylactery shifts to a more virulent crimson, the tech inside activating and charging. The woman turns the glass, so its pointed edge aims directly at Kai. Energy begins to collect at the point before releasing a laser-like bolt of energy straight toward Kai.

Wren moves faster than a thought.

She jumps over the banister and pushes her own mental power at the blast. The shock deteriorates, the remaining tendrils redirected to the ground.

So much for not getting involved...

Behind her, Kai's breath shudders on an inhale. With his guards dismantled, she can feel the shock rolling off him in waves. Shock and horror at her appearance with a touch of anger, at her maybe? Or at the situation?

"What the hell are you doing?" Kai hisses from behind her.

Clearly, he is not pleased to see her insert herself in this way. Well, bully for him! He's the one who dragged her here in the first place. She ignores him in favor of addressing the vampyric bitch in front of her.

"Since when do vamps use witchcraft? Not that I'm not impressed, but your blood really isn't suited for it. It tastes wrong."

The woman sneers at her, eyes lit with curiosity. "A witch. Impossible! The only witches still around are old hags too frightened to leave their swamps or children too young to know the difference between a spell and a fart. So, who the fuck are you?"

"Nobody important."

"Oh, perhaps you should mind your own business, then. What does it matter to a witch if the Miyazaki family perishes today?"

"I supposed it shouldn't, but I'm afraid I'm morally opposed to mass murder."

The woman laughs, the sound hollow and raspy, caught in her throat like a death rattle.

"How quaint! A witch protecting technomancers. Zero, it looks as though we've found you a plaything after all." She turns around and pats her cohort on the shoulder. "Take out the trash, will you?"

The vamp saunters over to the raised dais and sits in the monarch's Peony Throne. Wren's blood boils, her anger rising as she remembers another long-dead enemy who similarly sat in her father's Coral Reef Throne in her past life as her family's blood stained the floor, their bodies shredded to pieces for defending their home. A man who'd laughed as the last of her innocence was ripped from her.

These two are no different. Scum on her boot.

She sees red. 'Atalia's' brown eyes glow green.

Zero's fist pummels down toward her skull. She deflects the blow and throws herself across the room before casting a shrill whistle in his direction. The pulse barely shoves him a few feet from her. He recovers the distance with a bounding step, her bursts of kinetic force barely deterring him as he comes down hard on her. She blocks his downward swing, but not without taking a heavy boot to her sternum. She rolls away, the breath knocked from her lungs as she coughs.

"Stop! This isn't your fight!"

Kai's words reach her loud and clear, but she pays him no mind as once again Zero charges her direction.

Zero is fast, but she can be faster, and with her new physicality, it's all the easier. She gathers her wits and runs straight toward him. He laughs, seeking to catch her in a grapple, but at the last second, she slides to the floor and knocks his feet out from under him while reaching a hand to pull the pandora into her open palm. As she twists into a seated position, she takes a deep breath, unlocks the box, and starts to sing. It's a dissonant skipping song, childish in rhythm but morbid in lyric.

> All my lonely yesterdays,
>   I write them in a book.
>   And burn it page by page,
>   Until no one cares to—
> Look what Dolly brought me
>   A teacup full of blood.
>   I sip it bit by bit
>   Before I throw it in the—
> Mud stains on my stockings
>   I bought them from Tyrell
>   He took them from the corner lass,
>   She was as cold as a door—
> Bells on all my jewelry
>   I keep them with a swan
>   I broke its neck on accident
>   And I just can't glue it back—
> Honesty's a luxury
>   The rich cannot afford.
>   They'll blood the silks
>   And skin the ilks
>   Until there's nothing left at—
> All my lonely yesterdays...

THE TOWER

The notes drift over the hall, and shadows twist out of the depths of the pandora's box. Tendrils of green mist coalesce in her hand, screams of agony and avarice shudder from the darkness as the poltergeist from the asylum surges toward Zero at Wren's command. Her pitch ascends with the repeat of the verse, and as it does, the creature winds and digs shadowy whips into his arms and legs, trapping him spread eagle on the floor. He writhes as the poltergeist's malevolent energy sears into his being, tearing skin from muscle and sinew from bone. Zero clenches his teeth and growls as the entity throws him backward onto the ground.

"Zero, get up!"

Wren senses the vampyre's intention, ozone shifting malignantly as she prepares to launch some sort of ranged attack. Wren splits her focus and hurls a pocket of necrotic magic directly aimed at the witch-forged weapon in the woman's hand. Shock paints her features as she drops the phylactery. The resulting explosion tosses her sideways away from her seat.

She screams, gripping her charred and bloodied hand, bone twitching as the flesh is burned away by the liquid in the vial.

Kai shakes his head as the phylactery's destabilizing field of magic diminishes. He blinks twice, and his sights rev back to life. Many of the younger adepts still as their pained seizures cease. Wren continues to sing, focusing now on encircling the woman in the poltergeist's rage as well, but before even one of the green tentacles can touch the woman, silver flashes and pain ignites in her right bicep as a dagger slashes past her.

"Tanaka! You traitor!" shouts Kai, and Wren turns to see who he is yelling at.

A technomancer wearing Murasaki colors stands at the head of the hall, a kunai in hand and Faust slung over his shoulder like a sack of potatoes. Tanaka drops Faust to the floor and throws the second blade at Wren. Kai deflects the blade with his tanto, and Wren shoves him with enough telekinetic power to throw him backward through the wall.

"Xena! Get rid of this goddamn spell!" yells Zero.

Xena shouts in eldritch.

PRELUDE

"Afsanna!"

"Wren, move!"

She freezes at the shout of her real name. It's a mistake. The blast of the spell hits her solidly in the back, and she goes down. Wren's spells dissipate in the blink of an eye. All of them. Including the glamour. Her hair darkens and her skin lightens to a golden olive tone. Atalia's face disappears in a burst of light, and Wren stands barefaced and exposed. Damnit! For not being a witch, this vampyre has a good grasp on curse-weaving technique.

"It can't be..." she hears a voice whisper toward the back of the room. It's Hikaru. His naked shock makes her dizzy. Or maybe it's the dispel curse. It's been a while since she was last hit by one of those, dazed from having a figurative sack shoved over her head.

The vamp laughs, crazed spasmodic laughter, as Wren shakes the nullifier from her synapse.

"A witch who hides her face!"

The poltergeist, no longer under her command, hurtles toward the doctor. Kai deflects it, and a wave of cyber energy slams into the creature. It shrieks away from Kai's attack only to be struck by a plasma blast. Though his tech is still inactive, Hikaru has risen, an æther pistol revved to life in his hand. Hikaru fires on the malevolent undead and the poltergeist splits, its parts scattering around the room. Wren gathers her wits to wrangle the damn thing back together to aim it at Xena.

"Zero! Kill the witch!"

Zero tackles her, and she wrestles with him using her slighter frame to her advantage, dodging around and wriggling out whenever he tries to grip her. Out of the corner of her eye, she sees the rogue cut off Kai's attempts to get to her. A meaty hand wraps around her throat.

"I'm going to rip out your voice-box, witch."

Wren gasps as his hands crush her windpipe. The hair at the back of her neck rises as Kai's power surges.

"Wren!"

Kai's tanto, coated in an ultraviolet glow, hurtles toward Zero, and the hexen is thrown off her as Amatsu slams into his side. Wren coughs, bloody bile rising from her abused throat. She swallows it down with a wince. On the other side of the room, Tanaka bleeds out on the floor, slashed across the chest by Tsukuyomi. Kai's attention diverted, the man coughs and chokes, sniveling just a step away from mortal injury on the ground as he pulls a glass vial from his coat and breaks it on the tile. Dark energy engulfs him, and he disappears.

A reverse summoning.

Kaito lands in front of Wren, his sights skimming over her form in a cursory glance before directing his gaze to Zero, still wrestling with Amatsu. Kai summons the tanto back to his hand. Both blades shine with ultraviolet power. The technomancer is back at full power, and for all that she might pride herself for being a pain in his side, Kai is not one to be trifled with. He slashes at Zero who blocks the first strike. Kai's second attack opens his chest.

Wren rises from the ground, necrotic energy once more unfurling around her as she refocuses herself. Kai jumps back as Zero swings a clenched fist.

Wren's necrotic tendrils of telekinesis lock Zero in place, but his energy fluctuates, something coming alive within him. A blast from an æther pistol hits him from the opposite side of the meeting hall. Zero roars, teeth sharpening as the sound falls from his maw. Renki lands opposite her and Kai on the far side of the room, his own katana crackling with energy. Several other adepts enter the hall. She sees young Akari among them, recharging her pistol.

Xena moves for Wren, but Kai cuts her off.

Renki attacks, but the boy's blade does nothing, stalling at the beastly man's skin. The teen makes a surprised face, and Zero, getting bigger as he builds power, yanks out of Wren's magical hold and clotheslines Renki across the stomach, sending him flailing into Akari with a shout.

Wren tries to wrangle him back in, but Zero, his features now more animal than man, breaks the remnants of the spell. The backfire flings Wren backward. Kaito catches her and they both tumble to the floor. Kai preps to throw Amatsu as Wren regains her hold on the poltergeist.

Xena appears at Zero's back holding Faust by the back of his collar. She draws a vial from her belt, another reverse summoning.

"Enough, Zero!"

"But Xena—"

"No, now!"

Kai and Wren release their attacks together: Kai throwing Amatsu, and Wren throwing a curse laced with the poltergeist's toxic essence. Wren's spell coils around Zero's forearm. A deafening howl sounds as Amatsu's blade severs the limb. It flops to the ground with a splat as the three disappear in a flash of void. The remaining limb glows an eerie green as it decomposes right before their eyes. Necrosis setting in as a testament to Wren's rage until there is nothing left but bone, sinew, and grease.

In the absence of their enemy, most of the posties sit or stand stunned by the wreckage made of their throne room. They're either too shaken by the assault or too busy consoling the poltergeist back into the pandora to pay Wren any mind, something she takes full advantage of as she begins inching her way toward the exit.

However, Kai's hand closes under her bicep as she moves to stand, definitively halting her retreat. She holds her breath, looking at him in surprise as he helps her stand, gently lifting her to her feet.

"Are you alright?" he asks as she rises to his eye level. She stumbles a bit before her feet find themselves firmly on the ground.

She swallows thickly.

"You knew..."

His silence as he releases her arm is all the answer she needs.

"How did you know?"

If her voice trembles, she ignores it, backing away as much as she can. Hikaru's voice is delicate as he approaches, almost like he is trying to sooth a wild animal.

"Wren Nocturne?"

THE TOWER

As stripping as Kaito's gaze can be at times, it is far more unnerving to be studied by the older of the Miyazaki brothers. Hikaru's eyes, despite the warm, baked honey of his iris, are colder than ice. Hikaru regards her with chilly indifference as several posties rise and make their way to Fumiko. The older woman is coming around as well, albeit much slower than her two nephews. Hikaru stands with all the regality of his station despite the blood still present on his suit and face. His sights have not yet returned to their full power like Kaito's. They flicker in and out as he tries to reactivate and maintain his tech. If she possessed less of a spine, she would have attempted to hide behind Kaito. Instead, she stands proud and unflinching across from the standing Emperor of Murasaki no Yama. When he makes no move to attack her, she tilts herself into a lopsided bow.

"Emperor," she acknowledges before a smirk splits her face. "Forgive me. I didn't have the opportunity to present myself to you upon entry into your domain."

"And who would you have presented yourself as had you had the opportunity?"

She bites her tongue but stares him dead in the eye. His soft expression puts her on edge. Any moment now, she fully expects him to command her arrest. How else would one react to a long executed and dangerous witch wandering into their receiving hall? However, another voice chimes in first.

"Impossible!" Great! Fumiko's awake. Akari rushes to calm her. "Grandmaster, please. You're injured."

"What are you worrying about me for? Do you not see there's a witch in the throne room!"

"Good to see you're doing well, Sensei," Wren says, smiling brightly to the elder's horror. "Though you look like you've just seen a ghost."

"Wren Nocturne!" She says her name like a curse, and quite frankly she is a bit insulted. She isn't that bad, is she? "I see your sense of humor hasn't diminished in death."

"Gotta keep it alive somehow." She shrugs.

Fumiko looks positively scandalized, while Hikaru's expression deflates in exasperation. She doesn't need to look at Kaito to know he's glaring at her. The back of her head feels like it is about to burst into flames. Humorless as ever.

"Look," she says, addressing Hikaru and Fumiko. "You don't want me here, and I don't want to be here, so if it's all the same to you, I'll let myself out, and you can forget all about the fact that I was here, huh?"

She starts to tiptoe her way out, preparing to make a mad dash for it, and crashes face-first into Kai's chest, an unwavering barrier between her and freedom.

"Lady Wren's presence here is my doing," inserts Kai. "I knew who she was when I brought her to Snowfall."

Fumiko swoons on the spot. Hikaru's jaw tightens as his aunt faints. Something in his expression darkens, and Wren can feel flickers of both sadness, resolution, and—Oh, is that what hatred feels like?—drifting off him.

"I see," he says at length. "We have much to discuss, then. Renki, Akari, please, escort the Songstress of Lorelei to a holding room." His usage of her title is not lost on her. The two teens look taken aback, Renki especially looks particularly stunned by her appearance.

"I thought the Songstress of Lorelei was supposed to be dead," she hears Akari whisper.

"She is," answers Renki.

Kaito looks at his brother coolly before bowing his head and speaking. "Your Excellency, might I suggest the Jade Apartments be more appropriate?"

Hikaru's eyes slide over Kaito. The sadness in his essence intensifies at being addressed so formally by his baby brother.

"The Jade Wing, then. See that she does not leave before I am ready to deal with her."

"Hai, Miyazaki-heika," answers Renki.

Renki, who is so young he's probably only ever heard of the Songstress of Lorelei in horror stories, places a tentative hand on her arm before ushering her forward. She casts a backward glance at Kai before she is escorted from the meeting hall. This time, when the Jade room's doors close behind her, a barrier is erected, an anti-magic field set, and a lock slides into place. She well and truly won't be going anywhere until they see fit to let her out.

Merde!

13
FIVE OF WANDS

WREN LEARNED EARLY ON THAT MAGIC IS more about intention than fancy rituals or painted arrays. If you believe in something enough, push your intention forward hard enough, you can harness it. That's why songweaving is such a powerful form of magic, touching people at their very core whether it's a radio station pop song or an orchestral suite.

Magic lives in the soul. Everyone is born with it, whether augmented or not. Witches are just more attuned to it. More sensitive to it. Jessabelle said that once and then winked at her like the minx she was, purposefully tickling her with a dancing tendril of her own soothing magics.

The anti-magic field around the Jade Wing prevents her from doing much more than turning the lights on and off. It would seem Murasaki has indeed progressed by leaps and bounds in their ability to restrict magic within their borders. The ward is almost as effective as the one used during her trial by combat against Montwyatte, but that one had been larger and powered by several dozen technomancers. This one is smaller and less belligerent, designed to limit her abilities rather than nullify them. She tests this, making one of the pens on the desk levitate, able to flex her power enough to draw it to her, but even this gives her a small stress ache behind her eyes. Unless she wants to do some damage to herself, she is nowhere near able to give it enough force to harm a target should she decide to throw it at someone. A small courtesy, she supposes. At least she won't get a headache just being here, nor does she feel the same mind-numbing weakness she would normally expect.

No, this is just a precaution to keep her from escaping and/or casting anything potentially harmful to her captors.

Intention... Did they center the ward to target intention?

She contemplates hacking into one of the computers to gather some information, but she's too annoyed and her eyes hurt. Her cover is blown, not only to the Miyazaki family but also to some unknown enemy. A vampyre and whatever Zero was—lycan maybe? Then there's the rogue technomancer.

There are plenty of creatures the League classified as hexen—the spell-folk of Deus: witches and the peoples/species their magics created. Creatures like lycans and vampyres to name a few. There are plenty of others. Not all hexen are human, but Wren would argue they are all people.

It is hours before anyone comes, night long fallen since Renki and Akari left; so long, in fact, her stomach starts talking to her. As her stomach growls for the nth time, the wards are dismantled, and the door opens to reveal her two favorite teenagers, this time laden with trays of food.

She's left the room dark in her contemplation. The only lights are the icy blues and violets from the various monitors around the room. She watches them from her place in the darkest corner of the room, knowing full they can see the ominous glow of her eyes in the darkness, but then Renki commands the lights on. And AYA greets the young master.

Akari is a little on guard, understandably so, but Renki seems to be totally at ease. Surely, he doesn't think their conversation earlier counts them as friends. It would be a foolish mistake to make.

"Isn't it a little late to be paying a visit to your friendly neighborhood witch?"

Renki gives her a jarringly sweet expression before setting the tray on the table.

"We thought Lady Nocturne would appreciate company."

"And food," offers the girl, looking far too eager for a Miyazaki adept.

That's hilarious. Teenagers acting in deference to her. What's next? Will the emperor be kowtowing to her?

"Sweet of you both, really, but isn't it past your bedtime?"

"Miyazaki-sama suggested we come," says Akari.

"Did he now?"

"Yes," answers Renki with a sharp nod of his head as he takes a bite of a dumpling. "This way you would know the food isn't poisoned. He was concerned you wouldn't eat otherwise."

Concerned! That bastard! A sensible bastard, who knows her too well, but a bastard nonetheless. She flicks her wrist and one of the dumplings settles itself in her hand. Akari's eyes widen to comedic proportions.

"*Sugoi!*"

Renki elbows the girl in the ribcage.

"Ow!! Meanie! I'm just saying it's cool! Do you realize how much easier it would be to find the remote if you could just telekinetically summon it to you? I wouldn't have to get up and look for it."

"You're lucky Fumiko-sensei isn't here to hear you say that. You would be knee deep in extra lessons for a month."

"It would be worth it if I never have to get up to turn the light off again."

"The light in your dorm is a clap on and off."

"Well, sometimes my arms are tired, and my roommate's a weeb..."

"I'm your roommate!"

"Yeah, and you're a weeb."

The two devolve into a raucous slap fight. Wren can't stop her own chuckle from bubbling up.

These kids.

Renki sends her a small half smile at the fact that they are amusing her. She shakes her head and eats. The two bicker back and forth a moment longer, then Akari directs a question toward her.

"Is it true you once downed a whole coven of witches?" asks Akari.

Akari and Renki are both looking at her with unwarranted askance in their eyes.

"That's an exaggeration."

"But it is true! You took those monsters down for siding with Seraphim during the war. I read about it in a book in the library."

"They aren't monsters, Aka," scolds Renki. "They were people who chose the wrong side."

"They sure look like monsters in the pictures Fumiko-sensei shows us. One of them had leeches for fingers."

"You should never judge a book by its cover," inserts Wren, calling to her a bowl of rice. "Some of the most frightful looking creatures can be the gentlest beings you ever encounter while there are plenty of monsters who are pretty enough to eat and twice as deadly as the ugly ones. Imagine wearing the face of your prey. Would it not make the hunt all the easier? Why chase if you can lure?"

"Are there many hexen who mimic people?"

"They are people, Akari," stresses Renki, once more, and if she is being completely honest, it throws her off a bit. Since when does anyone in this family consider hexen to be anything other than savages?

"Yes," agrees Wren, looking at Renki. "We are just as human as you are, possessing in equal measure the potential to act as predator or prey. That's why, regardless of how many netherbeasts or dead things you face, always remember the most danger comes from monsters who look just like you."

"You mean other bionics."

"Bionics, humans, human+, witches, vampyres, lycanthropes... Can you distinguish them all on sight? What sets someone apart as being family or friend and others as being strangers?"

"I feel like there's a pretty obvious answer to that," says Akari, laughing a bit under her breath.

"Yes, familiarity's such a good distinguisher."

Sarcasm drips off Wren's words.

"How could it not be?" asks Renki.

"There are many people in the world who will find more comfort in a stranger's embrace than they ever will a mother or a father. Familiarity creates the illusion of safety. We like to believe our homes are the safest places for us, but how easy is it to break down a door or to leave a window unlocked? We like to think our lovers will always protect us, but the fact of the matters is that human emotions are fanciful things, and the more familiarity you share with a person, the more likely they are to hurt you."

The two stare at her, stunned speechless, so she finishes her thought.

"So, you see the greatest monster of them all is your own heart. Such a foolhardy thing it is. As cruel and as frightening as any boogeyman. It tricks us constantly and completely disregards all sense and reason. If you ever wish to truly protect yourself, you will never open your heart to something as banal as trust or, Gods forbid, love."

Trust and love, after all, were the sins that led to her own downfall.

"I do not agree with that."

Wren looks to the door to find Kaito now walking into the space.

Hm. How much did he hear? She expected he would be back at some point. These are his quarters. She probably even expected Hikaru to be with him to a degree. The person she did not expect to be present is Fumiko.

The two teenagers rise to greet their superiors with respectful bows. Kaito gives both youths a nod of affirmation, and they gather up everything they brought with them before exiting the room.

Wren does not move from her place, carefully watching the three as they move about the room.

PRELUDE

They stow their weapons away as they enter, Kai setting his blades in their rightful resting place while Hikaru and Fumiko set their own weapons down near Kai's. None of them have activated their sights, their integrated tech powered down. And while their efforts to put her at ease are well-intentioned, Wren feels more than ever like a caged animal, her palms sweating in the fabric of her skirt.

Fumiko looks haggard and more than a little displeased to see her, but she shuffles in behind her nephews, a limp forcing her to take a slower pace than normal, and takes a seat at the far side of the low table where she and Kaito had lunch earlier. While Fumiko seems somewhere between a headache and a full-blown aneurysm, Hikaru is the picture of a poise. He smiles winningly in her direction, an aristocrat on parade.

"Miss Nocturne," Hikaru says in askance.

The man gestures to the opposite side of the table as he settles himself next to their aunt. Kaito does not come farther than the entryway, face impassive as ever as he watches her watching them. She wonders what he is thinking, what he is feeling... Confusion, frustration, anger... Surely, he's not happy she's back.

She smiles, a lopsided, untrusting offering of peace as she unfolds herself from her place on the floor and moves to sit. The anti-magic field surrounding the Jade quarters may prevent her from exacting violence via supernatural means, but her power thrums just under her skin, and she knows they can feel it as easily as breathing.

Once she sits, Kaito takes a seat on the side of the table adjacent to her, between Wren and his brother. Nothing is said for a very pregnant moment. The witch watches them watching her until she breaks the silence.

"Are you going to arrest me?"

"No."

The answer comes quickly from Fumiko.

"But we do have questions for you," says Hikaru.

"And if I do not wish to answer?"

Hikaru exhales as though fully expecting this kind of behavior from her. He smiles at her, like a parent indulging a child's temper tantrum, a sentiment she neither appreciates nor has ever responded well to in the past.

"Wren."

Kai's voice is a soft chide. She looks at him sharply, ready to spit poison at him, but it sticks fast in her throat at the beseeching look in his eyes.

Hikaru speaks while her attention is on Kaito.

"It is the lady's prerogative to whether or not she answers our questions, but we hope Miss Nocturne will be honest and forthcoming since we mean her no ill will, and in fact, find ourselves somewhat in a debt of gratitude for her interference earlier today."

"I was bored," she says airily, winding a stray curl around her finger.

"Your reasons for interfering aside, your actions and our honor dictate we give you the benefit of a doubt."

Was it not Hikaru's honor that inspired him to sign his name on her death warrant with the other council members twelve years ago?

"They used to say deception was my bedfellow. What makes you think you can trust me or my answers?"

"If Miss Nocturne believes I deem her trustworthy, she is mistaken."

Wren nods her head in approval.

"Emperor Hikaru is indeed a wise ruler."

Hikaru continues as though she hasn't spoken.

"However, I do trust my brother's judgement."

"Hikaru," Kaito calls his brother's name in warning. Hikaru doesn't elaborate further to Wren's annoyance, and Kai gives away nothing in his expression.

"Fine. Ask away."

Fumiko asks the first question.

"How long have you been back?"

She counts backward in her head. "This is the third moonrise since I woke up in the sanitorium."

"Only three days."

Wren nods.

The three technomancers share a look.

"How is this possible?" asks the eldest Miyazaki.

"It shouldn't be."

Fumiko stares her dead in the face.

"Explain."

Wren inhales deeply.

"There is a resurrection spell. It's old and faulty and has never worked in the centuries since its invention. Before...everything, I had been tampering with it."

Fumiko's nose wrinkles in disgust. Wren gives the woman a long-suffering look. There were times in her last life too that she missed Kai's mother (may she rest in peace) while dealing with Fumiko. How the two were twins is beyond Wren.

"My research was entirely theoretical and unfinished on top of everything else. It should have been impossible to perform anyway because of the extreme price such a spell would have demanded."

"What price?"

"Life. Or in this case, several lives in exchange for one."

"So, they brought you back out of the goodness of their hearts?" asks Fumiko, skeptical.

"There's a cost for everything, sensei, but no. More like they wanted to make a pact with a dark entity."

An overdone trope really. Never thought she would one day be said entity.

"So, you are now in their debt?" asks Hikaru.

More like bespoke to a binding contract she never signed. Wren's silence is answer enough.

"And what kind of debt are you expected to repay?" demands the emperor.

"Use your imagination, your excellency. I'm sure you'll figure it out." She needs to get them off this topic now. "Regardless,

I'm more interested in finding out who gave them the tools to pull it off."

"What do you mean?" asks Fumiko.

"This was no witch coven. They were beaten up prisoners in an insane asylum with no magical history. It should never have worked, and where did they even learn the ritual from? I never finished my research, and all the spells I wrote in my Book of Shadows were left purposefully unfinished. I didn't want them mimicked if it ever fell into the wrong hands."

"Interesting security measure," observes Fumiko.

Wren smiles genuinely at that.

"You can hack a computer or copy a recipe, but you can't decode an organic brain."

Fumiko adjusts her glasses in thought. Hikaru nods in understanding.

"What were you doing on the light rail?"

"Trying to get somewhere."

"Where?"

"Anywhere, really." A half-lie. Just because she didn't quite know where she was going doesn't mean she wanted to end up just anywhere.

"Did you summon the kenku to the light rail?"

"I'm not a summoner."

"If not you, then who?" Fumiko's voice booms.

"Summer Helsdottir was there. Trying to get to Faust, I imagine."

"Helsdottir was executed nearly six years ago." Hikaru's voice is sharp with disbelief.

"Must have been a botched execution then."

"None of our people saw her there, including Kaito."

"She escaped before I could properly confront her."

"Out of a moving train?"

"Crazier things have happened... Besides, it was stopped when she teleported."

"The two from today. Do you know them?"

Wren shakes her head.

"The technomancer who was with them used his clearance to abduct Faust from his holding cell," explains Kaito. "We have no idea as to their whereabouts."

"Shame. I had some questions for him myself."

Hikaru says nothing to this. Instead, he bows his head to her and thanks her for her compliance with their questions as he reaches for a briefcase at his side. From it, he pulls a case file and sets it on the table in front of her.

"Miss Nocturne, you've answered to my satisfaction for the moment, but I am afraid before I can end our discussion, I must request your assistance with something."

"My assistance? Thought you were indebted to me?" she drawls, raising an eyebrow.

"I should think you would call it paid, considering I've refrained from throwing you in a locked dungeon."

"Touché, but still, a council member like you has access to all the assistance you could ever ask for. Why do you need little ole me? You certainly had no problem using that power before, or have you grown bored with sanctioning mass genocide?"

Hikaru, to his credit, does not wince at the jab. Kai's hand, however, clenches into a fist. Interesting...

"I will not justify my actions to you, Miss Nocturne, but you can rest assured I have not been a member of the council for many years now. I hope you will be amiable to my proposal considering I have no intention of turning you in or even revealing your resurrection to the public."

"And if I refuse, what then?"

"You're free to go whenever you please. You are not now, nor have you ever been charged with any crimes in Murasaki no Yama, and I am not interested in holding you against your will."

"The anti-magic field your students erected tells a different story."

"They were instructed to take precautions, but we all know very well that you are just as dangerous without your magics as you are with them, so my question is, why haven't you forced your way out yet? Renki and Akari seemed rather content to hold conversation with you. Why not take advantage?"

"Despite rumors to the contrary, I take no pleasure in harming children."

"When the wards went down, you could have easily fled," he continues, barely letting her finish her sentence. "Why didn't you?"

"Perhaps I should have. Are you complaining?"

"Not at all. Just curious as to your motives."

Wren doesn't even know what possessed her to turn around when the forcefield fell, so his guess is as good as hers.

"Disrespectfully, I don't owe you an explanation for my actions either, and I am not about to do the dirty work of a man who sat in a cushy, viewing chair while Montwyatte tried to pull my vocal cords out of my throat."

Interestingly enough, both Fumiko and Kaito shift with discomfort, both of them averting their gaze from their familial head. Hikaru, to his credit, does not rise to the bait. Instead, he closes his eyes—praying for patience, emperor?—and offers her a gentle smile. Wren will eat her own boots if that smile isn't covering up an intense desire to hit her. Well, the feeling's mutual.

"I can understand your reluctance. Which is why I am willing to offer you payment in exchange for your services."

"Whatever you're offering, I'm not interested, and since you claim I'm free to go, I will do so."

Wren gets up from the table.

"You will not last long on your own once the council discovers your return."

"Is that a threat?"

"Not at all, but if you leave here without even hearing my offer, the chances of them discovering you is 92.76%."

"The council doesn't scare me, and neither do you. I'm no stranger to being hunted."

She makes her way to the door, her pack over her shoulder.

"Full autonomy."

She stops in her tracks.

"Full autonomy and the privileges of a private citizen under the protection of the Crown of Murasaki no Yama."

"Not even an emperor has enough power to grant autonomy to someone as infamous as me."

Hikaru's chuckle sets her teeth on edge.

"There isn't a single person in the world that has that power. Wren Nocturne is long dead. Atalia Vaishi, however, is only missing."

Wren turns around, and Hikaru meets her gaze, the smile ever present on his face, one she is beginning to realize is a better poker face than any she has ever seen.

"Since when does the Miyazaki Royal Family forge documents for known criminals?"

"Miss Nocturne has a rather unique skill set, and between today's events and the details confined in this case, the circumstances are extreme indeed for us to even consider such a negotiation. Surely, you are smart enough to take advantage of the opportunity. Or are you so proud you'll walk yourself into a second grave?"

She has always been a relatively good chess player, and she knows when to recognize a checkmate when it is about to happen. Unfortunately, for all the self-confidence she pretends to harbor, she doesn't have enough pieces on the board to counter it.

"I was under the impression I never had a first."

"Wren," calls Kai, and his voice nearly makes her lungs collapse. "This is not a trap. We aren't trying to trick you."

There was a time when she trusted Hikaru solely on the fact that he was Kai's older brother. Not that she trusts Kai any further than she can throw him since he played her heart like a concert piano to cataclysmic effect.

"And you would know all about that, wouldn't you, Miyazaki-sama?"

The confusion that snaps into place on his perfectly blank expression is almost enough to inspire her to strike him, laugh, cry, or all of the above. *How dare he!* Fumiko and Hikaru recoil as though Wren did, in fact, just slap the youngest of them across the face.

"What are you trying to imply, Nocturne?" demands Fumiko, looking at her like Wren is mad as a hatter. Wren won't fight that opinion, since it is probably true, but rather than snip back she sets her bag back down.

"Nothing at all, sensei. Nothing at all."

Fumiko looks as though she is about to strangle Wren herself, but Kaito, his expression the picture of calm once more, sets a hand over hers and shakes his head. Anubis, what is she still doing here? She needs to leave before she chokes on her own convoluted emotions.

She turns her face away from the three technomancers. Her skin feels too tight all of the sudden. Her lungs too small. Her pulse too loud in her ears. Her eyes hot behind her eyelids, and when she lifts her hand to her temple, she sees her wild script flashing violently.

"Wren." The call of her name brings her back into herself. It's Kai, much closer, standing a few steps away from her left shoulder. "If you want to leave, you should, but before you decide, let me walk you through the case. You can see everything we have to show you, and if afterward, you still want to go, no one is going to stop you."

A hand appears in her peripheral vision, Kai's signet ring reflecting warm in the lamplight. Slowly, the phantom grip on her chest loosens, and she takes four steadying breaths. Maybe... maybe she's misremembering. Maybe it was all just a fever dream, an illusion, a cruel joke she played on herself. That's what she wants to believe. That's what she wants to think. Curse her memories for hanging on to that wretched detail but forgetting everything else.

"Wren," Kaito calls her name once more, gentle, beseeching, kind. The way most lies are... especially one she wants so desperately to believe.

She can't leave. But she can't take his hand either.

PRELUDE

Wren feels heavy and wrung out as she turns back around. Kai guides her back to the table without touching her, where she pulls the case disk to her. She pointedly ignores the way Fumiko and Hikaru are looking at her, like she is a freak, unstable, and a very real threat. Is exhaustion a side-effect of being dead for twelve years? She should probably write that down somewhere.

She scolds herself, swallows it down, and pulls the storm back in.

14

FIVE OF SWORDS

THE DATA DISK LOOKS NO DIFFERENT FROM any other she has ever seen. She flinches as Kai takes it from her hand and inserts it into a reader embedded into the table but covers it up by putting her hand in her lap. He notices anyway, keeping his eyes on her as he moves.

Almost instantly a holograph lights up.

The opening page of every technomancer casefile always details the location of the case along with the date of the case's creation. Wren's eyes widen as she instantly recognizes the location from the photograph, a temple compound nestled in the piney ridges of a mountain to the north of Murasaki no Yama. She turns to Kai in disbelief.

"Shinka Temple?" The very heart of the Miyazaki dynasty's data systems and adept training grounds is the location of a case? How could such a thing even be?

"It is compromised," Kaito says in answer to her unasked question.

If Shinka is compromised, the entirety of Murasaki no Yama could fall. No wonder Hikaru and Fumiko were desperate enough to enlist her help. This could mean utter destruction for their entire country.

Prelude

"How?"

Hikaru clears his voice and answers her.

"Two and a half years ago, on the eve of trial graduations, one of our passing adepts went missing. Nothing was found save for his tech and a carved-up skeleton in the woods surrounding Shinka, and this was several months after his disappearance. An investigation was launched to find the creature responsible, and when a werewolf was found in the vicinity, we assumed the case closed."

"You assumed werewolf because they were eaten?" asks Wren skeptically.

"We assumed werewolf because that is what was found," answers Hikaru, a touch of annoyance in his voice. "And the creature was mad with bloodlust when we found it. It made sense, so we assumed the two fit together. We now know we were wrong. Eight months ago, it happened again. Several others were found dead in the surrounding woods, half-eaten by some gluttonous monster. We opened an inquiry on it, but the technomancer who took the case never returned."

Fumiko continues the brief.

"Around the same time, we started to notice something was running interference in our network. Lights flickering, equipment shutting down, neural interfaces being scrambled along the outskirts of the temple. We eventually decided to vacate the temple six months ago after the security systems failed and one of the dormitories was attacked, resulting in the deaths of four trainees. We've moved all of our remaining students here until we can get to the bottom of the disturbances."

Wren swipes through the attached photos of the victims and case detailing. Torn up bodies, missing persons, and finally—she winces here—an attack on the temple dormitories that resulted in the deaths of several young trainees. Fumiko speaks up as she speedreads through the details of the last few missions to the site.

"What is worse is that not long after we moved the students, we lost all communication with the personnel left stationed there. Complete radio silence."

FIVE OF SWORDS

"Two months ago," continues Hikaru. "Kaito and I led an expedition to the temple, and what we found there proved dismal. The temple grounds are covered in a cursed miasma. Most of the adepts were brought to their knees on approach to the temple by the pain of their tech being scrambled by the curse. We could barely even reach the gate without risking total deactivation for our weakest human+. The only one who was able to enter the grounds was Kaito, but even he can't stay for long without serious injury. We are beginning to wonder if the attacks were a subterfuge to force us out of Shinka, so that somebody could cut us off from our most central resource."

"What I don't understand is why a werewolf pack would willingly work in junction with a witch to do this?" asks Fumiko. "The hexen are not exactly organized these days, and they avoid each other as much as they avoid us."

"Fumiko-sensei still believes the attacks to be the work of werewolves?" asks Wren, daring to offer a teasing smile toward her old teacher. The woman sputters, jarred by Wren's sudden turn of presence.

"One of the adepts said they saw a large beastly creature with human-like features running into the forest on all fours. Fits the description of a Koi Lycan if you ask me. I certainly don't know what else might be responsible, but my nephews seem to believe the Songstress of Lorelei could shed some light on the situation if she were so inclined."

Well, somebody's gotten bitter in their old age. Actually, Fumiko was always kind of bitter... Or maybe it's just her.

The woman isn't wrong though. The description given does match up with a Koi Lycan, a werewolf transformed under the full moon cycle of the larger of Deus' two moons. They are much larger than their Dei cousins who look much more like regular wolves than the horrific mixture of wolfish anthropomorphism their larger cousins claim. She takes a few more moments to review the various dates and autopsy reports on the various victims and attacks before turning to Kai.

"Well, they aren't werewolf attacks."

"What makes you so sure?" asks Fumiko.

Wren zooms in on a victim whose throat was slashed. His belly is ripped open, flesh ripped from the bones as though someone butchered him for the best cuts of meat.

"Much like real wolves, werewolves primarily attack with their fangs, not their claws the way the movies and the TV shows like to portray them. If it had been a lycan, this man's throat wouldn't have been slashed. It would have been torn out with a bite that would have broken his neck first. These look more like the work of a butcher. Hungry but controlled. A rabid wolf couldn't have done that."

"So, if it isn't lycans, what is it?"

"I don't know, but I can tell you the miasma around Shinka is the result of a curse. You're entirely right about the subterfuge part."

"What makes you say that?" asks Kaito.

"The timing of it is too perfect. Someone cast a curse on your temple grounds when your graduate went missing two years ago and left it to grow unfettered."

"Why did it take so long to form a miasma?"

"My guess? Your anti-magic wards were keeping it at bay, and with the diligent maintenance required of Miyazaki adepts to maintain their augmentations, it probably staved off any damage the spell was causing over time. Kind of like bandaging a stab wound, it keeps the bleeding under control, but without stitches, it doesn't completely close. When you vacated the temple, it was given free reign, so like any wound left untreated, it festered and became necrotic."

"So, this means..."

Wren nods her head.

"Someone planted the equivalent of a time bomb on your temple grounds and left it to do its job."

"Who could do something like this?"

She shrugs her shoulders and starts thinking aloud.

"Well, I could, but I've been dead for twelve years. Maybe there's another witch running around capable of it? Oh, like Summer!"

Hikaru and Kaito exchange a serious look before turning back to her. Fumiko brings her finger to her mouth in thought.

"Look, believe me or not about Summer. I know who I saw on the light rail."

"It is not that we don't believe you. It's just difficult to wrap our heads around the possibility that she's still alive."

"I'm alive, aren't I?" she deadpans, and Hikaru visibly withdraws. "And don't pretend like I've told you anything you didn't already suspect. I know exactly why you're showing me this case. You need a witch to cleanse the curse."

"We are aware of our situation," says Hikaru. "I will not hide that this is a mutually beneficial offer."

"Mutually beneficial, my ass! This is a suicide mission, and you know it. Countering a curse this strong could take days and would draw the attention of every ghoul and ghost in the vicinity. Even if I do manage to break it, I'll be a sitting duck for the next zombie rat to pick off, so you kill off two birds with one stone. Not only do you get your precious temple back, you get to tell the world you killed Wren Nocturne a second time, and this time you have a body to set on a pike because she was stupid enough to take a solo mission from someone who wants to kill her."

"You are misunderstanding."

"Am I?" She laughs.

"Wren, stop drawing conclusions and listen." Kai's command draws her attention straight to him, and she grits her teeth, just about ready to punch him right after she finishes with his damned brother.

"My intention is not to send you alone," Hikaru interrupts her.

"Did you not hear a word I just said? This is a suicide mission. I don't care how talented you think your more expendable adepts are—"

"Kaito will be going with you."

The hot air goes cold in her lungs. "What?"

"Kaito will be going with you," he repeats slower as though speaking to a five-year-old.

Well, if that isn't the most asinine thing she's ever heard!

"I can understand wanting to send me, but your brother? You must be crazier than I ever was if you think that is even mildly a good idea."

"No, Miss Nocturne. I think the two of you working together can accomplish exactly what is necessary."

"You're mental," she says. "Even if that were true, you're depending on my ability to break a curse that's been festering for more than two years. Any notes I had on countering a curse of this size were lost with my Book of Shadows, so sorry, but I am quite useless to you."

"Your Book of Shadows is not lost," says Kaito. "It is in Shinka's library."

Wren turns her head, staring at him wide-eyed.

"H-How?"

"It was recovered," he says simply without further explanation. "That's all you need to know."

"Kai," she growls.

Fumiko clears her throat.

"Yet another incentive for you. I'm sure the recovery of your grimoire would prove invaluable for you."

Fumiko, as tiresome as she is at times, has always been very good with reason. Hikaru takes the opportunity to speak again. His continence is pleading, eyes soft as he tries to appeal to her humanity.

"Miss Nocturne, we understand the danger you will be putting yourself in by taking this on. Murasaki will be in your debt. Our pride will not let such a debt go unpaid, and while I do not presume to speak for my brother, I am quite certain he would lay down his own life to ensure you accomplish this task."

Hikaru's gaze is firm, not a shadow of a doubt in his expression; Fumiko's shift in posture is subtle but glaring. The anxiety hiding in both of their expressions, too, strikes a chord as she glances at the aforementioned male. He makes no comment, despite being spoken of like he isn't in the room. Kai sits rigid and statuesque, shoulders set, and the lines of his face sketch a portrait of determination. Wren can find no fault in Hikaru's words. Kai's honor and filial piety would allow for no less. He will either walk out of Shinka mission accomplished with her alive as promised, or he will not walk out at all.

Wren's shoulders visibly sag.

"That won't be necessary."

"I take it we have a deal, then?"

Hikaru extends his right hand across the table toward her: manicured fingernails, gold signet ring, heavy and expensive on his ring finger, the ports where his weapons connect visible at the second knuckle of his thumb and opposite his pulse point. She notes idly that his fingers are just on this side of thicker than Kai's, whose hands are long and elegant from years of piano playing and callused from swordsmanship. His skin is also a touch paler than Kai's, clearly spending more time tending to his duties as a monarch than running cases.

She reaches her hand out and shakes his.

"I'll accept, provided you hold up your end of the bargain."

"Of course, Songstress."

"Don't call me that."

"As you wish."

With that, they rise. She should probably do the same. It would be proper etiquette after all. She rises from her seat and offers a half-hearted haphazard bow to the man currently holding her by a leash. Hikaru bows back to her. Wren burns at the meaning behind the gesture. Then all three of them make their way to the door, Kaito going outside with his aunt and brother briefly to speak with them, she imagines. Normally, she isn't above eavesdropping, but as soon as the door shuts, she wilts back to the floor.

She exhales heavily, flopping her head down on the table. She feels raw and exhausted and exposed, like a nerve flayed out from under the dermis, and being in front of the three of them was more trying than fighting legions of undead. At least Fumiko and Hikaru are leaving. Leaving her just Kaito to contend with which is both better and worse.

Her moment of respite does not last long as Kaito returns. She opens her eyes when he addresses her.

"We leave for Shinka in the morning. You should rest and recover your strength for the trip."

She stares at him, unflinching, trying to decide what it is she should be feeling right now. She's angry, certainly. Hikaru has backed her into a corner, and she would be reacting more violently were it not for the fact that she would be the surgeon walking into an operating theater to either finish an amputation or save a dying limb. But Kaito... Kaito was going with her knowing full well they would be walking into a death trap. It wouldn't be the first time, but...

"Why did you bring me here?" she asks, but Kai doesn't answer her. He fixes her with a cold stare, both of his hands firmly held behind his back.

"Go to bed, Wren. I will sleep elsewhere."

Her shoulders shake as she titters at his oh so honorable intentions.

"I'm not some vestal maiden whose virtue needs to be protected as you well know, though his highness is clearly still the gentleman I remember him to be."

"Wren, this is not a joke."

"If you're so concerned about propriety, wouldn't it be more appropriate to put me elsewhere for the evening?"

"That would make it difficult for me to keep an eye on you."

"Prince Kaito acts as a personal guard now, it would seem. First, he volunteers himself for a mission that is essentially a death trap. Then, he insists on keeping watch through the night in his own home. Surely, this one is not worthy of such an esteemed distinction?"

"I am the one who brought you here. You are, therefore, my responsibility."

"How cumbersome that must be for you."

It must be terribly off-putting for him to be seeing her again after all this time. I mean, who wouldn't be set off at having the closest living thing to a ghost drop into their lap without any warning whatsoever? She doesn't look a day older than twenty-one whereas Kai has lived in this world now more than ten years longer than she. While he looks younger due to his technomancer enhancements, he is still thirty-three years old. And now here he is standing there in all his too pale clothing, still torn up and a little bloody from the day's earlier events, serious demeanor hovering around him like a storm cloud, and tasked with the penalty of having to deal with her after twelve years of what surely must have been the most peaceful time of his life. He probably brought her here thinking he could get her to confess before throwing her in the dungeon, *ojos que no ven, corazón que no siente,* and yet here he is having to babysit her as recompense for going behind his brother's back on something so serious as the housing of a witch. A witch his brother apparently has a use for . The whole idea is hilarious.

She starts to chuckle as she responds.

"Weren't you the one who used to lecture me about making bad decisions? Really, Kaito, you should take your own advice."

"Wren, you can choose to behave as spitefully as you'd like, but there is nothing you can do to make me regret my decision."

"Your dedication to clan and country is ever admirable, Your Royal Highness."

The look he gives her is stale, and she howls with laughter. He watches her rip her seams for a bit before finally turning away with a disgusted curl of his lip.

"You never did know when to take something seriously."

She calms herself enough to get a word out. Goodness, her stomach hurts from laughing.

"I take everything seriously. I just don't feel the need to be so stoic all the time."

She leans herself back on her elbows, her legs extended under the table, a despicable posture she knows very well often got her in trouble with her tutors, her brother, and Kaito when they had been trainees together at the summit.

"Lighten up, your highness. I'll be out of your hair as soon as I close this case, then you can carry on as if nothing's changed.

You can forget all about my existence and continue living your perfect life without my interference."

"You do not remember how you died."

The change of subject is so abrupt Wren gets mental whiplash from the sudden halting of her line of thought. The teasing grin diminishes to a lopsided upturn of her lips, the previous darkly mood around her thickening again. Kai, infuriating as always, levels her glare with his own dead stare, and as quickly as it came, the mood passes, and she looks sideways away from where he is standing.

"I don't remember anything after stabbing myself through the gut to kill Montwyatte."

Kai's eyes widen a fraction of a centimeter, just enough to let Wren know he is surprised by this statement, but then his expression hardens and resolution sets into the line of his stance.

"Nothing."

"Nope. Nada," she says, popping her lips hard on the 'p' sound. "One minute I was fighting Montwyatte, the next I was... well I guess dead anyway, not that I remember much of that either. I don't know what happened in between, and I, quite frankly, don't want to know."

"Your memory is damaged. Does this not concern you?"

"Not much I can do about it, can I?"

He doesn't say anything to that. He just stands there for a very long time. Long enough that she leans forward and opens the casefile again. She has a lot of prep to do if they are leaving in the morning and only hours to do it before dawn. Pulling her pack to her, she opens it up and pulls out the talismans she was working on earlier in the day along with the locket, out of which she summons the violin.

"It's your bed. You should sleep in it. I don't imagine I'll be sleeping very much anyway."

The hard edges of his eyes soften.

"You've never liked sleeping."

She hasn't enjoyed sleeping since she was seventeen. Too many nightmares and too many sour memories. She'd rather stay awake, sleeping only when her body forces her into a merciful unconsciousness, neither tainted by dreams or nightmares. It's odd to her that he remembers this about her.

The instrument is out of tune. She thrums the strings lightly, adjusting the pegs as she goes trying to tune them by ear alone. It would be so much easier if she had something to compare pitches with. Kai watches her fiddle with the instrument a moment longer before he crosses the room to a far door that leads to another section of his quarters, a lounge/office of some kind. She tries not to pay him any mind, but soon she hears the tinkling notes of a piano playing.

Despite her stubborn determination to ignore him as much as possible, she goes to investigate.

Kai sits at a baby grand in a room that looks to be a studio/dojo for his personal training and practice. It takes her a moment to recognize that the notes he is plucking out are not quite a song. They are chords and scales in patterns that start from G and end on E, occasionally skipping through the fifths as he goes.

Fifths from G to E. Ah, he's helping her tune.

She lifts the violin again, and when she finishes matching the pitches to the piano notes, she raises it to her chin, brings the bow in hand, and plays a scale. This was one of the things she missed the most when she lost her mechanical hand in her past life. Without a left hand, playing most instruments became impossible, and thus, she became reliant on her voice, but sometimes it's easier to compose on an instrument, something outside of her body that she can manipulate with her hands.

Kai seems happy to leave her be for the time being as he notices she has finished tuning and can therefore move onto playing actual music rather than just plucked notes. She returns to the table, picks up a pen, and begins plotting arrays, blueprints for castings that may prove useful on their mission, etchings that she can analyze and then redraw from memory in blood. When she has an array set, she picks up the violin and begins to compose a melody for it, an activation hymn, if you will, that will create a resonance in the key the array ends up settling on.

PRELUDE

It is peaceful, surprisingly, working like this, left alone to her own devices, the sounds of the piano the only indication she has company.

Kai's fingers travel from one melody to the next, onward and forward until she loses track of the hours, and the day starts to catch up with her. An old familiar tune begins, tumbling through the wall. It takes her a moment to recognize it, changed as it is for the different instrumentation. It's an old lullaby she wrote a long time ago. Well, she didn't so much write it as hum an ever-changing pattern, a jumbled series of notes strung together when the mood struck her. No set rhythms or textures, just an idea that morphed and evolved with her moods, wordless but for the gentle cadence of a child's voice. She used to sing it all the time to little Fae when they lived in the wilds near Lorelei, but how did he even remember it? Kai would only have heard it a handful of times. Did he hear her sing it to Renki on the train? No, she only sang a portion of it.

It is quite effective, the gentle rise and fall of the notes. It always put her charges right to sleep.

Her eyelids grow heavy, the sandman's dust fogging her focus. She's gotten enough done for the night, right? She'll just lay her head down for a second, close her eyes a bit before she wakes back up to take care of the rest. She still needs to prepare a water spell and chaining talisman and a...

The music folds around her, and slumber blankets her before she can even finish her thought.

She stirs only a little as a feeling of weightlessness envelops her. Warm arms lift her from the table and settle her amidst what is surely a cloud of soft cushy pillows.

"Goodnight, Wren," she hears before sleep's embrace pulls her back down into its depths.

Despite Kaito putting the stubborn witch to bed with her own lulling melody, Wren sleeps fitfully. It really shouldn't surprise him considering everything he knows about her, but it catches him off guard nonetheless. She doesn't scream or cry out, but he hears the small, whispered pleas from his place in the sitting room and goes back into the bedroom to check on her. She is asleep, but her skin is clammy and cold sweat soaks the sheets. Caught in a nightmare. Haunted by painful memories or her own mind's twisted machinations, she twists back and forth so violently, he worries she's having a seizure.

He sets his hand on her shoulder, and her thrashing stills. Her breathing evens out and it seems as though the nightmare diminishes. He scans her lifeforce, finding it twitchy but stable. However, as soon as he lifts his hand from her shoulder, making to leave the room, she starts to fidget, the green glow of her energy becoming erratic once more.

"Give her back to me..." she murmurs, burying her face in the pillows.

He returns to her side and sits at the edge of the mattress, setting one hand on her head. She stills again, and all at once, he remembers her as a teenager in the times between her abounding confidence and her teasing flirting nature. Times when the outward façade dropped, and she showed him her vulnerability. She looks terribly small curled up amid the sheets and pillows of his bed.

"AYA."

"Miyazaki-sama?" answers the A.I. at a low volume.

"Play 子守唄 and overlay it with a seaside track while I leave the room," he says, and AYA complies, setting a track of white noise to play through the sound system over the lullaby. It seems to settle her, so he goes to the bathroom to change and dress for bed. His thoughts are a scattered jumble as he settles in beside her atop the covers, not touching her but close enough to intercede should she begin to stir again.

"*Mon rivage...*"

PRELUDE

Wren's soft voice whispers into the darkness, an endearment from another life, and Kai wonders how the same voice bit into him earlier.

And you would know all about that wouldn't you, Miyazaki-sama?

It doesn't compute.

She's been dead for twelve years. Her memories are incomplete. She's confused and on the defensive, and when Wren feels powerless, Wren gets hostile.

At least she still responds to him.

He doesn't know how his karma saw fit to give him a second chance, but he will not waste it, so as sleep overcomes him, he makes his vow.

It is said that the neutral zone between the Hexen wilds and the League Nations is haunted. Countless ghosts lurk, forlorn and forgotten in the shadows of a war waged for so long the tales of its origins have no recognizable overlap— the stories all attributed to myth and legend depending on which faction you are speaking with. Ghosts waiting to wreak havoc with the setting of the sun. Spirits that have accumulated over the centuries from dead both bionic and hexen left unburied on the battlefield. When the haunts began to spread to the nearby territories resulting in the deaths of many civilians from both sides of the war, a temporary truce was called between the Hexen and the Technomancers to clean up the mess. Thus, the catacombs were built, the largest underground tomb in Deus.

In the two hundred years since their construction, the city erected over it has grown in both size and population, a haven for anyone wishing to stay out of the war's path.

An Excerpt from *Lorelei, the Crumbling City*
By Heather Ables, 1874 A.P.

15

THE WHEEL OF
FORTUNE PART. 1

Sixteen Years Ago–18th Day in the Month of Fire 1861–4 Months after the 247th Technomancer Summit

A MISSIVE REACHES MURASAKI FROM LORELEI about mysterious killings of both human+ and hexen. Normally, such happenings in Lorelei wouldn't concern the League at all, but when an Aighnean technomancer's body is found on the outskirts of the city, somebody has to investigate. Kaito and Hikaru accept the assignment and travel via light rail to the city located just beyond Murasaki's borders. How Wren and Xipilli also receive the missive, he doesn't know, but this is already proving to be a trying reunion. The trip to Lorelei is filled with Wren's laughter and affectionate teasing toward her brother, who only ever seems to be in a good mood when his younger sibling is wholly focused on him. The dynamic between the Derivan siblings is vastly different from his own with Hikaru who he has always enjoyed an easy relationship with. Wren and Xipilli, on the other hand, are intense to the point of concerning, Xipilli bouncing back and forth between having a playful/intense rivalry with his sister and being overly protective of her.

The latter of which turns on in full force when Hikaru suggests the four of them split into two groups for reconnaissance. For maximum range of abilities, the Miyazaki brothers will each pair with one of the Derivan siblings. Based on their various fighting styles, they pair Wren with Kaito (Kai with his dual blades and Wren with her double-bladed ætherkalis) and Xipilli and his trident with Hikaru and his long sword, called an *o katana*. It makes the most practical sense but...

"Absolutely not."

They haven't even entered the city, and Xipilli is already fuming.

One thing is for sure though, Wren's love for her older brother is very apparent in the way she coddles him out of his darker moods. She employs this charisma of hers as a weapon against Xipilli's scowl.

Wren slings an arm around her brother's neck.

"Oh, come on, Xipilli. It makes sense to divide and conquer."

"I fail to see why it would be better to split up when we know how to work together better than with them."

"Complementary skill sets, *hermano mio*. We can help each other with our different strengths."

Xipilli doesn't argue back, but he does send a glare in Kai's direction. Clearly, the teen still remembers catching them on the roof. Wren says something in Derivan to her brother that somehow manages to soften him, and the teen relents enough for them to get underway.

"One day, your mouth is going to get you into trouble, and I am not going to be there to help you."

"That's fine. I'll be there to help myself."

Xipilli rolls his eyes at his sister's antics, mumbling under his breath as he turns and storms his way toward Hikaru.

"How was I cursed with such a sister?"

"Just lucky, I guess," Wren calls after him with a wide grin on her face.

Her brother makes a lewd hand gesture back to her in response, to her glee.

As Wren and Kai make their way through the city, they scope out several apartment complexes and cafés looking for information. They turn up nothing, mostly because no one seems willing to talk to them. There are a lot of reasons for that. Most residents of Lorelei want nothing to do with the League, even the non-hexen, augmented or otherwise. Voluntary outcasts, these people would rather live among hexen, dangerous, bloodthirsty hexen, than live within a League country's jurisdiction.

Kaito just can't comprehend it.

"Hey Kai, I was wondering..." Wren's voice comes through on his comm through her helmet. She's been quiet thus far, as focused on the task as he.

"Now is not the time, Wren."

"You don't even know what I was going to say."

He has a good idea, though, because the topic has also been on his mind. Their last rendezvous on the roof. He keeps forcing it down like a stubborn itch, a mosquito bite he knows better than to scratch.

"We have more important things to deal with right now."

He doesn't look at her, but he can hear the cadence of her laugh behind him as they park their cycles. It sounds just like the kind of laughs she gave during the summit whenever she knew she was about to do something that would guarantee her an extra assignment or task.

"Ever attentive to your task, highness."

Something about the words themselves bother him, even if she says them as teasingly and cheerily as usual.

The apartment complex is rundown: cracks in the foundation, peeling wallpaper, threadbare carpets. Most of the tenants are hexen and refuse to open their doors, distrustful of their augmentations, but they do speak to them via the call monitors on their doors. Most of them are scared witless about a beast that has been visiting nightly, its terrible shrieks and growls enough to inspire a self-imposed curfew among the residents.

Wren takes point when one of the women, a shaking transhuman with red-rimmed eyes and tear-stained cheeks, says one of her daughters was taken by the monster last night. She told them to get them to leave, but with a little persuasion Wren convinces the mother to allow them into her home.

Wren questions the woman about what happened while Kaito goes into the child's room.

His throat clenches.

The crib is overturned and shattered to pieces. A dried bloodstain smears through the center of the floor, splatters of reddish brown accented with claw marks.

How did the beast get in?

He checks the windows for signs of entry, but the pane is untouched, a thin sheet of dust still settled over it, and the lock bears no signs of being forced. There are no markings on the door, and the rest of the house has not suffered any damage. In the vent is where he finds his answer. The cover over the air duct has been bent in half. It is not a large duct; whatever made its way through would have to have been small. That or it had the ability to change its size or shape. Hanging on the edge of the vent shield is a scrap of skin and hair. When he analyzes it with his sights, it comes back as human.

There are several puzzle pieces here that don't quite fit together.

"Anything interesting?"

Wren stands in the doorframe.

Kai turns from where he kneels in front of the duct. He gestures with his head from the crib to the vent and the blood spatters in between.

"Whatever took the child came in through the ventilation system."

"What kind of creature could fit in there?"

"Not sure. I was just about to look inside."

"Here, let me. I can fit a little better," she says.

She walks over and crouches down next to him. Pulling what is left of the vent off the duct, she sets it aside while he moves back to give her room to work. Laying all the way on her stomach, she moves her left hand forward. The mechanical joints of the middle finger open, and a gold beam of light bursts forth. She aims it into the dark space of the vent, and all but sticks her head into the duct. A sound of disgust leaves her throat.

"There is blood everywhere. It definitely dragged the poor thing out this way."

"Do you see anything else?"

She rolls back to look at him before answering with a frown.

"There is something a little farther back just sitting there, but I can't see it very well."

"Can you pull it out?"

"Yeah, just give me a second."

She turns off the flashlight feature of her augmentation, then twists the limb until it detaches entirely from her forearm. She presses a button on the back of it and sets it on the floor. The mechanical hand springs to life and crawls into the duct like a five-legged spider. A few moments later, it returns, dragging/pushing a decaying horse's hoof into the room.

Wren picks it up, her nose wrinkling as the hoof continues to degrade in her hold, the skin flaking off and the hoof falling from the furry ankle as she holds it.

"Looks like whatever it is, it's wanting for parts, and not of the living variety."

"We'll take it for analysis. Maybe Hikaru can pull something up on his servers."

She nods and drops it into a plastic bag which Kaito tucks away into his pack. Wren picks her mechanical hand off the floor, and before deactivating it, she gives it a gentle "thanks." The device hops almost happily in her palm at the praise. There is something both endearing and disturbing about the way she addresses it as though it were a living creature.

"Do you often talk to your augmentations?"

"Well, of course!" she says and then reinstalls it to the insertion point on her arm. "Mano has got me in and out of some tight situations in the past. It would be rude not to acknowledge her for it."

"Mano?" he asks.

"Yeah, Mano, as in hand. My brother thinks it's stupid, but you have to name a friend who gets you in and out places."

She looks down at the attachment fondly as though regarding a well-kept pet. Kai tilts his head up and down slowly at her, a speculative look on his face before saying.

"And would Mano perhaps be how you were able to break into the firing range that night in Shinka?"

She abruptly looks up at him, lips puckered like a child caught with their hand in the cookie jar before chuckling, embarrassed at being caught out. She raises the hand in question to him, pointer finger extended toward him as she shakes it playfully, scoldingly.

"Prince Kaito is too astute."

He shakes his head at her.

"What did you find out from the mother?"

Wren lights up a holo in her mechanical palm and reads through the notes she took.

"Magdalena Villanueva. ID#64128T6. A citizen of Deriva. She recognized me from pictures of the royal family. That's why she decided to let us in. She said the night of the attack, she woke up to a crash and her daughter crying, but by the time her partner had grabbed a weapon and come in, the babe was gone."

"Anything else?"

"Her daughter was about a year old. Born in Lorelei, so no ID chip. Which is why she didn't report the attack. She wouldn't tell me why she is living in Lorelei to begin with, but I could ask again if you'd like."

He shakes his head.

"We should go. Leave the family to grieve."

She hums in agreement.

"Let me check in with the mother one more time. I want to thank her for letting us in."

She moves around him and out of the kid's room back toward the living area where the woman stands wringing her hands as she looks out the window. When she catches sight of Wren, she stirs, a bit panicked but trusting enough of the easy manner with which Wren carries herself. When she looks at Kaito, however, the sense of unease returns as though she is afraid of him.

"Did you find anything?"

Wren ducks her head.

"Yes, thank you for allowing my partner and me to go into the room. We are going to do everything in our power to find the creature responsible for this."

"*Gracias, señorita. Bendición sobre ti. No—*"

"Magdalena, what are you doing? Who are they?"

A feminine voice sounds from the doorway, and another woman stands there with a small child in hand, a little girl maybe six or seven years old. The woman who has just walked is a hexen. Even if she had managed to cover the small black circular indicia on her shoulder in time, Kai can see the faint ripples of magic that coat her form. Kai immediately takes his guard, sights whirling to life, putting a hand on Wren's shoulder and pulling her back and away from the unidentified witch as he reaches for Amatsu's hilt.

Magdalena, however, cuts the woman off even as the witch's meager energy reserves collect to create a shield.

"Olga, it's alright. They are friends."

"Maggie, they are technomancers. We've talked about this."

"They are trying to find the thing that took Lisa."

"And once they find it, what do you think is going to happen? You can't trust these people."

"Olga, please. They mean us no harm."

"They mean you no harm, but technomancers are killers. Do you want them to take Lucille away from us too?"

"Olga!"

Wren steps forward cautiously, hands in front of her.

"Ma'am, please, we aren't here to hurt you or your family. We just want to stop whatever is doing this so no more innocents go missing."

Wren's gentle charm cascades over the room as easily as a perfume, a balm that whittles the tension from the space, working toward diffusing a situation that could quickly turn into a bloodbath. Olga looks at Wren before glancing at Mångata resting at Wren's hip and Kai's hand on Amatsu's hilt at his back.

"If you mean that, you'll drop your weapons."

"We can do that."

Wren slowly lowers her hand to her hip, unstrapping Mångata and placing it on the floor.

"Wren," says Kai in warning. "This is not smart. We should leave."

"It's okay, Kai," she says and looks from Olga and back to Kai, her eyes pleading as she places her hand over his on Amatsu. *"Kanojo—kowai."*

She says the words carefully and purposefully in his native language, a broken sentence he can piece together well enough to understand. "She's scared," she's trying to say, sea-green eyes beseeching him to disarm if only for the moment, and indeed, he realizes, Wren is right. The hexen woman is far more scared of them than they ever could be of her, her magical abilities too weak to warrant anything more than a few parlor tricks. Kai wonders at how easily Wren chooses to trust the hexen woman not to try something against them, but he supposes it wouldn't be very wise for Olga to do anything. She is outnumbered and outclassed. She is clearly not an avid practitioner, and even without their weapons, Kai alone could subdue her if necessary.

The muscles in his face tighten, but he concedes, unstrapping Tsukuyomi and Amatsu from his back to place them gently on the floor still in their sheaths. He does not deactivate his sights though, poised for any sign of attack from the witch.

Now that both technomancers have disarmed themselves, the hexen woman relaxes, exhaling a long-held breath and setting down the child in her arms before addressing them. The little girl runs into her mothers' bedroom and away from the two strangers in the room.

"What does the League care if hexen children go missing?"

"One of our technomancers and several adepts were killed while on patrol in the area," answers Wren. "We didn't know hexen children were going missing until we arrived. It's possible the two are related, and since Lorelei is a neutral zone, we are happy to give aid to those in need regardless of blood or birth."

The woman, tall and muscled, her blonde hair clipped close to her head, nods.

"I'm sure my wife has already told you what happened."

"Yes," says Wren. "But I'm wondering if you have anything else to add."

"Lisa was just coming into her magic. She's been refusing her bottle by freezing it. Then the children started to go missing."

"How many children have gone missing?" asks Kaito.

"Six in the last fortnight. Two werewolf pups, a goblin infant, and three witchlings. All of them between 10 and 16 months old. Lisa is the most recent," answers Olga. The abhorrence! A monster that kidnaps and kills innocent children! Babies, hexen or otherwise, were precious, meant to be protected. "A group of us were going to go out hunting tonight to find and kill the thing."

"Do you know if any non-hexen babies disappeared?" Kaito follows up.

"Not that I am aware," answers the hexen woman crisply.

"What about your other daughter?" asks Wren. "Is she also hexen?"

"Our older daughter, Lucille, is augmented," answers Magdalena. "She sleeps in the same room as Lisa, and yet she was left alone."

Kaito turns to Magdalena and asks, "Did she see what happened?"

"She was awake when we found her, yes."

"May I speak with her?" asks Wren.

"She has not spoken since it happened."

Wren's eyes sadden before perking up once more as an idea enters her head.

"Does she like to draw?"

Olga and Magdalena share a look before nodding.

While Wren spends time with the child, Kai settles himself against the wall, idly dragging his fingertips over the necklace hidden under his shirt collar. He watches the activity not only in this apartment but the whole building through his virtual mapping. He has picked their weapons up off the floor and set them on the small coffee table in front of him in clear view of Olga. He keeps an eye on the witch as she moves about her home even as Magdalena, her augmented wife, sets a glass of water in front of him. Much less on edge now that the secret of her wife and daughter is out, she settles in the recliner opposite him.

"You don't trust hexen very much, do you, your highness?"

"I have little reason to trust them."

"They're people too, you know."

He doesn't answer, nor does he reach for the water she brought him.

"You think I am crazy to marry a hexen."

"My thoughts have no bearing on your life, madam."

Magdalena smiles at him gently, grief dulling the edges of it and darkening the skin under her eyes. She reminds him of his mother after his father died.

"A hexen killed my husband, Lucille's father, years ago before I even knew I was pregnant. They wanted to kill me too, but Olga kept them from killing me and Lucille."

His gaze drifts to her as she continues her story.

"I found out he was leading a mermaid pearling ring. You don't realize how wicked the practice is until you witness it for yourself. They catch them out at sea, and then they force them to cry. Do you know how badly you have to hurt a mermaid, a supposedly soulless creature, to get it to cry? They keep them until they reach their quota, then they cut off their tails and throw them back into the water to drown."

"Why are you telling me this?"

"My husband is lauded as a folk hero for what he did and how he died, but when I found out about it, I was so ashamed I didn't notice what he was doing. How could anyone do that to another person?"

"There are few who consider mermaids people or any other fae for that matter. Fae, regardless of species, are dangerous creatures, and the same can be said for hexen, condemned to evil by the blood in their veins and the uncontrollable nature of their abilities. The few that do not fall victim to that inevitability are anomalies, not examples to be held up and praised."

"You're wrong!"

Kai's sights spin a half rotation as he watches the woman's face. Desperation, determination, bold rebellion. She wants to convince him she made the right choice. Desperately wants affirmation from him, though why is beyond him.

She cows in the face of his tech, remembering herself and recoiling from the technomancer. Wren re-enters the living room as Magdalena apologizes.

"Kai, what's going on?"

Wren looks overly concerned, no doubt by the shout, but Kai ignores her question, gathering their weapons and tossing her Mångata.

"We're leaving."

She catches the hilt easily enough.

"Okay?" she agrees, confused, but for once she doesn't argue, sensing the sourness in his mood. She still takes the time to reassure the women Lisa will be returned to them if and when they find her, thanks them for their time and hospitality, and lets Olga know to cancel any plans she had with the other hexen to track down the creature themselves while Kai waits on the threshold. The cyborgean woman at least has the sense to bow to them as they take their leave. A small part of him wants to take Wren by the hand and forcibly remove her from the premises, but he restricts himself and waits until her bright gaze turns back on him, an apologetic smile on her lips.

He turns to leave, and she follows.

"What did she say to you?" asks Wren.

Kaito ignores her in favor of getting back out onto the street as quickly as he can without making a scene. If she is bothered by his silence, she doesn't show it, holding out instead the little girl's drawing.

"Well, whatever it was, I promise you it was worth enduring. This drawing is a huge help."

He looks over at it, squints, and takes it from her hands for a better look. The picture is blotchy and inelegant, of course, a child's masterpiece, the markers having bled through where the child pressed too hard or held too long. Surprisingly though, it isn't all done in one color, black and red and green comprising the vast majority of the image, but there are also greys and browns and a little bit of yellow tossed in here and there. He doesn't recognize the creature right away as any type of hexen, fae, or supernatural beast he has ever seen. Honestly, it looks like the little girl simply had an incredible imagination and didn't know what to do with it. Or rather someone didn't have enough parts to work with, so they stitched them all together to make this monstrous mosaic.

"A chimera," says Kai as the elevator doors slide closed before them.

Wren nods, pressing the button for the first floor.

"These attacks aren't as random as we suspected," she says.

"Someone is making these monsters."

"It's beginning to look like it, and what better energy source for them to procure than hexen babies?"

Kai looks at her, incredulous, as he puts on his helmet.

"Raw, unfiltered, wild magic," she emphasizes as though he didn't already figure that out.

"That's disgusting."

"What is?"

"Thinking of infants as batteries."

"Yeah, I know, so how about we find the boltbucket responsible and rip them a new one?"

He doesn't think he's ever agreed with her more.

The Thirteen Months of the Deus Calendar and Their Associated Festivals:

Month of Ice   *Start of the New Year*

Month of Frost   *World Liberation Day (WitchSlayer*
                             Celebration)

Month of Song   *Spring Equinox*

Month of Storms

Month of Planting   *Human+ Festival*

Month of Light   *Summer Solstice*

Month of Soil

Month of Fire   *Summer's End*

Month of Falling

Month of Darkness   *Autumn Equinox and Hexennacht*

Month of Harvest

Month of Cold   *Firefly Hearth Festival*

Month of Hearths   *Midwinter Celebrations*

16
THE WHEEL OF FORTUNE PART 2

HOURS LATER, AFTER RECONVENING WITH their brothers to compare information, Wren and Kaito are on the hunt, and they have found nothing. *Nothing!* Even on Kai's virtualscape. And Kaito's frustration is beginning to bleed into his posture. His jaw clicks every time he cracks his neck, and his back feels like someone shoved a hot coal between his shoulder blades.

He's anxious, his swords so eager to spill witch blood they vibrate with it in their sheaths, but without the witch they are looking for in front of them, he can only stay his hand, searching like a dog sniffing out a scent. And he can't even focus on that because he's too busy replaying his conversation with Magdalena over and over and over in his head.

The woman fell in love with a hexen and got her baby stolen from her because of it.

Wren most certainly is not helping. Wren has not stopped chattering on about something or other since they split off from Hikaru and Xipilli an hour ago. She isn't even talking about the mission. She goes on about the buildings, about a strangely colored butterfly, a goblin mission she took a month ago... It is unceasing and beginning to seriously grate on his nerves. It doesn't even seem like she wants him to respond. She just carries on and on and on and—

"Wren, will you be quiet!"

The biggest shit-eating grin he has ever seen breaks out across her face.

"He speaks! I have been blessed by the voice of a prince."

His eyes narrow and the irritation he was feeling peaks at her antics. Wren seems entirely unbothered by his cold glare.

"Oh, don't look at me like that. You've had your panties in a twist since we left the apartment."

He rounds on her, eyes flashing his hand going to Tsukuyomi before he has a chance to put his emotions on ice.

"You are the most infuriating—"

"So, what is it?"

The moment the question comes out of her mouth, his agitation dwindles, and Kai realizes she is being purposefully annoying to get a rise out of him and get him to open up. He scoffs.

"It doesn't matter."

"Mmm, I think it does."

He moves to walk away from her, but she snatches at his sleeve. In an instant, he whirls around and catches her wrist in his palm. Wren takes his momentum and redirects it, so they go spinning sideways like a fiercely executed waltz turn. She doesn't calculate correctly though as her back connects with a tree trunk, and he presses her wrist into the bark. He has her augmented arm in hand while her flesh hand is pressed to his chest. He glares down at her, nearly spitting with indignation, and she has the audacity to smirk up at him.

"At least you aren't ignoring me anymore."

Maybe she didn't miscalculate their rotation.

"Can't you be serious for once?"

"Can't you be open for once?" she deadpans. He frowns, looking away from her. "Come on. I know you're hungry to catch the witch, but something else is clearly upsetting you. So, tell me."

"You are the most vexing creature I have ever met." *And unbelievably perceptive*, he adds mentally.

He breathes slowly and surely. Steadying his pulse and swallowing down the unreasonable anger threatening to boil over, he lets go of her hand, stepping back and out of her space. She doesn't let him go far though, her hand already hooking back into his coat sleeve. It really shouldn't surprise him how strong she is. She has of course received the same muscular enhancements he has since their graduation. She could probably lift him over her own head if she really wanted to, assuming, of course, he doesn't fight back.

He closes his eyes and tells her.

"That woman was like us."

"She was hardly like us, Kai. Her augmentations were standard issue and years out of date. Not to mention she's a civilian with no combat training. There are a lot of people like that in Lorelei. They get fed up with technomancers and adepts and all the meaningless jurisdictions we impose on them, so they leave and find someplace where they can be left alone."

Kai glares at her much to Wren's amusement. She knows very well that is not even remotely what he means by his statement. The woman at the apartment is probably as far divergent from them as any hexen might be, but the fact remains that she is not a hexen. So why?

"I do not understand how someone like us can be with a hexen."

Interracial couplings between hexen and human+ were unheard of. It just was not done. How can two people with such different backgrounds and philosophies come together? How can they form any kind of functional relationship when one party is the fleshy embodiment of chaos while the other is the product of carefully executed science? It would never work. It would be like trying to marry light and darkness, fire and ice, earth and air. They could never coexist.

Just as he is about to think himself into a tizzy, Wren interrupts his thoughts.

"Is that all?"

Kai's eyes flash open, a storm on his brow.

"Is that not enough?"

"It may be hard to understand, but it isn't our business."

"It isn't right."

"You might be right," she says, a small smile on her face as she keeps a hold on his wrist. "But the heart wants what it wants, and sometimes not even we have a say in which direction the tides of our affections flow."

"And look what it's gotten her. A decrepit home and a kidnapped baby who, for all we know, may already be dead because of someone just like the woman she married."

"No, not like the woman she married," says Wren firmly. "There is a big difference between a witch who steals and kills babies, and a witch who walks into her home to find technomancers and instead of going on the offensive, she tries to make a shield. Those are two witches who couldn't be any more different, and if Magdalena feels Olga is her soulmate, who are we to judge her for it?"

"So, she sought refuge in chaos?"

"It's not like the League has given her many options. Her relationship would be condemned anywhere else, and in some countries, her younger daughter would have been taken from her the moment she started demonstrating magical ability."

"Deriva doesn't hunt witches."

"It still isn't legal to marry one. And the only reason we don't hunt witches is because most sea witches are pretty mundane, but we do hunt them. My father killed one after..." She trails off biting her lip. "Look, all I'm saying is they wouldn't have been safe even in Deriva, and they love each other. Is that such a crime?"

He huffs, turning his face away from her and closing his eyes. Yes...No...Maybe... He hasn't a clue.

"Kai, about what happened on the roof, I—"

"That was a mistake."

"Look, I realize Xipilli can be a total ass at times, but you really don't need to—"

"Enough! We are not discussing this."

"Wow. Okay. I didn't realize you disliked me that much."

He turns his head and finds her expression blocked off, eyes shuttered and a false smile on her lips. She ducks around him.

"Welp, glad we cleared that up."

I am an idiot, he thinks, realizing how unnecessarily cruel his words must have sounded. He grabs her jacket sleeve.

"That's not it," he insists.

"Let go!"

"I do not dislike you, Wren."

"Then why—"

"This is not the time or place to be discussing this."

"Well, too bad. I want to discuss it."

"You are being ri—"

"Ridiculous," she finishes for him. "Yeah, what else is new?"

He faces her then, meeting her eye to eye for the first time in months, every iota of his attention on her.

"Wren, please," he says firmly.

"What! You've barely looked me in the eye this whole time. I get it. The rooftop was probably my fault, but it's not like I planned it, and don't people usually talk about these kinds of things? I don't know. It's not like I've ever actually done something like that before."

The brakes slam down on his racing mind. Shame boils up from his stomach. He is surprised by this revelation. He shouldn't be surprised by this revelation. Rumors were terrible things to listen to, and Miyazaki principles would dictate all such gossip be deemed false until proven factual, but the whispers that followed her! Of her Firefly training, of the kinds of things such students are taught and supposedly encouraged to practice, her absolute ease around both boys and girls, of her easy charm, trusting personality, and overly affectionate mannerisms with others, her open countenance, her sugary teasing, and flirtatious disposition. He suspected most of the slander was a result of jealous girls and boys who she had turned away, slighted suitors trying to shame her, but to hear he was Wren Nocturne's first kiss... it's unfathomable. Surely, she should have gotten her first kiss from someone better than him?

"Y-you...That was...I was your first—"

Her left eyebrow raises at him incredulously before she laughs, boisterous and full and far too loud considering they're in the middle of a hunt.

"You think I make a habit of kissing people under the moonlight on isolated rooftops to sneak things into their pockets? Despite popular belief, Firefly potentials are supposed to guard their firsts very closely in order to bolster their worth. My stepmother would have flayed me alive if I'd done anything to diminish my value to her. Though quite frankly when you grow up learning about the 'proper technique' for those kinds of things, it kind of makes you want to avoid them like the plague. I was innocent before you stole away my first kiss, thank you very much." She tuts feigning annoyance and turning her head in mock anger.

His mind still reeling, he shakes the stupid out of his ears and refilters her words before responding.

"I-I'm sorry."

The smirk drops from her expression, and he continues his thought before she can voice any protests.

"My behavior was appalling. It was ungentlemanly and ill-mannered, and I beg your forgiveness if it caused you distress." As he speaks, he turns around to face the girl, bowing before her, bent nearly in half at the waist. "This prince should never have stolen such a precious moment from you without your due permission."

There is a sharp intake of breath from Wren, and then she sputters out protests at his actions.

"Kai, there's no reason to apologize, especially not so formally."

"You are owed as much," he says, without looking up, determined to stay here for as long as he needs until she understands this is no small matter to him.

Eventually, he feels her hands settle on his shoulders, coaxing him to straighten back up. Her eyes are soft and open, the greens in them darkened to the color of a forest floor while the blues highlight them in muted sapphire. He tenses as she steps into his space, but he doesn't retreat.

"The only thing that caused me distress was my dear brother being his usual angry self."

"I did not ask your permission."

"You didn't have to. You had it."

Her hands slide down his arms, her fingertips barely registering against his skin under the layers of his leather coat and long-sleeved shirt. Her fingers ghost over the back of his hands, and he twists his wrists so their palms touch. She pauses, her hands hovering over his.

"Regardless. It would have been proper to do so."

She smiles, but it doesn't reach her eyes.

"You would be surprised how many people ask even though they have no intention of relenting when they're told 'no.'"

He remembers the advance from Oswald and understands plainly that for her that was not an anomaly. Anger tings beneath the surface at this, but Wren remains ever unfazed. Clearly such individuals were unworthy of the barest respect, and he hopes deeply that they paid for their foolishness tenfold.

"I'm sure I don't have to ask how you made the clarification to them," he says.

She winks at him, a laugh falling from her lips.

"How do you think I built up such a good left hook?" She twirls away from him, rocking to a stop on the balls of her feet, hands behind her back and looking for all the world like a plotting pixie. "Though really, Kaito, if one of us should be apologizing for their behavior, it's me. How dare I infringe upon the virtue of Murasaki's most reputable Prince Kaito! This one humbly apologizes if she stole away his honor."

Indignation rises in him.

"Don't be absurd!"

She practically bounces in excitement.

"Oh, was I not his highness's first kiss? Oh, I simply must hear this story."

He shakes his head and stomps away firmly set to ignore her. She follows his trek through the woods, still teasing him but also looking around.

"Aww, Kai! Come on. I promise I won't tease. Was it a boy or a girl? I like both myself."

"Wren, this is not endearing."

"How old were you?"

"Drop it!"

"Was it a dare? It was a dare, wasn't it?"

"Wren..." he growls out.

She starts her next question, but abruptly stops herself as a noise to their left reaches them.

"Did you hear that?"

"Yes."

Kai unsheathes Tsukuyomi and Amatsu, hooking them into their appropriate ports but not quite activating them yet while Wren unbuckles Mångata from its place at her waist.

SNAP!

The sound of a branch breaking cracks through the air. Both teens tense, preparing for an attack as the leaves begin to part. A clawed foot appears followed quickly by the orange body of a fox. Wren and Kai drop out of their battle-ready stance. Wren chuckles, Kai feeling more than a little foolish for not realizing what it was.

"Well, that was anticlimactic."

"Keep your weapon ready, next time it might—"

A high-pitched shriek and an arc of forest debris comes from behind them, and a monster roughly the size of an imp barrels toward them. With a screech of power, *Mångata's twin beams scream into existence, and Wren spins the weapon in her hands. The creature reels backward and away from the bright flash of energy.*

Kai activates his own blades and lunges forward. The chimera's mismatched wings flap violently, dodging around Kai's swords. It hisses at them, smoke puffing from its mouth and pollutes the air around them. When the smoke clears, the chimera is nowhere in sight.

"Wren," he calls simply, and Wren understands, setting her back against his. Open and alert, they scan their surroundings. The fox is long gone, but the feeling of something thick sits heavy in the ozone around them. The shriek sounds again. One of Mångata's beams flies past Kai's left hand side to parry a set of mismatched claws, one cat's claw and one vulture's talon. He stabs Amatsu to his right to head off a second chimera aiming for Wren's flank as she bends out of the way.

The two creatures flit about them, and the two technomancers move in cautious sync with one another. While no longer entirely back-to-back, they guard one another's blind spots as they go on the offensive. For several tense minutes, they fend off attack after attack, moving in and out of each other's space. At some point, Kai ducks down so Wren can spin Mångata overhead like helicopter blades, throwing the weapon high enough to slice into the flesh of one of the chimera. Enraged, the creature dives for them. Wren catches her weapon and throws herself sideways as Kai delivers an uppercut, effectively slicing the creature in two. The monstrosity falls dead and in pieces to the ground as the second shrieks toward Wren. It lands on top of her, pressing down into the hilt of her weapon and pulling as though trying to snatch it out of her hands. She holds fast, kicking at the creature with her right leg only to receive a nasty peck to her calf. Kai throws Amatsu from his hand. The blade stabs the creature, knocking it away from Wren and embedding it into the ground. Wren turns over, whacks her blade down like a flyswatter, and Mångata lops the beast's head off. With the mechanical cables connecting the sword's hilt into his forearm, Kai pulls Amatsu out of the corpse and reels it back to his hand.

Despite the oozing gash on her leg, Wren stands firm, kicking the downed monster nearest to her.

"Nasty little pieces of work, huh?"

Kaito examines the one he slashed in half. A cat's head stitched to a torso that is half possum, half canine, with mismatched leathery wings. One of its front arms looks like it belonged to a primate while the other looks like a lobster claw. Both of the hind legs seem to come from a vulture or large bird of prey. Wren's is equally grotesque, a weird amalgamation of squirrel, rodent, bird, and wild dog with a head that looks a hell of a lot like an eagle.

"Who the hell put these things together?"

As Wren voices the question, a strange light begins to leak out of the creatures' seams. One glows purple while the other glows with a strange burnt amber texture. The light leaks from their bodies before forming a single sphere of blackened energy. It hovers in the air for a moment before the molten mixture of void-like magical energy hightails it forward through the woods.

Kai takes a split second to look from the orb to Wren's leg.

"Go after it. I'll be right behind you."

And he gives chase.

The disc of darkness weaves in and out of the trees, and he follows as closely as his augmented legs can carry him until the terrain shifts to hard asphalt and city streets. He barrels through the underbrush, tracking the thing while listening for the sound of Wren behind him. Kai's breath comes in short bursts as his lungs begin to feel the strain of running at top speed for so long, but he pushes himself forward, toward the chimera, toward its source, toward the witch he wants to kill. He runs past crumbling buildings in this deserted part of the city, ghosts made of concrete and glass.

He only comes to a stop when the cement below his feet takes an abrupt dive downward, a yawning mouth framed by the metropolis' metal bones. The orb of void energy tanks into a steep descent down the shrapnel ridden slope. He is about to drive Amatsu into the cement wall to lower himself down in an improvised rock-climbing maneuver with his weapons' cables when he hears Wren catching up behind him. Wren, limping from the chimera's beak, trips over a crack in the asphalt, and she goes careening forward with a yelp. Just as she is about to stumble past him and into the pit, Kai catches her by the back of her jacket to stop her from rolling completely off the edge of an apparent entrance to the catacombs below Lorelei.

"Shit!"

The sudden arrest in momentum throws both of them onto the hard ground, but the loose gravel sends them over the edge and down the jagged slope. They knock and swing into each other as they tumble. Dirt flies into Kai's face and mouth as the world spins violently around him before he comes to a sudden jarring but somehow cushioned halt at the bottom of the incline while his swords clatter noisily around them, and Kai is only thankful they weren't accidentally sliced to ribbons by his own blades or stabbed by the metal bars sticking out of the street's cross-section. He's a little cut up, but the contusions are minor. Not enough to merit wasting medical supplies.

A low moan reaches his ear from something soft below him. "Ugh..."

When he realizes Wren is underneath him, he bolts upright and back to let her breathe.

"*Shimata!* Wren, are you okay?"

Wren coughs as the weight of Kai's body, having landed wholly on top of her, disappears. Her leg dangles over the edge of a watery pool. Blood drips sluggishly from the injury into the muddy water.

"I'm okay," she says moving to sit up with a wince before a shit-eating grin breaks out across her face. "At least, I don't think anything is broken. This hardware comes in handy from time to time."

She gently knocks against one of the exposed nodes on her collarbone with her prosthetic hand to make a dulled metallic thunking sound. She then immediately reaches for her pant leg and tears the fabric away from where the beak had pecked her. He sheathes his weapons and scans her up and down with his sights as she palpates the bone. As she said, nothing is broken, but the both of them will be plenty bruised up come morning. The wound on her leg looks ugly, seeping blood and a black ooze, no doubt from the chimera.

"Gross," she says, squeezing around the hole in her leg to push the black substance out, cleaning it with her sleeve before she looks up at him. "There's a stim in my pack. Do you mind?"

He looks around and spots her satchel in the mud several feet from them. He walks over to it, wincing as his body protests the movement, and digs through its contents until he finds the aforementioned stim. He takes it, along with the pack, over to where she is sitting. Thankfully, she strapped her weapon back to her belt while they had been running, so it hadn't gone anywhere during their tumble into the underground.

While he was retrieving the stim, Wren stripped off her boot and stocking to submerge the injury in the water, scrubbing the blood and gunk out of it. When she finishes washing it, he powers up the stim and injects the medicine into her injured leg. She hisses a bit, but when the injury begins to close, she shakes it out and rolls back up to her feet. He gives her the space to move, backing up and looking around.

Well, the un-glowing ball is gone and to who knows where.

The room they've landed in looks like an isolated sepulcher without any entrances or exits. He tilts his head to peer up at the moonlight streaming in from the opening to the cave they have tumbled into. The height of it makes him dizzy, considering the unexpected and rather painful drop down. With his night vision active, he can make out the bones and skeletons that line the walls and the engravings etched into the stone, runic sigils for journey and transformation. Judging from the steep angle of their descent, he doesn't imagine they will be able to climb their way out very easily without spelunking equipment of which they have none. Which, now that he thinks of it, was probably a huge error on all their parts even if they hadn't planned on entering the underground.

He activates his neural comms and contacts his brother using his external comm unit so Wren can see and hear the conversation.

"Hikaru."

"Ototo? Where are you? Your reception is broken up."

"We killed a pair of chimera. Their life sources led us to a precipice into the catacombs which unfortunately, we've fallen into. I have a feeling they were heading for the witch we are looking for."

"You're stuck underground!" Xipilli's voice reaches him. "Where's my sister?"

"Lady Nocturne is here."

"We too have encountered some of those miserable little creatures," says Hikaru. "Much to the same effect. However, the entrance they took into the catacombs proves unpassable. We are circling around to a different entrance. We'll gather equipment and try to find you underground. Some parts of the catacombs are more maze-like than anything else. Xipilli is sending Wren a map now."

"That will have to work."

There is a chime of a file downloading. Wren opens up her left hand and activates a holographic map of Lorelei and overlays it with a known map of the catacombs.

"So, this is where we fell from," she says, pointing toward a portion of the city highlighted in red, an abandoned district. "It looks like the map we have of the catacombs doesn't have anything listed in that area. We must be over a section built by hexen."

"Well, that's helpful," says Xipilli.

Kai points to the map.

"It would make sense for our witch to try and hide in an undocumented portion of the catacombs. We may very well find them before you even get down here."

"Alright. Be careful down there."

"Affirmative."

Kai hangs up the call and turns back to Wren, once again standing and looking disdainfully around. She shudders, and he wonders what thought might have incurred that reaction from her.

"So, any ideas how we get out of here?" she asks when she too observes there are apparently no entrances and exits to the chamber they are in.

"I'm afraid I don't have much experience escaping tombs."

His deadpan expression would typically be enough to cow anyone for asking such an obvious question, but Wren takes it in stride, even going so far as to turn to him, wide eyed with a laugh hovering on her lips.

"His highness has jokes!"

He ignores her.

"There is either a secret door, or we will have to blast our way out."

Wren makes a small noise of agreement in the back of her throat and turns off the holo. She puffs her cheeks out at him and taps her temple as though in thought. Then she snaps her fingers as though an idea just occurred to her before stooping to pick up a piece of petrified bone from the floor. She takes several steps back toward the pool of water and tosses the rock into it. The rock sinks much farther than he was expecting.

"Underground tunnels flood all the time in towns that are on a relatively low sea-level like Lorelei. It's why Deriva has never buried its dead. Most families opt for cremation or a mausoleum storage until the sun turns the corpse to ash. Though the noble families set their loved ones out to sea. Anyway, when I was washing my leg earlier, I noticed it was deeper than I thought it would be."

She begins to take off her other boot and stocking, setting them beside their twins. Then her jacket comes off. This doesn't alarm him so much. It's when she reaches to unbuckle her belt, pants, and top that his face heats up entirely against his will, and he turns away from her.

"What are you doing?"

"Well, I'm not going swimming with a whole bunch of layers on. Unless of course, you plan on scouting out the water, but I figure between the two of us the islander might be more adept at diving."

"You don't have a bodysuit."

"Lorelei is in the middle of a wilderness. I'm sorry I wasn't prepared for scuba diving."

"Can you even swim with your leg injured?"

"Oh." She seems taken off guard by his concern. "It's fine. I've gone deep sea diving with worse. Besides, my tech will pretty much nullify it."

He keeps his eyes firmly fixated on the wall in front of him, trying his best to make himself deaf to the sound of her clothes rustling as she removes them.

"You can turn around. I'm not completely indecent."

In nothing but her underwear and a camisole, Wren busies herself with getting ready to go underwater, completely unbothered by his presence. He restricts himself to looking only at her face, hands, or feet as she moves around.

"You're sure you can swim alright?"

"I'm fine, Kai."

Her leg does seem better; she isn't limping, at least. He notices for the first time the brass anklets flush with the skin around her ankles. She sits down and begins tampering with the devices on her ankles. His sights whirl as he analyzes the tech. Derivan made leg enhancements of some sort. He notices the faint scarring of the skin around her tech as though they were integrated as the result of injury. He almost opens his mouth to ask, but then he remembers it isn't any of his business, nor is it his place to ask something so personal of her.

They pulse to life with the aquatic-blue glow typical of Deriva tech. From the base of the anklets extend twin beams of golden light. They fold over her feet and flare out from her toes like flippers, and when the filmy, iridescent structures are complete, the anklets make a locking sound and Wren stands back up, her feet now encased in a layer of her own lifeforce, harnessed and shaped to help her swim. She goes back to her utility belt and pulls a rebreather out of one of the pockets and a set of goggles out of another.

She sets the rebreather in her mouth and the goggles over her eyes. They click into place, connecting to one of her neural nodes. Wren wades into the water as though descending steps. She takes a deep breath and disappears under the inky depths.

A few tense moments later, she resurfaces.

"There's a tunnel alright. Looks like we'll have to swim out of here. I'll go down and see how far the tunnel is flooded. Hopefully, it isn't far. How long can you hold your breath?"

"Three and a half minutes."

"I can hold my breath for about eight. If the tunnel is much longer than that, we can talk about trading off the rebreather. Unless of course you have your own?"

He shakes his head.

"No problem. I'll be back."

"Be careful."

"Always," she says, throwing him the same look framed by her middle and index finger before she disappears under the surface.

Kai settles in and begins comparing the maps again while she is gone. He marks off the locations of each of the kidnappings. He finds, unsurprisingly, that the locations create a fairly even circumference. He connects them in his head space, looking for pentagrams, runes, alchemical symbols, anything that may pinpoint a possible location for the witch to be working in. After several minutes of work, he finds it. Two overlapping triangles, and if he leaves the bottom two points unconnected, he has in front of him the alchemical symbol for arsenic.

He looks to the point where the triangular points overlap and looks for the central point. He finishes sending the marked point to Hikaru just as Wren resurfaces approximately thirty minutes later.

"So good news, the other side is nice and dry. Bad news, it's a way's off. Are you comfortable swimming for that long without surfacing?"

He nods. Kai would never compare himself to a Derivan adept when it comes to swimming prowess, but he's comfortable in the water and scored decently in comparison to Wren, her brother, and the other Derivan potentials during the summit on underwater demonstrations.

He stands up and begins to divest himself of his jacket, boots, and socks. He pauses before deciding it would be best to follow her lead and also rids himself of his leather pants and outer vest. He tucks his clothes into his pack and ties his boots to the straps while Wren does the same.

Before he follows her under, she turns to him, offering the

rebreather.

"Do you know how to use one of these?"

"It is fairly self-explanatory."

"Yes, yes, you're very astute. Make sure you exhale completely through it before you breathe in. Whenever you need to trade off, tap three times on my arm or leg, and I'll give it to you. I'll do the same to you if I need it."

"Understood."

They dive together with Kai holding the rebreather in his mouth.

They make their way along slowly, switching who has the rebreather every few minutes until finally they break the surface on the far side. Wren takes back the rebreather and wrings out her hair and camisole before pulling her clothes out of her pack.

"I found the origin point of the creatures."

She turns her head to look at him as she pulls her jeans back up. "Oh yeah? Where do you think?"

When they finish dressing, he pulls up a holo screen and shows her where he believes the rituals are taking place. They estimate a direction and follow it, but navigating the catacombs is easier said than done.

The catacombs are a veritable maze. They encounter dead ends and roundabouts. They find themselves turned around on several occasions, and at some point after she insists they've passed the same arrangement of skeletons three times, Wren tries to take down a wall with Mångata which Kai prevents, not wanting to disturb the dead any more than their presence here requires. Nevermind the possibility of a cave in.

Eventually though, they come to a new chamber filled with the carcasses of dead beasts. Bats, birds of prey, cattle, cats, dogs, many of them have been dissected and quite a few are missing their heads and various limbs.

"Looks like chimera weren't the only thing our witch was trying to bring to life."

"Thankfully, they were unsuccessful."

At the center of the room, a summoning circle pulses with

black energy. There are also several cages around the room, each one containing some monstrosity Kai has never seen in real life. A kenku, a babadook, a kitsune, even a displacer beast, all creatures that he's read about in books. Creatures from alternate dimensions called to the waking plane via dark summoning witchcraft. It is a small blessing each netherbeast is dead at the bottom of the cage, all of them twisted and warped in ways no creature could survive. Faulty summonings cause as much pain to the summoned creature as they do to the fabric of reality.

Except for one.

A mewling growl draws their attention to an occupied cage, an animal still alive. *No*, Kai thinks correcting himself, *a netherbeast still living.* A large cat-like creature drips with viridian energy. The cat lies limp at the bottom of its cage, its tail barely twitching and its head lolling to the side, a chain wound tight around its neck glowing with magic black as pitch sapping the beast's strength.

Kai unsheathes Tsukuyomi, prepared to put the animal out of its misery, but Wren stops him.

"Wait," she calls as she rushes over to the cage.

Mångata's blade makes quick work of the lock and even though the creature begins to snarl at her, Wren makes her way into the tight space to kneel next to the large feline. Wren puts Mångata on the ground and lifts the chain from the beast's neck, and the netherbeast lets out a wild roar.

"It's okay," she says, soothing the creature. "I'm not going to hurt you."

She puts her hand on the beast's head and strokes down gently. Kai tenses as the beast's eyes open, yellow and phosphorescent in the dim light of the cavern.

"Wren, what are you doing? Just kill it."

"I don't think it's dangerous."

She gives it another stroke with her fingertips, and the creature's eyes slide shut almost as if it were enjoying the attention. She mutters something to the animal that Kai doesn't quite catch, something like "big fluffy house cat."

"Of course, it's dangerous. It's a summoning creature."

"It's fine."

The chain falls to the floor, and Wren releases the binding circle the witch etched into the ground. Within a split second, Wren is knocked backward into Kaito as the animal bolts upright. He catches her with a shallow grunt, pulls her back, and draws Amatsu as the giant feline takes off.

"Kai, don't!"

He throws Amatsu at the beast. The monster zips under the blade's arc and dives with a loud mewl into a dimension circle, Amatsu embedding itself into the center of the array. Wren pulls away from Kaito and closes the portal, nullifying the array. Kai pulls on the cable that connects him to Amatsu and the tanto whips up and back into his palm.

"I can't believe you just let it go. What if it kills someone?"

He is livid with her, but she doesn't seem even remotely concerned by the fact that she just violated at least four separate technomancer principles.

"I don't think it will."

"You can't know that."

"It went back home, Kai. It won't hurt anyone."

He is about to say something else when high-pitched laughter greets them from the next room followed by the beginnings of a chant. A lurid ebony smoke seeps from the passageway. They share a look, and Kai allows Wren to take point, as the smaller of the two of them. As she goes, he sets a virtual parameter tracing the caverns around them.

He closes his eyes and opens them to a world lined with coding.

Kai's virtual form steps into the large chamber that opens beyond the tunnel. At its center stands a hooded figure, a knife in hand. The code reads hexen, a girl not much older than they, and a witch, the runic indicia on her skin highlighted on his scans. Wrapped in a bundle on the floor is the infant, colicky and fussy but very much alive. No doubt the little thing is hungry and cold and nearly frightened to death being away from its mothers for so long. Additionally, Kai traces the limp body of a new chimera set to be made, similar in size to the two they killed.

Kai relays this information to Wren via the holo on her Mano, and his partner steps around the corner just as the witch raises an athame, a curved blade in the style of a scimitar, to kill the babe. Kai strikes first. Tsukuyomi deflecting the knife from the virtual realm.

"Argh!"

Saibāki lights up the woman's arm, a painful infusion of raw technomancy that makes her skin blister. He slashes again aiming for her head, but she ducks down to avoid his attack.

"Why hello!"

The chimera he thought still unanimated springs up. He tries to map it, but the beast is outside his scopes, his blade ineffective on a creature that can't be mapped. It attacks his virtual form. Just before its jaws close on his coding, he deactivates his VR, opens his eyes, and rushes into the room.

Wren is already there.

She moves around the baby, aiming a sweeping uppercut at the witch. The witch's hood is knocked from her face to reveal long copper hair and pale youthful features. She would look like an ordinary teenage girl, unaugmented and unremarkable, were it not for the obsidian indicia decorating her throat and the pair of goat's horns apparently embedded into her temples. The alchemical symbol for arsenic/transmutation and extreme body modification.

Witch!

"I don't remember inviting any guests to this party."

She laughs in Wren's face as Mångata spins in her hands the beams just barely missing the witch each time.

"Sorry," calls Wren in return. "I've always been fond of gate-crashing."

"Hmm. Perhaps I should call my bouncer then."

The girl clicks her fingers, and the chimera whirls on Wren. She blocks its attacks while Kai presses in on the witch. Amatsu whistles through the air as he throws her, and there is a clash of steel on steel against the girl's athame. Tsukuyomi in hand, Kai closes the distance between himself and the witch. She manages to deflect two more of his attacks, but his superior swordsmanship wins out. The third strike nails her in the shoulder.

"Jerk!" she cries out and shimmers out of existence as his blades slash the space she once occupied.

She reappears in the center of the summoning circle by the baby. She picks up the child as another chimera appears to take Kai's attention just as Wren kills her chimera.

"Identify yourself, witch," shouts Wren.

"Summer Helsdottir at your service."

The hexen gives them a sarcastic bow, and Kai offs the chimera, slashing its head from its body.

"Helsdottir!" shouts Kai. "You are under arrest for murder, kidnapping, and the illegal production of chimera. Put down the child and surrender before I carve you in two."

She turns her attention to Kai, her eyes black as coal. She gives him a twisted expression and licks her lips and hums like a hungry cat.

"Ask me nicely, handsome. I'll let you arrest me all you want, Älskling. Virgin sacrifices are always the most potent."

She extends her hand out and void magic shoots from her fingers at them. Kai blocks the attack, both of his swords crossed in front of him while Wren leaps out of the way of the attack, running toward the witch. Wren strikes at Summer who laughs in response and dances out of the way, still holding the baby.

"Give her back!" shouts Wren, brandishing Mångata. Summer holds the babe in front of her. The child's screams intensify.

"Ah ah ah. You don't want to hurt the little tyke, do you?"

Kai rushes her, swords flashing, and she extends her hand again and shouts.

"*Förstöra!*"

Kai finds himself thrust backward. The noise of shattering rock and debris floods his ears as Summer disappears into the ether. He hits the cavern wall, and the world around him goes dark.

Wren's voice shouting his name is the last thing he hears.

I got my period for the first time today. By the traditions of my mother's people, I'm not a kid anymore. Not of marriageable age, thank Gods, but not a child.

My mother sat me down, and we talked for a very long time about men and women and love. About how men and women make love. About how women and women make love. About how sometimes others will use love as an excuse to pressure me into doing certain things. And the entirety of that conversation, I can narrow down into one sentence.

Men are animals.

Entitlement is the first thing a boy learns growing up rich. He thinks he owns everything around him, and if he doesn't, surely he can just buy it. Some girls think this way too, but they're different about it. A girl's affections are gentler, more inclined toward invitation rather than possession. But boys, men... if they can't control something, they try to tame it, and if they can't tame it, they try to break it.

Mama, really shouldn't worry so much. I'm never going to fall in love! Not with a boy. Not with a girl. Not with anyone.

An Entry from Wren's Diary. Age 10
3rd Day in the Month of Hearths, 1854 A.P.

17
THE WHEEL OF FORTUNE PART 3

"KAI...KAI...CAN YOU HEAR ME? *AYE CABRON,* wake up!"

Consciousness comes painfully slow. The sound of water dripping. A voice calling his name, comforting in a strange way. His head feels like it has been split open, and his back is one big bruise. His eyes open to the glow of Wren's prosthetic hand shining in his face. The light burns his retina, and he flinches away.

"Thank the machine, he lives."

"Please, get that light out of my face." His voice is rough, dry. Speaking is like rubbing sandpaper over his vocal cords.

"And the prince is more frog when he wakes up from a nap. Don't worry. Your pupils are fine, and you don't have a concussion."

Wren's narration of his present state of being is not endearing in the slightest. As he is working to sit himself up, she places a hand at his back just under his shoulder blades where it feels like most of the damage is and holds a water bottle to his lips.

"Here. Drink this."

He does, without complaint, taking a few small sips of the cool liquid before turning his head away.

"Better?"

He swallows, glad his throat is no longer dry and scratchy.

"What happened?"

"She broke her own circle and shimmered out with the infant in hand. The backlash threw you against the wall. You've been unconscious for nearly an hour."

"An hour!"

"She brought the roof down on top of us on her way out. I've been trying to send a signal out to Xipilli and your brother, but I don't know if anything is getting through. I'm afraid we're stuck for the moment."

Stuck? Trapped, she means.

Bile rises in his throat. Dread boils up into the space behind his thoughts. His breath becomes strained as adrenaline floods his system. He has to move, to seek, to escape. An imperative he must follow. Get out.

Kaito shuffles his way to standing, his movements stuttered and jerky, so much so that Wren reacts worriedly to his efforts.

"Whoa, whoa, easy." She puts a hand under his arm and tries to help him up, but he shoves her away and uses the wall instead. "Hey, I'm just trying to help."

"I do not need your help."

He reaches back into his pack and pulls out the medi-stim. Without much preamble, he charges the device and slams the injection into the meat of his thigh, gritting his teeth as the needle pierces his skin. The nanobots make their way through his bloodstream, and already his pain diminishes, the bruising in his back dissipating, but the anxiety remains wound tight and thick in his stomach, nausea threatening to spill out mouth.

"Better?" she asks, one eyebrow raised at him incredulously.

"I'm fine!" He grunts at her, unfounded irritation, but the best he is capable of at present. He doesn't have the time or patience for propriety. Get out. He needs to get out. The ceiling is dark. The walls are dark. There's rubble everywhere. Water dripping somewhere, loud and muted at once. The drip, drip, drip of it like someone is flicking his synapses with their pinkie.

"Oh good, I would hate to watch you swallow your pride asking for help. Glad you are entirely self-sufficient, your highness."

Her mocking tone strikes an ugly chord in him, biting and sharp like the sour note at the end of a prelude.

"You know," he says through clenched teeth. "Anyone with manners would know to leave well enough alone when they aren't wanted."

"I find manners superfluous at best, downright dishonest at worst."

"Wren, why are you so purposefully irritating?"

"So long as it keeps you conscious and lucid, I'm happy to be."

"I am not in any danger of fainting."

"I'm not worried about you fainting, your highness."

His step falters, and he winces, head throbbing once again. She is there, instantly at his side, though she has the presence of mind not to touch him. The world is spinning. Whirling shadows, his night vision flickering on and off. Green then black then green then black. The edges of Wren's face blurs in the dark.

"Hey, hey, hey, just breathe for me, alright? You'll feel better if you breathe."

Every fiber of his being wants to fight the logic she's trying to instill in him, but the irritation from before keeps the panic at bay, so he listens.

"That's it. Deep breaths."

She guides him. The words are a half-song, light and airy. Gentle in the way his mother once calmed him as a child, so he follows her lead. As his lungs expand and contract, the panic subsides until he feels more level-headed.

"Better?"

He still refuses to look at her.

"I am fine."

"Mmm. Perhaps you should sit down."

"We are somewhat in a position where time is of the essence, don't you think?"

"To the contrary, I managed to set a tracker on Helsdottir, and I don't think there is very much we can do about this situation other than wait it out for now. Resting would not be the end of the world. In fact, we should probably sleep while we can."

"I will find no rest here."

"Hikaru and Xipilli will find us."

"Clearly, you haven't any lack of confidence."

"I trust my brother. I think you trust yours as well."

"I do."

"Then?"

The silence stretches. Kai's jaw clenches, and his fists tighten where they support him against the wall. He closes his eyes and breathes as the panic once again tries to claw itself higher into his being. The thought of being entombed and buried alive under a crumbling city of outcasts more terrifying than facing an army of ghosts. He screws his eyes shut and wills the claustrophobia away.

"My father was buried alive by a witch. His body never recovered."

He doesn't look at Wren. Doesn't want to see the disappointment no doubt gracing her face at his weakness. He just keeps scanning, keeps looking, keeps hoping that she's wrong and that they aren't trapped here.

"Hey..." she calls softly, her voice washing over him in a gentle cascade. He wonders idly if she is using a pheromone on him to set him in a synthetic ease, but then he remembers Wren is so naturally charismatic, she would have little need for such enhancements. His eyes rise to meet hers, and nothing he expected to find is there. "We aren't going to die down here."

"Optimism is for fools."

"Then call me a fool, your highness. I'll even dance and juggle for you if you'd like."

"Wren, be serious."

"Yeah, you're right. I'm rubbish at juggling, but I can dance." She sets a hand on his shoulder, gripping into the leather of his jacket, and tugs. "Come here."

He allows her to guide him to where she has set their packs down on the ground. She turns off the light on her prosthetic hand and pulls an emergency glow stick from her pack. She cracks it and the stick alights with a blue glow bright enough to nullify his need for night vision at least in their immediate vicinity.

He settles himself carefully against the wall, wincing only a bit as the lingering bruises press against the hard surface.

"It's okay to be scared of things, you know. I'm terrified of heights. When we fell down that drop, I thought I was going to have a heart attack. Here, eat this. Can't have you starving to death on me."

She tosses him a ration from her pack and gets up to look around further. He catches it easily, wondering why she feels the need to take care of him. They may be allies, but she has no responsibility to him. He doesn't voice this, however, choosing instead to take a bite from the ration, chewing slowly and swallowing before he resumes their conversation.

"Fear is a weakness."

Wren has moved away from where he is sitting. He can see her light flitting back and forth in the darkness from where he sits. After a prolonged period of silence, he assumes she didn't hear him, but then her voice reaches him from the opposite side of the cavern.

"If there was nothing to be afraid of, there would be no reason to be brave. Just like we wouldn't know happiness if we didn't know sadness, love if we didn't know longing, excitement if we didn't know boredom. Life would be pretty lackluster, I think, if that was the case."

"Such things are not suitable for a technomancer."

Wren's expression saddens at this, but she is far enough away in the dark that he doesn't quite see her expression fall. It seems like she is about to comment when her comm unit buzzes.

She hurries over to answer it. Her brother's face appears on the screen, staticky, his worry apparent despite that.

"Xipilli! Did you see my messages?"

"Yes, you _ound the hex_n."

"Yes, some mad bitch by the name of Summer Helsdottir. She got away and dropped the roof down on top of us. We're okay. We're just trapped. Did you get the coordinates I sent you?"

"Yes, Hikaru a_d I are on our way. We j__t don't know h_ long it __ll take to _ig you out."

Somehow, Wren is able to understand despite the broken connection.

"No, go after the witch. I managed to put a tracking chip on the infant. She's on the run above ground."

"Wr_n, don't be __diculous!"

"We can wait! The baby cannot. She is going to sacrifice her, Xipilli! Find the bitch and take her down, do you hear me?"

There is nothing but static and a broken slur of words in response. Wren curses in Derivan and raises the comm above her head, looking for a better signal.

"Lady Wren." Hikaru's face appears on the comm screen as the call reconnects. "May I sp_k with Kai_o?"

She nods as Kai makes his way over to her.

"Aniki?"

"Ka_to, are you alr__ht?"

"I am well. We are managing."

"G__d," answers his brother. "Try t_ get som_ r_st. We will be t_ere as soon as we c_n."

"Hikaru, you should go after the hexen. We will be fine for the moment."

"Ve_y wel_. Xipi_ has the trace. We will have yo_ out as so_n as we c_n. It may be sev_ral h_urs. Morn_ng at the la_est."

Kai nods. For all that his brother looks calm and put together, Kai knows his being trapped underground disturbs Hikaru as much if not more so than it disturbs Kaito. It's a different type of disconcerting when it's your family at risk rather than yourself. Hikaru passes the comm back to Xipilli, and the man passes on one last reassurance to his sister. Xipilli's eyes then turn to Kaito, but the predictable threat on his lips doesn't make it out before the connection is lost.

The call ended, Wren nearly wilts with relief, sliding down the wall she was just leaning against as though the adrenaline just went out of her. Looking at her now, he notices the worry lines on her face, the bruising around her neck and arms, and the shivering starting to envelop her form.

She's sopping wet, soaked from head to toe. She must have been thrown into the nearby pool. And this whole time she's been putting on a strong front for his sake. Shame fills him. He failed to pay proper attention to his case partner, too busy having his own private panic attack to notice she too might have need for help.

"Are you hurt?"

She shakes her head.

"The stim I took earlier is still working. Probably why I didn't pass out during the blast. The bruising should go down in a few more minutes."

"Are you cold?"

"I'm fine, your highness."

A full-bodied shiver racks her form. Right...he totally believes that.

Caught in the lie, she twists her lips into a simper and curls into herself. Her lips are turning blue.

Kai removes his leather jacket and offers it to her.

"You're shivering. Your clothes are soaked through. Take it before you become ill."

She eyes it suspiciously, but he merely holds it out to her in insistence. She takes it with a roll of her eyes and rises. He averts his gaze as she removes her wet clothing.

"Kaito is too much of a gentleman. It's okay to look, you know."

He is mildly thankful that when he turns to look at her, his jacket is firmly set around her shoulders and covering the majority of her body. The leather trench coat is too large for her and pools around her feet, making her look smaller than she is, but her shivering diminishes.

"Thank you for keeping me calm earlier."

"That's what partners do. We take care of each other."

"If I had remembered myself better, I could've paid better mind to you sooner."

"Claustrophobia is no joke, Kai. I'm surprised you stayed as calm as you did. I would have been a complete wreck."

"While your praise is noted, it is not accurate. I should have held myself to the proper standard."

She hums, nodding as he settles on the floor next to her in a loose lotus position, hoping to meditate for a while to pass the time because he sure as hell is not going to sleep down here. She is quiet for a long time. So long, he thinks she's fallen asleep.

"About that."

"I would rather not talk about it."

"Okay." The syllables extend long in her mouth. "Then what would Prince Kaito like to talk about?"

"Lady Wren may find the sound of silence calming in such a situation."

She makes a face at him.

"How boring."

He can practically see her pouting at him in his mind's eye. It's cute. His lips quirk up, but the amusement dies as quickly as it came.

A few minutes later, she presses on, despite his earlier rejection.

"I just wanted to say it's okay, you know. We're all human. It's natural."

"Your assurance is noted but unnecessary."

"My mother was killed by an ahuizotl when I was 10." Kai opens his eyes abruptly and looks at her. "The water dog had nabbed me while I was swimming in the shallows. It's how I lost my hand. It nearly drowned me. My mother wasn't an adept, but she swam out to save me anyway, and it dragged her into the deep. The sea dog belonged to a witch. My father sailed out personally to kill him, but that didn't bring her back."

She smiles sadly.

"I miss her every day."

"I'm sorry," he says.

"I am too, about your father. I'm sure he was a great man."

"He was."

In the blue glimmer of the glow stick, her eyes are more blue than green and her skin paler than its normal tawny tone, probably from the cold. She reaches out a hand and places it gently on his shoulder.

"We aren't going to die down here, Kai."

"I know."

If anything, her head tilts in curiosity and her fingertips reach out to caress the necklace still around his neck.

"You're wearing it."

Kai's face grows hot for an entirely different reason. Wren smiles gently.

"Yes, thank you. I should've said so sooner, but I couldn't figure out when a good time would be."

"The fact that you're wearing it is thanks enough, Kaito. I'm glad you like it."

She beams at him, and for a full moment, Kai can't take the force of it, closing his eyes again.

The truth of it is, while he should probably be a little more desperate to get out of here and a little more angry at the situation, at being trapped down here, at Summer escaping, at Wren herself for how she dealt with the netherbeast earlier, being in her presence is soothing. She'd talked him down earlier. The very sound of her voice, unceasing as it is, acts as a balm against the quiet of the dead space around them. How odd it is! She is the most annoying person he has ever met. The most unruly, unapologetic, and the most headstrong woman he has ever come across. She is by sheer force of her personality chaos incarnate, yet when the force of it washes over him like this, in moments when she is calm and pensive, he can't help but be calm himself even when less than an hour before he could have bloodied himself with disquiet and terror-driven frenzy.

"I appreciate that you made it for me."

The way her eyes light up as her smile blooms in genuine happiness so bright he almost forgets they're underground in total darkness. Her fingertips are ice cold where they brush against his skin. He reaches over and sets his hand over hers. If the touch surprises her, she doesn't give an inkling. Her hand is small in his and far too chilled for his liking.

"Are your internal temperature stabilizers on?"

"Oh, yeah. I set them with my unit over an hour ago. I don't know why they aren't working."

Kai sets his sights on her system to check her over, and she turns her head to the side so he can look at the neural network and its connections into her system. Looks like whatever magic the witch used to destroy the cavern managed to scramble parts of her mainframe. Everything is still in working order, but they need to be rebooted.

"You said you didn't fall unconscious after the blast."

"Correct."

"It looks like some of your augmentations were shut off in the blast. They should turn back on automatically next time you sleep, but if you'd like, I can reset them for you."

"You can do that."

"Not easily, but yes. I would be better than you getting hypothermia, and who knows what other parts of your tech were shut off without your knowledge?"

She shrugs.

"I'm not planning on sleeping any time soon, so sure."

He stands up and makes his way toward her. He sets himself in front of her.

"I'll need to hack into your system. Try not to tense up."

"Won't it hurt you?"

"It will, but so long as you don't try to fight me, the worst I'll have is a headache later."

"Here." She raises her mechanical hand up, presses a series of buttons, and a holo opens up. "You won't need to hack in. I can just grant you access if you're comfortable with it."

He is taken aback by the offer.

Linking in.

By connecting in this way, not only would she grant him access to her systems, she would have access to his as well. A two-way connection. Only his brother, his aunt, and his mother have access to his tech system in the event of emergency. It's how he's able to communicate with Hikaru in rapid fire without an external comm. Anyone else and he would need to wait for them to accept or answer, like making a phone call. With someone you're linked into, however, he can trace their GPS, upload information directly to them, even broadcast straight into their neural hubs without needing their permission. That's why you only ever link in with someone you know will never abuse the privilege.

It isn't forbidden to link in with someone, per se, but it is definitely something that isn't encouraged. Once the connection is made, it cannot be unmade, lest one of them performs a hard system shutdown on their augmentations which is A. painful and B. dangerous. As technomancers with full-body augmentations, their system integrations control and sustain various vital body systems. A total shutdown is not only crippling but downright deadly without immediate medical care.

So yes, he is taken aback by the offer, but he does not immediately reject it. In fact...

He nods and gives her the series of numbers and letters that quantify as the access code for his personal network while he integrates hers in turn. He maps her augmentations into his directive, and the full scope of her augmentations is revealed to him. Carefully, he coaxes each of her augmentations systems to reset to their original system processes. The process takes him roughly twenty minutes. When he's done, he sets her thermal controls to a reasonable body temp, extracts himself from her coding, and moves back.

"Thank you. That's already better."

She shakes herself out and stands, groaning as she settles back into her augmentations. She does some stretches and exercises, testing the range of motion on her physical systems.

"You really are something, Miyazaki-sama."

He hears a shift of fabric and a scrape of shoes against the dirt. Warmth settles in at his side, and he frowns even as his muscles defy him, relaxing at her proximity rather than tensing up and remaining on guard.

"Kai, can I tell you something?"

His silver eyes slide to her. He's listening. There is a mischievous lilt to her question, one that puts him on edge, reminds him far too much of her naturally flirtatious nature.

"You're really handsome."

Kai's head whips around so he can look directly at her. She is giving him the same kind of look as when he found her shooting targets at Shinka's firing range. His gut clenches, and he feels as though his leg is being pulled. She cannot be serious. If she is teasing him again, surely it must be to continue distracting him from their situation which is quite unnecessary at this point, and is this really the place for her to be acting up?

"Your flirting is not endearing, Wren."

"I'm not flirting," she pouts, indignant, her eyes looking up and to the right. "Well, okay. I am, but I'm being honest."

"Then I assure you, my mind is at ease. You need not divert my attention to stave off another moment of disquiet."

"I wasn't trying to do that either."

"Then what are you trying to do?"

She doesn't answer him right away. Her attention shifts down to her hands, and her fingertips play with the sleeve of her jacket—his jacket—her jacket—his jacket currently being worn by her. She looks down at her hands like they are the most intriguing puzzle she has ever pondered. She huffs as though steeling herself, building up some of that bravery she spoke so fondly of earlier.

But then she goes shy all of the sudden, and it's as jarring as her naked honesty. He isn't quite sure what the impetus for it is, but he watches, entranced, as the color of her cheeks darkens to a pinkish hue. She turns her face from him, and he immediately misses the soft coloring of her cheekbones. Her bottom lip pushes out slightly as she continues in a smirking tone.

"You know what? Nevermind. You're right. I'm wrong. I'll, umm, I'll leave you be. Totally wasn't thinking about anything like...you know. After all, we're in a tomb—"

"Wren..."

"—I mean, there are better ways to pass the time other than kissing. I mean, not kissing. I didn't say kissing. That's totally not what I meant at all..."

I was innocent before you stole away my first kiss...

Her words echo back to him, and heat dusts over his cheekbones. Innocent, indeed! She is a shameless flirt, and she has just expressed a desire to essentially make out with him in a graveyard, and shouldn't he be more morally opposed to this idea? It's concerning.

"Wren. You're making my head spin."

And his head is certainly spinning.

"I know. I'm ridiculous. I tease and flirt and am far too comfortable with displays of affection, but my mother always taught me to be honest with myself, so there. Here I am being honest. Though I can definitely see why my timing might be a little off, and I'm probably being rather inappropriate, aren't I? Don't worry, prince. I'm not planning on jumping your bones. Though I'm not sure I would be opposed to that either... Here, I'm probably annoying you. I'll stop. You don't have to look at me like that..."

She is talking so fast, he can't get a word in edgewise. She is kind of babbling to herself at this point, giggling every few sentences like she is trying to banish the awkward away by force of will. The confidence in her earlier statements slowly fading away as she rambles on. He's glaring at her? What? She is being honest with him. She wants to kiss him. Jump his bones? Isn't there a protocol to this kind of thing?

She shifts her weight, her shoulder bumping into his as she moves to rise. Probably for the best that she put some distance between them all things considered, but suddenly the prospect of her warmth disappearing from his side is unbearable, suffocating, and painful. The idea of her walking away from this conversation instilling a different kind of panic than the fear-clogged one of waking in a shut-in tomb. Gods, does she ever run out of air? He needs to think.

He places his hand atop hers on the floor, stalls her movements, and with his other hand, he pulls her in by the back of her head until she quiets on the sole reasoning that he has effectively sealed her lips with a kiss, and time slows down.

As far as kisses go, it is not anything salacious or hungry. He presses and molds their lips together and holds the connection through his fumbling. He pulls her in closer, and she somehow ends up sprawled on his lap before he pulls away. She pulls back and peers at him in the dim light, confusion and shock on her face.

"Your highness?"

She blinks at him, puzzled and waiting for him to say or do something as though she was not the instigator of this whole conversation. He holds her gently in place, his expression betraying nothing until she pulls back and away. When she draws her lower lip between her teeth, his eyes are drawn straight to the movement.

"You do not annoy me."

"What?"

Kuso! This woman is going to drive him insane, assuming she hasn't already.

"You speak too quickly, and you make my head hurt, but you are not annoying."

"Oh, that's a relief," she says with a light titter.

"I'm serious, Wren."

"Me too, Prince Kaito."

"I prefer when you call me Kai."

A small smile lifts at the corners of her mouth, and she settles back slightly, her green eyes penetrating through him in the darkness.

"Kai..." she says, toying with the hem of his coat. "So, if I'm not annoying, what do you think of me?"

A lot of things, he thinks, but he doesn't say as much because surely the words will fail to convey his thoughts entirely on how fascinating she is, how infuriating, how perplexing, how unerringly captivating her eyes are, and how the feel of her body next to his makes him warm but nervous. And does she know that she has a mole behind her left ear?

His fingers tap a rhythm into her hip, dancing over a piano that isn't there, a sonata he worked through years ago but never kept with because it was written for voice and a piano accompaniment. Could Wren sing it? It's in her range.

There is an earnest look in her eye, a blush on her cheeks, and a small tremble in her body that has nothing to do with the temperature of the room. *Anticipation*, his mind supplies for him... But for what? Suddenly, he thinks he wants for more than a chaste kiss in the dark. It makes him feel unnaturally warm, unnaturally tense in a way that is new and slightly frightening, different from when he needs to relieve tension in privacy.

He doesn't answer her verbally, but he does rise to meet her, studying her face and looking for any indication he is unwelcome. She does not retreat from him like she did with Llewelyn. She just looks at him quietly as he moves into her space. Her body language remains open, calm despite him closing their proximity. He can feel her heartbeat. They are so close, his breath rustles through her hair. She leans toward him and suddenly, the rest of the world seems terribly far away.

His eyes close as they meet. The space between them buzzes, and this time her arms wind around his neck. Her flesh hand snakes down the front of his shirt, toying with the leather-corded necklace, and he pulls her in tighter. His hands seek out the seam of her jacket (his jacket!) coming into contact with the soft, still slightly damp fabric of her camisole. She may as well be wearing armor though for all that he yearns to touch her skin. As though sensing his frustration, she pulls back to shrug away the outer garment entirely before drawing him in by the collar of his shirt. He goes willingly.

Her pull on his clothing tugs the fabric out of its normal placement, and soon he too is undoing buttons and tossing aside the belts that bind the fabric to his body. Her hands, both flesh and mechanical, find the skin of his chest, and he reclaims her mouth. Her teeth nip at him before her lips part, and he deepens the kiss all too readily.

The tightness in his chest he's felt ever since the first day he saw her, since the first time she set her gaze on him, the fiery look in her eyes challenging him all through the summit, unfurls into something he can't particularly name yet, but it floods his body, hot blood coursing through his veins, and he releases her mouth, opening his eyes to map a line of kisses along her jaw and throat. He could drown in her soft sighs. His name falls from her lips like a prayer, and suddenly she is pushing his shirt off his shoulders.

He rids himself of the rest of the garment, his hands returning to her hips where her camisole has ridden high to her waist though he makes no move to push it higher, admiring instead the texture of the crocheted coral patterns at the hem under his fingers. She meets him again in another kiss. Nothing but soft, giving fabric between them as he pulls her closer. Her knee brushes against his growing arousal through his leathers, and he groans at the contact.

She stills at his reaction.

"Kai, is this okay? Do we—Is this something we want?"

He is panting. Her chest heaves, coming flush against his own with each inhale. A blush starts at her collarbones and rises into her cheeks. She bites her lip.

"I will stop if you tell me, Wren."

He holds himself back with all the discipline his schooling has ingrained into him. Surely, she has come to her senses. This kind of intimacy should be kept between promised couples, not teenagers fumbling in the dark. At the very least, if they are going to say to hell with propriety and decorum, shouldn't they at least be doing this in a bed or on a couch? Hell, normal teenagers lose their virginity in the back of a car—or anywhere that isn't an underground tomb! This should terrify him, disgust him, shame him, and make him want to vanish on the spot. But he feels none of that, her body trembling under his touch. There is only need and the knowledge that he has never desired anyone like this, has never even imagined wanting this kind of closeness with another person. But...

"Do you wish me to stop, Wren?"

"No," she breathes against his lips, her chest heaving under the thin cotton of her chemise. He keeps his eyes on hers. She shakes her head, and her nose brushes against his throat as she buries her face into his neck. "I want you. Do you want me?"

It's barely a whisper, but he answers.

"Inexplicably."

She laughs in delight. He moves with her as she lays back into the haphazard blanket they've made of his jacket. Her knees part on either side of his hips, and surely enlightenment is a place that can be found here, nestled in the spaces between her curves.

And there they are. Two teenagers, fumbling in the dark into uncharted waters.

She guides him, nervously, patiently, and he is thankful, so terribly thankful for the wisdom imparted to her by her mother and trade teachers. She deserves better than his inexperienced fumbling, and yet she more than tolerates him—she encourages him. He follows a map of her soft noises, seeking more as he explores her body, and she discovers him in turn. Their skin fevers, their mechanical accoutrements chime sweetly every time they meet, and they synchronize, hooking into each other, body, tech, mind, and maybe even soul. Is it too soon to make such a presumptuous link between them? Are they too young to share such things?

He doesn't think too much on it.

When she opens herself to him, when he breeches her, she gasps wonderfully. Firsts: new, terrifying, exhilarating. Her heat surrounds him like a vise, and is she alright? Because surely...The pain is minimal, she assures him. Everything is fine. She urges him forward, and he is lost in her ocean. Carefully, he moves, caressing her like a delicate bloom warming in the sun, and she kindles his passion into an arduous blaze. Her nails leave red trails down the line of his back. His fingertips press into her hips with bruising force, and she accepts him, all of him, letting him lead. Relishes in his touches both harsh and gentle, gives of herself more than he could ever imagine while he works to do the same. She comes undone under him with a pitched cry, and the realization of it floors him, triumph and pride welling in his chest, like winning a fight or a race but different. Better. Something he could yearn for again and again.

Eventually, they fall asleep together, wrapped in each other's embrace, sated and whole in a wholly new way.

With the coming dawn, Hikaru and Xipilli dig them out, a captive Summer between them. They rise and gather their things after a message from Hikaru lets them know their brothers are clearing an exit for them now. There is a content air about her. He would have expected to feel nervous or awkward around her, but they fall into an easy quiet, a dance accented with soft touches and exchanges he doesn't second guess anymore. He only jolts once because she pinches him on the rear. He swats her away, telling her she drools in her sleep. She pinches him again, indignantly, and he pulls her in for a kiss.

When they are finally out, there's no opportunity for a heartfelt goodbye (not that there's any need for one), not with her brother standing right there looking like he is about to have a conniption at the prospect of rescuing a hexen child and ready for his long-overdue return to Deriva with his sister. Wren just nudges Kai in the shoulder companionably, offering a small curtsy to him and Hikaru (and if there is a small tint of pink on her cheeks when their eyes meet, he's certain he just imagined it, after all he looked away as fast as he could, lest his own face redden) while Xipilli shakes their hands on an accomplished case. Wren takes the baby, Lisa, back to her parents, the poor thing crying herself purple the entire time. Xipilli goes with her, and the four of them part ways.

Hikaru and Kaito escort the captive witch to Aighneas where the mission case originated. Summer spits curses at them, slurring lewd things to Kaito the whole way until his brother administers a tranquilizer to keep her docile through the transport to Ebele.

He is tired and dirty and in desperate need of a shower, but his brother is looking at him oddly from across the aisle of the train.

"You seem to be in bright spirits."

"Not entirely sure what you mean."

"You seem different is all, ototo."

He feels different but not at the same time. A part of him wonders if he should be feeling more different than he does at the moment. If we are being primitive about it, he's technically become a man.

"I am the same as always, Hikaru."

He avoids his brother's gaze entirely, even as the man gives him a knowing look.

"You and Lady Wren seem to work well together. I would not be surprised if you were paired together for more cases."

"That would be their choice."

"Would you be against such a pairing?"

Kai does not answer his brother, choosing instead to watch the landscape pass them by as the light rail speeds onward.

Over the course of the next few weeks, Wren and Kaito stay in contact via their comms and media apps, the hardware connection they made giving them nearly unlimited ability to contact one another on a private network. They would even, as Hikaru suspected, find themselves assigned a joint case. All seemed well despite the distance between them.

However, halcyon days crumble as the threat of war looms.

18

ACE OF PENTACLES
(REVERSED)

Present–3rd Day in the Month of Falling 1877

AYA WAKES HER AT AN UNGODLY HOUR. Wren grumbles her way out of bed (who put her here, anyway?) and into the sitting room where Kaito sits waiting for her, a plate of breakfast set for her on the table. She is surprised to note he is no longer wearing the mourning colors she saw him in the day before, donning instead a deep byzantine tunic and black leathers. He gives her one look, commands her to eat, and then lets himself out. She has half a mind to just not eat for the sake of being petulant, but it's going to be a long day.

Kai gives her a reasonable thirty minutes to eat before he returns, commanding her to follow him with a snipped, "Let's go."

Feeling more than a little put upon by his shortness with her and not quite sure what stick he shoved up his own ass, she decides to poke the wasp's nest.

"Yesterday, I was getting whole sentences. Now we're down to two syllables?"

"Don't be preposterous."

"Never, your highness."

Wren follows Kai to the palace garage. Hikaru, Renki, and Fumiko stand waiting for them with some supplies and equipment. A lone lightcycle stands ready for them. Annoyance tinges in her head.

"I have two hands. I can ride on my own."

"You do not have a license," Kai answers smoothly.

"Then wouldn't a car be a better option?"

"We'll travel faster by cycle."

Kai hands her a helmet. She takes it begrudgingly as Kai tucks her bag in the cycle's storage compartment before taking the materials Hikaru prepared for them and stowing them as well.

Hikaru looks her up and down.

"Lady Nocturne."

"Your Excellency."

When Wren gives the emperor an appropriately level bow, he acknowledges her calmly.

"I hope the lady has prepared appropriately for this case. It would be unfortunate if harm befell her due to a lack of proper planning."

A laugh threatens to escape her. Hikaru most certainly has mastered the uniquely sovereign ability of sounding both trite and sincere at once.

"Not to worry, Emperor. I can handle anything that comes at me. I'll leave the proper planning to Kaito-sama."

Hikaru gives her a dry look before turning his attention to Kaito.

"Walk with me, didi."

As the brothers walk away, Fumiko comes to Wren's side. The woman is dressed in an exquisite pink kimono with red accents. It is the most feminine Wren has ever seen the woman, far more accustomed to seeing her in battle or teaching attire. It's an interesting cognitive dissonance and makes Wren a little dizzy.

"Once you've broken the curse, we can send our adepts to deal with the backlash. Renki and Akari always enjoy helping Kaito with his missions when they can."

"Well, there'll be plenty of that to go around," responds Wren, watching the brothers exchange words, more than a little curious about what Hikaru does not want Wren privy to. There is tension between them, more than she has ever witnessed in the past. Then Hikaru's gaze finds hers, and she knows, beyond a shadow of a doubt, they are talking about her. "I'm only hoping whatever creature has decided to use Shinka as its den is easy to take down."

"We can only hope," agrees Fumiko.

Kaito doesn't say much to his brother, but when he finally does reply, Hikaru visibly sags.

"Are Renki and Akari even certified yet?" Wren asks as Hikaru moves away from Kaito, disappearing back into the palace proper while young Renki approaches Kaito who angles himself to regard the young man.

Fumiko turns to her.

"Murasaki no Yama prepares technomancers differently than Deriva, I would imagine. Our trainees are expected to assist on missions within our borders. Renki and Akari may not be certified technomancers, but they will be attending their first trial in the coming year. They are advanced enough in their training to take on missions with a partner or mentor who is."

As Fumiko speaks, Kaito sets a hand on Renki's shoulder, conversing with him gently in their native language. The pair of them seem awfully close, and they look so similar, albeit Renki's hair is darker and his eyes more vibrant, blue-green to Kai's silver. If Wren didn't know better, she would think they were father and son, but the boy is too old, probably born either just before or not long after the start of the war against Seraphim. Familial relations truly could be uncanny. It makes her heart hurt a little watching them, so she turns her attention to the emperor.

"Renki has been training under Kaito since he was six. He is young but capable and eager to learn."

"I noticed he wears the royal family seal. How is he related to you?"

Fumiko stiffens, her shoulders tightening so much the silks wrinkle around her shoulders.

"If Lady Wren truly wishes to know, she should ask the boy herself. She is after all the reason his family was torn apart."

Wren flinches.

"Ah, another Miyazaki who wants me dead, then. You all certainly know how to inspire family values."

Fumiko looks at her calmly.

"No one in this family wishes you dead, Wren."

Wren waves her hand at her old teacher.

"Your reassurance is kind but rather unbelievable. I know my place well enough, sensei."

"Believe what you like, Lady Wren, but I will say I am glad to see my nephew out of mourning colors."

And what the hell does that have to do with her?

She bows to Wren and steps aside as Kaito returns to the lightcycle with Renki behind him. The teen offers Wren a bow, his hands clasped together in front of him. Well, at least the teen has a good grasp on his manners even if he is a vengeful little gremlin.

Fumiko reaches up to set a hand on Kaito's shoulder to whisper something into his ear before Kai settles himself along the front of the cycle.

"Safe travels, Lady Nocturne. We wish you both good fortune on the completion of your mission."

"Thank you, but that's not necessary," she says, and the smile the woman gives her as she ushers Renki back to the palace entrance throws her off guard so hard she nearly trips over herself as she turns her attention back to Kaito waiting for her on the cycle.

He looks at her expectantly, and she waffles on the tarmac, hesitant.

There is plenty of room behind him for her to sit comfortably. No problem there, but still, she is loath to sit behind him. She masks this, of course, by teasing him.

"You really sure you want me behind you? I might very well stab you in the back."

"That would be ill-advised at high speeds."

Ace Of Pentacles (reversed)

Kaito's face doesn't shift a bit as he stares back at her, unreadable as though carved from stone.

"Oh, come off it! You've barely said a full sentence to me, and you want me that close to you?"

He sighs.

"I do not mind you riding pillion, Wren. You seemed reticent last night. I was trying to give you the space you seem to want," he says, putting on his helmet.

No one should be allowed to put on a helmet that gracefully, and Wren is sorely tempted to throw her helmet directly at his head. Reticent!? Humph! She'll show him "reticent"! So she stomps over and slings her leg over the seat behind him. She adjusts her hair and slips on the helmet while Kai revs the engine.

Hikaru (when did he get back?) gives Kai a nod which he returns while Renki waves from his place between the emperor and Fumiko-sensei.

"You should hold on." She hears Kai's voice through the helmet's embedded headset.

"I'm holding the handlebars."

"Must I remind you these have quite the kickback?"

"I'm not going to fall off, Kaito."

Yeah, this is going to be an awkward trip... He turns his head to look at her expectantly. Just to be petulant, she sets her hands loosely on either side of his hips over the leather jacket he is wearing. When she refuses to tighten her grip, she hears him huff in annoyance.

"Don't say I didn't warn you."

He revs the lightcycle, kicks off the brake, and takes off like a bat out of hell. Wren most definitely does not squeal. She's surprised, is all, and if she jolts forward, wrapping her arms fully around his waist, no one could blame her because street rash is not a good look on anybody. So, she holds tight for dear life, her front pressed flush to his back as he steers through the cityscape.

"You did that on purpose!" she shouts over the comm.

The noise of the engine is too loud for her to hear properly, but she is pretty sure she hears him laughing.

It's a three-and-a-half-hour ride to Shinka. They make three stops along the way, once to top off on fuel—which is absolutely horrible. Wren just about pukes the second the pungent odor of gasoline hits her nose—and twice to drink water, eat, stretch, and take a short rest. Even with that, Wren's back, unaccustomed to riding anymore, is stiff and achy from the trip. What makes it worse? Not only is she already sore from their little road trip, she is now staring up from Kai's parked lightcycle at a seemingly endless ascension of steps to get to the actual temple grounds, only instead of the beautifully crafted, pristine steps surrounded by foliage she remembers, her vision is met with viscous miasma oozing with malignant energy.

"This is as close as we can get before the miasma starts to take effect."

Meaning the lightcycle will be useless any farther, the tech nullified by the anti-tech field. Even if they did try to ride the cycle closer, it would probably fizzle out within the first fifteen minutes. Wren dismounts and steps toward the shroud of bruise-purple fog hovering just in front of the gate leading to the main temple. She whistles low, awed by the pulsing swirl of poison.

"You weren't kidding. I've never seen one this heavy."

Kai sets the kickstand down and comes up beside her.

"It has thickened," he observes. "80 percent increase."

"80 percent in two months. You're kidding?!"

Kai gives her a look that says plainly, 'does it look like I'm kidding?'

"Well, it's definitely malignant. How are you able to sustain this close to it?"

"Upgrades."

Upgrades?

She studies him closely, more closely than she has since encountering him again, and notices for the first time the additional nodes on the side of his head are not the only changes to his tech system. The seams and nodules at his temple are shifted. The holo-projection hub embedded in the back of his hand is shaped differently, as well, triangular rather than circular.

"Your tech design is different."

"Of course, it's different. It's been twelve years."

"No, it's *different*," she emphasizes, walking right up to him, determined to look at his augmentations. He tries to back up, but she closes the space as she looks.

"Oh, don't get shy on me now."

She grabs his wrist, pulling his sleeve up despite his protests. It's so strange; she's seen his tech before, knew it better than she knew her own, but she doesn't find the familiar patterns of it under his skin. The ports are in slightly different places, offset from their original placements, and the wires beneath his skin, while not visible to the naked eye, thrum with power she can feel and the lines of which are different. When she looks closer, she notices the scarring left from old nodes that have been completely removed. The scar tissue left behind reminds her of how her own arms and legs had looked after...

"Who ripped out your old tech?"

He jerks his arm out of her grip even as she reaches for his other arm to compare. He yanks that one away too.

"No one."

"Then where are your old nodules? Your patterns are completely changed. No sane person does a full system repavement just for an upgrade. Take off your shirt. I want to see."

"Stop, Wren."

She backs off, crossing her arms and more than a little put off at being shoved away.

"Fine! Keep your virtue."

He turns on his heel and walks straight into the miasma. Her eyes widen, expecting him to drop unconscious, but he seems entirely unaffected. For the moment at least. There's no telling how long his tech can withstand the cackling energy around him.

"Impressive," she calls moving to catch up to him. "Who designed your new system?"

"I did."

And if that isn't the most asinine thing she's ever heard! No one performs a full system redesign just for the hell of it. It's unheard of, and never done unless serious damage has been done to the previous system. And Kai would have been at least 21 which is beyond the age recommended for anyone to undergo a complete system integration, or in his case a re-integration. The older a person is, the higher the risk of infection, rejection, and death from technomancer level augmentations.

"So, you expect me to believe you tore yourself to pieces for a power buff?"

"If that is what you wish to believe, then you may believe it."

"Bullshit!"

"Leave it alone, Wren."

"No, I want to know who destroyed your original system."

"You do not!"

He says it with such severity her next question dies on her tongue, nearly running into him when he stops dead in front of her and whirls around to face her, sights active and glowing a darker purple than normal. She looks at him, studies his face, trails her eyes along his body, wondering how much pain he experienced having a full system shutdown and replacement, horror slowly creeping into her face.

Your memory is damaged.

"Did I do this to you?"

The tension cracks.

"No," he answers, gentler now. "Just drop it, Wren. It is in the past."

"But—"

"Drop it, please." There is a strain to his voice that leaves no room for argument, and Wren decides to leave well enough alone. What should she care anyway, right?

"Fine... How long can you stand in this before you start to feel it?"

He takes a moment and does a system analysis.

"Two hours."

"That's not long enough. Here, give me your ring."

"Excuse me?"

"Your signet ring. Give me your signet ring so I can cast a protection charm on it unless there is something else you would prefer I enchant."

Kai's hand wavers as though he is trying to decide this or that, but he does as she asks, removing the ring from his left hand and handing it to her. She takes it and resumes walking up the path, a hum on her lips as she holds the ring in front of her.

Kai walks beside her, listening and watching as she works. The ring begins to glitter. The clear, smooth amethyst that lays over the Miyazaki crest, too, shimmers with Wren's magical tune, the purple gem glowing amaranthine. As her song comes to a close, she pricks her finger and allows a single drop of blood to fall into the center. A small reaction occurs, a bright flash of light pulsing over the piece of jewelry before sinking into gleaming silver.

She inspects it once more before holding it back out to him.

"Here, it should keep you unaffected by the miasma."

Kaito takes the ring back from her and does a quick scan of the new energy revolving within. Like a mist unfolding or a lazy, sun-drunk feline uncurling from a nap, Wren's lifeforce moves around the ring in a spectacular show of controlled chaos. The light, however, bright as it was in Wren's hand, has dimmed in his own.

"It is linked to you."

"Yeah, sorry about that. So long as I'm within the vicinity, it will remain active. It has a radial reach of fifty meters. Farther than that and I can't guarantee it will remain effective."

"Hm."

Kai continues up the way, and Wren, not one to be left behind, follows quickly enough. They walk up so many steps Wren is certain she's going to be sore tomorrow, but Kai seems unbothered. Of course, he's unbothered. He grew up here. He's probably walked up and down this path hundreds of times. She, on the other hand, is functioning in an under-toned, untrained body. Thankful as she is to have it, endurance is not something one just pulls out of thin air. The miasma doesn't help either. While it may not have any effect on her magically speaking, it is still thick in the air, air already thin considering they are in the mountains.

The path they take to the temple winds them past the old training grounds and the lake. The grass has blackened, power lines sputter with crackles of lost energy as they pass, and ghosts drift here and there across the grounds visible only to Wren for the moment since she assumes Kai isn't actively trying to map the area, or maybe he is, and he just isn't looking for dead things right now. Wren stops to look when Kai makes a disgusted noise in the back of his throat. The lake water is blood red and stinks of iron. When she dips her hand in it, her fingers come back out dripping and bloodstained.

The miasma caused this? How powerful is this curse?

Bubbles rise up from beneath the surface of the lake, and Wren makes a mental note to avoid the water until they have the equipment necessary for going up against an underwater fiend of any kind.

Eventually they do make it to the actual temple grounds, the various buildings that make up the compound loom before them looking far more rundown than Wren remembers. Charred wood, broken windows, and rubble everywhere she looks where there was once elegantly painted tapestries, lacquered wood, and shining glass. Despite the sun being high in the sky, it is darker here, the sunlight unable to penetrate through the dense fog enshrouding the grounds. The dim light, while distressing in its own creepy way, is not what brings her to an abrupt halt at Kai's side.

"Goddess above..."

It's the smell.

The temple grounds reeks of death and decay. Sour and bitter, so much she can taste the decay on her tongue, coupled with the gut-clenching odor of excrement and noxious gases. It smells like blood too, a lot of it. The air is so saturated with it, the iron tang of it hovers in the back of her mouth threatening to crawl forward as bile rises in her throat. Flies buzz in the air relishing in the rot. Through the smog, she can see the corpses torn open and left to melt under the heat of the sun, all of them in various stages of decomposition. And they aren't the only things that greet them.

As Kai and Wren approach the bloodstained grounds, several small "living" creatures scurry away to the darker edges of the compound. Kai thrusts Amatsu forward, and it slices one of the grey creatures down the center of its body. It lets out an ear-splitting cry as it bleeds out. Wren walks up to the corpse eater to take a look: gray almost white skin, scaly and fish-like, drawn taut over ragged strips of bone and sinew that make up its six limbs. With serpentine slits for nostrils and large round eyes, the creature's face is not much for description. More notable is the large leech-like jaws that decorate the undead monster's torso, designed so it can latch onto a corpse and consume it bit by bit until it is either frightened away by an intruder or direct sunlight or it finishes its meal, leaving only the bones behind. This one is about the size of a toddler, and judging by its swollen abdomen, it has been eating well over the last few weeks if not months.

"Ptóma (πτώμα). Disgusting undead vermin."

Amatsu returns to Kai's hand, sickly purple blood dripping from the well-oiled blade onto the ground.

"Easy enough to deal with," Kai dismisses.

"The cowardly little gluttons will head for the hills the moment they catch sight of you, your highness," she says, teasingly.

Kai gives her the side eye as he steps forward. The grounds are saturated with death, looking more like a gory battlefield than a once sacred temple. It didn't occur to Wren there would be plenty of unburied bodies here, but it makes sense. After all, the temple was not vacated so much as overcome and made unapproachable by the curse, and there was bound to be at least some evidence of the massacre must have occurred to subdue the temple so completely. Some of the bodies are nothing but skeletons in the mud, the result of time and scavengers like the ptóma. Others...

"Toujiro-san."

Kai stands over the corpse of an older male. The cadaver is half eaten, butchered of its insides and meatier parts. There's barely anything left to identify it as a recent kill were it not for the fact that it still smells of blood and the limbs that haven't been feasted on yet appear perfectly decomposed in line with a three- or four-day-old corpse.

"This corpse is only days old."

"But he went missing weeks ago?"

"Correct."

"So that means something kept this poor sod alive long enough to flay him, and it wasn't the ptóma."

"I am aware."

"Any guesses as to what?"

Kai looks sidelong at her.

"That is what we are here to figure out."

"True enough. Was this one of the adepts sent to gather reconnaissance a few weeks ago?" asks Wren, bending to get a closer look at the body. There are several bite marks along the neck and torso, but one of the marks sticks out as being of a different patterning. Less sharp toothed and fangy as expected from a carnivore, more omnivorous, but warped, like something that used to be such but was no longer.

"Toujiro-san was a technomancer. He was one of our best."

"Not good enough, it seems."

Kai gives her a stern expression for the callous remark. She raises her brow at him, daring him to scold her.

"Am I wrong?"

A long-suffering look. Poor man... Think he regrets kidnapping her yet?

"Hikaru thought he could lead a team to investigate the miasma, but he wasn't supposed to enter the grounds." She snickers under her breath.

"Well, let's hope his teammates were smarter than him or at the very least luckier."

The cheeriness in her voice is borderline disrespectful, and she knows it, chooses to use the inflection on purpose just to goad him further. She stands there looking at him out of the corner of her eye and waits for the angry response, but nothing comes. The rigidness in Kai's stance suggests he most definitely wants to berate her for her indifference to death. So why doesn't he? Perhaps because he knows it would be futile to try and sensitize her to it. There isn't much sympathy she can harbor for a technomancer she never met who was old enough to have played a role in her having been dead herself not so long ago, but that's probably unfair... After all, the man's spirit is standing but a few meters to Kai's right looking at the man like the sun wouldn't shine without him.

Toujiro's ghost is nearly as ghastly to look at as his corpse. The dead man stands just a bit shorter than Kai, bloodstains trailing from a bite wound at his neck. His hands are torn up, and there is what looks like a puncture wound at his jawline, as though he was strung up like a hooked fish. He was stripped of his clothing before he died, and she can see the gruesome state of his body at the time of his death. Pieces of flesh shredded from his bones as though peeled away, the way one would butcher a deer or a cow for drying jerky.

Looking at the ghost before her, Wren doesn't doubt for a moment that his death was painful and drawn out.

She scoffs.

Who cares? He's not the first person to die a torturous death, and he won't be the last, and it sure as hell is not her job to help his spirit be put to rest. She has other things to do, and if she wants to go do them, she needs to wrap up this case as quickly as possible, so bully for him. Let the Miyazaki clean up their own mess.

Anyway, nostalgic as it is standing in the middle of a bloodied courtyard, she has more concerning things to get started on.

"My book?"

"In the library." The reply comes stiffly.

"Shall we, then?"

Her eyes flash and without sparing him a second glance, she steps over the corpse and heads in the direction of the temple library, the doors of which, they find, are hanging off their hinges, the heavy-duty steel dented and the wood splintered from impact with something capable of exerting a whole lot of force.

Kai's sights activate immediately.

"You've got to be kidding me..." Wren curses and rushes into the space.

The Lunar Cycles of Deus:

Koi, the larger of Deus' moons, is about the same size of Jupiter's moon Io. Cold, composed primarily of ice and silicates, Koi is slow moving, reaching its zenith once every six months where it will shine full for approximately five days. Whereas normally Koi shines full twice a year, every seven years or so, Deus will get to witness Koi's full purple glow three times in a single year, called a leap year.

Dei is much smaller than Koi, less than a quarter of her lover's size and quite a bit hotter. Volcanic due to its dense, radiating core and composed mostly of heavy metals, Dei glows dull red in the night sky and orbits Deus at a much faster pace, circling around the planet every twenty-two days. Because of its volcanic activity, Dei is always full.

Because of their vastly different timetables, it is rare to see both moons of Deus in the night's sky in a perfect eclipse. An occasion rare enough, the pagans, to this day, still believe miracles can happen just because two pieces of rock manage to avoid a third ball of rock's shadow long enough to catch the sun's reflection.

An excerpt from *Moondance*
By E.X. Icarus, 1724. A.P.

19

THE CHARIOT REVERSED

THE MIYAZAKI FAMILY SIGNET RINGS ARE simple in comparison to other royal families. Silver to his brother's gold and smaller, at the center of the Kai's ring, the ookami howls under a smooth, clear amethyst, outlined with engravings of winter peonies. The divine wolf, a symbol of piety and loyalty, is the age-old animal representation of his family's spirit. It reminds him of the importance of discipline and family, of patience and perseverance, of trusting your instincts and sharpening the mind.

It was his father's, given to him by his mother for his seventeenth birthday. The day marked not only his coming of age in Murasaki but also his ascension to technomancer.

He's carried it with him ever since.

Now, sixteen years later, Wren's magic folded into the ring makes his skin tingle, her aura warm even if the woman herself is chilly. In the face of her ire, he reflects on those lessons over and over and over again lest he do something he'll regret later.

The library is a mess of literary carnage, books scattered and torn all over the floor.

Kaito scans the room for clues as to who may have done this while Wren rips through the space looking through the books and various broken pieces of metal and technology on the floor to see if her spellbook is among the wreckage. There are no claw marks or traces of any kind of monster, so that is out as a possibility, and the destruction with which the room has been treated indicates someone was here looking for something. There are also smeared fingerprints, humanoid in appearance. With Shinka's main servers down, trying to match them now is fruitless, so he saves them to his database for later analysis. He scans the main computer, knowing that if someone were truly determined, they could rip the station open to abduct the hard drive from the system's heart. It's intact, not even a scratch to the console, which tells him that whoever came in here was looking for something very specific that could not be uploaded onto a mainframe.

Kai walks around the computer station toward the back of the library, bypassing the stairs to the second and third floors on his way, and is relieved to see the bookcase concealing the lift to the family vault is still standing even though all the books have been torn off. On closer inspection though, he notices the shelf is ajar. When he pulls it open, doors to the elevator are open, the shaft vacant save for the cables that run the car, meaning the elevator is sitting up the lift in front of the vault. Someone rode it up and left it there. How they managed that is to be seen. Hopefully, the car is secure enough not to fall considering what they are going to have to do if they want to reach the vault.

Wren mutters something obscure under her breath, and when he turns back around, she hurricanes around the room, looking through the debris, panicked and uncharacteristically unmindful of the books.

"Wren," he calls, attempting to call her attention, but she's too busy tearing around to even look at him.

"Wren, calm down. You're going to damage the books."

"They're already damaged and I—"

"Your spellbook is not in this room, so would you, please, stop that and come here?"

His tone isn't enough to cajole the irate witch—Ha! When has it ever been?—but she does stomp over to him, the little ball of hellfire she is.

"What is it?"

She eyes the elevator shaft.

"This is the lift to the secured ward of the library. That's where your book is being kept."

"But the elevator is down."

"Correct."

She shifts her weight from foot to foot, eyes looking around for other options that are nonexistent at this point lest they want to waste even more time.

"Are there stairs we can use? A ladder, maybe?"

"Unfortunately not. We will have to go up the shaft."

"I'm a witch, not a bird. I can't fly."

"You can climb well enough."

Wren sputters and starts ranting about why that is the worst idea she has ever had and how absolutely stupid could you be to not structure an emergency means of getting in and out of a room that doesn't require scaling a death trap. The expression Wren makes alongside her rapid gesticulations would be funny if he didn't know exactly how she feels about heights.

"I can help you," he says, cutting her off mid rant.

She goes quiet, the words caught in her throat, a stormy aura settling around her in stark contrast to her previous foolery. She doesn't say anything to him, but the air about her becomes nearly oppressive. The shift in mood is so jarring, he has to backtrack a moment to check if he said something wrong or outright offensive to her, but he can find nothing, unless Wren is now so petty that a simple reassurance would set her off. Probably the latter.

"I don't doubt that you are capable. I was merely saying—"

"Well don't!" she snaps at him.

In response to her anger, a shudder rips through the miasma curling through the room. It writhes like a living creature, a high-pitched sound emanating from it as though experiencing some sort of torture. She withdraws back into herself at that, and the miasma calms. "Just don't...If you have rope, I can handle myself just fine."

Kai steps toward an emergency panel on the inside of the shaft and cracks it open with a sharp jerk of his wrist. From inside the panel, he pulls the fire hose, cutting it from the faucet with Amatsu.

"It's not a rope, but..."

"It'll do," she declares. The triskelion at the center of her brow appears and begins to glow faintly as she lifts the hose from the floor and up into the shaft to tie off on one of the bars under the elevator car.

"Damn," she says once she's tied it off.

It is a touch short, the end dangling too high for Wren to reach even if she were to jump, but...

"I can lift you. You can jump from my shoulders."

She looks at him like she wants to protest, but thinks better of it, walking up to him as he bends to offer her his thigh as a stepping point. The hard rubber at the bottom of her boot grinds into his quad. It is the closest she has gotten to him willingly since they left Snowfall, outside of having to hold onto his waist while they rode through the countryside earlier today, and he's not quite sure 'willingly' is the correct term to describe the motions they are going through now, but she is close enough he catches her scent, like the forest before a rainstorm with just a touch of sweat. He offers her his opposite hand over his head. She takes it and pulls herself up higher until she is standing on his shoulders. Once she is balanced, he straightens.

"Ready?"

"Don't coach me," she snips. Then without any warning, her feet press into him, forcing him to push up at the last moment to keep from stumbling. Wren catches the hose line and begins twisting herself up the tail of it as easily as an aerial dancer. She winds in and out of the weaving she makes with her legs and torso, carefully making her way up. The higher she gets, the more determinedly she refuses to look down.

Despite her apparent disdain for him, he watches her, especially when she pauses midway to catch her breath. Tangled and hanging by her legs, she trembles slightly, shaking her hands out. When she resumes her climb, he steps forward in case she falters. She is about three quarters of the way up when he too begins to climb. With a pair of leather gloves to protect his hands, he pulls his way up the lift's pulley system. When he gets to the top, Wren has already thrown aside the escape hatch into the elevator and pulled herself up. He hears her breathing, heavy and tense as he lifts himself up and through the opening, and as he enters, he catches a brief glimpse of her huddled close to the floor trying to calm herself down, but by the time he is all the way in, she is upright and so composed, he wonders if he imagined the brief moment of weakness. Regardless, it is not for him to bear witness.

Why are you treating me like a stranger?

"Took you long enough," she says, mocking and cold. "Care to open the door?"

"Is Lady Wren not capable?"

"I didn't feel it was my place. After all, this is your domain, is it not?"

He rises to his full height and gives her a resolute look. No, he's wrong. She isn't treating him like a stranger. She's treating him like an enemy.

He pries the doors open with some cabling and Amatsu's sheath as a lever. The doors open to a dimly lit room that looks more like a vault than a library. Artifacts scattered throughout the space on shelves and tables. There is a wand taken from a wizard centuries ago. A cursed doll lies on its side next to a haunted dollhouse that was once used to trap people while the witch who made it prepared to turn her captives into dolls themselves. A few weapons line the walls: a glittering shield made from iridium, several katana long retired after the technomancers who once wielded them passed away, a few of them Kai's ancestors, and a nine-tailed whip capable of lashing a person's very soul to pieces. It sits warded and caged in a glass dome on a high shelf.

PRELUDE

Near the back of the vault is where Kai expects to find the text they have come looking for. In a cabinet, fortified with magical depressants, they keep various magical texts that have been found and seized from witches over the years. There are old tomes, older even than the first crusades, leatherbound and black as the night, seated on a low shelf, also warded. Black magic drips off them like a pestilence.

There are also Miyazaki texts, passed down from father to son and mother to daughter for as long as the Miyazaki name has existed. Books containing his family history, their duties, their lineage, and most importantly, the secrets of their abilities and how those abilities have progressed through the generations. Beside all of these should rest Wren's Book of Shadows, set there personally by his hand for protection and safekeeping until it was needed again.

It really shouldn't surprise him when he reaches the cabinet to find its doors ajar and the book they came to find missing from where it should have been. It makes no sense. The disarray of the lower floors of the library. The destruction as though somebody had decided to make a mess on purpose down there, taking nothing in the process, just trying to make it look like something had been taken, but up here, everything is spotless. Untouched save for the one text that has actually gone missing, the Songstress's Book of Shadows, protected against the prying eyes of strangers by lasting wards. The question is, how long ago did someone steal the book? Was it before or after the curse on the temple?

"It's gone."

"What do you mean it's gone?!"

Wren, who has been perusing the artifact aisles, appears behind him at his words. She sees the cabinet and the various books left, half of them scattered on the floor, and rushes forward, kneeling to inspect the texts on the ground.

"Someone has been here."

"I thought you said this room was impenetrable."

"It is."

"Then do you mind explaining to me how someone managed to break in?"

"I don't know."

"Well, you better figure it out because—"

"I said I don't know, Wren."

She grumbles something under her breath before stalking away. Kai, in the meantime, scans the books on the floor. The tomes on dark magic are untouched, as are the Miyazaki clan texts. He picks a few up and flips through them just to make sure pages haven't been torn out, but he finds no such thing. Why take just one spellbook when there were so many available to steal? What could they have possibly been looking for?

He tries to recall the different arrays he had seen inside of it during the short while he had been referencing it, but he had mostly studied her notes regarding technomancy, ignoring completely the witch-specific spells she had been working on.

"Wren,"

"Yes?"

"How many new blueprints were you working on in your Book of Shadows?"

"A few," she answers. "Why?"

"What were they?"

"What do you care?"

The deadpan she gives him is enough to make him climb the wall. She is being difficult on purpose, and he does not appreciate it.

"Just answer the question," he snaps back at her.

She huffs, crossing her arms over her chest.

"Mostly nonsense spells I never had the opportunity to cast like the resurrection spell. Most of it was potions drafts and seancy bullshit. You know, undead mayhem and all that. A few curses, but I never tested any of them. Mostly to ward away technomancers from entering an area." She cuts herself off suddenly, and Kai's eyes widen at what she just said.

"You were crafting curses that specifically target posthumans."

"No! I mean, yes, but none of them were finished!"

"Wren, this miasma is the result of a curse just like that. What else did you have in that book?"

"It doesn't matter what was in there. Your thief has done nothing but dash their own hopes and piss me off. They wouldn't be able to open it no matter what they tried. It's completely sealed to anyone other than me, myself, and I."

"I wouldn't be so sure about that."

"Excuse me?"

"I was able to open it just fine after..."

"You! How?! You aren't a witch. It should have zapped you the moment you touched it."

Quite the contrary. The book had all but fallen open in his lap the first time he built up the wherewithal to handle it in that first year after Wren's death, during the time he kept it in his quarters. Imagine his surprise when, after revealing the text to Hikaru and Fumiko, neither had been able to open it while he had flipped through its pages as easily as a magazine the night prior. Its pages shut tight to all but Kaito at the time, not that he ever made that fact known. He had yet to see if Renki could open the book, but it's been housed in the vault for nearly ten years.

"You tell me," he says.

"But that doesn't make any sense."

"Is that so?"

"Yes!"

"And why is that?"

She doesn't answer him, her teeth grinding down hard on her lips.

"So, the protection lock can be broken. Wren, be honest with me. Is there any chance you made the curse that was set on Shinka?"

"No," she hushes.

"You're positive?"

"None of the curses I invented were fatal."

"What are the chances someone altered one to make it so?"

"I am telling you: this did not come from me! I am not responsible for this curse or for the deaths of the people here, and screw you if you think I am."

"That's not what I am saying."

Wren, true to form and, really, maybe he should start expecting this kind of reaction from her, whirls away, ignores him, and stalks away, turning the corner to where the aisle changes.

Kai looks outside the nearby window and notices just how dark it's getting. The sun will be setting soon. It will take them a good while to get back to the lightcycle, and he would rather not stay here after dark. He goes after her slowly, confident she won't just throw herself down the elevator shaft.

Her behavior is disconcerting, he thinks, remembering with no small degree of discontent the last time she treated him with such reticence. It had been during the war, and Koi knows there had been plenty to deal with at the time for the both of them, and Wren... Let's just say he'll never blame her for behaving the way she had. It had taken time for them to fight it out properly so they could actually talk and return to seeing eye to eye again, but this... He feels like he's missing something. Something important, but he has no way to broach the subject without garnering more of her hostility.

"Wren, it's almost sundown. We should leave."

When he rounds the corner, he stalls, nearly plowing clean over Wren who barely even moved past the corner turn, stopped abruptly and seemingly transfixed by something in the corner of the room. Eerie how still she's become.

"Wren, let's go. We'll come back tomorrow and start looking for the source of the curse then."

"Hold on."

Kai stops at Wren's call, wondering what kind of absurdity she is concocting now.

"We cannot stay here past sundown."

"Just hold on," she hisses at him. She then turns to the direction she was looking before and hisses out, "What are you doing here?"

Kai frowns in confusion.

"You know very well what I am doing here."

"Not you, Kaito," she snips, not looking from the corner of the room. Her attention is squarely fixated on what looks like a vase or perhaps something past the vase he can't see.

The next time she speaks, she does so in Hexspeak, guttural and hoarse, sounding like dying flowers and rotting flesh were such things audible to the ear. It makes his hackles rise, and his hands itch to draw his blades. Wren continues along in this for a while longer, anger rising in her voice and posture as she goes. There must be a spirit in the room with them, and Wren is not pleased to be speaking with it. He sets a virtual boundary and maps the area for spirits. There are several around, but the one in the room with them is obscured from his base mapping system which can only mean one thing. A hexen ghost. Kai activates the next layer of his system, pulling over the present layer a blanket detection for necrotic magic. It does not fail him, and the spirit Wren is conversing with comes into sharp definition. A face from the past so starkly connected to Wren's destruction that it takes him a moment to rein in the immediate desire to destroy the ghost on impulse.

Yggfret Bloodfang, the Goblin King, who joined ranks with Seraphim during the war. The half-goblin witch whose execution Wren carried out herself.

It would seem that since his death, he has become a Villdød, the wild dead, a spirit who is formed from the remnants of a powerful witch's soul after dying a particularly agonizing or torment-filled death. Left untethered, they can wreak havoc on the living, their magics still powerful enough to kill, maim, and destroy even in death. In rare instances, a villdød could be chained by a living witch and used to exact a variety of tasks at their master's command. The casting for it is easy enough. All the summoner would need is a personal artifact of much import to the deceased and enough power to call them from the grave.

Kai has never seen one before, but there's no mistaking it. The undead before him is a villdød. It was a fate he long feared might become of Wren's soul when he learned that proper burial rights would not be observed for her. It was one of several reasons he had fought diligently to maintain custody of Wren's Book of Shadows after everything. Artifacts like that are incredibly personal to the creator, containing any number of personalized blueprints, research, castings, and, in Wren's case, musical compositions for songweaves.

But how could Yggfret be a villdød? Wren had killed him with her athame, Lacuna, the soul-eating bone dagger. The weapon lost without a trace after her death and wherein his soul should be trapped for eternity, yet here he is and far more than a run-of-the-mill ghost.

Painted and outlined in rapidly descending and sliding lines of code, Yggfret's villdød hovers larger than life, a good two feet taller than Wren but thinner than Kaito, long limbed and towering like the half-goblin he was in life even as he regards her with all of the disdainful reverence he once showed her toward the end of his life before Wren cut the skin away from his chest, broke his ribcage open, and pulled out his heart to rest in his mouth until he suffocated to death.

The witch and the villdød go back and forth, Yggfret seeming to goad Wren on until he lifts his hand and shoves dark energy in her direction. Wren blocks the attack easily enough, but the distraction is all the spirit needs to take off down the hallway.

"Get back here, you fiend!"

"Wren, stop!"

If she hears him, she ignores him as she races down the aisle of artifacts after the spirit of Yggfret, practically shoving Kai out of the way in her hurry. She dives for the exit as though the devil were at her heels. There's a loud crash behind him, but he pays it no mind, taking off after the witch.

"*Kuso!*"

They do not have time for this. It is almost nightfall; they've been here too long as it is. No telling what new surprises await them with the setting of the sun.

PRELUDE

Just as Wren reaches the elevator doors, he catches her from behind, pulling her off her feet.

"What the hell, Kai?"

"We do not have time for this."

"Let go!"

"What are you going to do? Jump down the elevator shaft?!"

"No! I want to know who dug up that bastard's soul and set it here."

She elbows him in the ribcage, and he drops her, pain shooting up his side. She falls, sputtering to the floor, twisting as she goes. She seems entirely unbothered by him and even kicks at his left leg for good measure. He blocks her kick by grabbing her ankle which she pulls roughly, bringing him down on top of her. Their heads crash together, bony joints knocking against the wooden floor and each other. An ear-piercing scream sounds to his left. A soundwave hurls into them, and they are shoved sideways into the elevator, almost straight down the emergency hatch. Kai's sights spin wildly, and he hears Wren coughing underneath him, the wind knocked out of her from landing flat on her back. His added impact not helping in the slightest. Neither is the fact that her upper body is hanging halfway out of the emergency hatch.

He moves to pull her up, and another soundwave ricochets through the shaft, only this time it is not them. It's aiming for the elevator's locks. The car shudders beneath them, and a loud snapping sound comes from above them. Kai's stomach lurches as the elevator plummets. Wren gives a sharp shout and latches onto Kai's shoulders, her nails digging into the flesh there.

He pulls back, dragging Wren along with him. She is screaming, panic in her eyes as she thrashes in his hold. He shakes her, willing some semblance of sense back into her. Her scream subsides, and she looks at him.

"Wren, slow it down."

She nods her head wildly, and he lets her go.

Wren rolls herself onto her knees, palms pressed flat into the metal flooring and begins to channel energy into the rapidly descending car. It doesn't stop. It doesn't even slow down enough to matter. She needs more time. He has approximately five seconds before they end up as nothing but rubble at the bottom of the shaft. He draws Tsukuyomi from her sheath, coats it with saibāki and thrusts her through the metal of the car into the outer wall. He grits his teeth and hardens the energy over the blade of his sword, praying the steel doesn't snap in two.

The car slows.

He hears Wren's voice. A fevered song falling around the space and the car slows just as they reach the first-floor doorway. He looks over to see Wren straining to hold the weight of the lift against gravity, sweat beading around the triskelion and the spiraling designs that fall around her temples. Kai dislodges his katana from the wall, grabs the back of Wren's jacket, and pulls her with him out of the falling elevator and onto the first-floor landing. They land in a heap; this time Wren's knees land directly in his gut. Her song chokes off, and the elevator falls straight down and through the base boards. A loud crash rises to meet them when the car meets its final destination underground.

"Shit! Sorry!"

Wren moves off him as Kai coughs his airway clear and plops down to curl up on the floor holding her head in her hands.

"It's fine," says Kai as he moves to stand up. Wren coughs, and when he looks, he finds her wiping fresh blood from her nose. "Are you well?"

"Just the usual headache," she answers with a wince, but she unfolds herself, sniffles once, and lying on her stomach, looks over the edge of the landing. She whistles.

"Wow. I didn't realize there were subterranean caverns under Shinka."

Kai looks up, unsure what she means. Other than the underground waterway that bridged the mountain to the sea, there are no caverns under Shinka. At least not any Kai has ever been made privy to, and as the heir presumptive to Murasaki no Yama, it is his duty to know these things.

"We don't."

Wren turns back to him, still lying on her side and rolling across her stomach to look at him.

"Then you should probably take a loo—"

Wren's words are cut off by a strangled cry as something grabs her from behind and pulls her straight down the now vacant elevator shaft. Kai is up in a flash and dropping down after her. Wren is kicking and twisting in the grasp of a large beast. It hunches down and drags her with it, and *kuso!* It moves fast. He gives chase, not even taking the time to ponder that yes, there are indeed caverns under Shinka, considering he's running straight through them, rotten wood and debris kicked up in his face in the wake of the creature's mad dash into the underground.

Kai covers his eyes as the beast barrels through a planked wall and into an open chamber. Wren manages to swing herself around and poke the creature in the eye, her sharp nails causing the beast to rear back in pain. She pays for it when the monster shrieks and throws her into a wall. Bloody water drips down into the cave, blood red and splashing everywhere as Wren lands right in a puddle of it.

With Wren out of the way, he moves forward, Tsukuyomi slashing the space the creature inhabits, and Kai gets a good look at the monster. It's tall, at least a meter taller than Kaito. Humanoid in shape with clawed hands and feet, legs looking lycanthropic in nature, but the upper body is distinctly human, dark skin thatched with pockets of coarse fur, and the head! An elongated snout and jaw lined with razor sharp teeth, black beady eyes crowned by a treacherous decoration of antlers sizable to a great stag and pointed enough to run a person through. Kai strikes again, but the creature ducks its head down, and Kai's sword falls into the tangle of hardened keratin, stuck fast. Amatsu finds its way into Kai's hand, and he uses it to deflect the claws looking to eviscerate him. One of the swipes catches him across the lower ribcage, but he also gets in a slash across its hind leg.

Kai pulls on Tsukuyomi to dislodge it, and the sword comes free much to the rage of the monster. It lunges for him, jaws snapping for his throat. He lifts both of his blades up in an X in front of him, and teeth come down on both blades. To his right, he hears Wren stagger up with a groan, and ozone pulls taut she draws on the tides of chaos.

"Kai, move!"

He kicks the creature in the gut and jumps away as the ceiling comes down on the beast's head. It thrashes under the weight of the rock until it is buried completely, but even under the rubble, he hears it roar along with the furious scratching sounds— already digging its way back out.

Time to go.

He catches Wren, unsteady and angling sideways, under her bicep and pulls her forward, leading them in a race through uncharted tunnels. Kai activates his virtual mapping, miles worth of tunnels, beaming, and trashed equipment unfurl in his code-readers. These tunnels are ancient, older even than the temple. Lavender coding flickers over everything in his range, and he finds a means up to the surface. Kai throws Amatsu to use the connecting cable as a rope to climb the steep slope. Wren takes hold of the cable with both hands, pulling herself along too, Kai pushing her forward every time she falls onto all fours in front of him. There is a bite wound at the junction of her neck and shoulder where the creature nabbed her. Her skin is flushed and hot to the touch. The bite may be toxic.

When they reach the top of the slope, he hears the raging monster clamoring behind them. He breaks apart the wooden planks that keep the soil above their heads from falling in, and the dirt falls into his face. He covers his eyes, reaches into the dark earth, and starts to bore his way through, using Tsukuyomi as a makeshift shovel. There is at least half a meter of earth between them and the surface.

"Wren, push the ground up!"

She takes a moment longer than normal to process his words, but then, limply, her hands rise, and she pushes her magic up and breaks through. Kai lets go of Amatsu, and the blade automatically settles itself into its sheath. He looks back to find their attacker already climbing up the slope after them, hands and feet in the dirt, clawing its way up rapidly. Too rapidly. Kai grabs Wren under the armpits and heaves her up and out of the hole before following after her.

Wren grabs his arm and gives him a single sharp tug to pull him out as well before falling backward onto her ass. She starts to laugh uncontrollably, clenching her stomach and gasping for air even as she can't stave off the fit. She looks like a shrieking ghoul, covered in blood and mud from the curse-polluted pools. When she looks at him, her pupils are blown wide, the early onset of delirium.

"It's a wendigo!" Wren howls. "You have a bloody wendigo in your temple!"

Kai pulls her back to her feet, a sharp curse on his tongue, but she keeps laughing, shuffling along as he makes his way to the temple stairs just as the wendigo breaks the surface right behind them, saliva dripping from its fangs, hunger apparent in its cold black gaze.

20

TWO OF PENTACLES
(AN UNEXPECTED DRAW)

KAI DRAGS HER DOWN THE TEMPLE STEPS BY the arm. Wren shudders and her teeth chatter even though it feels like her skin is on fire, fighting to keep running until her feet give out from underneath her. The ground hurdles up toward her, but Kai scoops her up like a sack of potatoes just before she eats it. (Heh, a sack of potatoes! Kai's never lifted a sack of potatoes in his life!) She doesn't know how he manages it, but he has one arm under her back, the other under her knees, and Tsukuyomi hovers vibrating with power alongside. If she blacks out, she doesn't remember. What she does remember is seeing teeth about to close down on Kai's arm, and she lifts a hand to force it away. Even when she's high as a kite, her telekinesis doesn't fail. The wendigo howls as her magic slaps it in the face, cracking off an antler. Tsukuyomi coils around her body to strike at the creature and delivers her own strike to the beast's flank.

The wendigo relents long enough for them to reach the lightcycle. Wren calls the antler to her hand and clutches it to her side.

PRELUDE

Kai all but chucks Wren onto the front of the bike, not trusting her to grip him strongly enough to stay on riding behind him. He winds his arms around her to reach the handles, activates the engine, and takes off down the mountain, Wren cursing at him in her own loving little way, as the beast gnashes its teeth at them, a swipe of its claws finding Kai's bicep as he grinds the gas to get them out of there, the wendigo hot on their treads. Wren, despite the pounding in her head, grabs a pistol from behind Kai's hip and aims over Kai's shoulder at the wendigo. She fires off three shots. The first beam goes wide, the second hits the beast square in the leg, and the third impacts it in the shoulder. It's just about all of the concentration she can manage before her vision swims.

Eventually, the distance between them and their pursuer becomes too great, and the creature gives up the chase.

At the foot of the mountain is a small town by the name of Heion. It's about twenty-five minutes from the temple grounds. Kai pulls them into the parking lot at a small inn. In the darkness of the night folded around the city, the streetlamps seem painfully bright to Wren's eyes. She is more than a little queasy, her shoulder and neck feel like they are on fire, and her head hurts something wicked from being pulled through several wooden planks face first, and she is fairly positive she looks half dead on her feet between the sticky feeling of the blood soaking into her side and the sweat dripping into her eyes. Though when she thinks about it, that is probably minor. The look of abject horror on the innkeeper's face reminds her that she is covered in mud and gore from the blood pool, something she probably should have thought about when she decided to walk up with Kai rather than wait outside.

Well, it was less her walking up with him so much as him half carrying/dragging her limp body after she made it very clear that she would gladly crawl her way after him if necessary. He's got her hiked up high against his hip so that her feet just skim the floor, not that she is trying to walk very much anyway despite her protests to the treatment.

"It's my shoulder, not my leg. I can walk just fine."

He gives her a look that reminds her that she quite nearly faceplanted right after stepping off the cycle, but that's not really her fault. The blood had just gone out from her legs for a second. She is fine!

The innkeeper even offers to call an ambulance or the police for her if necessary, which she quickly passes up with a laugh and joke, much to Kai's chagrin.

"Oh, no, no, no. I doubt they'd know what to do with me, and I hate needles anyway. And look, I know this gorgeous hunk looks scary with all his fancy augmentations, but I promise, he only beats me when I ask nicely."

To which Kai promptly lets her drop to the floor where she cackles like a hyena for a good two minutes, much to the woman's horror.

Poor Prince Kaito! He has to flash the innkeeper his Technomancer ID before she leaves them well enough alone, (Hehe, she nearly bludgeoned herself on the countertop, she bowed so fast!) but she still looks like she wants to call the local police on Kai for domestic abuse or something, or maybe she's wondering if she should be calling the nearest loony bin. This is not helped by the fact that he quickly ushers her up the stairs and out of sight once he has their room confirmed.

And what's the big deal, anyway?

Kai looks just as dirty as she does. He may not have been physically dragged into a secret underground basement, but he's been wrapped around her and manhandling her plenty since their flirting with death. Why is the innkeeper only staring at her like she's a walking corpse that has just walked into her establishment?

Probably because even covered in viscera, Kai is still way too pretty.

She does shout down that a few extra towels would be appreciated if they can spare them. When the innkeeper makes a strangled noise, Kai apologizes profusely while ushering her into their assigned quarters for the evening. Wren honestly doesn't have it in her to care. Kai trudges his way into the room, and all but tosses her, torn clothes as all, into the shower. For a second, she thinks he is going to get in there with her and bathe her himself so she offers for him to join her; he all but slams the door on the way out, leaving her under a very cold spray of water with a terse statement that he will have clothes brought to her.

A resounding "no" then.

She laughs in his wake, but it isn't long until she calms under the cold water. Crimson circles the drain, and with it the adrenaline rush that has been burning through her veins since those jaws closed on her neck and shoulder. Eventually, she figures she should probably rid herself of her clothes if she plans on bathing properly. She realizes idly that she is more than a little loopy from the pain and wonders with a dull sense of concern if the creature's teeth were the cause of her strange mental space. That would account for her unreasonable behavior, ricocheting violently from the scared-shitless end of the spectrum to the everything-is-coming-up-daisies end. Hell, she'd nearly thrown herself off of the lightcycle during their flight just because an oncoming semi had honked at them as they went, then promptly, after said crisis was past, attempted to grope Kaito, who really is a better man than she gives him credit for because how he managed to deflect her and keep the bike stable at the same time, truly must be a superhuman feat.

Ah, he truly is the definition of human+.

She never turns on the hot water, choosing instead to let the cold sober her back up before actually making any such attempt to get the blood out of her hair and skin. It's nearly thirty minutes later that the blood stops circling the drain, and she has scrubbed the bite wound so hard it is bleeding again, which to her only means that she can get the injected endorphins out of her system all the faster.

When she finally turns off the water, it with a heavy sigh, a lackluster enthusiasm, and maybe a twinge of embarrassment at her antics. Had she really tried to feel him up while they were running from a wendigo! And that's another thing! A wendigo. A snarling, gnashing, rotting-ball-of-cannibalism wendigo. How did a wendigo find its way into and den itself under Shinka Temple? It is unthinkable.

She shakes her head and leans heavily against the sink where a pair of loose black pants and top have been set for her, but she doesn't reach to pull the clothes over her head right away. Instead, she studies her reflection. It is the first time she has really looked at herself since her resurrection, and it's a little jarring. Other than the gaping wound at her shoulder, the cuts on her forearm, there is not a single scar on her. It feels wrong, naturally. Her scars were her story written in pain and blood on her body. The tiny scar on her knee that looked like Deriva's largest island if she turned her head and squinted at it a bit. She got it the first time she went coral diving. It's gone. The little scars on her knuckles from when she was nine and she and her brother started practice sparring. She jammed her fist on Xipilli's teeth and split her knuckles open. She got several stitches for it while Xipilli got a double visit from the tooth fairy as the last two of his front teeth came right out on impact. Those were gone too. There are others absent, of course. Some she vaguely recalls, others that stood out starkly in the dark, some she will not miss in a million lifetimes. To be missing those scars now, she questions if any of those memories even happened or if maybe they had happened to another person separated from her entirely by time and space and death.

Maybe she is still dead, and this whole thing is all just a dead dream, a fantasy dribbled up from pent up energy making her hallucinate through her last sleep, and any moment, she'll wake back up as one of the damned.

But then she pinches her arm and remembers. The dead don't feel pain, and the body she is in currently is very much living and breathing. A total system reset couldn't have been more perfectly executed. It's mind-boggling to her still, how a coven of non-witches managed to accomplish making, summoning, and recreating her.

Prelude

Katrina, LuQin, Atalia, Sarah, Emilio, Hoshi, Amani, and Nadia... Humans, fledgling witches, little sisters/brothers, tortured souls. A coven of victims attempting the impossible. And voila! Here Wren stands in a body that is hers and not hers at the same time.

But not everything has been reset.

She channels a bit of power, and the flowing viridian designs of her wild script bloom to life on her brow and temples. They wind down the sides of her throat, over her shoulders and end at her middle fingers. Wild script flows across her skin more deeply ingrained into her network than any tattoo or piercing. Her Indicia: the triskele at the center of her forehead shines as bright as the first day she woke with it.

She remembers clearly when her markings used to be much, much simpler, starting and ending with the three interlocking spirals at the center of her brow. The Triskele symbolizes the spiraling connections between three seemingly opposing forces, realms, or ideas like life, death, and rebirth or spiritual, physical, and celestial, or even the three parts of humanity: physical, mental, emotional. She's never read too deeply into why this was the source design for her indicia. At the time, it seemed rather arbitrary and strange that she would carry it. As a telekinetic, she always assumed the triad of calling, rejecting, and keeping the three states of movement were where the significance of the symbol laid with her, but Jessabelle had merely looked at her sagely when she'd voiced this aloud one day in the midst of recovery. The older witch once told her that only a very special witch could bear such a mark.

Looking at it now, five days into her resurrection, the meaning of it becomes too heavy for her to properly process right now.

Over time, a witch's indicia can expand and grow, creating more markings under the witch's skin linked to the original indicia. The more markings the more powerful the witch. Wren had many markings, and a teenage Wren watched in horror as more and more appeared on her skin despite her best efforts to reject the flow of magic in her veins. She tried to hide them at first, but that was another thing that had been entirely unfair at the time. Most witches can hide their indicia with clothing, but not Wren! Wren's indicia is in the middle of her damn forehead for all the world to see if she so much as laughs too hard. Some things never get easier. Better to accept things for what they are than try to hide any ugly truths.

With a sigh, Wren pulls on the clothes left for her and leaves the bathroom, feeling a little more human but even less sure, especially considering the man waiting for her outside the door.

Kai stands in the middle of the room, a comm unit in hand as he speaks in the flowing language of his home tongue to his brother and aunt, no doubt relaying to them the events of the day. The missing Book of Shadows, the wendigo, the cursed miasma, Yggfret's damned ghost showing up at the temple, and *¡Mierda!* What's up with that? Who gave that asshole any kind of permission to become an undead? She had taken great pains to make sure that did not happen after she killed him and still! She will murder the person whenever she finds out who they are, and she will find out. She can guarantee it. Will she actually murder them? Who knows? But they better have a damned good explanation for this.

She scoffs at herself, drawing Kai's attention. When he turns around to look at her, she shakes her head halfway between wanting to laugh and sob at his appearance. He is covered in dirt, and if it weren't for the smear of blood along his face and torso, she probably would have laughed. Instead, she swallows thickly around the lump in her throat and moves farther into the room, gesturing that the bathroom is all his if he wants it, which, considering the fact that he disconnects the call not long after, is probably very much the case. He takes his bag with him into the shower room and shuts the door.

Wren plops herself down on the lounge, but she doesn't stay there for long. She still feels a bit feverish, and her shoulder is throbbing something wicked. She should probably clean and bandage it before her insane capacity for healing closes the skin over a festering wound, but she can't exactly see it well enough to clean it herself, and besides, her head is too filled with too many whos, whats, and whys to sit still, and she is fed up with Kai manhandling her, which is kind of funny to her for some asinine reason she is so not going to think about right now, so the moment his back is turned, she stands right back up.

Who took her book? Who could have had access? No one according to Kaito, and while he is certainly pretty guarded with the truth sometimes, he is not very practiced at lying.

At least not face to face... she thinks bitterly. Elements be damned! She just wants to finish this and be on her merry way.

A wendigo! What else had antlers and sharp fangs and an unceasing hunger for human flesh! How is there a wendigo in Shinka? Did somebody put it there? How does one even deal with a wendigo, *anyway*? To her knowledge, no one had seen one in decades. They were more myth than monster, and there was only one way to kill it. And it was just her luck too, the only way to kill it would be to burn it alive with fire. Fire! You know, the element that killed her some twelve years ago. Burn it alive with fire. Light it on fire while still alive so that its screams are very audible, very apparent, and the smell of burning flesh gets charred into her nostrils as much as the day she died.

And so her thoughts progress, one after the other after the other, and maybe it's because of the toxin from the wendigo's bite, but her blood pressure is rising, and she feels more than a little panicked for no reason whatsoever. She keeps glancing toward the window, half expecting to see beady black eyes staring back at her while she plots the death of the stupid thing.

Oh! And don't even get her started on the miasma. Or the damned villdød! How can there be so many problems in one stupid place? Didn't these Miyazaki plusies do anything to maintain the safety of their so-called sacred temple?!

She is pacing fervently around the room by the time Kai returns from the bathroom, clean, wearing fresh clothing, and toweling his hair dry. Her hands grip her hair and face and head as she walks back and forth across the space, muttering to herself. Her spoken thoughts are so erratic, her movements even more so, that Kai looks at her with worry lining his brow like she is going to cause herself even more damage if she doesn't sit down. That's probably true, but she has too much bottled up energy to sit.

"Wren?"

Wren cuts him off before he can voice a question or tell her to calm down.

"Sorry about my antics, by the way. Pretty sure the thing's venom made me pretty stoned. Did you happen to get a recording on its lair while we were down there?"

"It is in my memory banks."

"Can I check something?"

"Only if you'll sit and let me bandage your shoulder while I rerun it."

She screws her face up at him.

"So mean, highness."

"Sit," he instructs, a stern look on his face, and she pouts as she goes to settle on the lounge. She won't admit it, but sitting down feels incredibly good right now. Her shoulders slump, and even though it pulls on the bite, she rolls the muscles out. A satisfying pop sounds in the wake of the action, and she settles, eyes feeling dry and overly sensitive when the light of the holoprojector flips on at Kai's command.

Most of the sequence is a blur of rapid movements and discombobulated glances around the space as the wendigo races down into the caverns with her in its jaws. Kai passes her control over the playback, and she rewards him for the action with a dazzling smile before she begins to stop and start the recording, rewinding and fast forwarding as Kai's vision tracks through different parts of the underground and onto the creature as they fight. The moment when Wren sees herself get thrown into the wall, Kai's recorded gaze immediately follows, and Wren pauses the frame. The basement wall is etched with runes, and Wren pulls over a piece of paper and a pen to start jotting them down.

As she studies the still frame, she notices that Kai, despite having settled down next to her, has yet to begin treating her shoulder. In fact, he seems to be watching her work.

"I thought you were going to bandage my shoulder?"

"I need you to move your sleeve."

Oh, right. There is that. She kind of expected him to do it himself. Not like they hadn't once been far more than familiar with each other's bodies, but, she supposes, that was lifetime ago for her, and a long time ago for him. She rolls her eyes and tugs down the shirt until her shoulder is exposed, and surprisingly enough, it feels strangely intimate. She shakes the thought away and returns her attention to the recording.

"It's discolored," he says.

"I can't see it. Is it purple or green?"

"Yellow around the edges and its swelling."

"That's to be expected. Don't worry. Witchy healing. I'll be fine by morning."

Kai says nothing more as she zooms in on another sigil. As she begins to copy it down, Kai's hand grasps her shoulder, and the strength of his grip makes her lose focus, headiness blurring her vision, but then he begins to clean the bite with an alcohol swab. She hisses as he works but maintains her attention on the holo, getting through three more sketches as she finds them.

"You should take a stim."

"Don't need it," she says off-handedly. She doesn't. Once she finishes working the toxin out of her system, her natural healing abilities will take care of the rest.

"Must you be so stubborn?"

"You mean to tell me you didn't miss that part of my sparkling personality?"

There is a moment where Wren imagines Kai's gaze opening with a strange vulnerability. She might have mistaken it for yearning had it stayed long enough, but all too quickly, Kai's expression closes, not that it was terribly open before, but it's like a shutter slams shut behind his eyes with such finality that she definitely believes she imagined the brief moment. Wren almost regrets her words, but when has she ever been one to linger in regret?

What does put her off is the sudden dismissal of the holograph.

"Hey!"

He ignores her, and lest she decide to act even more like a petulant child, she is forced to sit there while he finishes dealing with her shoulder. When the bandage is finally in place around her shoulder (She should say thank you. Should she thank him?), Kai gets up and makes to walk to the opposite side of the room where he set their bags earlier. She would have let him too were it not for the stutter-stop first step he takes when he stands.

"You're hurt."

He grunts at her.

"Really? Aren't you a little too technolyzed to be giving me caveman responses?"

"Leave it alone, Wren."

"No," she says sharply, standing up and trailing after him. She crowds into him and snatches for the hem of his shirt. His hands catch her wrists in a deadlock. Kai's silver eyes lock onto hers. To any sane person, the hard look in them would have read plainly that this was most definitely a back off and retreat kind of moment. Wren, however, who laughed at the very idea of sanity numerous times in her life, only translates his look for the challenge it is. "Who's being stubborn now?"

He twists away from her, but the movement must pull on the injury because he cuts his movement midway.

She shakes her head.

"Come on! I can heal it for you, and you can save yourself the stim."

"You should worry about yourself."

I'd rather have you worry about me. The thought comes to her unbidden and entirely unwelcome. It smacks her mental space hard enough that she reels backward, thankful she didn't just mouth off again. Irritation tingles under her scalp.

"Will you just let me heal you?!"

Kai holds her gaze for a long still moment while she fumes at him. Stubborn man. Eventually though, he exhales and pulls his shirt up and off.

Wren stops breathing. Not because of the sight of his injury or anything superfluous like his muscular physique. No, she stops breathing because around his neck is a very familiar necklace. The very same corded-leather necklace she wove for him, complete with the three beads of malachite and a pair of seashells. It looks well-worn, the once black leather now off-shade and closer to a gray, but taken care of, the clasp too new in comparison to the leather, and the malachite as glossy as when she first threaded them through the cabling.

Why does he still have it? Shouldn't he have thrown it away?

She coughs around the ball in her throat and looks to the real reason he has so graciously removed his shirt for her.

The gash on his back is pretty gnarly. Four long swipes, not deep, but they reach from the top of the posterior side of his ribcage and curl around to near his front hip. He must be in far more pain than he is letting on. She is almost impressed. To think he lugged her sorry ass around with this on his side. Ok, nevermind. She is a little impressed.

She whistles in admiration.

"Wow, your pain blockers must be out of this world."

No response.

"Like seriously, did you add an adrenaline boost somewhere into your upgrades because damn!"

He grunts at her. She keeps babbling.

"Holy starfish! Any deeper and you would have lost a kidney. Wait, do you still even have both kidneys? Doesn't matter. It would have gotten your spleen for sure. I hear wendigo like phlegm."

"More like a chunk of my liver."

He speaks!

"Well, thank your lucky stars it wasn't. Jaundice would not be a good look for you."

"Lady Wren is too kind."

She quips something equally sarcastic back and stops actively following the conversation even as she continues to goad him. The banter is good. It's familiar but not at the same time. At least he is letting her touch him. She reaches forward and hums.

Magic blossoms from her fingertips, and she feeds it into his skin. It's an easy casting, returning to her as clearly as the day Jessabelle first taught it to her back in a time when she had still been wrestling with her new identity. Her heart clenches, remembering the witch who saved her life a lifetime ago, and her hands ache remembering how the woman had guided her one step at a time into her new life as gently as a lover.

Whose fault is it she's dead? A voice growls at her, and Kai hisses as the intensity of her spell fluctuates into something almost malicious.

"Sorry," she whispers, agitated with herself for getting worked up.

She screws her eyes shut in a harsh blink, banishing the grief and the anger with a prayer to the dead before she can lose focus on what she's doing.

The torn flesh begins to knit itself back together. Wren doesn't look at Kai's face as she does it. She's never actually healed someone else like this before other than the one time little Fae took a tumble and scraped her knee. The toddler had been screaming more from the shock of the fall than anything else, but the soothing flow of a quick healing spell over the injury calmed her down and not even the smallest scar remained afterward.

Kai's injury is a little more substantial. It takes longer, requires more focus on her part, and by the time she is finished, she feels a little lightheaded, but the skin is repaired without any sign of scarring, and while she imagines the area is still a bit tender, it shouldn't cause him any problems.

"You still have that ugly old thing."

He stiffens.

"Does that surprise you?" he asks, cautious. Cautious in the way a snake charmer approaches his basket, his flute at the ready should the serpent decide to strike.

She doesn't answer.

Her fingers ache, wanting to brush against smooth skin, to touch the leather of the necklace and test if it is warm from his body heat, but she dismisses the urge with a shake of her head, retreating to the far side of the room to stew in her own festering regrets and bitter thoughts. Perhaps the bantering had been a bad idea.

"Thank you."

She turns back to look at Kai, surprised. He has put his shirt back on and is looking at her, the necklace tucked safely away under his collar. She shrugs her good shoulder and says, "You bandaged my shoulder. It's only fair."

"Even so."

Her skin is starting to feel hot and clammy again. Maybe she exerted too much energy on Kai. Her hands are shaking, and her vision keeps blurring. She can feel her pulse behind her eyelids.

"Glad my magic tricks could be of service to you, highness," she singsongs.

"Wren, that's not—"

"See you tomorrow," she says, dismissing him and the rest of whatever conversation he might like to be having with her in favor of wandering into the bedroom area of the suite. The door shuts with a sharp click. Pulling out the bedclothes and sliding in among the cushions, she notes somewhere in the back of her mind there is only one bed in the room. Odd... She settles herself right in the middle anyway, uncaring of his comfort level. It's going to be a rough night of tossing and turning anyway.

Clad all in white, upon a violet bank,
I saw thee half reclining; while the moon
Fell on the upturn-d faces of the roses,
And on thine own, upturn'd—alas, in sorrow!
...And in an instant all things disappeared.
(Ah, bear in mind this garden was enchanted!)

An Excerpt from "To Helen"
Edgar Allen Poe, Old World, 1831 A.D.

21
DEATH PART 1

W REN'S ACQUAINTANCE WITH DEATH DID not start and end with the date listed on her death certificate. It started long before.

The first time Wren met Death was the day her mother died. A seadragon, barely more than a fledgling, had latched onto Wren's hand and pulled her under the water after the little girl had fallen in from where she and her siblings had been sitting on the dock. Wren's mother had been watching the three children from a nearby rock ledge, and when Wren's head disappeared from the surface coupled in junction with Atzi's scream, Freya Nocturne dove into the water. Wren's mother wrestled Wren out of the *ahuizotl*'s mouth, but the creature caught her instead dragging her under as one of their guards pulled a screaming Wren out of the water.

She had been ten years old.

Her second meeting with Death was the accident during the combat trials that killed Oswald Llywelyn. She doesn't think too long on this one. There isn't any remaining guilt there. It hadn't been her fault, but she had still watched him die.

Prelude

The third time though, the third time had been more than any seventeen-year-old should ever have to face. After that, Wren's relationship with Death changed.

And Kaito...

Kaito watched her embrace death like a lover.

Sixteen Years Ago–The Month of Falling 1861

The day after returning home from his latest case, one that he was assigned with Wren, Kaito is nervous. He has been thinking this over and over in his head. There are more pressing, more immediate things he should be concerned with, but every time he goes to review what they found during their mission, he can't help but remember the warmth of her smile, the softness of her touch, and how it had felt to be there for her when sickness weakened her momentarily. About asking her to dinner followed by a nervous proposal that she spend the night with him since the case wrapped up later than they expected. Waking up with her. Seeing her off in the morning.

Her laughter still rings in his ears from when they'd been fooling around, wrestling and play-fighting before finally making love again. He knows himself, and he knows what he wants, knows that his mother will support him even if his aunt has a conniption at the prospect of Wren returning to Murasaki no Yama in any capacity, but she'll survive. He has no reason to be nervous about wanting to discuss such a minor thing as his relationship Wren Nocturne, but he is as he looks for an audience with his mother where she sits out on the deck during the time she usually takes her tea. She is there just as he expected, perusing emails and reports as she sips daintily from a pretty teacup.

"Mother, do you have a moment?"

Empress Mirai looks up from the monitor to meet his eye. The blue glare of her sights clears, the holo in her hand disappears with it, and the clear chocolate brown of her gaze finds him. She smiles gently at her youngest son.

"Kaito, of course. Sit."

He settles himself gracefully on the settee. A nearby attendee offers him a warm cup of tea which he accepts gratefully. He sips carefully, jasmine, his mother's favorite, before speaking.

"Seraphim has declared war on Aighneas. President Gewalt has been taken into hiding. Her generals rally around her while General Llywelyn drops missiles on her major cities. They have managed to deflect a major portion of the attacks, but Seraphim's drone technology and robotics research surpasses Aighneas' more primitive means of warfare. Their pilots lose their lives while Seraphim only loses scraps of metal."

His mother hums.

"That's right. You and Lady Wren, wasn't it, overheard a transmission from Seraphim. I've read the mission brief you wrote. You two did well together."

"Wren and I foiled the operation they were trying to launch along the coast."

"Unfortunately, the situation continues to escalate on the other side of the continent. Our remote hacking technologies protect us from further invasion for now, but they do not seem to be focused on us at the moment. I worry who their next target will be. I don't think Murasaki no Yama will be able to stay neutral for much longer."

She takes a sip of her tea, clears her throat, and settles the cup back on the saucer with a gentle clink. There is a finality in the gesture that Kai reads easily.

"But this isn't the reason you have come to see me, is it, *akachan*?"

His throat clenches, and the nervousness he has been feeling since his return to Snowfall returns in full force. He is not afraid to voice his request. Not at all. He would shout it out from the rooftops, were the idea not so readily frowned upon by his aunt. No, he is afraid of what her answer will be, what she will think of his choice.

He nods his head with a small hum in the positive.

"Mother, I realize it is highly untraditional of me to seek this audience with you while my elder brother is yet still unwed; however, it is a cherished rule of our people that we listen to and obey the directives of our heart."

She settles her teacup in its saucer.

"Oh... Please, continue."

"In the last year, I have met and grown close to someone of my age. Another technomancer, who I have now shared much of myself with, and she has reciprocated in turn."

His mother hums. She slides her hands into the open sleeves of her kimono.

"And who is the young woman who has captured my son's eye?"

"Lady Wren Nocturne."

"Ah, yes, I remember Lady Wren. House Moctezumo of the Derivan royal family. She is the daughter of Vulcan Tlanextli and his dearly departed Firefly, is she not? A bright and talented young lady. She drove your aunt quite mad with her constant questions. My poor sister has always hated dealing with students who are as inquisitive as herself, but that's karma for you. She is quite the beauty if I remember correctly."

That's certainly true enough.

"Yes, kaa-san. I wish to court her publicly and in the open. If she would have me, I would ask for her hand in marriage. With your blessing, of course."

The empress's smile remains warm, but her eyes shift as she looks at him.

"I knew her mother, did you know?"

He shakes his head, patiently waiting for her to continue.

"I was still young when I first met her, and she really wasn't much older than your aunt and me. Your father and I were soon to be wed, and your grandparents were still alive. My responsibilities were to myself and my soon-to-be husband more so than to the crown in those days. My mother brought her to court to act as a mentor to me, a guide, if you will, as I took my first steps into marriage and starting a family. She was my teacher, my friend, and eventually my midwife. She stayed right here in Shinka until your brother reached his first birthday. It was here she met Tlanextli.

"The gossip surrounding Freya's marriage to Vulcan Tlanextli was salacious. 'How cunning she must have been! Such a talented seductress to inspire a king nearly ten years her senior to take a second wife despite the ire of his first.' Freya Nocturne was a smart woman, indeed. Powerful in her own way. No one quite knew where she came from before she made her premiere as a Firefly. Fair skinned, light-haired, and indeed quite beautiful. As an organic, she was mysterious and entrancing, and her patrons loved that about her. There was not an eye left unturned when she entered a room, and when she sang, it was like a spell was cast over the audience. She made her way from nothing with the careful gesturing of her hand. Some even said she practiced witchcraft, but they were mere rumors.

"The lessons she departed on me during her time here seemed limitless, but I knew that what she taught me could only be a fraction of her experience and knowledge. Knowledge I know without a doubt she would have bestowed upon her daughter before her death so Wren would be armed and armored when she decided to walk onto love's battlefield. And having seen Lady Wren myself during her time here, I can certainly attest that she is as enchanting as her mother."

There is a glimmer in his mother's eye that he doesn't quite understand. An accusation or a cautionary gleam?

"The number of men and women I saw fall in love with Freya was no small number even in the short four years she spent here. Those kinds of fancies, when not reciprocated, are heartbreaking, Kaito, and Freya was very good at not reciprocating affection, but she was also a Firefly, ready and able to offer companionship and company, even fulfilling their desires when she so chose. She let their affections run their course until all that remained was fond friendship and intimate camaraderie. It is my understanding that Elisabeta made sure Wren passed her Firefly assessments before allowing her to attend the Technomancer Trials."

"I don't understand."

She reaches across the tables and takes his hand.

"Kaito," she starts. "You are young. Beautiful young girls are dangerous waters to tread. Wren, I hear, takes after her mother, and your aunt tells me her charms caused quite a few ruckuses during the trials. A pretty smile and a coy glance are all it takes for the most skilled students in the arts of companionship to lull a man into believing he's in love."

"Wren is not manipulating me, mother."

"And Freya did not manipulate Tlanextli. She loved him as much if not more than he loved her. She would not have accepted his proposal otherwise. That was the kind of person she was."

"Then why..."

"You may or may not be aware of this, but Elisabeta explicitly brought Wren to the summit to present her to politically advantageous suitors. I do not want for either of my sons a loveless marriage."

He fingers the necklace hidden under his collar. All this worry from his mother for that.

"That's not the way of it, Kaa-san. Wren worked hard to pass the trials so her stepmother couldn't marry her off. What I feel for her it's... I..."

He grits his teeth, frustrated. Neural nets! Why is this so difficult!!

Mirai watches her son carefully as he prepares his next words. This is not the first time she has had such a conversation. During Hikaru's teenage years, he had on two separate occasions expressed a desire to pursue a crush, and it had broken her heart each time Hikaru had found his affections returned not for who he was but for his station and what he could offer them. And by the end of each dalliance, he had learned his affections were not so deep as he could live with one-sided affection. Each time he had come to her and sat with nervous energy before her to make these requests. A boy approaching manhood, fidgety and blind, uncertain of his heart but eager to explore. Each time, she recognized the childish signs of puppy love and foolishly given her blessing, and her eldest boy had paid the price. She does not wish the same for her youngest. However...

Kaito does not look like Hikaru.

There is certainty in the line of her younger son's brow. A firm setting in the length of his shoulders and the ridge of his spine. He looks at her with the deference and respect of a son to his mother, but it is no longer a boy looking back at her. Sometime recently, right under her nose, her *akachan* had become a young man. There is still uncertainty there, he is seeking her approval, after all, but something in his determined stare tells her he may very well be prepared to venture forth without her blessing.

"Between Wren and I... I've never met someone like her. I wish to know her. To learn her. I believe this is something she too would welcome."

"This is not a passing fancy, then."

He shakes his head, mouth set with conviction.

"And you are not simply lusting for the girl? It would not do for any son of mine to seek a conquest out of another."

She knows how easily such a charismatic beauty can inspire lust.

Kaito bows his head to her.

"Forgive this son, kaa-san, but I can assure you my affections run deeper than the pleasures of the flesh. Wren is not a mere conquest to me."

"Oh...?"

Something in the way he says this puzzles her. He can practically read the question across her face.

"We have lain together."

His cheeks flush as he speaks, and he averts his gaze to something over her right shoulder. She is a bit taken aback at first, the rug pulled from under her as it were by this unexpected revelation. So much she has learned about her young man today.

"Well, then, far be it for me to not support you, Kaito. I have raised, indeed, an honorable prince. You have my blessing. When you are ready, we can send the intention of your courtship to Deriva to Vulcan Tlanextli and Vulcana Elisabeta for Wren Nocturne."

"Thank you, Kaa-san."

They finish their tea in silence, and still, she feels a small melancholy. Both of her boys are grown now. They will not need her much longer. Hikaru takes his duties as the heir to the throne very seriously. She has already begun entrusting much to him, preparing him for the weight of the crown he will one day wear on his head. Hikaru has been grown up for some years now, but Kaito, who had, it seemed, only just turned seventeen, seems hellbent on showing her just how quickly children become adults. She'd thought she would have a few more years of her baby, her *akachan*.

"So," she says as he settles his teacup to the side. "How was it?"

"How was what?" he asks cautiously.

"Well did you enjoy having sex for the first time?"

"Okaa-san!"

She chuckles as she finds the floor back underneath her while he excuses himself, red-faced and indignant. All is still well with the world so long as she can embarrass her sons. And who knows... perhaps she'll be able to welcome a grandchild sooner than she expected.

The next day, Kai finds himself in a video conference between his mother, Pharaoh Rameses, Orisha Absko, and President Morrigan Gewalt. There is no representation from the smaller territories and countries. This meeting is to be held in absolute secrecy. Seraphim has begun to make moves toward invading Sekhmeti, and Rameses is not for allowing the pontifex to continue this bloody crusade unchecked. The conference today will determine whether Murasaki no Yama, Ebele, and Deriva, the three major countries at this point left unaffected by Seraphim's assault, will be joining Sekhmeti and Aighneas against the pontiflex. They are waiting for Vulcan Tlanextli of Deriva to log onto the meeting.

"It is time to begin. Should we proceed without him?" asks The Morrigan.

"I've never known Tlanextli to be tardy to an important meeting," says Empress Mirai.

Orisha Absko speaks, "I spoke to Tlanextli not three days ago. He said he was looking forward to this conference. That he is late is rather odd and disappointing. Princess Atzi had been so looking forward to seeing her family."

"Let us hope it is not an urgent matter that keeps him," inserts the pharaoh.

"Indeed."

"Unfortunately," says Kai's mother, "our time is limited. We should begin."

More tones of agreement resound, and Hikaru begins to debrief the world leaders on the outcome of his most recent case involving a nest of cyber ghouls that had been unleashed into the mainframe to attack unsuspecting citizens through their computer monitors and linked tech. Prince Jamar too recounts the border disputes along Sekhmeti and Seraphim that have begun to escalate. President Gewalt unhappily details the defense efforts her military has put into place to keep Seraphim robotics at bay. For his part, since Ebele is mostly unaffected by these skirmishes, Absko listens, his domo taking notes as the meeting goes on, Prince Chike, Princess Atzi, and Princess Chiamaka at his side.

"As you can see, Seraphim has far overstepped their bounds. The pontifex hides behind his religious honor and the autonomy of his technomancers, saying it is divine will that dictates

Seraphim extend its borders to encompass the entirety of Deus. If Ebele, Sekhmeti, Deriva, and Murasaki no Yama would offer us aid, we could avoid further loss of life, and push the pontifex back to where he belongs."

Pharaoh Rameses looks on impassively before shaking his head.

"I'm sorry, Madam President, but I cannot justify to my council extending assistance to Aighneas when we too have Seraphim forces banging on our doors."

"I empathize with you, President Gewalt. I do," answers Absko. "But my country is recovering from drought and famine. I cannot spare the resources to enter us into a war that does not concern us."

"Does not concern you! How long do you think it will take before Seraphim turns their eye on Ebele? You cannot avoid this conflict."

"I too can see the point The Morrigan is making, Orisha Absko," says Mirai. "Murasaki no Yama has too just expelled a small occupation from our borders. Seraphim, while they seem content to leave us alone for the moment, will not leave us be for much longer."

"Their goal is to take us down one by one beginning with Aighneas," argues Jamar in his father's silence. "We must unite if we are to retain our liberties as nations of the League. They cannot stand against all of us."

"But think of the destruction their weapons could cause us," inserts Chike. "Do you think they will hesitate at all in bombing us all once they have realized that we have united? We haven't a chance. Better to remain neutral in the face of adversity."

"They could choose to bomb you tomorrow while you're sitting on the toilet, and you will die a coward and fool!"

Arguments ensue. A cacophony of shouts abound, and Kai winces as the noise penetrates his comms. Eventually, with a look from their mother, Hikaru flexes his hacking sensors through the various holos erected throughout the room and silences each and every leader.

"Ladies and Gentlemen," begins Mirai as all of their muted mouths shut, and they look incredulously at Hikaru. "Arguing will get us nowhere. We either unite as one to address this situation, or we will all fall to Seraphim control. Now..." She lifts a hand to unmute each leader's microphone. "Shall we carry on this discussion like adults?"

Rameses opens his mouth to reply, but as he does so, the head of Shinka's security systems pops in, interrupting the broadcast for every world leader in attendance.

"A nautical from Deriva has just entered our borders. It is emitting a distress signal."

"A nautical from Deriva?" asks the empress, looking to Kaito. "Allow it passage. Supply it directives to dock at the lake."

"Yes, Empress."

"Kaito, go. Activate your sights and report back to us."

Kai is already rising from his seat to race down the hall, out into the courtyard, and to the lake. The nautical is already docked next to the pier. Its hatch peeks out of the water to the open air.

Several adepts and technomancers have already gathered. They make room for their prince to move through, and he jumps from the dock to stand atop the single passenger craft. He overrides the locking mechanism, and the hatch opens with a hissing pressure release. Inside, is an unconscious Prince Xipilli. Someone wrapped him in blankets and cloaks to warm him before strapping him into the pilot seat. He crouches down in the cramped space and checks the older boy's pulse and breathing, both barely there at all.

"Summon the medic. Now!"

He moves to reposition Xipilli's head to open his windpipe. He unstraps him from the pilot seat and begins a cursory examination for broken bones and open wounds. He is covered in bruises, his clothing bloodstained and torn from battle or torture or both. He sees Wren's visor nestled among the blankets wrapped around the other prince.

PRELUDE

Out of his earpiece, he hears the conference attendees exclaim their horror at the Crown Prince of Deriva being found in such a state. Atzi, on her husband's monitor, holds her breath, her younger brother's name a frightened whisper on her lips.

The medic arrives with a stretcher, and he helps lift the unconscious man up and out of the craft. Once Xipilli has been safely strapped down onto the stretcher, he examines the visor. There is a crack along the left side of the glass lens, but it functions just fine when he powers it up.

"Kaito, is that Prince Xipilli's visor? Can you hack into it?"

"No, it's Lady Wren's. I can access it." He slips it over his head and unlocks it. "There is a recording on here from two days ago."

He plays it and broadcasts the video into the conference meeting. The recording begins unfocused as the visor is moved around frantically until Wren's face comes into focus. She is scraped up a bit, but otherwise she looks fine. She speaks as her hands work the control panel in front of her.

"This is Wren Nocturne of House Moctezumo. Technomancer ID#2787B65, reporting Cresta de Corail has fallen."

Her voice breaks.

"My father, Vulcan Tlanextli, and Vulcana Elisabeta are dead. My brother, Crown Prince Xipilli Moctezumo, now vulcan, is severely injured but alive and the sole survivor of the assault. I am setting an auto-piloted course for Shinka Temple with the hope that Empress Mirai and Murasaki no Yama, please, help my brother. My plan is to follow behind on my own, but in the event I am unable to, I request that whoever is watching this deliver a message to my brother and sister that I love them and will find them as soon as I am able. In the meantime, please, Miyazaki-heika, save my brother."

She offers a bow to the camera, but as she returns to upright, the sound of a weapon firing draws her attention. She turns to look, draws Mångata from her side, and drops the headset into Xipilli's lap. The last thing he hears before the recording is cut is the scream of Mångata activating.

Xipilli is rushed to the dispensary, their head medic already ordering x-rays, blood tests, and CAT scans. In Kai's audio headset, the conference continues, Princess Atzi sobs a soundtrack in the background.

"This is too far!"

"Nearly the entire royal family slain in cold blood."

"How dare they!"

While the monarchs go ballistic, Kai goes internal, reaching for Wren's access codes.

Wren!

He sends the message straight into her servers. She doesn't have a visual hub, but she'll get the message through Mano.

Wren, Xipilli is here! Where are you? Are you on your way?

Curses! He hadn't even thought too much on the fact that he hasn't heard from her in several days, but it wasn't like they spoke daily, and he's never reached out to her like this, through their linked networks.

Wren, answer me!

Nothing comes. Not even a ping of acknowledgement like he is used to receiving from her when she's seen his message but doesn't have time to respond. But maybe she simply can't see them. So, he tracks her GPS.

Nothing. There's nothing. She is just nowhere. Either out of network or...or... No, that's not possible. Maybe she turned it off to prevent them from tailing her.

Kai's mother is silent for a long moment. Kai's thoughts are in complete turmoil as he follows Xipilli's stretcher to the dispensary. The prince, the vulcan, is cut from his garments. At the first sight of torn and burnt flesh, Kai averts his gaze. It is not his place to witness the evidence of this man's ordeal. He owes him this dignity, at the very least. His sights whirl as his mother's voice addresses him.

"Kaito, tell your aunt to stop what she is doing and report to the meeting hall. Hikaru, summon every technomancer on our roster to Shinka. Notify the military generals as well to make preparations for mobilization. I want every adept, both trainee and active duty, prepared."

"Empress Mirai?"

"President Gewalt, Orisha Absko, Pharaoh Rameses. I do not know what your plans will be moving forward, but today, in deference to the fall of Deriva, Murasaki no Yama calls for arms against Seraphim."

Each leader in turn nods their head at the empress's declaration.

"Deriva was our loyal ally both in marriage and in friendship," declares Absko. "Ebele too will go to war. Justice will be served on behalf of House Moctezumo."

"As will Sekhmeti."

"Aighneas' banners already fly."

"Then it is settled."

And Murasaki no Yama goes to war.

In the weeks following the arrival of Xipilli to Shinka, and subsequently the arrival of Prince Chike and Princess Atzi from Ebele, Kaito keeps a lookout for Wren's coming in the wake of her brother. He looks for her searunner, another nautical, anything that might indicate a Derivan approach to the temple, but nothing comes. His messages to her network go unseen and unanswered, and her GPS trace never turns on. He wants to go to Cresta de Corail and scout the palace himself, but there is no time and not enough resources, and the scouts they do send report back that the place has been claimed as a fortress by General Llywelyn, the naval technologies of Deriva seized for Seraphim's use.

Xipilli wakes from a two-week coma, demanding the location of his younger sister, but no one can answer him. Atzi, nearly brought to tears at the confusion on his face, could only answer that they knew nothing, had heard nothing of her since his arrival to Shinka.

Kai, who is in the room with the two siblings at the time, stiffens when Xipilli's intense stare meets his silver gaze.

"I will not rest until I find my baby sister."

Kai says nothing to this.

"Will you help me?"

Kai nods slowly and deliberately. He has already made his decision.

Contrary to popular opinion, Fireflies are not, nor have they ever been, whores.

To be a Firefly is to be a friend and a teacher, a guide and a confidante, a supporter of women, a midwife, and a caretaker for those who cannot always take care of themselves. A practitioner of love in all its incarnations: both platonic and carnal.

An Excerpt from *Love Bugs:*
Deus' Fireflies and their influence in World Politics
By Madame Kali De Vrie, 1747 A.P.

22

FOUR OF CUPS

Present–4th Day in the Month of Falling

WREN DOES NOT SLEEP. SHE CREATES FOR herself the illusion of sleep by closing her eyes and willing her body to still, but it is not a true sleep. She sweats cold, and her eyes throb behind their lids. Her limbs feel boneless and gooey, and when she finally blinks herself out of the temporary stupor of surface dreaming, it feels like someone has shoved gum between her ears. Yet even through the thickness of it, still she can hear muted screams of agony and avarice. The sensations of the other people in the inn, somnolent and helpless to their dreams and their nightmares. A few wakeful emotions are there too. Angsty thoughts coupled with drunken stupors and frantic, probably prepaid coitus. There is a couple upstairs pinging on her radar. The man's fervor tastes like sweat and anxiety, probably a cheating husband while the woman reeks of apathy.

It's enough to make her want to smash her head against the wall. That and the ghost who apparently decided to follow them down from the temple.

PRELUDE

It is dark outside, dawn not yet edging the horizon. Koi and Dei have both set, and the darkest part of the night, gloomtide, when neither sun nor moons grace the sky, blankets Deus. The witching hour, when even the most devout of servants slumber and devilry abounds. The time of night when even the most docile of magics stir and become agitated. Electricity tingles at the base of her spine.

There is an itch under her skin, gnawing and squirmy like maggots looking for death.

Her earlier fever is gone for the most part, but the bite at her shoulder still aches something awful. It throbs like a bruise more than a bite, a hickey left over from a particularly volatile lover, one who'd wanted to eat her in a way that really was not her idea of a good time.

With that last thought, she flings her legs over the edge of the bed and pads her way out into the main room. Kai, apparently, chose not to join her in the bedroom. She finds him laid out on his back on the chaise lounge. It isn't nearly long enough for him, and his feet dangle off the end. She moves forward to check if he really is asleep, and finds that yes, the man is very much unconscious. She even waggles her hand in front of his face just to double check that he isn't faking. When she receives no response, she taps him gently in the center of his chest. Once again, he remains unbothered.

Was Kai always such a deep sleeper?

Well, he's a fool anyway, letting his guard down this much in her presence. She could run a knife through him right now, and he would be none the wiser as to who slit his throat. Or maybe it's just that good old highborn arrogance these royalty types always, and she means always, embrace one way or another. She should know. She used to be one of them.

No matter. Not her problem. Not her issue.

She slips her boots over her feet, glancing backward to the rather noisy problem that woke her in the first place, before deciding firmly that before she is going to deal with anything else, she needs a drink. A strong one at that. Upon careful consideration as to whether or not she wants to spend her own hard-stolen cash or swipe Kai's credit chip, she digs through the man's wallet and slips the hard plastic into her breast pocket. (She is here on Miyazaki payroll, after all.) She unlocks the inn door with the room scanner and leaves the quiet of the space behind.

Surprisingly, there is a swanky dive/lounge not too far from the inn still open. She was expecting to have to find a 24hr convenience store or something.

This late, or this early depending on how you want to look at it, there's no one really around, save for a pair of hooded strangers seated at the corner table. Other than the brief tensing of their auras when she walks in, they pay no mind to her, so she waltzes up to the bar where a pretty older woman stands, cleaning out a glass tumbler.

She isn't stupid enough to walk around in public wearing her own face, so she donned Atalia's glamour before actually leaving the hotel room. Her eyes light on several posters hanging around the lounge. There are framed panels of the Miyazaki royal family: Kaito, Hikaru, and she even recognizes an old photo of their mother from when she was first crowned empress, and whoa, is that what Fumiko looked like when she was younger? What happened there? There are also panels dedicated to various Murasaki no Yama technomancers, their status granting them more than a bit of fame and celebrity in light of the dangerous undertaking they take on. She recognizes her ghost in one of the posters. A little younger maybe, but he was plenty handsome back then. Shame his face was gnawed off by a wendigo.

Though technomancers weren't the only being represented among the decor.

Paintings of lycans and goblins, vampyres and witches also decorated the walls. Unusual... From what she saw on their way through town yesterday, the place was mostly inhabited by normals, humans who were neither augmented nor magical. There's a painting of the Dei pack alpha Muracko Whistlewind next to the ageless vampyre queen Hecate. Notable leaders of hexenkin from wars past. There is even a portrait of her, Wren

Nocturne, settled in a place of honor near the forefront of the lounge.

She picks up a menu, scans the list of spirits and tonics, and is surprised to find her preference, so when the bartender checks in with her, she asks for absinthe. Nothing like summoning the green fairy at this time of night. A fancy colander is placed in front of her with a small pot of water and a serving vessel filled with the bright green alcohol next to it. She takes her time filtering it through the sugar before watering it down just a hair. When she tosses it back, the sweet, sharp, sting of black licorice and fermented wormwood burns down her throat.

"You know, the bionics in these parts don't much like that I serve absinthe here."

The bartender is a gruff around the edges but a sweet-sounding forty something human+ with a glass eye and vocal transplant. Wren can make out the nodes on either side of her temple that assist her with social cues and interactions. All the better to please her customers. She doesn't look Murasakan, precisely. Her eyes are less almond shaped, her skin darker, and her ebony hair is threaded through with braids and cornrows. A calm mood blankets her, a bit of exhaustion there, but she perked up when Wren walked through the door.

"Shame," Wren says, after clearing her palate. "It's a good spirit. Strong and tasty. Hits the spot and burns just right going down."

The woman takes to cleaning a glass at the sink. Wren refills her tumbler with a second serving and downs that in one gulp as well. She fixes herself the third and final shot. This one she sips, not needing the immediate infusion of alcohol anymore. Two shots have already burned away her over-sensitivity to other people's moods, the spillover more manageable now. She feels a little more like herself and a little less like a garbage disposal for other people's icky feelings.

"A girl after my own heart," says the barkeep. "Not even the local normies will drink it."

"Some people call it the witch's drink."

"Superstitious buggers," scoffs the woman. "Not like there gonna be a witch waltzing through this here city anytime soon."

Her accent is closer to what Wren would expect to hear from someone in Ebele than in Murasaki no Yama. Wren eyes the posters on the far wall.

"Is it normal for the local bars to keep artwork of famous hexen around?"

"Thus the basis of my establishment's appeal. We don't turn anyone away, and the reason we open so late is for the hexen who dare come into town."

She nods her head toward the two hooded figures near the back of the bar.

"Two of my regulars: goblins. They keep to themselves whenever ordinaries or other plusies are around, but this time of night is when they can relax and enjoy their drinks in peace. They tip well, too. Most hexen who come here during the witching hour do."

"Most small-town businesses don't much cater to the sleep schedules of hexen."

"Well, I do. The Hollow Nozzle is open from an hour before dusk to an hour after dawn, and we serve small breakfast and dinner appetizers during that time period. We catch the ordinaries and the bionics before their nightcaps and call in the party hour for the hexen."

"You must be popular with the city council. I'm surprised you haven't been shut down."

The woman gives her an incredulous look before setting her hands on the bar top.

"You're not from around here, are you?"

"Just visiting," answers Wren, taking another sip of her absinthe.

"Yeah? You hexen or human+, cause you sure as hell ain't a normie."

"I'm human," answers Wren, a small smirk tugging at her lips.

"Tsh, you sure know how to be cryptic, doll."

Wren chuckles as the woman rolls her eyes and carries back to address Wren's earlier inquiry. "Whether the city council likes me or not don't matter much to me. They can't shut me down for allowing hexen in my bar. Murasaki no Yama passed sanctuary legislation several years ago in response to the League-wide witch hunts. A lot of hexen moved here to escape persecution or came out of hiding afterwards."

Wren stares at the woman wide-eyed.

"You mean to tell me that Murasaki isn't actively waging war against hexenfolk?"

"Only for the last eight years! Where you been living? Under a rock?"

That wouldn't be entirely inaccurate though she supposes she technically wasn't buried either.

"There's still plenty of tension between plusies and hexen though, and it's not like hexen have any claim to citizenship. They got no rights like you or me, but so long as they maintain a low profile and stay out of trouble, the technomancers leave them alone in favor of dealing with other more pressing problems, but the normals are as scared as they've always been of things that go bump in the night."

Well, color her impressed! It isn't much, but baby steps are steps. It's nice to know just existing isn't a crime anymore at least in some places. She'll need to figure out who to thank for that. Kaito? His brother?

"So, there are witches in Murasaki?"

"Not exactly. Or if there are, they aren't overt about it."

"What do you mean?"

"By the time Emperor Hikaru got the support to pass the legislation, it was too late for most of 'em. Witches went all but extinct after the Songstress died. Occasionally, you get word about some new coven or other, but they're too weak to be of much use to the rest of the hexen community. Most of them can't even properly cast spells anymore. Magic has become more of a religious observation than an actual craft. Nothing like what the Songstress and her followers could do."

FOUR OF CUPS

"The Songstress didn't have followers."

"Oh? But the stories say she had an army of witches under her command. Hand-trained by her and destined to tear down the League or some nonsense like that. I forget how the stories actually go. There are so many, and they're all just a little different."

"That a fact?"

"One of them said she used to steal naughty children from their beds at night. Some stories say she would eat them or feed them to her familiars. Others say she kept them, amassing a hoard of potential witches under her care. I buy the first one more. Why would a woman so bloodthirsty want to raise a bunch of snot-nosed brats?"

No, Wren thinks sadly, *certainly not a bunch, but maybe just one...*

"People will spin stories so long as they have a brain with which to craft them," declares Wren, spinning the half-empty glass in her hand. "I never take anything I hear at face value. Between magic and media, there is too much in this world that can be manipulated, warped, and presented as this pretty fabrication we all want to believe. Video editing, photo manipulation, nevermind how rumors spread like wildfire on social media. At least when it comes to magic, you know it's an illusion."

"Wise words, Miss. You should write that down."

"No need."

She finishes the rest of her drink and looks the barkeep in the eye. She licks her lips and leans forward, extending the credit chip out for her to run.

"So," she says, drawing out the vowel. "Why keep absinthe in stock if the 'borgs dislike it and the norms won't touch it?"

The woman hands her back the credit chip with a flourish. The woman's eyes trace her body up and down.

"I supposed on the off chance a pretty young thing like you might wander in here asking for it."

Lust wafts off the bartender like a sugary perfume, just strong enough to color her mind with a pleasurable zing under the alcohol. With the drink warm in her belly, Wren is all too happy to indulge the woman the spark of desire that she feels.

PRELUDE

That's how she ends up in the backroom, a dim light bulb flickering above her head as she presses the woman back against the shelf, one hand hiking up the plusie's skirt and pressing past a thin elastic band to the woman's most treasured place. The barkeep makes pretty noises. She tugs a little on Wren's hair, and Wren doesn't mind that, but she dodges the woman's attempts to kiss her in favor of biting down high on her throat.

Kisses are meaningful. This isn't.

It is as Wren is about to drop to her knees that the single lightbulb in the closet bursts in a shower of glass and electrical sparks. This alone wouldn't deter her, but the shattered bulb in junction with the frosty whirlwind that rips through the room... Wren looks up to find Toujirou's ghost. Even without the vast majority of his face, the spirit looks positively livid.

She sighs and extracts herself from the barkeep, whose name she never bothered to get. The two hooded figures in the corner are still there, but they seem to have startled from the noise in the backroom. One of their hoods has fallen, and the patron is indeed a goblin. She leaves a small tip on the bar and hightails it out of the lounge, an irate ghost on her heels.

In the cool night air, the spirit is still anxious, drifting up and down and phasing in and out of her field of vision. Even with her empathy dulled from the alcohol, she feels the irritation rolling off him in waves. The air around him buzzes with agitation, and whenever he drifts too close, her ears ring.

"Is it because I stepped over your body? Are you punishing me?"

The spirit fumes, mute as a silent film which is pretty normal for spirits. Able to affect their environments with psychic/mental/spiritual manipulation while actual verbal communication is impossible due to the lack of vocal cords. It's why ghosts don't actually say "boo" despite what the cartoons say. She can see him well enough though to know that he is probably cussing her out. She knows she would be if their positions were switched.

"Tojirou-san, eh?"

The spirit nods stubbornly, a scowl crunching his remaining facial features together.

"Well, lead the way. Whatever is it that you want to show me?"

The ghost stomps his foot and gestures back at the inn, insistent and angry.

"I'm not going back to wake his royal pain-in-the-ass. You bothered me, so you get me. Understand?"

Without another gesture toward her, the spirit drifts off down the street.

The ghost leads her to the edge of town where a cemetery stretches out along the highway. Tojirou flits his way into the cemetery and begins weaving through the maze-like lines of ceremonial plaques and tombstones and offerings left for lost loved ones. Wren tries to run after the ghost, but the cemetery gates are deadbolted and lined with some mean-looking spikes.

The question here is, should she climb over or astral project herself into the cemetery? She could use a teleportation spell to cross the distance, but that would leave her drained of resources, and she doesn't know how long she'll need to be in there. Not to mention, she'll need to get back out as well. As far as climbing over goes, the spikes don't look very appealing to her. Perhaps scouting out the area would be a better option.

Wren settles herself against the iron railing in a place where her form is obstructed by tall grass and underbrush. Pulling her locket from where it rests against her skin, she opens it and summons her tarot deck once more. She looks for the Page of Swords, the traveler and the transverse wanderer. She holds the card between her pinky and ring fingers. Her index finger is extended while her thumb holds down her middle finger. A harsh variation on the Shuni mudra, but necessary here for her channeling.

She sings softly, the elder tongue dripping from her lips like fog until the card alights with her power. She closes her eyes and directs the weave.

A projection of her consciousness forms just outside her meditating personage, and with a slight tickling sensation, she steps through the iron bars and into the cemetery.

She walks in the direction Tojirou's ghost vanished.

The grounds are old but well cared for. There are offerings left for the dead, fresh flowers recently placed, even a few candles scattered throughout the grounds—she avoids these, giving the tiny inconsequential flames a wide berth as often as she can. She can see many of the memorial plates have been set up with AfterLife monitors as well for families who wish to interact with the cyber presence of their loved ones given audible voice without the need of a seance. It's a complete simulation, a pre-programmed smart computer possessing the deceased's decision-making patterns as documented by their online presence.

She taps a few of them. They don't react to her of course because she is more ghost than person in this state, but she can feel them through the connection. She drifts her way through the maze of graves and shrines. There are even a few ancestral halls scattered throughout the plots. Eventually, she reaches out with her empathy to track down the spirit and heads that direction.

Tojirou is hovering on the roof of a shrine which is rather disrespectful if you ask Wren, but she supposes he's not actually touching the shrine so it must be alright.

"So why exactly am I astral projecting into a graveyard at, near, the crack of dawn?" she calls up to the ghost. The man's head spins around so quick, she is worried it will flip right off. Thankfully, he isn't a ghoul, otherwise she is sure it would have. He makes a frantic gesture for her to be quiet, and she looks at him quizzically before looking around. Nothing sticks out to her or strikes her as odd, so she moves around to the far side of the shrine that Tojirou is hovering over.

That's when she spots it. Her voice catches in her throat.

It's the wendigo.

It followed them all the way down the mountain.

Merde!

It's sniffing around the graves, clearly smelling the decay and the rot below the surface, but she is a bit confused as to why it's here rather than terrorizing the living further into town. Perhaps it just hasn't gotten that far.

She ducks down behind a grave and keeps an eye on it. Mere hours since their last meeting and Kaito's earlier strikes against it are already healed. Even the antler that was cut off has begun to regrow. It's still an hour until dawn, she is by herself, and these things are invulnerable to most forms of attack. She needs to keep it here somehow, prevent it from hurting or abducting any humans for a fresh meal, and more importantly, she needs to keep it away from her physical body.

Slowly, Wren inches her way closer, hands extended as she lifts a fairly large marker (Many apologies to the deceased) out of earth slowly, ever so slowly, to prevent the beast from noticing. Once she has it hovering about a foot off the ground, she psychically shoves at the creature's head as hard as she can manage. There is a rush of wind being displaced and the tombstone makes contact.

However, the wendigo is hardly even stunned. Beady black eyes turn on her, and a loud screeching sound falls from the creature's mouth loud enough to make her wince before it jumps for her. Wren tenses and the beast slides straight through her projection knocking its head directly into the brick wall of the shrine behind her.

Maybe, if she can distract the creature long enough, she can keep it above ground until sunrise. The sunlight will burn it to a crisp, and then there will be no more wendigo to worry about. When the creature reorients itself, she calls it over and starts to make noise. Lots of noise.

There are bells and wind chimes and all sorts of fun dangling talismans hanging all over the cemetery. She gets them to start chiming, moving the air and space until a cacophony of metal rings throughout the cemetery. It's disorienting even for her, but she runs as the wendigo gives chase. She has to pace herself if this is going to work. The more magical power she expends while in her astral projection, the more likely she'll be forced back into her physical body early, and for her plan to work, she'll need to milk this for as long as she can.

Her tactic works for not nearly long enough despite the countless headstones she's thrown at the thing. At some point the direction of the wind changes, and the wendigo stops chasing her. It turns its head toward the wind, angling its nose this way and that way. It lets out a low growl, then races off in the direction where, she realizes, her physical body is.

Double merde!

She takes off as fast as her spiritual form can allow, and it's more than a little frustrating that her astral form is so limited. At least she can run through the headstones, but the wendigo can literally jump over them all in one powerful bound, the thing is so long. She sees the iron railing of the fence and pushes. The wendigo is already climbing up and over the metal, teeth gnashing at the spikes, all but ripping them off their posts before it lands directly in front of her unsuspecting body.

Wren is too far away to do anything but watch as the monster's jaws open wide to clamp down on her head again. She closes her eyes and waits for the pain even as she keeps pushing forward, because this is going to hurt.

"Wren!"

There is a flash of violet power as Tsukuyomi crosses its blade with the monstrosity's teeth once more, and then Kai is there, Amatsu in hand, forcing the beast back and away from her body. The wendigo shrieks at him, recognizes him as its earlier nuisance, and dives forward. Kai is better prepared this time though. He twists and turns in and out of the creature's attacks, continuing to force it back.

Wren's astral form stops moving, opens her mouth, and sings. The wendigo freezes in place while she directs one of the torn off spikes to embed itself in its side. At the same time, Kai stabs both of his swords into the creature's torso. It screams and thrashes against the binding spell until it rebounds back into Wren. She sees Kai get thrown backward as well as she goes sprawling through an above ground sarcophagus into the skeleton of somebody's aunt or uncle. Who? She doesn't know, and she doesn't care because he was apparently buried with a sword, and she's not about to look a gift horse in the mouth. She begins to sing her danse macabre to the skeleton until the bones reassemble and start to dance.

She pushes the lid of the sarcophagus open, the skeleton rolls itself out, weapon in hand and it begins rattling its way toward where the wendigo is hovering over Kaito. She climbs out of the sarcophagus and keeps moving to reach her physical body.

Kaito is yelling at her to wake up.

She commands the skeleton to attack. She half expects Kai to try and destroy the undead himself, but he doesn't, choosing instead to work in tandem with her thrall, using the skeleton as a distraction to land several hits to the wendigo. Seeing this, Wren begins the process of resettling into her body. It's always a bit of a bump and grind switching from incorporeal to corporeal. Not dissimilar to being reborn actually, but not nearly as agonizing, and there is far less bloodshed involved. It is dizzying, though, and she nearly pukes when she opens her eyes and sees a large hairy wendigo land directly in front of her. There is a rank stench about it, and she watches as the contusions Kai and the skeleton landed on it are already healing.

It looks directly at her and swipes for her with a roar.

Wren barrels backward, draws the dagger from her belt, and stabs down into the creature's flank before yanking it away. As she pulls the blade out, Tsukuyomi and Amatsu slash forward as a unit. The bite on her shoulder throbs painfully almost as if in response to the beast, and she falters as she tries to stand. One of the wendigo's claws catches around her ankle to pull her toward it, but Kai's arms wrap under her arms and around her shoulders and he drags her back and away while she kicks at the monster's head hard enough to discourage it from maintaining its grip. When she is far enough back, Kai lets go, and she stands up and begins to direct the skeletal warrior again. The undead moves forward and begins trading blows with it, but the wendigo lands one hit to the skeleton's ribcage, and the bones scatter to the ground. So much for that spell. Kai makes to recall his blades, but Wren tells him to wait. She stretches her right hand back and flings it forward toward the wendigo, a bright streak of magic flying from her fingertips to shove the wendigo hard enough to send it back through the iron grating and into the cemetery.

"Are you injured?"

Kai's question comes from her right. Amatsu and Tsukuyomi return to his hands easily.

"I'm fine. What are you doing here?"

She is snappish and wholly ungrateful to the fact that he just saved her from being eaten for the second time in less than twenty-four hours, but she doesn't care. She rushes forward after the wendigo, already pooling energy in her palms while he charges his swords.

"You left."

"Oh, so sorry. Your friend, Tojirou, insisted."

"Tojirou?"

"Well, his ghost anyway. Machines! Are all Murasaki technomancers so insufferable when they need something?"

An agonized inhuman scream reaches them, and Wren looks up and stops cold in her tracks. The wendigo is on fire. Less than five meters in front of her, the creature's entire arm is alight with flame. Wren's pupils dilate and sweat beads across her forehead. She stops so suddenly, Kai barrels into her, sending both of them to the ground. The smell of burning flesh sears into her nostrils and this time Wren really does heave.

She screams. Pain alights in her senses. Her skin starts to peel, blistering back from her bones. Her hair is on fire, being melted straight from her head. It is scorching, burning, torrid agony that racks through every one of her nerve endings, flaying off the outer layer and diving into her very synapses. An acrid taste in her mouth, a series of mind-numbing paroxysms, and she is dying. She is dying again, and this time there will be no heaven, hell, or even limbo for her soul to go to. She keeps on screaming.

Something shakes her so hard her brain rattles in her skull.

There is a deafening shout of her name, and the hallucination dissipates. She goes limp, panting and bleary eyed on the ground. She lays there still for seconds, minutes, hours. Time has no meaning. There is the taste of bile on her tongue, her throat hurts badly, and she realizes, belatedly, the reason why. She'd been screaming for the entirety of her attack. The sky is beginning to lighten. She can feel it on her skin; she sees it on the insides of her eyelids, painted orange with fire just seconds ago. There are hands on her shoulders, and her head hurts, probably from the shaking, whoever responsible, trying desperately to pull her out of the waking terror, their hands still clasped around her shoulders. She opens her eyes to see who it is.

Kai hovers over her on his knees beside her. His lips are moving, possibly around a word that might be her name, but her ears are still ringing.

There is no wendigo in sight.

"What..." she trails over, her voice thick and gravelly. She clears out the remaining bile, coughs, and turns her head to spit the rest of it up. "What happened to the wendigo?"

"Nevermind the damn wendigo."

When she looks at him, his expression is pinched with worry and fear. He is looking at her like she is the most breakable piece of glass he has ever seen, fine porcelain that's just been dropped on the floor, something precious worth fussing over and protecting. This pisses her off. What right does he have to worry? Afraid his precious hostage won't live long enough to unravel the curse!

"You let it get away!" She hates how rough her voice sounds. She pushes him back and off her as she comes to standing. "What the hell, Kaito?!"

"Am I expected to abandon my mission partner when she is vulnerable?"

"Yes! The mission comes first. And who are you calling vulnerable?"

She starts to scrub at her face with her sleeve. Ick! She has puke on her chin. That's a great look!

"I disagree."

"This isn't some weekend outing for pleasure, you know! This is business."

Kai's expression closes at that.

"Business? Right."

"Yes, business. Though I supposed even that is a rather gentle term for this transaction, don't you think? Blackmail, kidnapping, and we can add wasting my time to the list."

He shakes his head at her, disregards her anger, and begins to say, "Are you—"

"If you ask me if I am alright one more time, I'm going to cut your tongue out of your head."

"So, I should not inquire as to my partner's well-being."

"You should leave well enough alone, is what you should do. I'm not some amateur in need of coddling. I don't need you to pretend to care."

"Are you really going to carry on with this tirade?"

"Until you start using some common sense. You don't need to waste energy on acting. It isn't like I'm here to build a working relationship with you or any other technomancer in Deus. You should've done the smart thing and actually, you know, killed the wendigo. The creature has probably gone to ground by now. It will take a whole day before it even dares to venture back out. So, please, Miyazaki. Keep wasting my time with bullshit excuses for not doing your job."

She is huffing, her chest heaving up and down at an embarrassing rate. She's let her emotions run away with her. She blames the absinthe and Tojirou and possibly the wendigo again. There is a candle flickering to her left. She kicks it over to snuff out the damn flame and moves to storm away from the man still glaring at her.

His hand catches her around the bicep, stalling her rampage away. She turns around, spitting venom. "What?"

"Is being on the mission with me so horrible to you?"

They are in the middle of a graveyard, on the tail end of dealing with a wendigo attack that his dead comrade led her to, and he has the audacity to accuse her of being... whatever exactly he is accusing her of being. She isn't quite clear on that right now, but she has a right to be offended, so here she goes.

"You'll forgive me if I don't find joy in being your brother's lap dog. The sooner this is over with, the better, but I can grin and bear it so long as he keeps his promise."

"My brother is a man of his word. He will fulfill his oath."

"Oh ho! He certainly is! Hikaru has always done exactly what he says he is going to do. It's the younger brother who lives his life entirely unbothered by the effect his lies have caused."

"What are you insinuating?"

She turns to him then, her eyes tracing up and down his form.

"Nothing," she says. "Kaito Miyazaki would never jeopardize a case with petty qualms. Personal matters are above the Miyazaki royal family. They are so shameless, their pride so untouchable, they take no issue blackmailing someone they once stepped all over just to maintain their power."

"Wren, if you think—"

"What do you even care what I think? I am here in service to you as demonstrated. Now let's move before the damn thing gets too far away."

She rips her arm out of his grasp with a slight wince, pivots away from him, and keeps on walking.

"Stop."

She freezes mid-step as he catches her by the other wrist and holds, firm but gentle. Cautious and careful. She can feel the tremor in his hand around her wrist.

"Wait."

She turns around, her smile a cruel, twisted thing on her lips.

"What do you want now?"

She spits the words out like a curse. Despite the tenseness in his body language, his facial expression remains calm and collected. His eyes study her, puzzling through her behavior as though he had any right to be confused about her hostility toward him!

"I want an explanation right now."

"For what?"

"For your contempt for starters."

She laughs, mad and more than a little hysterical at that. She laughs so hard, she has to hunch over herself, clenching her stomach against the cramp that begins to stitch itself together across it. Her wrist twists in his grip which stays firm enough to keep her in place but not enough to bruise or cause harm which strikes her as odd.

Why should he be concerned with hurting her? She's just a wicked witch after all. He's hunted her kind his whole life, hasn't he!

"You want an explanation for my contempt. You! Hahaha! You're hilarious. You want your precious temple back. Fine. I'll do it myself without your help. Then you don't need to subject yourself to my apparently misplaced contempt. You need an explanation for it, well too bad. I don't owe you anything, so code off!"

She tugs hard on the arm he is holding, but he holds fast. There is no anger in his voice when he responds. No ire, no heat, nothing. Just calm, steady conviction to force this whole charade to a head at last.

"That is not an option."

Her expression closes instantly, the false smile dropping from her features. So, he wants to tear off the ruse then. Fine. If he wants to be an immovable object, she'll barrel into him with all of the force of something that is unstoppable.

"Excuse me?"

"There was a time when you trusted me. What changed?"

Excuse her! Did he forget? Did he delete it from his servers? How dare he! How dare he not know what changed when she can never forget it!

Her eyes narrow, and anger sparks in their depths.

23
TWO OF SWORDS

"YOU REALLY EXPECT ME TO BELIEVE YOU don't know the answer to that question!"

Kai's muscles are tense enough to cut steel. Knots forming in his shoulders and back as he holds fast to her hand even as he feels Wren's ire rise. While most of the time Wren is happy to grin and bear whatever is bothering her, once her button is truly pushed, she bites and she bites hard. That's fine. He'll let her, but if she is foolish enough to think he will stand by and accept her abuse any longer, she is sorely mistaken.

She wears Atalia's face, but the twist of anger on her brow and in her eyes is wholly Wren's. The essence of it is palpable on the air around them. Tendrils of her power curl and pulse around her; it actually crackles against his fingertips where he holds her wrist. Her skin is hot to the touch, and the bite wound at her shoulder has reopened, bleeding through the bandage he set earlier in the evening.

"Drop the glamour," he demands. The dysphoria of arguing with Wren while she is wearing another person's face is too much to ask.

"Fuck you!"

She unleashes without warning, a pulse of power that should by rights knock him flat on his back, but he holds fast and absorbs the blow into his palm with a wince, teeth gritted.

"I said drop it, Wren!"

"Make me!"

Frustration on his side, he turns it back on her and activates his dispel. Atalia vanishes, and Wren stands before him, pale and tired and so, so angry it's a relief. She isn't pretending anymore. There is no grinning mask. No false pleasantries. Just Wren and her storm.

"Explain yourself this instant!"

"Explain myself? How dare you! You know exactly what happened. Your brother's wretched signature is probably still drying on that death warrant. Tell me, did you ink the pen for him, too?"

Her voice is deadly quiet and dark; she says it through her teeth.

"My brother's actions are not my own."

Her eyes darken, glimmering in the muted light of dawn as the spark of her temper smolders dangerously at him. He sees that expression, and he recognizes it. Feels his heart clench seeing it directed at him again. In that gaze is all of the underlying hostility she has been edging at for the last forty-eight hours.

"*Che!* And you call my memories damaged! I guess it was so long ago for you, you must have forgotten. Here I thought you would be proud of the part you played in the massacre at Lorelei. My apologies. Such small matters clearly mean nothing to the crown prince of Murasaki no Yama."

The part he played?

"I played no part in what happened to Lorelei. The council made that decision."

She tries to thrash away again, but he holds fast.

"Just because you weren't there doesn't make you any less guilty for what happened! You know what you did!"

"What I did? I spoke out against the raid. I tried to save you!"

"You tried to save me!? You're the reason they caught me in the first place, and now you want to take it back and say that you tried to save me. Twelve years later and you think you can just pretend nothing happened, wearing the necklace I gave you, convincing your brother to make a deal with me! What! Did your system reset wipe your memory banks? What kind of an idiot do you think I am?! You're the reason I was dead."

He's the reason? He's the reason!

"I'm the reason you died?! You killed yourself, Wren!" He's shouting, shaking with fury at her onslaught of accusations when she is the one who left him. "You gave up! You committed suicide! And for what? To spite me! I wanted to be there for you, but you didn't let me, and you dare to say I'm the reason you were dead for twelve years!"

"I didn't kill myself..."

He hears her words, quiet as they are, but he doesn't register them. Too many years of grief and anger and resentment bubbling to the surface in the face of this person who stopped fighting, who gave up, who left him as permanently as she possibly could because she didn't have the strength of will to keep going.

"You've always been impulsive! You never stop and think. You never sit down and process; you just act!"

She left him behind. She left them both behind!

"I didn't—"

"Twelve years, Wren! You were dead for twelve years. I never thought you would ever be so goddamn selfish. You killed yourself, and I have had to live with that for twelve years. I have mourned for you for twelve years! Now you come back and have the gall to accuse me of being responsible for your death? You made that choice all on your own, and you don't even remember making it!"

"I remember fire!"

She shoves him in the chest, and Kai's sight's whirl, the need to puke clenching in the pit of his stomach. Fire?

"Fire and gasoline. I was burned alive!" she all but screams in his face, and Kai relents. "I didn't kill myself. What kind of idiot lights themselves on fire? No one! That's not how it's done. Someone killed me! Someone set me on fire!"

Kai's voice hardens.

"Wren, if that's—"

But Wren isn't listening, too busy spitting venom at him.

"And how dare you say that you resent me for dying! I don't remember a lot of things, but there are some things that I remember very clearly, and I remember every word from your cursed letter:

"Dearest Wren."

She sneers the words out like a cursed recitation. "

I know who is responsible for Zazu's death. Meet me at the southern edge of Lorelei Forest. We can handle them together, and after, you and Fae can return with me to Murasaki. I can protect you. I can protect both of you. You don't have to do this alone. Please, Wren, let me help you. 我爱你。

"Forever your shore, Kai."

Tears streak her face.

"Ring a bell?"

Kai's anger at Wren drains out of him, a stopper pulled from a bath, as she recites, word for word, his greatest wish, composed over and over again in his servers but never put to paper.

"Wren—"

"You! With your flowery words and pretty cursive! You wrote that to me, and like a fool I believed you. I believed you, and I was so tired that I went, and who did I find waiting for me? Your cursed brother and a slew of technomancers, but where were you? Nowhere. Were you too busy celebrating how you tricked me?!"

No, no, none of that is true. He didn't write those words. He wouldn't do that. Not to Wren. Not to anyone.

"I didn't write that letter."

His greatest wish and his greatest regret, never expressed because he couldn't figure out how to arrange a situation that truly ensured Wren's happiness, where the witch wasn't treated like a shameful secret. Wren, as free-spirited as the songbird for which she is named, would never be able to live a life where she was little more than a prisoner in her own home. Should never have to live such a life. A life restricted from the rest of the world because the world hated her so. So, he never voiced his wants to protect her, never wrote them down, never sent them.

And the first bit about Zazu... The true lie. Despite his best efforts to find the person responsible for her nephew's death, he never found anything. Not even after she was gone.

"They trapped me, and they killed Fae, they killed Jessabelle, they killed Silje, and Lisa, and Magdalena, and Lucille. They killed everyone! They taunted me with a bloodstained stuffed animal, and you didn't even have the spine to watch them do it!"

This is her truth. This is what she knows, and it is terrible. A crippling blow that would break anyone's spirit. And none of it is true. Not the way she thinks it is. Deus, she died thinking he had forsaken her in the worst possible way.

"Wren, please. That's not what happened."

"*¡Mentiroso!*"

She steps into his space. The sigils around her temple glow violently. She raises a hand as if to strike him, but he catches her wrist in his other hand. She struggles against him, and he braces himself knowing full well that she could send him headfirst into the nearest headstone with the flex of a thought and a note on her tongue, but he doesn't move to block her ability to sing. Instead, he pulls her into him.

"Wren, listen to me. I didn't write that letter."

"Stop lying to me! It was in your handwriting!"

"I am not lying. Listen to me!"

He opens his mind to her, dropping the neural wards guarding his emotions from her and letting the pent up sensations cascade over her. Because of their skin-to-skin contact, he may as well have slapped her across the face with his very being. Abruptly panicked, she shakes her head violently, fighting to get away from him.

"Are you crazy? Let go!"

He doesn't let go, but he does temper the connection between them, pulling back so as not to overwhelm her. He only has an inkling of an idea of how deeply she can probe somebody's consciousness when touching them like this, and there was never a time in the past when he had dropped his guards like this. Can she feel his regret, his grief, the painful clench of his feelings for her that he has kept curled up and quiet in his heart since her death? Can she feel his hope, the naked euphoria and disbelief that still strikes him now that she has somehow miraculously been returned to the world of the living? Or can she only feel his surface emotions, the nervous fear, the confused anger, the desperation to understand, the frustration with being treated like a stranger, an enemy?

The little he does know is a good starting point. He knows she will be able to tell whether he is lying to her or not. He knows she can feel his determination to get to the bottom of this decade old misunderstanding. Of the lie that poisoned her to him.

"Wren, I don't know how that letter came to be, but I would never betray you. Not like that. Not ever! Please, you must understand that. Can't you feel it?"

He remembers the hostility she greeted him with when he finally made it to the combat grounds. The look of betrayal in her eyes. Her contempt for him, chalked up at the time to magic-induced madness. She had called him "svikari," the Hexen word for a traitor, attacking him on sight, and until now, he has never known why. The violence against him amplified by her rage and grief. It's echoed in every biting remark she's made toward him in the last two days. All their interactions have been colored by it, distorted by it.

Her breath quickens as his emotions unfurl for her.

"Stop broadcasting! I can't think!"

He wills himself to calm.

She too calms, somewhat anyway. He can't be sure whether it is a synthetic response to his own aura, her empathy allowing her to embody his emotions as much as alter them.

"Wren, listen to me," he stresses, bringing his forehead down to meet hers. Then she gets it. He is not asking her to listen to his words. He is asking her to listen to him, to his heart.

"You want me to touch your aura?"

"I am inviting you to."

"You don't know what you're asking."

"I trust you."

"You have no reason to trust me."

"Even so."

"I'm a monster."

"No, you aren't."

She stares at him hard, eyes puffy and swollen, and he meets her gaze with his own molten silver. He notices belatedly that she is trembling. A long conversation happens between them in the span of a moment. Wordless and too intimate for any language to properly capture. Aquatic irises soften to a cooler blue, and just like that, the argument is over.

"You are not a monster, Wren."

Wren's eyes sparkle like shined aquamarine in the light of dawn, glassy and unsteady. Up until two days ago, he never thought he would see those eyes again outside of his scraped memory-servers. He wipes the tears from her cheeks with his sleeve.

The triskelion at her third eye chakra point glimmers, the pulse of her power spiraling from the center point to trace each of the three swirls. He lifts her hands to either side of his head, and she presses barely-there touches into his temples. She hesitates. (Is she afraid to do this?) But it is only for a heartbeat, and then he feels the moment her mind sinks into his.

PRELUDE

It is an odd sensation letting someone into his head in this manner. He has read descriptions of it, anecdotal research written by technomancers and posthumans who have hunted and interacted with empathic witches, cautionary tales of the ability's potential to maim the psyche as the empath rips through the mindscape to grip the person's very being. To leave a person an invalid, out of their minds, their very sanity shredded. The texts talk about the feeling of being violated, the push of a probe, the charring burn of the neurons being ripped apart and vivisected. Of how emotions can be drained away, morphed and manipulated, and artificially recreated to suit the witch's needs.

He would not describe what Wren does as any of these.

There is a sensation of being pressed upon, but it is not overwhelming or even terribly uncomfortable. It is like she is coaxing the information from him, a hand held out in invitation for a cat to brush against. Cautious and careful as though she is touching something precious and fragile, she works his mind open. A gentle prod here, a stroke there, it almost makes him sleepy how calming it is to have his emotions milked from him in this way. But then she stops, and an empty chasm of lethargy settles over him. This is the worst part: an empty, hollowness too similar to how grief starts. His heart stutters in his chest, and once more he feels as though his implants have been forcefully torn from his body, taking with them all semblance of who he once was. He drowns for seconds before mercifully, Wren pushes some of himself back into him, and it's like coming up for air.

"You're not lying."

Kai just about sags with relief. Finally, she's listening. The glow of the twining sigils on her skin dims as they disappear with her more turbulent emotions. Her hands drop, and he adjusts his own so that his palms support hers, maintaining the empathetic connection between them.

"I have been trying to find the people responsible for Zazu's death for years, and the rest...well. When I found you living in Lorelei, I wanted more than anything to ask you to come to Murasaki with me, but how could I ever ask you to cage yourself for me when you told me yourself, 'The easiest way to kill a witch—'"

"'—is to keep her from the sun.'" She wipes a tear from her face. "You made Murasaki a sanctuary for hexen."

He nods slowly. That victory had been hard won, an uphill battle against his brother's (and his own) ingrained beliefs that hexen were dangerous, little more than monsters, but with Wren gone from the world and the rest of the League waging war on every hexen man, woman, and child, someone had to stand firm and demand better. It was the least he could do after failing her first.

And to learn now that she was, indeed, murdered by witch-killers... How could he have ever believed the reports of her suicide just because they came from her own brother? Xipilli, who would more than earn the name witch hunter in the years to follow, supposedly out of some self-professed need to avenge his sister's fate by eradicating the witchcraft that drove her insane.

"So, it was a forgery... But how could they..."

Anger, cold and biting, builds in his throat, but it is not directed at her. The language of the text, the handwriting, the knowledge of Wren's hideout. Like someone hacked into his head.

"I don't know, but when I find out..." He trails off, fingers clenched tight around Wren's hand.

Somehow, someway, someone hacked his system. And whoever they were, may some deity save them if he ever finds out who, because they would answer for this. In the meantime...

Wren looks around dazed as the sun continues to rise. The tears cling to the edges of her lashes, and Kai can't possibly fathom what might be going on in her head.

His hands shift and soften, interlacing their fingers in front of his chest. It is a confirmation that she is not some mirage or illusion, sent here to torment him like so many dreams and nightmares he has experienced over the years. She isn't one of the hallucinations fabricated by his own mind while bereavement suffocated him: Wren's ghost taunting him, raging at him, beguiling him, manipulating him into reliving the best and the worst of the time they had together, until it warped and twisted, turned into something grotesque and cursed.

It has been less than four days since he first caught 'Atalia Vaishi' in his arms. Barely more than a day since he saw Wren's actual face again, revealed in the midst of battle with an enemy she had no reason to face. Just days since her resurrection and he keeps waiting for her to disappear again.

"Wren, you can trust me."

She looks down, forlorn and aching at their hands.

"All this time, I thought you wanted me dead."

He cards his fingers into the hair at the nape of her neck, slick with sweat and warm with fever. She is still fighting off the toxins from the bite, too stubborn to rest properly. He tilts her chin up with his thumb until he finds the blues in her too-green eyes.

"Never."

Their faces are closer to one another than is probably appropriate. He should pull away, give her back some of the distance she has so purposefully placed between them in the last two days, but something in her gaze has shifted, so he holds on with bated breath. It's softer and reminds him of a stolen moment from so many years ago. Two teenagers swaying together in a rooftop gazebo under a double-moon eclipse, newly commissioned as technomancers and a promise unfolding between them that not even they were privy to. The openness in her gaze, decorated with a touch of vulnerability, returns after being closed to him for so long.

Her eyes drop to glance at his lips.

He leans forward as she tilts her head back. When she exhales, he can feel the warm brush of her breath on his lips. It is a shuddered breath. His hand lifts, his fingertips just barely grazing the curly wisps of the ends of her hair. He so desperately aches to close the distance, the vast chasm between them, to hold her and support her, but he doesn't. It is not his place, not his privilege to push this on her, even if it hurts. Wants and desires that have laid quiet and buried for years, old feelings and dreams tucked away in the dark for a long time now can wait for however long she needs.

He holds still, and when she next speaks, averting her gaze from his, he is thankful for his restraint.

"Do you mind shuttering? It's...You're... You're a lot."

She sounds overwhelmed.

He has no illusions on the fact that she has just felt his want. What she decides to do with that now is her decision. He reactivates his neural wards, and Wren nearly swoons. Her head drops to his chest with a dull thud. Her indicia disappears, and she whispers into his chest.

"Kai, I'm sorry. I...I didn't... Ay, *pinche pedo*, why is this so hard?"

Her voice sounds thick with emotion. She closes her eyes and sinks into his hold which morphs into a true embrace as his arms wind around her petite form. Tears soak into his shirt. Kai just holds her through it. His lips ghost over the top of her head, and when he breathes, the scent of an ocean mist drifts through him.

Eventually, she quiets with a sobbed laugh. She wipes at her face and shakes herself, already pulling away.

"I have been a right monster to you, haven't I? You didn't deserve that. My apologies, highness."

He notes the usage of his title. Her age-old way of creating distance between them. She steps back and away, and the chasm yawns wider than ever, but he lets her go. He has had twelve years to reflect. Twelve years to pull out his fragmented memories of her and examine them. To look back in hindsight and wish he'd handled things differently. To yearn for someone who was no longer there.

He understands. He understands implicitly.

She has not had that time. She is just now learning him. He aches, but if there is anything he can give her, it is time. Could anything else be so precious to someone who has had so little?

"Your ire, while misplaced, is not uncalled for. Whoever sent that letter knew they would set into action a chain of events that would result in your death one way or another."

A bark of laughter falls from her lips. It's hollow and sarcastic, and he wonders what she is thinking.

"Wren, are you alright?"

"Sorry, sorry. I just... This whole resurrection thing isn't a cakewalk. Goddess, I feel like an idiot."

She waves it off like it's some joke. Like the last hour hasn't been anything more taxing than a discussion over tea. Like he is suddenly supposed to stop worrying just because she's pasted on this fake smile and waved it away like some cheap magic trick. He didn't realize the weight of everything she had been carrying. The weight of her own grief. Grief for the ones she lost. Her grief for Fae, when—

"Wren, there's something you need to know. It's about—"

"Aww, no kiss and make-up? Really, *min dronning,* don't you think you should show the man a bit more appreciation?"

Kaito turns to find Yggfret hovering, visible even to his naked eye roughly five meters away.

"Yggfret," growls Wren. Before she or Kai can move, the villdød hurls a casting directly at her. It hits Wren square in the chest and pushes her into Kaito where it explodes into a surge of power which envelops both of them.

Kai's stomach drops out of its place, and the world condenses to a single point before rapidly expanding once again. He loses his physical self, becoming nothing more than a thought before all of his parts, flesh, mech, and all, are shoved back together. He and Wren collide into one another as the ground hits hard against his back while Wren's elbow slams into his diaphragm, but he has no wind for her to knock out anyway. He can't breathe.

"Shit! Kai, breathe. Deep breath in. Come on. Breathe!"

The glow of his tech flickers and goes out, and Wren's voice becomes an afterthought.

He fights to suck in air, but nothing. He can't do it. His lungs have stopped working. Wren's voice and face start to darken and fade, pupils blown wide with panic before the world blackens. Fingers pinch his nose shut and air is forced into his lungs. And the breath returns.

His neural hub lights back up like he's been restarted. He coughs and sucks in lungfuls of cool air, sitting himself up, but Wren forces him back onto his back.

"Don't move! I need to check and make sure you're in one piece."

He doesn't even ponder what that might even mean as her hands begin to swipe over his head, neck, and shoulders. There is magic radiating from her palms as she quickly checks over his chest and legs. When she is finished, she checks his head one more time before sighing in relief and sitting back on her haunches.

"Okay, it looks like you're all there. You can move."

Kai sits up with a pained wince. Everything hurts, but the longer he waits and breathes, the less the pain lingers, and slowly he comes back into himself.

"What was that?"

"That was a teleportation spell. They aren't designed for 'borgs. I needed to make sure none of you got left behind."

He opens his eyes once the dizziness dies down. It is pitch black in the room; the only thing he can see is Wren's eyes reflecting his tech lights back to him and the neon glow of her indicia. He activates his night vision, and even though there is a twang of discomfort, the setting turns on without a fuss, giving him the ability to look around. They are in a wine cellar of some sort. There are barrels throughout the room in racked stands. Toward the back of the chamber, a door has been ripped off its hinges, opening into a darkened space that no doubt leads farther underground, possibly into the caverns they found themselves in yesterday. Around the periphery of the chamber, there are dusty, old-fashioned torches lining the walls, archaic things: lengths of smoothed, twisted iron topped with steel cages and a propane tank designed to fuel the flame, similar in design to a flamethrower but less refined. The fire resulting from these torches would blast out with the purpose of coating the entire head of the torch in a messy burst of flame more like a mini explosion than lighting a fire. Everything is so dusty, too. He can imagine no one has been down here in decades. There are sigils all along the walls and an open circle in the center of the room. It is a yawning hole that leaks sinister energy. Placed at five separate points around the circle are five phylacteries of varying shapes and sizes, fashioned just like the one used during the attack on Snowfall Palace.

"Where are we?"

Wren, who had been focused on him up until now, looks around for herself and shakes her head.

"I don't know."

Kai immediately does a virtual scan of the area both above and below them, but the interference prevents him from reading much farther than the confines of the room.

"I can't scan past these sigils. It's like this place is hidden from the network."

Which means the magic in this room is dense enough to create a dead zone.

"Are you functioning well?"

"Yes, I believe I am whole."

"Good," she whispers, relief in her voice. She stands up and approaches the active array. "Yggfret, you better show your sorry face now! You have some explaining to do!"

The undead witch appears before Wren, his upper body bent in a deep bow. Kai picks himself up off the ground. When he wavers slightly, Wren settles a hand between his shoulder blades.

"Of course, *min dronning.*"

"Stop calling me that."

"What is the meaning of this?" demands Kaito of the spectre.

Yggfret, as though noticing Kaito for the first time, sets his hands together and offers the prince a mocking bow.

"Of course, your highness. I just thought I would save you the trouble of a return trip here. After all, did you not wish to know where the miasma was originating from?"

"This is Shinka?"

Wren and Kai trade glances. Kai has never seen this part of Shinka.

"Yes, *min dronning.*"

"I said, stop calling me that!"

"But it is your title," the ghost sneers at her. "Of course, I'm happy to rid you of it, if you'd prefer."

The villdød hurls another blast of power toward Wren. This time she is ready for it, reflecting the blast back at the undead witch, who shimmers out of the space before reforming on the far side of the chamber. Kai draws Tsukuyomi from her sheath. Yggfret's laugh echoes through the chamber as the villdød hurls himself forward and disappears into the array. For a moment, nothing happens. Then a low hum begins to sound.

Wren's eye twitches, and she approaches the circle. She strokes the array's aura with her fingertips.

"It's a trans-dimensional circle."

Kaito walks over to look at the markings. They look old. There are several markings along the outskirts of the array that indicate sealing or caging something away.

"Something was locked away in here," says Kaito.

"And someone decided to unlock whatever it was. See how they reversed the seals? The wendigo?"

"Maybe," answers Kaito. "This place certainly looks like a holding cell for something that doesn't like fire."

Just then a torch alights on the wall right behind Wren. She startles forward, stepping fully into the array as more of the torches ignite. Standing in the middle of the array, void magic oozes out around her feet, curling around her boots like seaweed, but Wren, terror-stricken by the flames around her, doesn't even notice.

"Wren, get out of there."

She doesn't move.

"Wren!"

She turns to him wide-eyed, shaking where she stands. Pyrophobia. Of course. Kaito reaches over the array line to pull her out just as one of the tendrils wraps around her ankle. There is a harsh yank, the sound of popping bone, and Wren is pulled into the array. At the same time, a gust of chilled wind billows through the cellar, jerking him into a barrel. It shatters on impact, and the acrid tang of oil burns the lining of his nostrils. These aren't wine barrels at all. The oil soaks into his coat, and Tsukuyomi's blade slides through the puddle.

He has little time to contemplate this as a shrieking ghoul angles his direction, claws outstretched and teeth gnashing for his pulse point. He swings upward with his blade, and the undead dissipates into grave ash. His sights whirl to life, and he scans the room. Wren is nowhere to be found. He adjusts his scanners and looks for her magical markers. He finds something that reads like her, but the coding is warped, upside-down and flipped as though she is standing on the other side of a mirror.

Her coding disappears through the ceiling, and in the physical realm, Kai follows via the trapdoor. He can't open it. It is either locked, or there is something on top of the door. Wren's code is getting farther and farther away, and if he lets her get beyond the scope of his VR perimeter, he'll lose track of her, entirely. Kai sheathes Tsukuyomi and focuses his internal processors on his muscular enhancements. He balances himself on the ladder as solidly as he can before he pushes up. It gives a bit. There is definitely something on top of it. He hits the latch, and it breaks clean off the door.

Taking two more steps up the ladder, Kai braces his shoulders under the door, and with a mighty heave, bursts through the floor to find himself in Shinka's reception hall. Since when has there been a trapdoor in the reception hall? He is standing on the dais where the ruler of Murasaki no Yama sits when holding an event in Shinka, the same seat from where his mother presided over the opening ceremonies of the 247th Technomancer Trials. When he turns around, he realizes the weight he needed to push off the door was the temple throne, a humble version of the peony throne back at Snowfall Palace. Has this trapdoor been hidden here this whole time? He doesn't know.

The hall is a mess of bodies, adepts and human+ trainees dead and decaying amongst the long tables and various statues.

He does a quick scan for Wren's magical resonance in the virtual plane, but there's nothing to be found. Wren has disappeared from Kai's virtual sights, and he knows without a doubt she is out of range for the protection spell on his signet ring which means he has two hours to either find Wren or get out of here, preferably both. The effect of losing Wren's protection is starting to make itself known already. His limbs start to feel heavier, his senses sluggish.

He steadies himself and switches his systems to safeguard mode, reviving himself somewhat as the magical compatibility of his hardware increases. An undead pings on his radar, heading his way. Yggfret flickers into the room as he draws, hurling a swirling ball of dark energy at him.

Kai dodges to the side and flips over the edge of the raised platform. Another blast heads his way, and he races his way through the bodies littering the floor toward the villdød. Sights on, Kaito sets his territory, mapping the undead into his virtual field so that he can destroy the damned thing. Saibāki coats his blades.

"Come now, highness. I promised Lady Wren I would take good care of you."

"Where have you taken her?"

"Just led the lady to a vital piece of information I'm sure will come in handy later. Don't worry. I'm sure she'll be just fine. She may even make it back here in time to save your miserable existence."

Yggfret dodges this way and that, maneuvering himself out of Kai's range, so he lets the swords fly, the mechanical whirr of the forearm attachments buzzes as they become prehensile extensions of his arms. Zinging outward, the vertebral cabling arcs the blades toward the ceiling where the specter hovers, gloating.

"Twelve years, huh? That's a long time for a hot-blooded man like you to grieve, wouldn't you say? Tell me, did you ever seek out a replacement, or was visiting your memory banks enough to keep the desolation away?"

Yggfret moves around the spaces like a monkey, ducking in and around the various banners, draperies, and chandeliers that dangle from the rafters.

"Though, I suppose, you've been busy. Chasing ghosts and raising the next generation of witch killers. Tell me, what were you about to tell her before I interrupted?"

A deep growl expels from Kai's chest, and Amatsu connects with the undead's being, stabbing it from the ceiling all the way to the ground to anchor it to the floor while Tsukuyomi returns to Kai's hand. Kai pushes forward with a surge of speed and cuts the space the villdød occupies, and the specter howls as the metal catches its outstretched arm. Black seeps from the strike point. Dark magic descends like fog from the undead creature's wound. Yggfret pushes another energy strike forward and hits Kai square in the chest. His armor absorbs the majority of the blast, but he goes careening into a table. The carved wood splinters as Kai flings his legs out and up in a kip-up to return to standing right as a blast of fire hurtles toward him.

"Catch, lover boy!"

Tsukuyomi and Amatsu hover before him in an X to block the blast, and Tsukuyomi's oiled blade alights in flame.

"Follow me, *gemål*. I'll take you to her."

Not knowing what Yggfret just called him, but not exactly caring right now, he catches his blades once more and gives chase as Yggfret races out of the door. He pants as he runs, scanning and rescanning, looking for some trace of Wren as he weaves through the various hallways after Yggfret. Nothing. It's like she isn't even in the temple anymore.

He closes one eye and extends his virtual signature beyond his physical body. His coded self flickers forward and tackles Yggfret. The villdød crumbles beneath Amatsu's coding as the tanto is stabbed through the spirit's core. The goblin king grasps the virtual blade and sends a shockwave through the lavender-coated weapon and through Kaito's virtual signature.

Rriiing!

Ringing in his ears as phantom pain blisters through his synapse. Teeth clenching, he forces his tech to keep working, but he's misjudged the effectiveness of the curse, and his VR extension has drawn too much of his power. It winks out, his sights powering down.

"You should be more careful, *gemål*. You can't protect *min dronning* if you're dead."

Kai rounds the corner, and a pair of large jaws snap for his face. He bends backwards, ducking under the wendigo's putrid maw. A familiar shriek sounds, pain and fear tempered by hunger and rage.

He swings Tsukuyomi's flaming blade forward at the wendigo and cuts it across the chest before backing out of range. The monster still bears the marks of its earlier flaying, scorched flesh and fur along its left flank. Where Tsukuyomi strikes, the skin peels, blackening to char. The creature moves to run, but Kaito throw himself forward. The heels of his boots dig into the creature's back, the momentum behind his body weight sending the wendigo crashing face first into the ground.

Tsukuyomi sings as she beheads the pitiful beast.

A low whistle sounds behind him along with a slow clapping. It's Yggfret.

"See, easy as cake when you've the right tools."

"What are you playing at, *villdød*?"

The dead man tsks.

"Is that anyway to address someone who just saved you a lot of time and effort?"

"Answer the question!"

"Ah ah. I think you have more important things to deal with right now."

Kai hears the howl of another wendigo.

"You technomancers... Honestly. So concerned with slaying one monster, you forget to question whether it might have a mate. This is why witches are far superior to 'mancers."

A large claw busts through the paneling of the wall beside him. Kai leaps back just in time to avoid being pulled straight through the plaster. Another claw joins the first as the other wendigo rips its way through the building. This one is even larger than the first, more emaciated, gaunter, without antlers, and sporting blackened teats. A matriarch, and she is not happy.

Kai ducks behind an alcove. Concealing himself from view, he reactivates his scanners and searches the area for further surprises. Yggfret has disappeared again to Deus knows where.

Colorless eyes find her fallen mate, and the creature sniffs at the corpse. She shakes the body, sniffs it, even takes a bite out of the other wendigo's shoulder as though to see if she can get a reaction from him before she finally, almost blindly pulls the head off the floor into her grizzly hands. She stares at the dead skull of her mate for several heartbeats. The noise she makes is a wail akin to a dying deer and a sniveling hyena, but despite the ghastly nature of the sound, there is no mistaking the grief behind the cry.

Kai closes his eyes and tries to focus. The world is getting spongy around him, thick and hollow and lead-filled, like a poorly made stew with no substance.

Suddenly, the pain hits him. It slams into him like a tidal wave. Has it been two hours already?

He must have made a noise because the wendigo's cries have stifled. And she is moving toward him. He runs. As hard and as fast as he can, he runs. His neural network goes down, and he presses his subconscious out, calling for Wren psychically. He has no practice in this. All he remembers is the feel of her sliding into his mind just hours ago, and he tries to mimic that now even as he races to the edge of the compound. He isn't sure he can make it.

Wren... His witch. She's still here somewhere. He knows it.

It's the last thing he thinks before he collapses into the dead grass outside, Tsukuyomi still a flaming blade in his hand while Amatsu is flung out to land in the dirt.

Kai feels the heavy weight of the curse on his senses, pressing down and digging into his core. His tech begins to flicker, one system shutting off at a time. He doesn't have long before he enters a total system shutdown. Already, his muscles cramp and seize at the shorts beginning to race through his system. He tries to stand, hears the wendigo doe behind him growling, hungry for revenge, screws his eyes shut as another wave of agony crashes into him.

Tsukuyomi leaves his hand on autopilot, tracing some path beyond his cognizant command. The wendigo screams loudly at whatever the blade does.

He takes another step forward and crumbles. He heaves into the dirt, and it tastes like oil and ozone. His neural net flickers and dies. The sky above him darkens, and his eyes lose focus on the world around him. There is a ringing in his ears again, staticky and persistent—a broadcast gone offline. His body numbs, and when an electric shock rocks his body, he knows exactly what is going on.

System shutdown.

24

THE EMPRESS REVERSED

WREN FINDS HERSELF HURTLING THROUGH darkness and into blinding white light. When her vision clears, she is upside down, curled on her head on hard tile.

"*Faen!*"

She rights herself with a curse and looks around, blinking at her surroundings and freezes. She is smack-dab center in a large reception hall that she instantly recognizes as Shinka's main greeting hall, and it is not the Shinka of the present day which would be better described as a standing burial ground than a temple.

The world is tinged in a bloody red and touched as though peering through the lens of a camera obscura. There is something other about the way the light streams through the hall that reminds Wren of looking through broken glass. Everything is split or cut off, doubled up or blurry in her vision, and no matter where she looks, the texture is off. Otherworldly or perhaps vintage would be a better word for the filter with which she seems to be experiencing this time and place, but these aren't the only clues that tell her this is not the present day.

The hall is packed full of people, so much so that it reminds Wren of the closing banquet of the technomancer trials she attended as a teenager. There is music and dancing and conversation, fine wine and food and all the elegance required of such an event held in Shinka Temple.

For a moment of disorienting panic, she thinks she's been swept back in time, but then a trainee steps right through her on the way to a nearby table—a trainee she recognizes as Renki, looking a year or two younger than he is in the present.

So, she is intangible in this space.

The boy bows deeply to the technomancers seated at the table before initiating a hushed conversation. She notes with a small chuckle that he is much shorter than she thinks he is now. He's not quite filled out either, more bone than muscle, baby fat still clinging to his face. It's kind of cute seeing him so small, the testosterone not quite having kicked in yet to bulk him up.

She smiles.

"Zenza, stop slouching, and sit properly."

Wren turns her head and is further affirmed that this most certainly is not her own graduation banquet. Xipilli, looking older and grumpier, sits at a table with a Zenza who is too young and boyish for the fluffy ball gown she is wearing. She looks to be just budding into her pre-teens as a young lady, holding herself in that awkward way that tells Wren she is hyper-aware of her body even though she is still more straight lines than curves. Wren's brother is already graying around his temples, but he is as straight-backed as ever, dressed in accents of Derivan finery. The loose silks draped fashionably over his form in a tasteful sweep over his black tuxedo.

"You're not my etiquette teacher," snips the girl back at her uncle. She straightens up anyway, tugging her shawl tighter around her. "I don't understand why mom couldn't come. She wanted to."

The mention of Wren's elder sister is jarring for a multitude of reasons, none of which Wren wants to think about too deeply. Atzi had been a casualty of good intentions, and Wren's good intentions carved out her sister's damnation.

"You know very well why your mother is not here, nor will she ever be able to attend an event like this."

"But she's been getting better. I-I think she recognized me the other day. She touched my face."

Xipilli raises his eyes heavenward.

"Zenza," he says, voice flooded with exasperated pity. "Your mother's mind was shattered when—"

"The Songstress of Lorelei attacked her, I know. But—"

"But nothing! Any illusions you may have about her recovery are just that. Illusions. There is nothing that can be done to repair her mind."

Because Wren can't face the truth of it, she moves away from the phantom echoes of her family. Renki is shuffling toward the raised dais, so she chooses to follow the boy. She sees Hikaru seated at the throne speaking with a man she recognizes as Donarick J. Thames, an older, very regally dressed version of the adept that strikes her as a little overt for his station, at least for his previous station. Perhaps he's advanced since her death. Not that she could see how. He's always been a squirrelly sort of person.

"Another summit closes. It's a promising group, don't you think, Hikaru-san?"

Hikaru looks worried. More than a little worried.

"It's the smallest group of graduates the League has ever welcomed. Less than five new technomancers. We've never had such a small group."

"Only four, yes," Thames concedes. "But you should be proud. Two Murasakan graduates. Your country continues to thrive when it comes to training technomancers."

Curious...

"I am afraid the ability is dying out."

"Oh, don't be ridiculous, Emperor. We are simply going through a lull in qualifying technomancers. You'll see in a few more years the numbers will pick back up."

Just then Renki reaches Hikaru. The boy bows deeply to the man who places a gentle hand on his shoulder to guide him back to standing.

"Renki. What brings you to me?"

Renki nods his head.

"Father has returned."

"I'll be right there. Thank you, Renki."

Hikaru rises from his seat. He bids farewell to Thames, then glides down the stairs, Renki following after him. A few moments later, Chiamaka sways her way toward Thames. The tall woman walks like a panther, beautiful and graceful. She exudes power and strength, a far cry from the girl Wren remembers as a teenager. Chike's little sister had always been more concerned with the gossip column than technomancy. She used to go on about her future wedding and future husband and future children. But time does change people. She looks a little different too. Where previously Chiamaka always styled her hair into a gorgeous afro, she now sports a head full of braids that fall to her waist from under a silk turban. There also seems to be something odd about the woman's proportions. Did she have a growth spurt or something? Or is Wren misremembering how tall the Ebelean princess was?

"Hello, husband," she coos to Thames, and the floor drops out from under Wren's feet. Chiamaka and Thames are married. What the...

"*Ololufe*," the white man acknowledges. His tongue trips over the Ebelean term of endearment, but Chiamaka beams at the man anyway, though there is something off about it to Wren. "My Orisha."

That's not right...Zenza is the rightful heir to the throne of Ebele. It's her birthright as the oldest living child of Chike Nagi, the first son of Orisha Absko. Chiamaka was never the direct heir to the throne and should only be acting as a figurehead until Zenza's coming of age.

"Careful, consort. You overstep," she acknowledges back to him with a playful smirk. "It would seem this party is beginning to disperse."

"It would seem. We should turn in for the evening."

He holds his arm out to her. She takes his elbow, and he begins to lead her out of the reception.

"Two Murasaki no Yama graduates out of the four certified. The emperor must be proud," says Chiamaka.

"You would think," says Thames.

"Is he not?"

Thames shakes his head.

"It is certainly suspect that Murasaki no Yama has consistently turned out the most technomancers at each summit over the last six years."

Chiamaka trades a look with Thames, and the two drift from the hall. Wren attempts to follow, but she doesn't seem capable of exiting the hall. Must be a binding of the portal's magic. Wherever she is or *whenever* she is, she is confined to this room. It isn't long before the lights to the hall are dimmed, the band of musicians packs up, the waitstaff begin to clear away plates and cutlery. Young trainees and temple students enter and begin to pack up the extravagance. She notices Renki and Akari among the young adepts, and she watches them with a fond smile on her lips. They do more play than work until one of the older students chastises them for it. Tables and chairs are stacked up, floors swept, and arrangements made for the event to come the following morning. Before long, Fumiko appears to inspect their work. The woman seems to approve, dismissing them to their beds for the evening.

After their exit, the hall is silent and still, but not for very long.

As the sky darkens into the blackest part of the night, Wren sees as the doors to the hall slide open despite the lock she saw Renki place on them. A figure clothed in black enters, their feet barely making any sound on the stone flooring. The person steps into a shimmering beam of starlight, and Wren recognizes Chiamaka instantly.

Without the finery of an evening gown and heels, Chiamaka's appearance is far more understated, looking more like the farm girls that populate her country than the would-be "Orisha" of Ebele.

PRELUDE

Chiamaka doublechecks that there is no one behind her before sliding all the way into the reception hall and to Wren's surprises, tugging a nameless adept in with her. He can't be older than nineteen or twenty, so not young-young but still younger than the Ebelean woman. She then slinks her way to the dais. Wren doesn't remember Chiamaka being anything other than honest in personality. She wouldn't sneak around in the dark like this, especially not with a man who isn't her husband. Something smells fishy.

Made more so when Chiamaka calls a fairy light into her palm.

Green eyes widen. Chiamaka, the ruler of a country of the League, using magic? Unspeakable!

"Your highness, what exactly did you summon me here for?"

"You'll see."

Wren watches as the woman uses the light to mind her footing on the way up the stairs going until she finds her way to the center throne where Hikaru had been sitting earlier, guiding the young adept the whole way.

Without much more ceremony, she shoves the young man onto the throne. He is notably surprised by the treatment.

"Orisha!"

"Don't call me that, boy. We are not our titles here. Now take your pants off."

The youth's eyes go wide, but as can be expected of any young hormone-riddled male, he is quick to comply. Chiamaka shoves her skirt aside and without much preamble mounts him. She moves fast and heavy over the boy she is right then and there making a man in the middle of a deserted reception hall on the very throne of the new technomancer's emperor.

Wren's jaw drops and horror floods her gaze as, when the youth reaches his peak, Chiamaka draws a dagger from her belt and slashes the youth's throat wide open. Blood spurts everywhere. It drenches Chiamaka, the throne, the dais. Chiamaka heaves herself up twice more before she too reaches a far less morbid end.

And they used to call Wren a necrophile!

She rises off the corpse and studies the stone carved seat. The boy's pants still dangle around his knees, his sex limp, skin pale and pallid from death and blood loss. His eyes are glazed over, the last dredges of his orgasm still reflected there, tainted by the terror of seeing his own death hurtling toward him in the eyes of his lover.

Chiamaka lifts the dagger once more. She cuts a long line across her forearm and blood wells, dripping down to mix with the boy's blood pooled already at her feet. Wren hears the elder tongue fall from Chiamaka's lips, coiled power darker than pitch pouring from her mouth like oil as she recites the incantation. Suddenly, the throne, which must easily weigh half a ton, is shoved backward along the stone to reveal a trapdoor.

As she works, Wren sees the haze of a spell cast over her whole being. Similar to the glamour spell Wren used to impersonate Atalia.

Could it be...

The woman continues the incantation, and the trap door swings up and open. She tugs on the corpse and tosses it into the pit. The corpse lands with a squelch, and if she had a physical stomach at the moment, it would have turned. The woman's teeth gleam in the darkness before she lowers herself into the hole. Wren follows, drifting down into the same basement/cellar Yggfret brought her and Kaito, where she had been sucked into this otherworld to bear witness to this night in history.

The room is just as dusty now as it is in the present. The only difference is that the torches are lit, the fires in them blazing through the haze of this plane's atmosphere, and the seal at the center of the room is unaltered and sleeping in inactivity. The only thing she can hear from the array is a gentle lullaby meant to keep something from waking up.

And there most certainly is something sleeping down here. Tied down in the center of the array is a wendigo doe. A broodmother. How long has this thing been chained up down here? Judging from the emaciated physique and near dead visage, at least several decades. Probably before Kai's aunt and mother were even born.

Wren doesn't look too closely at what Chiamaka does to the boy she just sacrificed for the sake of whatever ritual she is about to conduct, but when a heart splatters down in the middle of the array, Wren knows exactly what the witch is about to do.

The cut on her arm is still bleeding. She dips her fingers into the wound and uses the blood that pools over her fingers to begin altering the array. It is gruesome work, taking over an array with nothing but blood, a few stolen body parts, and willpower. She speaks in Hexen at the array, guttural and harsh.

"Jeg er mesteren. Stå opp og gjør mitt bud. Du er min."

I am the master. Rise up and heed my bidding. You are mine.

Chiamaka paints over the sigils, morphs the array, alters it to her liking, a void-like magic that Wren recognizes but can't quite place.

"Min!" she screams.

The array's song changes instantly, the lullaby becoming a harsh white noise. Not enough to wake the creature yet, but enough that this array will not remain placid for much longer. Where the sigils had lain dormant before, they blacken like ink spilling over paper before the energy begins to leak out of them, oily and thick like squid ink. It is small and contained, the kind of casting that acts like a timed bomb. It will be months, two years precisely, before the spell takes full effect, but the groundwork has been laid, and unless someone interferes, which Wren knows they won't, it will burst once it's acclimated enough power.

The footfalls of someone coming down the ladder pull Wren's focus toward the trapdoor. An Ebele adept descends the ladder into the basement. He reaches the floor and bows deeply to Chiamaka.

"I am ready, my lady."

"Did you clean up upstairs?"

"Yes, ma'am."

"Good. You will be the blade that cuts down Murasaki no Yama."

The adept moves to the array and settles. Chiamaka approaches him and kneels in front of him.

"You will be lauded in the halls of our ancestors for centuries to come."

The adept beams, shoulders squared with pride for his country.

"Murasaki is a traitor to the League. They've allowed hexen sanctuary within their borders and still they excel beyond other countries in their ranks of technomancers. They deserve to be brought down."

"Yes," says Chiamaka. She lifts a piece of raw flesh to the man's lips, and he takes the meat from her like a babe suckling at a teat. While he chews, Chiamaka chants once again in the Eldritch tongue.

The man swallows slowly, and Chiamaka backs away. She raises a hand, and the torches along the walls are snuffed out in a violent burst of wind. She says one last thing in Eldritch to the devotee who responds in kind before she lifts herself up and out of the cellar, closes the trap door, sets the lock magically, and returns the throne to its resting place. The Ebelean adept's screams, if there are any, remain unheard beyond the thick stone.

When the world resettles, Wren is lying on her back in the middle of the array. She's a little dizzy, but a few quick blinks to clear her vision settle that well enough. What's unsettling is the fact the Yggfret is hovering right in front of her face.

"Goddess be damned! Yggfret!"

"*Min dronning,*" says the villdød with a bow.

"I told you to stop with that stupid title."

"Forgive me, my lady, but it is your title."

"No, it isn't."

"But you're ready now. Don't you see. You are the center point of it all."

"Shut up!"

"You were too stubborn to embrace your duty in your past life, so we left you alone, and look what's become of it. The same won't be said for this life. You are obliged to your responsibilities."

"Responsibilities *mi culo!*"

"And perhaps, just perhaps, if Lady Wren had taken the appropriate measures to fulfill her responsibilities, she would not have lost her witchling."

"*¡Bastardo!*"

Wren pushes a pulse of power at the undead witch, and it hits him in his exposed ribcage. The villdød flails backwards with a resounding stream of laughter.

"Still angry with me after all this time, *min dronning*? I saved your life, remember? Have you no gratitude? Or perhaps it is your grief that fuels your rage?"

She hits him again. The spirit wheels through the air until it collides with one of the barrels.

"I've made peace with their deaths. Fae's and my nephew's."

"But you never told him, did you?"

"Shut up!"

"You never told the truth, and you've regretted that every day. Why not come clean now?"

"It's in the past. It doesn't matter."

"Is it? The past has a way of haunting us."

"You won't be haunting me much longer if I have anything to say about that. I'm going to bind your soul to the most miserable circle of hell I can find."

"That a fact? You might want to attend to something else before that though."

"Like?!"

"Notice anyone missing?"

For the first time, Wren looks around and realizes Kaito is nowhere to be found. She's been in another plane this whole time. How long? How long has she been gone from the physical plane? Kai told her his tech was only able to sustain itself in the miasma for two hours. Her protection spell won't hold through a dimension shift, especially not if he moved away from the array. She reaches out with her mind, tugging on her connection to Kai's signet ring. There is hardly anything there. Her eyes widen in panic.

She takes off up the ladder and through the open trapdoor. Her pulse beats in her ears as her feet pound against the ground. Please, let him still be alive! Kai needs to be alive! Do not let this be another death on her hands. Not Kai's. Please, anyone but Kai's!

She passes the body of the male wendigo, still smoldering, but she pays it no mind. She runs past destroyed corridors and tarnished furniture until she is falling onto the dirt outside the temple. She grips the grass, soil clogs into the pits of her nails, and she all but rips the dead foliage out of the earth in her haste to get back up, blackened blades restoring to a lively green in her wake beyond her perception. The connection to the ring is stronger out here. She can feel it now just ahead of her. She runs frantically forward only stopping when a wall of fire greets her.

Her throat closes up and her heart rate skyrockets. Fire. Deadly, destructive, killing fire. And on the other side of the flames, Wren sees Kai, unconscious, tech inactive, face down in the dirt, and she needs to get to him. Her read on him is faint, but it's there. He's alive but barely, clinging to the precipice between life and death. She needs to restart his tech, heal him, stabilize him, something, but she can't get to him. Fire, cursed, burning, hellborn fire blocks her way.

"Hhhrrawwwgg!"

A clawed hand catches her around the throat and lifts her from her feet, and she comes face to face with the wendigo matriarch she saw caged in the alternate plane. Its jaw opens, and the shrieking sound that spills forth is enough to deafen her. Wren rams her boots into the creature's face. It jerks back but doesn't let go, so she kicks out again and again until it drops her hard on her ass. She scrambles back, freezing when hot flames lick at her shoulders. Her indicia pulses to life as she draws on her power. The first wave of telekinetic force goes wide, but the second and third nail the wendigo in the chest. They do nothing to deter it. The creature strikes Wren's outstretched palms, and the force of the blow knocks her hands into the fire. She screams, jerking her hands back so fast she barely feels the heat.

In her haste, her hand knocks up some of the ignited grass into the wendigo's eyes. The beast screams in pain, grabs Wren by the shoulders, and slams her into the ground. The connection of the wendigo's hands on her skin opens Wren's empathy to the matriarch.

The grief hits her synapse, poignant enough that Wren's eyes tear up. A sob wrenches its way out of her chest. The wendigo screams in her face. She shakes Wren like a doll, back and forth against the ground. The rocks burning into her back, the heat of the fire at her head, and the faint tug of the spell connecting her to Kai, all of it keeps her lucid in the face of the wendigo's emotions.

"We killed your mate."

The wendigo continues to scream.

"I know it hurts. I'm sorry."

She pleads in her head to the creature. Saliva drips from the wendigo's jaws, hunger and rage and sorrow feeding into her psyche hard enough to drive her mad. But instead of succumbing to the familiar embrace of madness, she bears down. She braces her barriers and sets her intention. Magic is intention. The triskele at her forehead glows. The space between mind, body, and spirit. A prayer between her, her own blackened soul, and the earthly vessel she's been gifted. She'll face the fire again, she'll burn again, but only if it means that Kai lives. A burning falsetto spills from her vocal chords. The circle of flame collapses in on the target point of Wren's voice, slamming into the wendigo like a speeding train. It shoves the matriarch backward, and Wren throws herself over Kai's body and chokes down a sob when his lifeforce doesn't greet her.

"No...No! Kai! Don't you dare die on me, *cabron*. Wake up!"

His tech is completely muted. No pulse of power, no radiation of energy. She turns his head and moves his hair out of the way to find his central nodule. She needs to reboot his mainframe, a recharge. Electricity. Lightning. Lightning is just plasmic fire, right? She slices her wrist open with a sharp fingernail. She drips her blood onto the nodule and traces the alchemical symbol for lightning into his neck. She builds up the songweave with a lyric, then sticks her hand back into the flames.

"A spark for a life. A bolt for a light. Lightning precedes the thunder."

She repeats the haiku over and over until the tension has built in the pit of her chest, then she presses her index finger into the central node at the back of Kai's neck. A visible line of voltage connects her finger to his tech system. She pushes as much of her magical essence into him as she possibly can, as much as he can take before she burns out or before he overflows. The fire licks at her hair and skin, but it doesn't catch. She focuses instead on feeding her power into her technomancer. She focuses on the pathway of the power she feeds into his system, enervating the connecting nerves and the muscular tissue, she repairs the flow of the wiring, reroutes the blocked synthetic arteries, and pushes until his system is awash with ultraviolet saibäki, her magic converted to him, and his chest expands under her hands.

"Kai!"

When she pulls away from working through his servers, his system is relit and sustaining itself with his body's own power. She turns him over onto his back. She listens at his chest and finds a steady beat. She clears his airway.

He's breathing slow and steady. And the breath she herself has been holding is released.

She looks up for the first time since throwing herself on top of Kai. Toujiro's ghost hovers just a few steps away. He gives her a plaintive nod before he closes his eyes and disappears in a haze of light. The wendigo is dead, its corpse still burning, the flames incinerating the creature. She becomes aware of the smell of burnt flesh (Not her own, not this time), and she weeps.

PRELUDE

She weeps into Kai's jacket. Oil taints the leather. She cries for the dead. She cries for the living. She mourns for her sister, her brother, her niece, her nephew, her brother-in-law, her father and mother and stepmother. She mourns for Fae, for Jessabelle, even for Toujiro. She mourns for Kaito.

But most of all, she mourns for herself.

25
DEATH PART 2

Sixteen Years Ago–3 Months After the Fall of Deriva–The Month of Cold, 1861

K AI SEARCHES WITH XIPILLI FOR ANY TRACE of Wren, but their efforts yield nothing. They fight side by side against Seraphim robotics to take back Aighneas. The siege against Seraphim's occupation in Aighneas is a long, drawn-out thing, but with Ebele, Murasaki no Yama, and Sekhmeti combining their might, they manage it.

In the aftermath of the battle to extradite Seraphim from Aighneas, the Alliance, as they have come to call themselves, is in the midst of a battle planning meeting when the first news of Wren arrives.

The Morrigan stands at the head of her war room, a vision of composure and strength in her reclaimed domain. Mirai, Hikaru, and Kaito stand to one side of the war table opposite the Sahra and Nagi leaders. The newly crowned Vulcan, Xipilli stands next to Chike with a small contingent of surviving Derivan technomancers and adepts including Irene. Atzi, Chiamaka, and Rhiannon make steady circuits around the room with refreshments as the hours pass while they pore over battle plans for the upcoming raids.

"Madame President!" calls a young private as she rushes into the room.

"What is it?"

"A package, ma'am. Addressed to the Alliance Council with Vulcan Moctezumo as the attention."

"Who sent it?" asks Xipilli.

"Archibald Llywelyn, your majesty."

The Morrigan takes the package from her private's hands, placing it at the center of the conference table across from Xipilli. Kai's sights spin, looking from the carved box to the new vulcan.

"Has it been vetted?"

"Yes, ma'am, but it may perhaps be wise to exhibit discretion on who is in the room when you review its contents."

"Brief us," she commands.

The private swallows as though she is about to be ill.

"It-it concerns Lady Nocturne, Ma'am."

"Get out, all of you." Her order to the extra personnel in the room is sharp and unquestioning. Adepts and aids stumble over themselves to exit the battle hall, leaving only the technomancers and world leaders. "Xipilli, it is your call. If you wish us to leave the room while you review the box's contents, we will do so without hesitation."

Xipilli stares long and hard at the box before opening it. A shuddering breath escapes him as he sees its contents, eyes wide in horror.

"Atzi, I need you to leave this room right now."

"But Xipilli..."

"I cannot have you witness this firsthand."

Atzi looks as though she would wish to argue further.

"Chike, take your wife out of this room, right now."

This and the insistence in her brother's eyes has her inclining her head while Chike ushers her out gently.

Kai watches as Xipilli steels himself before pulling a bloodstained cloth from inside the box. The cloth, Kai recognizes, is the same material as the type of chemises Wren wore on a daily basis. He knows it is hers from the seashell pattern at the edge of the torn fabric. The fabric is nearly soaked through in crimson, and the metallic tang of iron permeates the room. Xipilli's hands shake as he unravels the distasteful wrapping, and Wren's mechanical hand, Mano, is placed on the table.

The appendage is severely damaged and various parts tumble to the tabletop as he sets it down. At the base of it, decaying flesh still clings to the attachment point as though the device was ripped from its owner's wrist by extreme force.

Kai's fists clench at his sides, eyes narrowed.

Xipilli's hand dips back into the container. Mångata, the ætherkalis quiet and rusted bloody, is pulled from the box next. Wren's weapon. The whole room flinches, seeing the hilt without its owner. The third time Xipilli reaches into the box, he almost seems reluctant, this time pulling a gold-plated beacon from its depths. When he sets it on the table, the device activates automatically and a holograph flares open. Archibald Llywelyn's smirking face in a smear of digital formatting appears.

"Ah, your highness, or should I say 'Your Majesty'? It was unfortunate that your stay with us was cut so short. What an improper host you are, leaving without so much as saying goodbye! Shame on you."

Xipilli's eyes rage down at the holo.

"No matter. Your sister, Wren, was perfectly happy to entertain us. Well, she wasn't happy to, that is probably an overstatement, but she certainly was obliged to considering how she so sneakily spirited you away. Which by the way, I caught wind that you have been searching diligently for her these last few months. I thought it would be best to let you know the status of your dear baby sister. Such a treat getting to know the technomancer who killed my son months ago. Of course, I'm afraid your search has been in vain. Her fate has long since passed."

The screen flashes from Llywelyn's face to a recording. It is Cresta de Corail's meeting hall dated two days before Xipilli arrived at Shinka half-dead. Blood decorates the floor and bodies litter the ground, including those of Vulcan Tlanextli and Vulcana Elisabeta. A guard stands in the frame, hands open making a 'gimme' motion with his fingers. Wren, bruised and bleeding, is pushed into the man who lifts her off her feet with a lecherous grin on his face.

"*Alright, boys, who wants 'a go first.*"

Another guard moves forward, hands outstretched to grab at Wren, but she kicks him in the gut, sending him rolling to the floor before throwing her head back to break the nose of the man holding her. He drops her like a sack of potatoes, curses and derogatives falling from his mouth.

Wren moves to crawl away, but the large bulk of Montwyatte, Llywelyn's right hand, more machine than man, enters the frame. His boot meets her face, laying her flat on her back.

"*Gentlemen, please. Show some decorum.*" Archibald's voice comes from behind the camera. This is his neural recording. "*It would be a shame to damage such a pretty face.*"

Wren spits bloodied saliva at his face.

"*Suck on grease, Archibald.*"

"*Hmm, that isn't very ladylike, Nocturne. Perhaps a lesson in manners is necessary. Montwyatte!*"

Montwyatte's steel foot slams into Wren's torso. He kicks her once, twice, three times with a sickening crack on the end. She falls onto her side, clenching her, no doubt, broken ribs. Llywelyn grabs a fistful of Wren's hair, and he drags her across the floor before throwing her into a table hard enough to break it down the center. He sets a booted heel into the center of her back and lowers himself so Wren's face takes up the whole of his sight.

"*Does that feel good? Getting kicked around like a piece of dirt? Time you had a taste of your own medicine, wouldn't you say? My son told me about you. How you would flit around the trial grounds like a bitch in heat. Tell me. Did you enjoy tempting my son only to reject him later? Is that why you killed him?*"

"*I didn't kill Oswald. He died because of your own vanity and stupidity. Maybe if you'd been less nepotistic, he would still be alive.*"

He growls, rising to grind his boot into her broken side. Wren's body shudders but not with pain. The sound of her laughter spills from the holograph.

"You poor, arrogant, pathetic man! Does it make you feel big, beating up on teenage girls?"

She continues to laugh. Llywelyn winds his mechanical hand around her neck, squeezing hard enough to choke off her laugh.

"The Lady Wren will do well to remember who is in control here, lest she end up like her dead compatriots on the floor."

Wren grits her teeth, trying to breathe. She shakes herself to try and dislodge him to no avail.

"You don't frighten me."

"I made a bid for your whore mother, did you know that? I was willing to pay a good price for her, too, but she rejected me like I wasn't good enough for her. And here I am, years later, with her progeny in my lap like a consolation prize. I think you'll make up for that little slight, nicely."

Wren thrashes harder.

"You vile piece of shit!"

"Hn. If I am so vile, what will that make you once I've taken my fill of you?"

"Get off of me!"

"I am going to break you so thoroughly you'll be screaming for death before the end of it."

She brings her tied hands forward and shoves him back hard. Llywelyn's view goes wide as she makes a break for it but centers as Montwyatte catches Wren around the waist, twisting her arm back until a pop is heard loud and clear. She screams as Mano is yanked from her wrist. He twists her around again to push her face down on another table and drives a knife into the back of her flesh hand to hold her there.

Montwyatte pulls her head back by her hair, and her mouth falls open with a gasp. Blood pools on the table at her trapped hand. Just then, Mano, Wren's cybernetic hand, appears at Montwyatte's head, trying to rip out his eyes. The cyborg reels, cursing at the automaton. Wren rips out the knife still embedded in her hand with her teeth. She takes it in hand, aiming to thrust it directly into her own heart.

"Stop!"

A new voice shouts, and the descent of the knife stops. Wren's hand shakes as though fighting an invisible force. Llywelyn's attention turns, and the gathered council watch in shock as the Goblin King, Yggfret Bloodfang, enters the frame.

"They're consorting with witches," hisses Rameses.

"Yggfret, you bastard! Finally decided to join us," calls Montwyatte, now sporting several bruises and scratch marks along his face and arms as he crushes Mano beneath his boot. The little bot gives a sad fizzle as its lights die.

The witch nods and approaches Wren, the dagger still hovering a breath away from her chest. The witch leans down to whisper something in Wren's ear that is inaudible. She makes a strangled sound in response, a mix between a shocked gasp and a sob. Her fingers, one by one, are pulled off the hilt of the dagger. It clatters to the ground, forced from her hand by psychic magic.

The Goblin King reaches a long, gnarled finger up to the back of Wren's skull and forces chaos magic directly into the central node there. Wren screams as the visible tech on her body sparks, sputters, and goes out with a fizzle. She drops to the floor.

Total system shutdown.

"Well, that certainly makes things easier."

"And you technomancers call us 'heathens,'" sneers the witch. *"You should show better respect. This girl is worth more than your limited intellect could ever understand."*

Llywelyn laughs, sarcasm dripping off his words as the witch wisps out of the room.

"Yes, yes, I'm sure she's worth her weight in gold. Fucking freak! Someone, clean this scrap metal off the floor. I'll deal with her later."

Llywelyn's face returns to the screen.

"I will spare you the gory details, dear Vulcan, but my word! I will cherish the recordings of that pretty trinket. If Freya's prowess was legendary enough to garner her a marriage to your father, your sister would have felled nations had she endeavored to follow in her whore mother's footsteps. But I am not without my mercies. I do promise that I was a gentleman, though my man Montwyatte was a right beast. Sadly, she expired at some point. I've so kindly delivered to you the most presentable bit of what remains of her. That and that worthless piece of junk she called a weapon. Not sure how it passed summit. None of my people could get it to work. Condolences for your loss, your majesty. If you care to look for whatever's left of the corpse, you'll have to take it up with the Goblin King. I'm sure he's ground her bones to dust by now.

"For anyone else watching this recording, let this be a warning. I'm sure you're all feeling quite confident in yourselves now that you have pushed us out of Aighneas, but please, this is a false sense of victory. Dismantle your so-called Alliance. Deriva's fate will be a mercy compared to what will be done to you."

The holo vanishes, and Xipilli's gauntlet goes through a nearby column.

"No! I don't believe it. I don't fucking believe that!"

It is a testament to Wren's character that this vile message is a blow to nearly everyone in the room. The Morrigan's jaw is clenched with rage, Jamar's sword hilt sparks, a tear falls down Irene's cheek, and Hikaru's eyes are closed in restraint. Kai's aunt looks up at the ceiling, her own eyes shining with tears. Chike, Wren's brother-in-law, and his father, Absko, trade determined looks before addressing Xipilli. Even Art Lionheart, who barely knew Wren, looks ready to wage war on Llywelyn.

And Kaito...

Something breaks in Kai. He refuses to believe this farce they've been fed. Wren can't be dead. Not like this. He envies Xipilli's lack of restraint. If he could, he would demolish the whole world.

At his side, his mother closes a hand over his wrist. Sorrow laces her dark brown gaze. Kai slides his wrist out of his mother's gentle touch, leaves the war room behind, and grieves.

Four months later, on the 2nd day in the Month of Songs, he would discover Llywelyn lied. Wren was not dead. Instead, he finds her, imprisoned but alive, trapped in a virtually generated memoryscape. He traces the signal and finds ruins, a medical facility left to char in magical fire and Wren nowhere to be found. She is alive. He knows she is alive. Alive but missing.

Kai clings to hope with everything that he has, and his search begins anew.

"...and the witch drew from her belt a double-edged dagger, shimmering with magic, the blade she would use to carve out the hearts of hundreds of humans."

The Witch's Athame—a ritual blade, usually made from wood, silver, or obsidian. Similar to a technomancer's weapons, a witch may choose to craft a blade that will act as her wand, her conduit, her instrument of destruction, her own personal athame that resonates with her magical abilities. While in the hands of a mundane witch they are mere decoration, some athames have special abilities. The blade Weeper, wielded by Herik Lokison, set a curse on anyone it cut that would make them cry themselves to death.

An Excerpt from *Hunting and Identifying Hexen*
by Finnick Lockecraft, 1852 A.P.

26
DEATH PART 3

18 Months Later–5th Day in the Month of Planting, 1863

WITHOUT A BODY OR A CONFIRMATION OF Wren's death, Kai still has hope. Every raid, every mission, every conquered battlefield, he searches. The war effort pushes on, and they are so close to reclaiming Deriva from Seraphim occupation, the Alliance is reckless with it.

It's raining. Lightning in the sky, the ocean a turbulent crash of waves against the beach. It churns angry and violent, an elemental reflection of the battle waging along the shore just out of his parameters. Kai stands at the bow of a ship, waiting to disembark at his brother's signal. Xipilli stands anxious at his side, thirsty for blood, Opochtli sparking uncontrollably in his hand. Llywelyn has been spotted among this group. He is their target.

"I'm going to hang the bastard from his entrails for what he's done to my family."

Kai doesn't respond. He doesn't respond because the same desire for vengeance pulses in his circuits, but Kai's vengeance will be served cold, calculated after so much time spent searching for a lost love. Kai's vengeance will come on Wren's behalf. Xipilli's is for himself, as hot as the first day he woke in Shinka Temple. The man is entitled to his revenge, heated as it is after all this time. Kai isn't sure any amount of time will cool the man's rage. He has learned in working with him that Xipilli's temper is at once the most reliable and most volatile aspect of him. He had seen it in action three days ago when they had closed in on the general but found the bastard had already flown the coop with his men. He'd left in a hurry too, as though something had frightened him away—something that had left a small pile of corpses in its wake.

When the cue resonates in his head, he signals his unit of adepts and they disembark. Kai makes a beeline toward his brother's coordinates. The other adepts and technomancers fan out toward the war zone. Seraphim operatives and their robotics defend against their attacks, but Kai bypasses them to reach where his mother and brother are fighting.

It's bloody work.

There are too many enemies, the rain too thick. One of the enemy technomancers fires at him while Kai parries a blow from an android. He twists the droid around, and the shot short circuits the bot, but as he is about to throw Amatsu at the technomancer, a decapitated corpse rises up and attacks the technomancer. Kaito reels back in horror as the Seraphim operative's head is twisted right off of his shoulders, the headless creature claiming the body part for itself.

Witchcraft...There is a witch on the battlefield.

Lines of green necrotic power pulse along the undead's flesh. The color makes sick bubble in his stomach as it turns to face him, the mismatched head lolling to the side anchored by the dark tendrils of magic animating the corpse. He prepares to defend, but to his surprise, it bypasses him in favor of attacking a cyborg from Seraphim coming in on his right side.

All around the zone, undead are rising and attacking, but they aren't attacking Alliance forces. At least for the time being.

Then he hears the singing. A haunting melody coats the battlefield. The song takes shape as a virulent green light, a fog hangs in the air, humming and pulsing with the siren's magic. It weaves through the rain and settles over everything it comes in contact with. As soldiers fall, it raises them up and pushes them forward. A dance macabre, poppets on musical strings led in a deadly waltz.

He wastes not another moment; he runs.

When he reaches his mother and brother, they are in a darkened warehouse surrounded by walking corpses. Not far from them, a person is cowering in fear at the feet of a dark cloaked figure. He can't make out much of the hooded figure, but he can see the outreaching hand and immediately recognizes the glowing sigils for what they are. He hears the song and pins its origin on the figure. This is the witch controlling the corpses. This is a witch with the potential to kill all of them, Alliance and Seraphim, in the span of one night.

He strikes first before the witch can fully maul the person at her feet. They must sense him because they rear back. The witch ducks away from him before his blade can strike.

"Kaito!" he hears his mother shout to him. "Wait!"

He doesn't listen and continues to press the witch. They are smaller than he is, probably female, especially when he takes into account the smooth alto of her voice. He has the physical advantage, but he has no idea what other powers she may have. If he is going to win this, he needs to do it quickly lest he lose the high ground. He cuts horizontally toward the witch's torso, and she twists out of the way as gracefully as a ballerina. The familiarity of her movements nearly stalls him. Like this is a dance he's danced before. The strike doesn't land, but he follows it with a kick to her sternum. The kick does land, and with a sharp cry, she tumbles, knocking the hood off the witch's head to reveal dark hair and a face obstructed from view by a lace mask. The song ends, and Kai sees the poppets drop to the ground, dead and inanimate once again. As soon as the notes die, he realizes he knows this voice.

It can't be. It's not possible.

"Take off the mask," he shouts, turning to face the downed witch.

She curses at him in a language he can't understand. The sound is like nails on a chalkboard, a knife scraping against glass. With a low growl, the witch is back up and on him.

A pulse of power lifts a piece of furniture off the floor, and he is forced to flip back. The table lands in front of him, and he jumps over it, swinging Tsukuyomi upward. She dodges and knees him in the stomach. He keeps on her, almost manic now. It can't be her. It isn't possible, but she moves like her, sounds like her, sings like her. No!

"Get out of my way!"

"I said take off the mask!"

While the witch is focused on him, the person who was huddled on the ground makes a break for it. The witch sees this and immediately shifts her attention, flinging out a hand. The person is pulled backward by the ankle and dragged across the floor. It's Llywelyn. The witch's target is Llywelyn. Kai flings out Tsukuyomi, and the blade stabs into the man's shoulder and holds him to the ground, reminiscent of a much smaller hand being stabbed into a bloodstained table.

The witch flinches, and Kai takes the opportunity to close in on her. He wraps one arm around the witch's torso and with the other, he rips the mask away from her face. Lightning strikes and aquamarine eyes stare back at him under long dark lashes.

"Wren!?"

He lets go of her so fast, you would think he'd been struck by the bolt of electricity. She meets his gaze only for a breath before she bows to him respectfully, ironically.

"Prince Kaito Miyazaki."

Her usage of his title cuts through him as sharp as any blade. Kai's gaze fills with steel as she returns upright. His sights whirl. There is a witch's indicia on her forehead, glowing a bioluminescent green, venomous and viral.

"Wren, what have you done?"

"Whatever do you mean, your highness?"

"You know what I mean!"

He gestures to the carnage behind her. To the corpses she was possessing. To Llywelyn whimpering on the ground. Looking over at the man, he sees just how messed up he is. This skin of his face is blistered and decaying right off his skull. The top of his head is seared away like he's been scalped. He notices, as bile curdles in the bad of his throat, that Llywelyn's feet have been twisted backwards.

"Answer me."

It's a demand this time. Wren's mouth opens in a scoff, and her tongue scraps over her teeth.

"I think you know the answer to that question, Kaito-kun."

"Witchcraft, Wren! Do you realize what you've done?"

She pouts.

"Must you be so invasive, *mon rivage*? I'd hoped you would be happier to see me."

He isn't sure if it is the endearment or her expression, but another imaginary knife stabs into his chest.

"I am," he whispers. It is beyond his spoken tongue how over the moons he is to see her again. Ecstatic and surprised and so relieved to see her alive and in the flesh that his heart pounds hard in his chest, the blood rushing loud in his ears. But magic?! At what cost was this miracle bestowed? What did she sacrifice, what did she give up to stand here before him wielding wild, necrotic magic? Raising the dead, casting curses like a witch of the waste, ready to tear out hearts and bowels and spirits for cold-blooded vengeance.

"You've a fine way of showing it, Prince."

"Wren," he growls.

Kai, tanto still gleaming in hand, takes a step toward her. Wren immediately backs away from him, her eyes flashing to his blade. He sheaths the blade with a curse, realizing his error. *Kami,* she thinks he's going to attack her, and he can't think straight.

His head feels like it's going to burst any moment. There is too much, too many thoughts, too many feelings. There is horror, there is joy, there is shock, there is despondency. Their reunion, which he'd dreamed and fantasized about, should have been joyous and momentous, soaked with passion and love and everything a reunion between lovers should be. Instead, here it is, tainted and warped by death and undeath, by witchery and mayhem, and where he should be happy, he is instead horrified; where he should be reviled, he feels elation and intrigue. He doesn't know which he is supposed to choose, both sides pulling him asunder in a sick game of tug-o-war.

"You! I killed you!" Llywelyn is screaming from his place on the ground. He points straight at Wren. "How are you alive? I killed you! I know I did."

Wren rounds on the general, a cruel smile on her face. Her boots click against the cement as she walks to the pinned man, more afraid of the witch approaching him than the sword cutting deeper into his shoulder as he struggles. When she gets close enough, she steps on his face. The pointed heel of her boot digs dangerously close to his eye. He makes a strangled sound as she applies pressure.

"You should have made sure."

She extends a hand, and magic curls around her fingertips as she takes a breath in preparation to sing once more.

"Lady Wren, patience, please."

Wren halts at the Empress's command.

"Your Excellency," she growls.

Both Kaito's mother and brother have made their way toward them. Hikaru's sword is drawn, wary as he looks at Wren. He does not address her, choosing instead to place a hand on Kaito's shoulder.

"Otouto..."

It is a gentle reminder, an attempt to sooth the turmoil within him. He does not appreciate the gesture now and pulls away even as Wren turns to properly bow to his mother.

"Lady Nocturne," starts Mirai. "I am surprised but gladdened to see you alive. We owe you our thanks."

"Your thanks is unnecessary."

"Even so. Your reappearance is quite spectacular. I would be interested to hear your debrief on how you've managed to achieve these new abilities."

Wren chuckles airily.

"I assure you, it's quite boring. Hardly worth inquiring about."

"I insist."

"As do I, Empress."

Archibald, having seen the empress approach, yanks himself off Tsukuyomi's blade and crawls on hands and knees toward her.

"Please, Your Excellency. Have mercy. I have done nothing against Murasaki. I beg you, have mercy."

Llywelyn clutches at Mirai's skirts, his bloodied head dirtying her clothes. Wren watches impassively as the man pleads on hands and knees, waiting for Mirai's response. The empress doesn't spare a glance for the man begging at her feet; her dark eyes alight on Wren, who stands across the space from the most powerful monarch in Deus and meets her, eye to eye, unflinching.

"Archibald, I'm afraid mercy is not mine to give."

Archibald, pathetic and in pain, goes wide-eyed before Wren's power surges. Whatever ghostly touch she now has drags the cowering man away from his mother's skirts. The green tendrils lift the man up by his broken ankles until he is suspended upside-down about five feet off the warehouse floor. She psychically slides a nearby bucket underneath him as his blood begins to drip to the floor.

Wren's nails are sharp, blackened at the tips like some of the witches in his aunt's lecture class.

"Hikaru, Kaito. We will wait for Lady Wren outside."

"Kaa-san?"

Kai's gaze remains steady on Wren's face, unwilling to look away. Her indicia glows around her face, far more intricate than he has ever seen even in pictures taken of witches over the course of history. At the center of her forehead is the triskelion: three interlocking spirals swirling away from each other in three separate directions. Trailing away from them to decorate her temples and down the sides of her face are more sigils: spirals interlaced with circles, triangles and squares framed in stars, crescents, and runes. The markings on her face stop just below her cheekbones, but the motifs echo on the exposed flesh of her arms, stopping at the glove she wears on one hand and the amputation of the other. The design is beautiful in an otherworldly way.

Wren's eyes glow, not just with chaotic energy. Hatred, cold and frozen over, shines from her eyes, and this is what makes Kai's mouth go dry.

"Wren?"

His voice is quiet as a whisper, but she hears him anyway and turns her gaze on him. At least, she doesn't look at him with the same visceral rancor with which she regards Llywelyn. Instead, her gaze is just cold and empty, like a shark. He searches for some semblance of the sixteen-year-old who once ran amok in Shinka, and he doesn't find her, not here in this haunted warehouse in the middle of a war zone. She is shuttered to him, a wall fortified by her desire for revenge.

"What is it, your highness?"

He wants to plead with her, beg her not to do whatever she's planning, but the words turn to ash in his mouth. As they look at each other, the glow of her magic diminishes enough he can see the blue in her eyes despite the dim light of the warehouse. Something shifts. The frost in her eyes cracks and there she is! He sees her. There's Wren! She is there just for a moment, then gone again as she averts her gaze.

"This situation is not for us to interfere, Kaito," his mother calls, "and if you hold any respect for Lady Wren, you will let her do what she needs to do."

Wren lifts her head to Kaito once again, and it is as though he hallucinated the previous moment. The green gleam is back in her eye, and Kai cannot stomach looking at it.

"Lady Wren," his mother calls her sharply, and the aforementioned woman, at least, has the decency to turn and acknowledge the empress. "Your vengeance is yours, but remember who you are."

Wren scoffs, and a smile twists across her face as she draws a dagger from her hip. Carved from bone and black as pitch, the curved blade is inlaid with emeralds, and it shimmers in Wren's hand. An athame, the ritual blade of a witch.

"I'm not sure what you mean by that, Your Excellency."

"I can imagine you've had much taken from you in the last year and a half."

Wren scoffs.

"Don't," continues Mirai firmly, "let him take your humanity from you as well."

Wren stays quiet as Mirai turns to leave, Hikaru following behind. Kai remains rooted to the spot. Finally, she laughs, manic and dark, though Kai's mother hasn't said anything even remotely funny. The empress pays Wren's fit no mind. Hikaru doesn't say or do anything either, looking back sadly before continuing out. Kai's fist clenches, and he grits his teeth so hard he hears them creak in his mouth. Eventually, Wren notices him watching her.

"Oh, pay no mind to me, Miyazaki-sama. I just found something funny is all."

"There is nothing funny about this."

"I never said there was."

She draws her blade, her athame, to her handless arm, and Kai's eyes flick to the blade.

"Admiring my Lacuna. She's quite stunning, isn't she?"

She slices a long line down her forearm. As the blood drips to the floor, sick wells in his throat, and the wild script along her exposed skin pulses.

"What are you going to do?"

"I'm going to destroy his soul."

"Nocturne," he all but snarls.

"You should go to your mother, Prince. You won't accept what comes next."

"This is madness!"

"At least madness is a steadfast companion."

He wants to argue, wants to shake some of the sense she's lost back into her. He wants to have the last word, maybe he even wants to yell at her—fight with her, and resisting those impulses is absolute torture.

He does none of these, striding forward to pull Tsukuyomi from the floor. Wren watches him carefully, warily, and once more, he can't read her expression, so he lets her see his. Anyone else would have missed the subtle narrowing of his eyes, the tightening in his jaw, but she is not anyone. She sees it plain as day before he closes off his expressions to her completely and leaves, Tsukuyomi clenched tight in his fist.

Kaito walks away, and while he does not bear witness to her handling of Llywelyn, the screams resonate loud and clear to where he waits with his family outside the warehouse.

"She is too dangerous. Do not let her disappear," his mother instructs them as the horrific sounds of Llywelyn's torment dulls. "And report this to no one." There is finality that Kaito was not expecting to hear, and she leaves to inspect the state of the battlefield and settle the adepts in their charge.

He isn't sure how much time passes with them waiting there. Several Alliance adepts come and go, the battle over, won the moment Wren's corpses took control of the field, not that anyone else knows that. There are shouts and confused orders being tossed around, technomancers scrambling to search for the witch responsible for the carnage defining this zone, but a single dismissive word from Hikaru, and the thought is dropped.

Eventually, Xipilli finds them. He is blood-flecked and savage looking. Opochtli still hums with power in his hand, and he has no reservations about demanding answers to his questions.

"Well," he demands. "Where is Llywelyn?"

Hikaru answers the irate king.

"It has been handled."

"What the hell is that supposed to mean? The general's fate is Deriva's to decide. Not yours."

"I assure you, Vulcan, the general's fate has indeed come to pass under Derivan jurisdiction."

Xipilli opens his mouth to argue but snaps it shut immediately as the doors to the warehouse slide open. Wren, bloodstained and wan, steps out of the deserted building. There is no pulse of power around her, no glow of indicia, not a trace of necrotic power. She appears ordinary. Simply human, unremarkable and uninteresting, and yet even the blindest person in the world would be unable to look away. Kai's world narrows once more, and he wonders if the witch he met just moments ago was a trick of the light.

"Wren," chokes Xipilli.

Wren's eyes close to crescents as she smiles at her brother, a far cry from the smiles she once gifted Kaito under the moonlight, in the dark, in the glow of the setting sun. Smiles that seem a lifetime ago, gone and lost to the cruelty of war. It's unbearable.

Faker... Liar...

"Hello, *hermano mio*."

Xipilli rushes forward. Before anyone can move, the man has his arms wrapped around his sister in a tight embrace. He pulls her into his chest and holds her.

She does not hug him back.

Wren tenses violently at her older brother's touch, her hand clenched into a fist, her head thrust back to maintain as much distance as possible. Xipilli pulls back to look her in the face but keeps a firm grip on her shoulders like she could drift away into smoke at any moment.

"How are you...Shit! Where the hell have you been?"

Wren relaxes a bit at the increased proximity, but she winces at the question.

"It's a long story."

She starts to cough.

"*¡Maldicion!*" exclaims Xipilli. "You're freezing."

He removes his jacket and drapes it around Wren's shoulders over her cloak, drawing the hood over her head and huddling her into the fabric until her fit subsides. Her eyes glimmer like a cat's in the dull light of the approaching dawn. During the fit, her indicia begins to glow, modulating bright and dim, bright and dim, enough that Xipilli gives pause. It's an affirmation that Kai did not imagine her earlier state of being. Xipilli studies his sister for a long moment. He fully takes her in for the first time, and it's as though something clicks in his mind as he looks from her hand to her eyes, to her clothing, and finally to the surrounding field of corpses.

"You did this."

Wren doesn't answer, nor does she meet her brother's eyes. Xipilli visibly shakes himself before reaching back for her.

"Never mind. It's good that you're back. We need all the manpower we can get. Mångata is back at camp. I can get it to you when we get back."

Wren makes a strangled noise in the back of her throat.

"A two-handed weapon isn't much use in the hand of a cripple, Xipilli."

Xipilli looks down and notices for the first time that Wren is entirely without augmentations, including the lack of her prosthetic hand. He shakes his head and reaches for her amputated wrist.

"It's alright. We'll get you fixed up. I'll call a surgeon for repairs—"

"I'm not broken, Xipilli."

The man flinches.

"Of course not. Come on. Let's get you somewhere warm."

A few more coughs wrack Wren's form. Hikaru steps forward with a stim in hand that will help regulate her temperature, but when Wren sees it, she withdraws farther away. Xipilli all but slaps the medicine out of Hikaru's hand with a reminder to mind his own business before he turns back to Wren who looks so small next to her brother.

"Vulcan Xipilli, Lady Wren has demonstrated some rather incredible abilities. It would be best if—"

"With all due respect, Hikaru, this matter is none of Murasaki's business."

Wren starts to cough again, violent hacking coughs that bubble blood up and onto her hand, and Hikaru backs off at the venomous look Xipilli shoots in his direction. Xipilli winds an arm around Wren's shoulders and starts to guide her away, and if the man shoots Kaito and Hikaru a seething glare on the way past, Kai doesn't notice it.

He only has eyes for Wren.

Goblins—The Hexen Wild Cards

There is much debate as to whether or not goblins should be truly classified as hexen. Usually the result of the mixing of Lycan or Vampyre blood with that of a witch's, goblins are rarely born with an affinity for magic and typically lack magical ability.

Most are pretty mundane and relatively shy, not to say they shouldn't be put out of their misery—they are still plenty dangerous with their sharp claws and teeth and human-like intelligence, but the ones with magical ability are not to be trifled with. They have all the abilities of witches and twice the barbarity as these goblin witches can go rabid at the drop of a hat.

An Excerpt from *Hunting and Identifying Hexen*
by Finnick Lockecraft, 1852 A.P.

27

TEN OF WANDS

Present–7th Day in the Month of Falling–Shinka Temple

KAI WAKES UP SLOWLY. COGNIZANCE trickles in like an ache to a hurt limb. It is bright, but he is not outside. There is a creaking sound underneath him as he shifts. His throat and mouth are bone dry. When he moves his arm, his hand butts into something solid and living, and a moment later, the soft caress of a breath drifts over his skin.

He opens his eyes in a jolt.

It's Wren.

She is curled up on the floor, her head resting on her arms on the small bed he finds himself in. The room is dusty, of course. It is one of the standard student dorms, a bed low to the floor, a dresser, a desk, and a lamp. He sees his swords resting on the dresser, his jacket draped over a chair, and his shoes set on the ground against the door. Even in here, the miasma curls through the room, and Wren has pulled up a cloth over his mouth in deference to that.

"W—"

His throat is so dry, he can't get a word out. He swallows sandpaper and attempts to clear his throat.

"Wren."

The witch stirs at the sound of his voice, blue-green eyes blinking in the light before she looks up at him and sees he's awake.

"Kai!"

She is up in a flash, reaching for a nearby water bottle. She twists the top off and brings it to his lips. She guides him through taking several small sips, the water a heavenly balm on his parched throat. When she deems that he's drunk enough water, she pulls back, screws the lid back on, and sets it on the floor next to her hip. The next thing he knows, her hands are hovering over his face and chest, emitting a gentle green glow as she hums. The feel of it is not unlike when she healed his side wound earlier, warm and soothing like being dipped in a hot spring. Between that and the sound of her voice, his eyes slide shut. Sleep sounds very tempting.

"How are you feeling?"

The question throws him off for a second. He isn't in pain. Physically, when he flexes his muscles, he isn't stiff or anything. The discomfort of disuse sits in his limbs, but the more he moves around, the more the kinks begin to smooth out. Other than that, he feels surprisingly good. He sits up slowly.

"What happened?"

Wren makes a face.

"We got separated. I—the curse shut down your tech. I barely got to you before..."

"Hm."

His sights turn on easily enough, and when he goes through his systems, everything is in working order despite the system shutdown. Though when he sets a virtual mapping, it takes longer than it should. Once they get back to Snowfall, he'll need AYA to run some maintenance on him, but he can make due for now. When he scans her, he can see that she is edging on being depleted.

He puts his hands over hers and lowers hers down.

"I'm fine, Wren. Stop wasting your magic."

She drops her hands with a sigh.

"You've been recovering for three days."

"Three days! The wendigo!"

"It's dead, Kai."

She killed the wendigo—the wendigo, a creature that is only vulnerable to fire, despite her fear of fire. She must recognize the questions drifting across his face because she lifts herself up and settles on the bed next to him.

"Yggfret's been quiet. Haven't seen him in a day or so, and I haven't found what's keeping him here."

She hands him a ration with the explanation that she found some foodstuffs in the kitchens that were still good before she continues as though Kai doesn't have a million questions buzzing through his head.

She fills the space with her voice, telling him about the last two days as he eats quietly, listening intently. When he finishes, she wraps up her detailing on the curse and what she learned while she was inside of it.

"You saw Chiamaka set the curse."

Wren nods.

"She is the one who killed that Shinka graduate. Poor kid never saw the knife come down. Then she left one of her own adepts down there with the female wendigo to become its mate."

"Why would Chiamaka want to curse Shinka Temple?"

"I overheard her and Thames talking, something about how Murasaki no Yama is the only remaining country to produce new technomancers so steadily. Is that true?"

Kai nods.

"It has been a concern of mine. Ever since the raid on Lorelei and the witch hunts that followed, fewer and fewer adepts have been able to demonstrate an aptitude for technomancy."

"So why is Murasaki unaffected?"

"I don't know."

Wren makes a disappointed sound and reaches for a stack of papers on the desk near them. They feature hand-drawn arrays and the various musings and scribbles Kai remembers as being part of Wren's brainstorming process.

"I've been scouting the caverns under Shinka, mapping out the array better. I think I have a good idea how I can close it. The sooner the better, don't you think?"

Kai does another scan of her.

"You are drained."

From taking care of me, he doesn't say, but the implication is not lost to her. Her eyes soften.

"It's nothing."

"It is not nothing."

Her lips quirk up at that.

"I can manage. Besides, we are kind of stranded here thanks to that bastard. If we want to get out of here anytime soon, we need to get the comm systems back up and working. I don't know about you, but I don't want to spend another day stranded here."

"Are you sure? It is my understanding that dispelling the curse will leave you vulnerable to attack."

The slight slant of her lips turns into a full-on, close-eyed grin, pouring over with light and reassurance.

"Why should that be a problem when I have the great Kaito Miyazaki to protect me?"

Trust.

Bright and coruscating, her expression and her statement, teasing as it is, is awash with her faith in him. The force of it renders him speechless. She must take his silence as assent because she continues her line of thought.

"I'm going to need some supplies first."

That is unexpected.

"What do you need?"

"You won't like it."

His brow furrows at that. He pushes himself up and out of the bed. He resets his armor, buckles his boots, and straps his swords onto his back while Wren watches him. He is outside of the network, but if there is something she needs...

"Tell me, and I will provide."

When she speaks, it's with an air of caution and hesitation.

"It isn't something you can just go out and get. You have to draw it to you."

He gives her an expectant look.

She finally stands up and moves to gather her own things. She's swiped a knapsack from somewhere around the compound it would seem, and she shovels a small bowl and a kitchen knife into it.

"Are you sure you're ready to do this? You just woke up."

"I've been sleeping for two days, have I not?"

She chuckles at that.

"Alright. This way, your highness."

Kai follows Wren beyond the edge of the temple into the surrounding forest. He draws his blades as the forest gets darker despite the sunlight drifting through the trees.

"Wren," he calls when they've strayed from the beaten path into the foliage.

"Just a little farther," she says.

She finally stops in a small meadow. Late summer blooms are sprinkled throughout the clearing nestled in soft, crisp grass. Wren settles down in the center. She closes her eyes and starts to sing. He recognizes the tune. It's a meaningless pop song from when they were children. He can't possibly imagine why she has chosen to sing it now of all times, but he settles in the grass beside her. As the words tumble from her lips, the energy around her thickens and releases in small wisps into the air, like feelers reaching out looking for something. As she conducts the songweave, he keeps his focus outward, on guard against anything that may appear out of the woods. There is no reason to doubt that any spirits haven't wandered into the forest from the temple grounds. When she finishes singing, she settles back to lay in the grass, her hands behind her head and her legs crossed before her. He looks at her expectantly, but she does not open her eyes to look at him.

"Now we wait."

"What are we waiting for?"

"For an answer."

Several long moments pass. They don't speak, nor do they really move. In fact, Kai would wonder whether Wren had dozed off in the grass were it not for the constant back and forth motion of her right foot, like a cat's tail swishing back and forth, denoting her tension. Before long, a pleasant preening twitter graces his ear. When he looks up, a pretty little songbird with gold tipped feathers is landing just in front of them.

Kai looks on in wonder at the bird.

"That's a Golden-Tailed Cardinal."

One of the rarest birds in Murasaki no Yama. They are legally classified as extinct in several countries, coveted as they are for their blood-red feathers dipped in pure gold.

Wren's attention is drawn to the small bird now puttering about in the brush.

"It is, isn't it?"

Her eyes follow the creature sadly before she rises from where she is sitting. With careful steps and quiet movements, she approaches and holds her hand out to the small bird. It chirps at her, studying her fingertips before hopping up onto her hand. She scrunches her nose up at the cardinal, lifting it so that its beak touches her nose. She whistles to it, a little call and response to the animal's song.

"How did you..." His words trail away as she holds the bird out to him. She gives him an encouraging look, so he lifts a hand and gently brushes his finger against the bird's feathers, soft as a cloud, as it titters at him and jumps onto his hand.

"When a witch calls, the forest listens."

"They are supposed to be extinct."

"Yes, this little bird is quite special, isn't he? Don't worry. There are others. He told me as much."

"You can understand him."

"If I listen well enough. It's the least I can do since he answered me."

She takes the opportunity to wrap both hands around the bird's body, plucking it from his hand and gently stowing it in her bag.

"Let's go."

Wren moves carefully to return to the temple, and Kai follows her. The bird's calls are barely audible through the cloth of the bag. When they make it back to the seal, Wren sets her bag gently on the floor, and the bird flutters out to land on her shoulder. She has indeed been working while he was unconscious. He can tell from the additional sigils that have been carved around the room. She has also relit the torches that line the walls. She's managed her pyrophobia this much. The seal is no longer dripping with power. It is not quite asleep, but it isn't fully awakened either. Wren pulls out the knife and a small bowl which she sets in the center of the seal. She turns to him suddenly, her eyes shifting nervously between the space beside his ear and his shoulder rather than directly at him.

"You should probably go outside."

"Why is that?"

He stares at her long enough that she finally meets his eye.

"You won't accept what comes next."

"You will do what you must."

"Kai, please. Sometimes something beautiful needs to die to banish something ugly. I don't..." She looks away from him and to the side. "I don't want you to see."

Silently, Kai makes his way to the far side of the circle. He doesn't touch the border, kneeling instead at its edge in clear view of Wren and any actions she may be about to take. He will accept whatever her coming actions may be.

Wren makes a pained sound in the back of her throat before kneeling at the center of the array. She pulls the bird from her shoulder and holds it in her palm. It chirps and flits happily enough in her hand. She says something under her breath that he doesn't quite catch, then her other hand moves. Long dark nails, steady fingers, and a thin wrist. Her fingertips stroke the bird's head lightly, her palm resting on the little creature's back as it flutters beneath her hand. Without warning, her fingers grip and twist violently, breaking the bird's neck, and the spark of life fades from the little body.

Kai watches, unflinching.

She picks up the knife and opens the bird's belly, letting the contents, blood and organs, spill into the bowl. She stirs the bowl with the blade before lifting the bird's heart from its contents. It's a tiny thing, unbeating, four chambered, steaming from what remains of the bird's body heat. Wren begins to chant and sing in the elder tongue, words that sound like curses, *mallachts*, and all the darkly things in the world before she swallows the heart whole.

Kai sees this, and though something twists in his gut as she swallows, he does not look away.

She dips her fingers in the bowl of gore, and with bloodied fingertips traces runes into the stone beneath her with her eyes closed. The seal begins to glow, a thick pulsing black and red, as her own viridian energy begins to seep from her body. The triskele burns bright on her forehead, the origin point as her wild script starts to shine. When her chant ends, there is complete stillness, Wren doesn't move, doesn't breathe, doesn't so much as even allow her heart to beat. Time stretches long and brittle as Kai's pulse pounds in his ears. He is hard pressed not to get up and shake her back into the constant motion that is Wren Nocturne, but just as the impulse is about to win out against his discipline, her head flings backward, eyes open, overtaken by glowing green power. A silent scream freezes on her lips, body bowed as though in ecstasy and agony as one.

Kai looks on as Wren's body collapses onto the floor, and her energy begins to seep into the array. A dull vibration emits from the carved markings as a silent battle unfolds between the existing intention and Wren's as she fights to take over and remove the temple's curse. Kai is an observer, here to stand vigil and protect her against anything that would attack her limp body.

I accept this.

Now is the time. He rises to his feet as the energies in the air begin to coalesce, so thick he can barely breathe, the red trails of his tunic scraping the ground as he rises. He pulls up his face mask and unsheathes Tsukuyomi, waiting to see what is drawn to them before drawing Amatsu.

I accept you, Wren.

Just days ago, she asked him how he knew it was her, and Kaito hadn't answered, the truth of it both simple and unspeakably complex. Because the fact of the matter is, no matter what mask she dons, no matter what face she wears, Kaito will always recognize Wren, and this... The magic unfolding around him. ...this is Wren Nocturne.

It isn't long before the first malevolent ghost finds its way into the cellar.

Kai rises, ready.

It's a lot like sinking underwater, entering the astral plane. Her bones become the earth and her breath the air. Her blood turns to water and her heart a raging fire. Wren's spirit glides through the array only to make a U-turn and step back out into the other side of the mirror where effecting change requires flexing the very foundations of her will. The air is thick and difficult to tread through. If she exerts too much, her breath will be stolen from her. If she takes too long, the waves of energy will wash her away.

Wren stands in a sea of black, viscous pitch. The darkness writhes like a living organism, and when she reaches into a thick patch of ink, it reacts. It curls around her hand with a snarl before flinching away, violently retreating as her essence floods viridian light into the immediate area.

It pushes against her, barreling her direction with reinforcements, newly acquired hatred and rage solidified into the sludge that coats this version of Shinka. She whistles as it closes in on her, and a sweet chirp answers back just as it is about to connect with her torso. The cardinal's spirit, glowing gold through the dark, flutters forward and into the coalescing hatred, and with an audible scream, it disintegrates against the bird's pure energy.

Wren holds her hand out to the bird's spirit, and with a sweet tweet, it alights on her hand.

"Thank you, little one."

The bird hops happily across her knuckles before settling on her pinky. It is warm, a pleasant energy against her own pulsing, often overwhelming, power. There was a time when her lifeforce was that same pure gold, but that was before. Trauma and loss darkened it first to a sickening burnt amber. It would have blackened completely were it not for the dormant magical blood in her veins, awakening to heal in her damaged essence and turn it a bright virulent green. It went from being the dark reflection of her thirst for vengeance to a blooming reflection of the new reality of her existence as a witch with new responsibilities.

Green—the color of life and nature or death and poison. Such a dichotomy.

She used to hate the color, so different from her original golden lifeforce, a lifeforce for the innocent and carefree, but time and acceptance have made her grow fond of it, and the coloration stayed with her through death.

The space around her that she has cleared off is a mirrored reflection of the cellar where the array is located in the physical realm. In this subspace, she can combat and destroy the curse piece by piece until with the help of the bird. It'll be slow going, but she can manage it, she thinks, even with her energy reserves low as they are. One patch of darkness at a time.

She runs forward into the darkness.

For a while, things work well. She moves slowly and steadily from space to space. Each new encounter drains more of her power, and though she is pacing herself, she begins to tire.

It comes to a head when she faces off against the main brunt of the curse. The amalgamated energy has gathered to push against her in large force. It fights against her like a beast, cornered and protecting its young with all the ferocity that can be expected of a feral mother. The longer the struggle goes on, the more she realizes that she made a calculation error.

Wren is flagging.

She underestimated the amount of time it would take to banish the various branches of the curse from Shinka. It's bigger and more stubborn than anything she has ever worked against, and she is not at her peak power-level. The bird is a hero in his own little twittery way. He darts in and out of the atrament, pushing it back and back as she focuses on caging and coaxing the malignant force into the array so she can destroy it.

The closer she gets to winning, the more intensely it fights back.

A tendril of darkness swipes her feet out from under her, and she slams down on her back on the floor, lifting her hands just in time to prevent it from quaking down to strike her. Her astral body is burning up and flickering. She doesn't have enough juice left to fight off the assault. The bird flits in long enough for her to get away, but she stumbles as she goes. The emerald glow of her astral form starts to falter as more of her power is sucked from her and into the miasma.

It folds over her face and mouth, begins to devour her, making her power a part of its own.

She closes her eyes and gives in.

Kaito is dealing with a group of four ghouls when he feels the shift in the air behind him. Something audibly shudders in the array as he cuts one of the ghouls in twain. When he turns to look, he finds the villdød hovering above Wren's supine form. Yggfret's rotting finger, crooked and broken, aims a stream of red power into Wren's temple.

"Get away from her!"

He throws Amatsu out. The blade doesn't meet its target physically, but Kai's power laces through the blade and ricochets out in a violet echo which hits Yggfret in the side. The undead is forced out of the array and away from Wren's body.

"*Gemål*, I am only trying to help."

"You said that before. I've yet to see how any of your intentions have helped."

Yggfret's mouth quirks up in a snarl as he clings the rafters at the top edge of the cellar.

"You may not see, blind as you are by your science and technology, but my influence is there."

"Your influence is unwelcome."

"Says you. What does Wren say? Should we ask her when she gets back? If she makes it back, of course..."

A sudden cry from Wren and the witch's head is flung sideways. A trickle of blood spills from her lip. Kai swings around to strike down another ghoul reaching into the array. Another astral strike flings her head to the other side.

"Are you doing this?"

"Not at all, highness, but if you would allow me, I can lend her some of my power. You continue your valiant duty out here, and she can continue her struggle to get rid of the curse on your precious temple."

Kai lifts Tsukuyomi and points the katana at Yggfret as the villdød moves forward again.

"No."

"Really, *Gemål*. Be reasonable. I would never endanger the life of *min dronning*. She is too precious. Especially now."

It's ominous the way that sentence hangs in the air. He doesn't read too far into it.

"That may be true, but it doesn't mean she would welcome your aid."

"Ah, yes. Miyazaki-sama is probably right about that."

Kaito shifts his stance and stabs his blades into a pair of spectres. They shriek in agony before dispersing in a haze of smoke. How much death has gathered to Shinka since the wards went down? How many people's lives have been claimed by this mess? Wren resettles herself as though whatever was just affecting her in the astral plane has passed, but her breathing is labored, shallow. Sweat builds at her temple from exertion.

Worry creases his brow.

"Well, if his highness will not allow me to offer aid directly, perhaps I can give an alternative. One that would set his mind at ease on my intentions."

Yggfret smirks. Another ghost screams over Kai's head, and he sets his virtual boundary despite the burn to his synapse. The ghost and its brethren snuff out the physical plane, banished back to death's embrace where they can find peace.

"There is no alternative that you could offer that would convince me to allow you to so much as touch her."

"Then you leave her to death! She is running out of power."

"Then I will give her some of my own."

Yggfret's expression sours further.

"You! A technomancer! You don't have the capability!"

Kaito steps into the array. Almost immediately, the flood of energy on his synapses makes his head pound, his body unaccustomed to this kind of exposure to chaos magic. He digs deep into the root of his augmentations, reaching for the switch at its base that he designed into his system himself that will allow him to withstand the force of it long enough to channel out his own energy into Wren. The gentle hum of the foreign marrow in his body alights with enough power to stabilize his tech systems against the beating of unsaturated necrotic energy.

He kneels at Wren's head and sets Amatsu and Tsukuyomi down on either side of Wren's shoulders before settling his hands on either side of Wren's temples. Kai's mapping systems light up violet, and the cellar is his, lines of code unfolding around him as his virtual territory sets. Tsukuyomi and Amatsu rise to defend their master on autopilot.

"What are you doing! You're going to kill the both of you!"

"If you are truly concerned, keep the cellar clear."

Yggfret sputters at being given such a command.

Kai ignores Yggfret, closes his eyes, and concentrates on syphoning his energy directly into Wren's meridians, lending her the power unique to the tech he designed specially from Wren's research.

He's not sure how long he can sustain this dual state, but he has to try.

When he opens them again, minutes, hours, days later, glowing green eyes greet him.

The forests around Shinka, long quieted from the effects of the curse even though it doesn't reach all the way into their depths, stand still along the outskirts of the temple. The stairs that lead to Shinka's peak, crumbled as they are from the rampages of the wendigo's reign over the temple, lay as a challenge for any who would dare venture up them toward the cursed grounds. The arches over the temple entrance, still majestic even if they have been discolored from the malignant energy coating the grounds, stand guard over the entrance. The twin wolves that sit on either side of the arch continue to bestow their wisdom to any who might approach them. The dead strings of lamplights carry not even enough power to flicker, and the once beautiful lawn spreads out dead and battle torn, decorated with the bodies of the dead, fodder for the carrion feeders. Windows that always exuded a soft glow before are broken husks of darkened glass and sill.

And draped over all of it is the miasma.

To an onlooker, Shinka Temple, Murasaki no Yama's training grounds for adepts and technomancers and the royal family's long-held sacred space, is abandoned, ravaged by time, rage, and death, a haunted temple for the spirits of the restless dead, the spirits of the same human+ warriors and adepts who one day hoped to become technomancers. They met their ends violently and without any hope for rescue or rest.

Until days ago, two strangers walked the steps toward the temple, a witch and a technomancer. People who stood on two sides of a chasm. A partnership of opposites. Of enemies. Of estranged lovers.

The two disappeared into the temple to banish the curse and have not emerged since, probably dead by now if the presence of the miasma is any indication. The miasma continues to reign like a conqueror over the once proud expanse of Shinka Temple.

Until...

The miasma over Shinka temple shudders and quakes angrily. In the shadows of the astral world, a witch battles against it with a technomancer at her back, feeding her strength and support. Glowing green power, violet streaks of light, and a tiny gold ball of energy flit in and out of the miasma until finally, it gives.

A small shockwave of light coats everything, a purifying wave of magic that banishes the curse. With a shuddered shriek, the miasma over Shinka Temple dies.

Minutes pass, hours maybe, and the clouds part. Sunlight dances over the temple gardens for the first time in months. The smooth sand of the zen gardens reflects the sunshine back across the broken windows. The bladed grass, brown and dead, twitches, hungry for the sun and green coils along the grounds once more to the rising notes of a bird's song.

A Golden-Tailed Cardinal lands on the temple gate, and life returns with the flutter of wings.

Jessabelle called me an empath today. She was fussing about in the kitchen, more than a little blustered. She cut herself, but I'm the one who said "Ow."

I suppose she's right. It would certainly explain a few things.

Oh! Fae is hungry again. It feels like she's knocking on my skull. I should go...

An Excerpt from Wren's Book of Shadows, Age 17
Lorelei Forest, The Month of Planting, 1862 A.P.

28

SIX OF PENTACLES

WREN SURFACES TO KAI'S SILVER GAZE.
He kneels at her head, his hands resting on either side
of her face, warm and gentle and strong.

"You're awake."

She nods carefully, eyes heavy and swollen. Her whole body
feels numb, like she's been running nonstop for hours. Lap 101
of a hundred lap marathon. Only this race was entirely spiritual,
leaving her soul-weary and bereft, her nerve-endings frayed from
swimming against the tides of chaos for so long.

"You're drained," he proclaims as if she didn't know.

"You're not much better."

And it's true. He looks as tired as she feels. His tech is dark
around his face, his systems reduced to a low-power state in
the wake of his energy expense. The cellar floor is littered with
all manner of viscera: monster, ghoul, and what-have-you, the
evidence of Kai's own battle on the physical plane.

How long has she been in the array? Minutes? Hours? Days?

She lifts a hand and touches his face, brushing aside the hair
stuck to his chin with some kind of muck.

"You helped me," she says.

"You were fading. We should have waited until you recovered more from keeping me alive these last few days."

"How?"

"Your Book of Shadows... You had several unfinished schematics in it."

"I remember."

"I used them to design my new system."

"Glad to see I did something right before I died," she says, grinning weakly.

Kai's expression softens.

"You have always been brilliant, Wren. Nothing could ever change that."

Wren shifts herself—her shoulder blades are giant bruises now that she's moving—and Kai helps her stand. He keeps a firm hold on her waist and she on his shoulder as they walk their way back to the little dorm room she found days ago. With the miasma vanquished, Kai takes a few minutes to re-establish the network and contact his brother.

She dozes on her side as he does this, so tired she thinks she could sleep for years, dimly aware of his warmth blanketing her back as he settles in behind her, his arm a dull weight over her hip.

The helicopter Hikaru sends is fast and accompanied by the two teenage adepts under Kai's instruction. Akari and Renki are truly adorable, chattering on and on, asking Kaito about the mission the moment they get the opportunity, and Wren gets the distinct impression this is a usual occurrence, a ritual greeting between Kaito and the pair after a dangerous mission. It seems especially important to Renki, who seems to idolize the Miyazaki prince in a way that is most endearing. There is a moment of awkwardness when they recognize her added presence for what it is, something foreign and atypical of their usual reunions with their mentor. It's to be expected. Her last interaction with them wasn't the most positive, and Fumiko's words still echo in her head about Renki's family.

Whatever the truth of that, it doesn't seem to deter the teen's interest as he begins to direct questions her way: about the protection spell, the curse seal, her face off against the wendigo matriarch, even about Toujiro's ghost... The boy's green eyes light up, inquisitive and curious, and, just for a moment, he reminds her so much of...

No.

Her heart weeps with nostalgia, but she pushes the thought firmly into the past and distances herself from a grief that doesn't feel even remotely as old as the calendar would dictate it is.

Akari seems a bit more wary of her than Renki, but she eventually grows bolder and starts asking her own questions with all the air of an investigative reporter. Wren answers their questions carefully, though Kai doesn't seem at all bothered by her answering their questions.

It is late by the time they return to Snowfall Palace, dirty and tired. Still early for a witch but late for Kaito and the teenagers. One of the palace staff meets them to let Kai know a room has been prepared for Wren since surely she would prefer her privacy for the evening, but Wren declines the offer for two reasons: Firstly, she doesn't trust Hikaru or Fumiko, or anyone else around here for that matter, not to try something while she sleeps. They wouldn't dare try anything in Kaito's presence. Secondly, it's just her preference at this point. Kaito is...well, he's Kai.

Kai neither protests nor supports Wren's decision verbally, but when the attendant starts to stutter about things like propriety and expectation, Kai shoots the man an icy look that has him shutting up and scurrying away very quickly.

Wren just laughs. Propriety is an illusion humans craft around themselves because they are scared of being seen for who they really are. Wren is not so disillusioned, nor does she have anything to hide.

Once they reach the Jade quarters, Wren insists Kai shower first since she'll take longer. He looks at her a bit warily, but she offers him a reassuring smile and physically nudges him toward the washroom, a hand pressing gently into his waist, while she goes back to the sitting room to pick at the food that was brought to them.

She doesn't have much of an appetite though. Her head is too stuffed full of echoes from the last few days for her to focus on anything else, so she sings instead, a dizzying, meaningless melody to clear her thoughts enough to look into the cards. She spreads the full deck out in front of her, drawing at random, not even really reading them: a cup here, the world over there, a promise in the swords, and a kiss from the magician.

As predicted, he doesn't take long, and she packs up the tarot as he re-enters the room wearing a simple pair of loose sweats and a red undershirt. He has a towel draped across his neck to catch the water still dripping from his hair which falls loose to brush the edges of his jawline. The esteemed Prince Miyazaki gone, replaced by soft fabric, damp hair, and a relaxed countenance in the safety of his own home. The safety of his own solitary piece of the world. Well, not so much solitary. After all, Wren is in the middle of his sitting room.

"You haven't eaten much?" he asks gently, settling down next to her.

The fabric of his pants skirts against her arm. She shifts, setting the tarot deck on the table next to the locket, not even glancing at the card she left face up on top.

"I ate my fill," she answers, not quite yet ready to meet his eyes.

Twelve years ago, she would have cracked a joke or teased him with some superfluous sphallolalia just to get a glance of one of his adorably frustrated expressions. It feels wrong to do so now. So, before he can engage her properly, she flits away, shutting the bathroom door behind her.

She stands under the spray of warm water for a long time, trying to gather her thoughts together, but everything is so disjointed. She thought he hated her. She died thinking as much. She'd been wrong. Clearly. Blaringly. Demonstrably wrong.

He removed his guards. He shut down his primary defense against her, asked her to penetrate his psyche, and his emotions washed over her confusing and painful and wretched and so, so terribly wonderful, she didn't know how to breathe anymore from the sheer agony of it.

It hurt the way looking at your own reflection sometimes hurt.

Then he'd leaned forward as though to kiss her, and she'd nearly met him halfway. He certainly looked as though he had wanted to, and he has been incredibly patient with her this whole unspeakable time, to no thanks whatsoever from her. She had fought him and bruised him and cursed at him, and he had taken every abuse she rained down on him without complaint. And for what? Duty. Responsibility. Because she knew a thing or two about whatever the hell was going on in that temple. Ha! Unlikely. The Miyazaki may be pious in their devotion to their familial disciplines, but no one is that much of a masochist, and Kai most certainly would not put up with that kind of shit from anyone.

Least of all her.

He had seen through her petty anger right down to the insecurity and hurt that blackened her heart to him twelve years ago. Angry and devastated by his perceived betrayal, she was blinded by a lie fed to her before her trial.

Goddess, how could she have ever believed him capable of something so horrible? Didn't that make her the traitor? Wren, the faithless. What a perfect addition to her titles. She died hating him and loving him in equal measure. All because of a lie.

And yet Kai stood there, undaunted by her rage, looking at her in the blood-tinged dawn of a lonely graveyard saying he would never hurt her. Would never wish for her death.

Kaito was wearing lavender the day he wrangled 'Atalia' to Snowfall. Lavender and grey. Mourning colors. And then the morning after her ruse was pulled aside, he showed back up in the powerful reds of his family.

But she's been dead for twelve years! Had he really mourned her all this time? Twelve years! Who mourns for someone that long? Who holds onto something that long? No one. That's who! No one. It's impossible. But... he said he did.

She lets her head fall forward and thunk against the tile.

The truth of it is she missed him.

She still misses him. Kaito Miyazaki, the one person she had trusted beyond all others. The person she once fought beside as easily as she had laughed with, danced with, and fallen into bed with so long ago. When she had been considered more monster than human, he had been the only one to see her as a person, to challenge her to uphold a morally right operandi in the face of bloodlust and vengeance. Later still, he was the person who gifted her with gentle words and gentler touches during her darkest moments when everyone else seemed ready to lock her in a vault, sheathing the weapon until she was needed again while they prepared to throw her to the wolves.

She misses his touch, the heated steel behind aroused silver eyes, careful nudges juxtaposed by untethered passion. She misses all of it so much, and why the hell doesn't she just walk out there and tell him as much? It's not like she didn't do the exact thing once upon a time while they were stuck in a godforsaken tomb.

What the hell does she have to be scared of? Nothing! That's right! Nothing!

She had felt his desire herself when he let his guards down. He opened himself to her in the most intimate way anyone could open themselves to an empath, and he had done it without fear of what she would find. His deepest, darkest secrets laid bare just for her.

She screams into the flesh of her hand wanting to pull her hair out of her head, but then the fit passes and some semblance of balance returns to her.

Resolutely, she finishes cleaning herself and turns off the water. She snags a towel off the rack and gives herself a rough towel dry. There are some clean bandages in the medicine cabinet, and she binds her left forearm again, careful not to agitate the still open slashes. Wren takes one last look at her reflection in the mirror, cementing her resolve.

Con ganas, Wren. ¡Con ganas!

Wren leaves the bathroom wearing nothing but a towel.

"Wren, my darling, one day you are going to meet your
soulmate. And you may not love them right away—you
might even hate them when you first meet them—but know
that time makes clear all things. Your father and I were not
an easy match. Our marriage was hard won and still his
people question it. You are the daughter of a second wife,
and people will discredit you for it. Pay no mind to such
dark words, for you are the living proof that a Vulcan could
love a Firefly."

Freya Nocturne to her daughter
Cresta de Corail , 1851 A.P.

29

THE LOVERS

KAI IS TURNED TOWARD A HOLO SCREEN when she enters the sitting room, the door she came through not quite in his line of sight. No doubt reviewing what he'll be reporting to his brother tomorrow morning.

His head angles ever so slightly toward her.

"Wren?"

She doesn't say anything, just pads over and settles herself behind him. She leans her head against his shoulder. His breath catches as her lips brush against the back of his neck.

"Wren, what are you doing?"

This time she does respond.

"Nothing, *mon rivage*," she answers, praying she isn't about to be rebuked.

The holo screen goes dark, and she lifts her head as he twists to face her. He notices her lack of dress with a start but doesn't allow his eyes to trace down her form. He searches her expression instead, observing the droplets of water trailing down her skin, flushed a rosy gold from the heat of the shower. What he's looking for, she hasn't a clue, but she might have an inkling of what he's feeling.

She's tasted his desire, felt it settle in her core. Were Kai anyone else, she would expect to see it here, in his gaze and posture. The prospect of a beautiful woman with whom you've shared carnal pleasure with kneeling before you wrapped in nothing but a flimsy towel is too much for any hot-blooded male to handle without reaction. But there's none of that in Kai's gaze: no lust, no excitement, no anticipation, and this is what she has always loved about Kaito. He doesn't expect anything from her the way most men expect things.

She toys with the edge of the terry cloth, suddenly uncharacteristically shy, averting her eyes to the floor.

"Wren, what is this?" He sounds as frightened as she feels, but it's not a rejection. Years ago, she might have mistaken it as such, but not now. She kneels before him, open and in askance, his full, undivided attention on her as though she were the brightest star in the sky and he a planet trapped in orbit. It's akin to the way he looked at her in the catacombs when they first made love, him an inexperienced seventeen-year-old, and she, sixteen, just as inexperienced yet headstrong and determined enough to tear down every boundary he held erected around him.

There's a difference, though, in the way he looks at her now, the intensity of it tempered with sorrow and loss. And looking at him like this, dressed in casual night clothes, hair undone and falling loose about his face, the fatigue of a long day clinging to his joints, she begins to understand the person sitting before her. This is not the youth she left behind. This is a man who has known love, known loss, known her.

Want tempered by grief. Desire tempered by brevity.

This is a man who held a place for her in his heart when she was gone from the world.

"Kai..." A thousand questions and prayers in the simple call of his name. "I-I miss you, and I wanted to... I don't want to miss you anymore."

I want you, here.

She sounds so cryptic. Why can't she just spit it out? She waits patiently while he looks at her, analyzes what she's offering, and decides whether to accept or deny it, the tension palpable on the air and knotting between Wren's shoulders.

So, she cuts through it with a disarming smile.

"Look, if I need to go put some clothes on, just tell me. It's kind of chilly in here."

His lips quirk at her jest, and finally...

"I'm right here, Wren."

He moves, palms lifting in offering to her. She takes them, sets them on her body. One comes up to tangle in damp, blue-black curls while the other curves around her waist. She leans up and kisses him. A soft sound escapes the back of his throat, a release of everything he's been holding back. He pulls her flush to him, grip tightening, broad palms burning through the terry cloth, holding her like a promise that could disappear at any moment.

"*Te Extraño. Te Quiero.*"

He hums, his chest rumbling under her hands. He understands. "Wren, *ore no kaiyō.*"

She doesn't catch the meaning right away, too unfamiliar with the language after all this time, but the expression on his face is fond, and that's enough for her.

Her eyes slide shut in relief. Leaning her forehead heavily against his, she trails her hands down the firm plain of his chest over the fabric of his shirt. He shudders at her touch, but no sound escapes him. When he calls her name, her eyes slide open, and she could fall into the molten silver staring back at her.

"I want so many things."

His words dance over her cheeks as her fingers thread through his hair. She likes this longer length on him. She wonders how he would react if she pulled it. His chest expands and contracts slowly under her hands. The world around them seems to narrow, the lights of the room darkening until just a twinkling of star lights gleam down from the ceiling.

"They're already yours," she whispers.

The space pulls taut, presses in, and snaps, a breath held too long.

Kai surges forward, reclaiming her lips. Fervent. Insistent. Desperate. For her. Hot hands, roughened with callouses, run over her skin, exploring her the way a sculptor touches a finished treasure, caressing every dip and grove and curve. Like being known for the first time, she squirms under the assault of those hands on her body, at once remembering how he likes to touch her, how she likes to be touched. The magic under her skin quivers. His need presses into her inner thigh. (When did she move into his lap?) Her arms wind around Kai's neck and her lips part, allowing herself to be consumed from the inside out while her hips grind into the heat of his arousal.

He groans, and her world tilts.

Kai dips her onto the table. Something clatters to the floor, and she doesn't know if it was her or Kaito who knocked it off. A sharp tug on the towel unravels it. He releases her mouth and descends, lips and teeth carving a path down the length of her torso. The chill of the air inspires goosebumps across her skin and a shiver down her spine when he pulls away, and she chases after his body heat (How dare he disappear from her!), scrambling to pull him back. But strong hands find her first, prying her knees apart and guiding them to his shoulders.

The prince goes to his knees before her and dips his face into the apex of her thighs.

She makes a startled sound, hands finding purchase at the edge of the table. Hands caging her hips, Kai devours her, unhinging her, her senses lost and found entirely in his ministrations. The pitch of her voice rises despite her struggles to control her noises, the coil in the pit of her belly draws tight, and her legs spread further.

She whines—Actually whines!—tossing her head back and trying to press further into the heat of his mouth, but he holds firm, a punishing grind of his fingers into her hip—she hopes they leave bruises—and she unravels.

"Kaito!"

Her eyes screw shut as he rips her climax from her body, continuing to work her as her muscles spasm. Those piano fingers pluck at her keys, dipping into her core, while he moves up her body, murmuring into her skin. Her lips part for him when he kisses her. Wren breathes and sighs under him, blissed out, brain cotton between her ears. She can taste herself on his tongue, tangy and sharp until the flavor dissipates, letting her taste Kai instead, smoky and herbal like a spiced tea. She drinks him, suddenly dying of thirst, until he pulls away.

"Open your eyes, Wren."

Dizzy from the descent of her first high, her eyes slide open at his request, aquamarine gems glitter in the moonlight filtering in from the window. Her breath hitches when she finds him watching her, lips swollen from worshipping her. He licks his lips, pleasure shining from his eyes like a cat that caught the songbird.

Time stills under Kai's gaze, more titillating than any orgasm. Even the constant hum of chaos under her skin quiets. She is bare to him. Kai's eyes rove over her, his sights on, absorbing every detail of her. The inky spread of her hair against the scattered paper on the tabletop. The flush of her cheeks. The rise and fall of her chest. The peaks of her breasts. The sway of her back. The curve of her thighs. Goosebumps rise along her skin under the pass-over of his eyes. She falls up and into the shining silver of his eyes.

She brings her hands up to his face and traces his features with her fingertips like a blind woman. Kai's features, like carved marble softened with honey and edged in amber, are too ethereal for this world. Her thumbs curve around the arch of his cheekbone, while her index fingers trace the line of his brow. The nodes at his temples glimmer cool silver in the blue-violet glow of the starlights around the room as she circles the metal. Her pinky brushes through his hairline, and she glides her hand under the strong edge of his jaw.

"You're beautiful," she declares.

Kai's sights spin, the familiar violet shine the equivalent of a sunburst. This man is focused so intensely on her it's like being at the center of a nebula.

"Not nearly as beautiful as you."

Okay, she really is going to burst into flames if he keeps talking to her like that, but before she can properly scold him, he quiets her with a kiss that makes her forget what she was embarrassed about to begin with.

"Wren..."

She hums to let him know she is listening.

"May I take you to bed?" he asks. Right, because a table is probably not the most comfortable place for this kind of thing. Though, historically speaking, it's not like they've ever been picky. Did she mention she lost her virginity in a tomb?

"Please..." she murmurs into the line of his throat, and Kai wraps his hands under her and effortlessly lifts them, holding Wren flush against him, her legs wrapped around him.

Wren's towel falls to the floor, abandoned, as Kai carries her to bed. To his bed.

He lays her down in the soft bedding before stripping his shirt off to reveal a firm muscled torso.

Two ports at his collarbones frame the long-ago gifted leather-corded necklace. Broad shoulders taper down to narrow hips. A faint trail of hair begins just below his belly button and disappears into his sweats. Kai's skin, pale as seashells and decorated with scars, shimmers sapphire in the moonlight filtering in through the blinds. A warrior's body, hardened and tested over the years. There are a few new ones, of course, scars she hasn't seen before. The most pronounced sits at the very center of his chest, an electrical burn that begins at a point and spreads to cover nearly a third of his chest.

Wren's new body is scarless, soft and unaccustomed to hardship and battle. It still surprises her sometimes to remember she now has a left hand. She reaches out with it now. Her fingertips graze over the electrical scar before he captures her hand in his.

Bringing her palm to his face, he plants a kiss, feather-soft against the sensitive skin of her wrist. He descends, leaving a trail of barely-there kisses and soft bites along her forearm, her bicep, her shoulder, the line of her neck, across her jawline, like a trail of butterflies lighting on a sea of flowers. It tickles when he murmurs into the skin under her right ear.

She hooks her fingers into the waistband of his pants, and he indulges her this much.

His pants drop to the floor, and Wren's eyes flash in the dim light of the room. Kai's member stands erect, and not that he would have been considered small before, but his length and girth are more than she remembers. He looks heavy, the organ filled with blood, standing proud and ready for her. She swallows at the prospect of taking him into her body, nervous but aching with anticipation.

"Is that for me?" she asks, raising her brow.

"Does my lady have doubts?"

"Not at all, highness."

He shakes his head at her antics with a breathy laugh as he raises a knee to the bed. She wants to touch him, but he cuts her off, lacing their fingers together. She pouts prettily at not being allowed to touch.

"Kai," she whines.

Hushing her with a kiss and a promise of next time, he guides her up the bed. There is reassurance there for both of them. There will be a next time.

She slides backward to settle amongst the pillows, her knees coming up to frame his waist as he lowers himself over her with a sweet kiss. Her right hand traces the line of his spine, the tips of her fingers gently touching each bony landmark and brushing over each of the glowing tech nodes.

"Are you sure?"

His musk enfolds her, earthy and cool like a mountain breeze mixed with bergamot and spiced incense.

"Very much so. Yes."

He presses into her. She moans as a mix of sensations wash over her.

Wren, for all her power and personality, is still very petite next to him, has always been petite, Kai standing taller and wider than her. The girth of him shakes her to her core, and she struggles to control her breathing as her body opens for him. There is pain and pleasure, the same mix she felt the first time she lost her virginity to him. Now, again, it returns in this second body, untouched and new as it is, more intense this second time around. The feeling of being invaded for the first time, of accepting such an invasion wholeheartedly and welcoming all that comes with it. She forces her muscles to relax, and as he draws up flush with her pelvis, she quavers around him. Her ankles cross behind his back, his muscles clenching and contracting between her thighs. His pulse pounds under her touch.

"Miyazaki-sama, what an extraordinary gentleman you are... Taking a girl's virginity not once but twice."

He drops his head into the crook of her shoulder, breathing heavily. Strong arms fold around her, solid and warm.

"You are a terror." His voice is gravelly and deep, his bedroom voice, a smile in the words. He is just as affected and desperate as she is, his pupils blown wide, sweat beading at his temple, and a flush dusting his ears and cheeks.

"Would you have me any other way?"

"Never."

The blush in her cheeks blooms further, embarrassed but wanting. His length a scorching pulse within her, she swivels her hips, wanting nothing more than for him to move.

"Kai, please."

He drapes himself over her body, hips pressed hot against hers, resolutely not moving.

"Tell me what you want, Wren, and I will give it."

Her eyes flashing with delight, she cards her hands in his hair, lifting up to kiss him insistently.

"Don't hold back."

So, he doesn't.

In a languid push and pull, Kai washes over her like a sea song. Hands, lips, body crashing into her. The low tide. Making love to her, pulling her into his depths as she allows herself to buoy in his rhythm, a largo for two. The intimacy of being known, inexplicable, floods her with terror and ecstasy at once. She wants the tide to sweep her out to sea. To pull her under, drown her, and never let her surface from the ocean that is Kaito Miyazaki again. He lays claim to everything she is: her sense, her reason, her heart, her pain, her pleasure, with all the pent-up passion of years lost.

His lips brush against the shell of her ear, and her fingers clench into the sheets as Kai's tempo increases, forcing the breath from her lungs.

"Sing for me, Wren."

So, she does.

She mewls and moans and screams, nonsense spilling from her lips as she sings his praises for the world to hear because he clearly has no desire whatsoever to quiet her, soaking in the sounds she makes and testing just how many notes of pleasure he can incite the songstress to sing. When he finds the right place, she lets him know, crying out for him when a second peak grips her. She arches into a perfect bow under him, lips stained red from abuse, hands looking for purchase in the sheets, the pillows, his hair, his skin.

Tears prick at the edges of her vision, and the markings on her body pulse to life.

She blacks out, all her senses shutting off to make way for the electricity releasing in the base of her spine, and her body goes numb. For half a heartbeat, she exists suspended in time and space. The heavens above. The world below. Both flowing in and out of her body while she is worshiped by them. *Le petit mort.* Her body torn apart and then put back together as a vision flashes through her.

Golden banners, desert heat.

Mångata screams to life in her hands. Blood spilling. Someone taunting her.

"You truly are marvelous, my lady…"

A girl with Atzi's eyes. A weapon firing. Pain in her side. Kai shouting. "Wren!"

Golden banners, desert heat, a spire that reaches for the heavens.

Kai before her. Raindrops trailing down his face as her life's blood seeps away.

She finally says the words, but they are too faint, too late, and too far gone to make any difference.

Golden banners, desert heat, and blood in the sand.

The fermata collapses. and her senses collide back into her. She is in Kai's lap grinding down in a fever pitch of her own design. She is alive, so desperately alive in Kai's arms; she holds tight, a sharp gasp falling from her lips. He embraces her, one of his arms curled under her buttocks, the other wound tightly around her back, as she rides out her high.

"Wren..."

His lifeforce shines like Ör, a life-giving warmth in the cold of space.

She comes down in parts, breathing hard and ragged. Her eyes flutter, her lungs expand, and she sinks boneless into his hold, head thrown skyward, hair damp with water, sweat cascading down her back. His pace has slowed in deference to her being overwrought.

"Come back to me, Wren."

Kai's lips dance velvety soft against her temple, continuing to build toward his own release with small, shallow thrusts. The wild script along her body goes quiet, and she calls out for him.

"Kai?"

He kisses her cheek, her neck, her jawline, his touch tender.

"I'm here."

She hums, shifting her hips forward and changing the angle of his movements.

"Me too."

Her long hair trails down to brush over the tops of his hands; several strands arch daintily over her nipples. She leans forward and kisses him, breathing him in, coming up for air, the dark sound of his groans in her ear. With both hands, he guides her hips. Her breasts bounce beautifully, and he takes her left nipple in his mouth, swirling his tongue over the pert flesh.

Kai pulls his mouth from her breast with a kiss and lays her back on the bed.

"Kai," she hushes.

THE LOVERS

He finds his release with a shout of her name. She holds him through it, wrapping arms and legs around the man as he rides the waves. She feels him pulse and twitch within her, her own muscles gooey and lax as she pulls him down for another kiss, long and drawn out. Kai's hands come to either side of her face, resting on his elbows so as not to crush her under him as they luxuriate in the feel of each other.

A long moment stretches between the lovers filled with hushed whispers, barely there touches, and the coiling together of star-crossed souls. The space between them chased away and banished as surely as a curse. Impossibly close and unendingly quiet.

Wren curls into Kaito's side, content and spent, allowing sleep to steal her away, and for the first time in a long, long time, she feels safe.

"I love you," she whispers into the sweaty span of Kai's collarbone, so soft and sleep-soaked, she doesn't even fully realize she's said it.

Great stones they lay upon his chest until he plead aye or nay. They say he give them but two words.

"More weight," he says.

And died.

From *The Crucible*
Arthur Miller, Old World, 1953 A.D.

30

THE EMPEROR REVERSED

8th Day in the Month of Falling 1877–Jade Apartments–
Snowfall Palace

SOMETHING WAKES WREN CLOSE TO FIRST light. Kai's arm is thrown over her waist, and he is curled around her. Despite the darkness, she can see Kai's face clear as day. He looks so much younger when he's sleeping. She lifts a hand. Gently tracing from his brow down to his cheekbone, Wren wonders what it might be like to have this every night, to wake up to this every morning.

Kai's breath fans over her fingertips as she outlines the bridge of his lips, the slight scruff of his facial hair grown out in the night. Kai shifts into her palm. Wren shifts to replace her fingertips with her lips but winces as the cuts on her forearm throb.

She sits herself up and examines her left arm. The bandage is soaked through with blood.

She scrambles out of bed quickly before she can bleed all over the sheets and stumbles into the bathroom while ripping off the gauze. The three cuts on her arm are dripping blood at an alarming rate. She turns on the cold-water faucet at full-blast and shoves it under the stream. The chilly water is a shock to her heated skin, but she grinds her teeth and bears the sting as swirls of red spiral down the drain.

The bleeding does not slow.

She hisses before she pulls her arm out of the water and looks under the sink cabinet for something, anything she can use as tourniquet. Unbelievably, the cuts bleed more, and her vision swims.

Shit! How long has she been bleeding that she feels like she is about to pass out?

There is blood on the floor now. It paints the ground she sits on, stains her skin, covers everything, and she can't find a goddamn tourniquet. A sound above the sink draws her attention.

She raises her head, and out of the mirror Chiamaka's dead hands reach for her throat, the woman's face scorched and twisted in rage.

"Betrayer!"

She screams as charred fingers wind around her throat.

Wren wakes close to twilight with a jolt. Kai's arm is tight around her waist, and he is curled around her protectively. His breath rustles through her hair while the whispers of the dead echo in her head.

Sweat beads along her brow. Wren raises her left hand to her face, and while her bandage is not soaked through with blood, she can see red bleeding through the bandage. Kai's face is peaceful in slumber, and she is glad her nightmare hasn't disturbed him. She extracts herself from Kai's embrace and pads her way into the bathroom.

It is strange. The wounds haven't bled since her first day back among the living, but now it's been a week since her resurrection, a week since the three slashes on her right arm disappeared in the wake of a partially fulfilled oath, and now, one of the cuts on her left arm is bleeding persistently, not enough to kill her, but enough that if she lets this go on for much longer, she'll be in trouble. Is she running out of time or is the curse trying to tell her something? Maybe both? She growls in anger.

She washes and rebandages her arm before leaving the bathroom.

Re-entering the bedroom, Kai has shifted over to where she was lying. He looks comfortable and welcoming, and a part of her wants to worm her way back into bed next to him, but the other part, the more practical, less impulsive part, knows that she won't be sleeping again tonight, so she slips her way into the sitting room.

The monitors around the Jade Wing's sitting room are powered down in slumber. As Wren sets foot on the tatami, a few floor panels light up.

"Wren-sama, has something disturbed your slumber?"

AYA's mechanical voice is surprisingly gentle at this time of night. The A.I. does not turn the lights all the way up.

Wren does not answer, much to the A.I.'s apparent discontent.

"Would you like me to wake Miyazaki-sama?"

Chiamaka's scorched face flashes through her mind.

"No, thank you, AYA," she answers, trying her best to make it sound like a command as she powers up one of the computer monitors.

Betrayer!

Chiamaka had shouted it, but at who? At Wren? The term certainly is a descriptive that has been used for her in the past, and Wren is responsible for both Chike and Absko's deaths. Hn! Responsible for? She'd killed them with her own hands, not that they'd left her much choice in the matter, but something in the way Chiamaka shouted in her nightmare makes Wren feel as though the word was not being flung out as an accusation. It was more like a shrieked explanation.

As the computer finishes booting up, Wren opens a search engine and types in "Chiamaka Nagi."

The first thing that pops up is a news article: CHIAMAKA NAGI TO ATTEND SHARD CONFERENCE WITH HUSBAND PRIMARCH DONARICK THAMES

She follows the search down a rabbit hole of information, a circling pit that winds around a coup d'etat centering around a gifted jar of herbs, Chiamaka claiming the Ebelean throne, and Donarick Thames's ascension to Primarch. Wren settles back in the chair she sits in and huffs, blowing her hair out of her face.

"I see you are catching up on what has happened during your absence from the world."

Hikaru's voice filters in through the monitor, and when Wren clicks over on the screen, the man's face pops up for her.

"Emperor!" Odd... It's three o'clock in the morning. What's he doing awake? "Trouble sleeping?"

He ignores her.

"My apologies for interrupting your research, but I was hoping to catch you awake when I saw someone using the network. If you wouldn't mind, I would like to discuss something with you in private."

"At three o'clock in the morning?" asks Wren cautiously, suddenly hyper-aware of AYA. Does Hikaru know how to bypass her system? How long has he been spying on her?

"You know your way to the conference room, yes?"

She nods.

"Meet me there in say five minutes."

"Alright."

Wren rises from the computer chair and moves to the bedroom.

"And, Miss Nocturne, I would rather you not disturb Kaito with this."

The screen goes blank.

Curiouser and curiouser...

"Ah, Miss Nocturne. Please, help yourself," Hikaru greets her, gesturing to a simple breakfast spread of fried eggs, tofu, rice, and fruit.

Hikaru sits at the head of the table with a tablet in hand. His eyes shift back and forth as he skims through something on the screen. In front of him on the table are her promised credentials, her prize for accomplishing her custodial duties at Shinka Temple.

"Your people are certainly quick."

"I assure you, Songstress. I would not have trusted anyone other than myself with this task."

He sets the tablet down on the table, and Wren briefly catches a glimpse of what looks like an intel report, but the screen goes black at Hikaru's touch.

"You have my thanks, excellency, but your reticence is showing."

"It is a truth that extraordinary times call for extraordinary measures," says Hikaru, exasperation dulling his eyes. "You should verify the details on those cards in case anyone asks you any questions."

Ah, fair point.

While Hikaru returns to his reading, she looks at the driver's license and passport. Both look indisputably above ground. Wow, she could get used to having a hacker or two on her side. She notes the birthdates, ID numbers, and citizenships she apparently possesses. They even list Atalia Vaishi's occupation as...

"Firefly?" She looks up at Hikaru, skepticism reading comically on her face. "Atalia was a Firefly-in-training, barely a chrysalis. You expect people to believe she ascended while in the loony bin?"

"She was training to become a Firefly, yes," says Hikaru. "It is the simplest stretch that can be made. Assuming you keep your head down and don't inspire anyone to go digging on Ms. Vaishi's history, it should work just fine for you."

Wren laughs.

"The gods have a unique sense of humor, don't they?"

"I imagined Miss Nocturne would be unopposed to holding true to Ms. Vaishi's originally intended occupation since you yourself undertook Firefly training in your youth. If I am remembering correctly, you passed your examinations just before your technomancer summit. In fact, despite being relieved of your status as a technomancer, you are still listed as a Firefly in accordance with the records kept by L'amour Lux."

"That's because Lux does not discriminate on the basis of race or creed for their Fireflies. It's basically a sorority, and once you pass initiation, you're a member for life."

"If this is an unfavorable circumstance, I could have it changed for you."

"Not necessary. It's a convenient cover."

"I'm glad you think so."

She tucks the cards into her bodice.

"But this isn't what you wanted to speak with me about."

At her words, the temperature in the room seems to drop, Hikaru's eyes turning steely.

"I take it you and my brother have reconciled."

As if that's any of your business, thinks Wren, well aware of the hickey presently on display at the junction of her neck and shoulder, so graciously put there by his little brother and a clear answer to his question. She wonders what he's feeling. Curse Miyazaki tech! Never before has she wished she could get a read on someone as she wishes she could on Hikaru at this very moment.

"I'll take your lack of response as all the affirmation I need."

"All the affirmation you need for what?"

"That your presence here is no longer necessary."

And no longer welcome, Wren finishes for him silently.

"I believe it would be best for you to continue on your own. Now I'm not so cold as to simply dismiss you from the premises without transportation or supplies."

Hikaru places an ignition card for a lightcycle in front of her beside a credit chip.

"Thank you for your assistance and for keeping my brother alive in the process. It is with a great regret that we part ways."

"Of course. Always a pleasure," she says, halfway tempted to tell him where to shove his pretty manners.

"Glad we understand each other."

Wren draws a hand up to her face and bites down on the meat of her index fingers. She takes a moment to draw the necessary sigils on her skin, and Atalia's glamour reinstates itself. Hikaru, to his credit, does not flinch at the grizzly display. He merely looks on, impassive. Any contempt he may be feeling toward her is well hidden under his indifference, and maybe he is indifferent to her. Maybe he truly doesn't care one way or the other about her decisions and choices, whether good or evil. What he does care about is the person he distinctly told her not to wake before she came to speak with him.

"I thought you trusted your brother's judgement."

"My brother's judgement has always been clouded when it comes to you."

"I suppose a 'see you soon' would be inappropriate, then?"

The expression on Hikaru's face is as severe as she has ever seen.

"Miss Nocturne, I don't care where you go. I don't care what you do, but let me be clear when I advise you not to return here."

Wren's hand extends forward to collect the ignition key and credit chip.

"Crystal."

It's better this way, Wren thinks as she revs up the cycle, Hikaru looking on from the top of the garage, arms crossed and stance unyielding.

PRELUDE

The sun hasn't even risen yet.

Wren can't begrudge him this. Not really. He's right in any case.

The cut on her arm still bleeds, and the cost to make it stop is not something she is willing to share with anyone, so she rides out into the yawning darkness of gloomtide, alone once again.

Ever alone.

And even though her heart aches, she does not let the tears fall.

Epilogue

THE KING OF SWORDS

THE MONITORS IN THE JADE APARTMENTS alight at the usual time their master commands them on. AYA's monitoring systems activate fully to prepare for her master's day to properly begin.

"Good morning, Miyazaki-sama."

Kai sighs as wakefulness trickles in. He feels heavy and warm, unwound in a way he hasn't felt in years. Loose-limbed and pleasantly sleep-soaked having stayed up late into the night minding a certain witch. His muscles ache, sore from more pleasurable activities, as he rolls over, eyes still shut, toward the opposite side of the bed. Still drowsy, he reaches out a hand, expecting to find Wren's warmth, only to encounter cooled sheets instead.

"Wren?"

His hand trails up and down as his eyes open to confirm his lover has indeed risen already, though her scent still lingers on the pillows.

Other than the buzz of various devices, it's quiet. Too quiet.

Kai rises, pulling on a pair of trousers before moving to locate his missing witch. She is not in the bedroom or the en suite, though there are bloody bandages in the bin. She hadn't been bleeding last night. Did one of the cuts on her arm reopen?

Worry starts to edge at him as he enters the sitting area.

One of the computers shows a search history, but he doesn't go to investigate quite yet. The table and floor have been picked up, and judging by the haphazard way things have been set on the tabletop, he can safely assume Wren was the one to do so rather than one of AYA's housekeeping drones.

Wren is absent from the space, no sign of her.

He swallows down the stitch forming in his throat.

Wren's tarot cards sit untouched on the table, The Lovers card still face-up at the top of the deck. Next to it is the locket Wren has carried with her since her resurrection. Wren wouldn't have left them behind, not unless...

"AYA, where is Wren?"

AYA answers, and Kai takes a moment to process what his A.I. tells him.

He dresses calmly, forgoing the more formal attire he would normally wear for a meeting with his brother and donning his battle leathers and riding gear instead. He does not contact Hikaru. He does not contact Fumiko. He will not be telling them where he is going.

Twelve years ago, he would have angered at his brother's actions. Twelve years ago, 'anger' didn't even begin to describe what he felt when Hikaru's good intentions cost him the love of his life.

Now though... Resignation. He was foolish to think his brother had grown at all in the last twelve years.

"You've maintained a relationship with her all this time!"

"She has been in total control since leaving the League."

"You think she has been in control. You can't know that."

"I know."

"You know nothing, brother. Your judgement is clouded by affections that are naught but illusions at this point. The child can come with us, but that thing behind you isn't capable of love anymore. Return to Murasaki at once."

THE KING OF SWORDS

"I don't believe that, and I will not."

"Then you leave me no choice."

The scar on his chest, long healed, aches at the memory.

Kai has had twelve years of wondering what he could have done differently. Twelve years of regret. Twelve years of loneliness. Twelve years of grief. Wren died, and life moved forward. Time, unyielding in the face of death, had continued to tick on, putting her firmly in the past. A nightmare best forgotten and a dream he never wanted to wake from. Ashes in the wind.

But by some miracle, Wren, his witch, has returned to him. Impossibly alive. Returned to him in a rat-infested asylum on the 32nd day in the Month of Fire. Her touch still lingers on his skin. Her whispered confession dances through his heart.

He'll be damned if he lets that die again.

There is a storm brewing on the horizon. It surges and lashes at his meridians. A storm is coming, and if Wren is the center of its eye, he will be the barricade that keeps the flood from rising while she calms its rage.

He collects Wren's tarot deck and the locket from the table, carefully stowing them in his utility belt. He commands AYA to shut down the Jade Wing, then transfers her into his visor. He locks up the apartments, granting access to Renki and Renki alone should the teen come looking for him. Who is he kidding? He knows Renki will come looking for him, for Wren, for both of them. (He hasn't told her yet. She needs to know.) The boy is as intuitive as his mother and twice as stubborn. He'll explain everything to him later.

First, he has a witch to find.

LA FINE DE *PRELUDE*

Wren and Kaito's song will continue in
SONATA
Book 2 of The Nocturne Symphony

GLOSSARY OF CHARACTERS BY FACTION

Deriva:
- Tlanextli Moctezumo – Vulcan of Deriva – Father of Atzi and Xipilli Moctezumo with his first wife, Elisabeta De Claré and Wren Nocturne with his second wife, Freya Nocturne
- Elisabeta De Claré – Vulcana of Deriva – Mother of Atzi and Xipilli Moctezumo
- Freya Nocturne – Second Wife of Tlanextli Moctezumo – Firefly and Mother of Wren Nocturne
- Atzi Moctezumo – Princess of Deriva – Eldest daughter of Tlanextli and wife of Chike Nagi. Mother of Zenza Nagi
- Xipilli Moctezumo – Current Vulcan of Deriva – 247th Trials Graduate – Wren's older half-brother
- Wren Nocturne – The youngest child of Tlanextli Moctezumo – 247th Trials Graduate – Known Alias: The Songstress of Lorelei
- Quetzal – Captain of Xipilli's Guard and technomancer of Deriva
- Zenza Nagi – Princess of Deriva – Wren and Xipilli's niece via their elder sister
- Irene – A Landless technomancer who graduated with Wren and Xipilli. Declared loyalty to Deriva.

Prelude

Murasaki no Yama:

- Mirai Miyazaki – Empress of Murasaki no Yama – Mother of Hikaru and Kaito Miyazaki
- Fumiko Miyazaki – Grandmaster of Shinka Temple's Adept Training Program – Twin sister of Mirai and aunt to Hikaru and Kaito
- Hikaru Miyazaki – Current Emperor of Murasaki no Yama – Elder brother of Kaito
- Kaito Miyazaki – Crown Prince of Murasaki no Yama – 247th Trials Graduate – Younger son of Mirai Miyazaki
- Akari – Miyazaki trainee under Kaito's tutelage
- Renki – Miyazaki trainee under Kaito's tutelage
- Tojirou – Technomancer under the Miyazaki family
- Tanaka–Technomancer under the Miyazaki family

Ebele:

- Absko Nagi – Orisha of Ebele – Father of Chike and Chiamaka Nagi
- Chike Nagi – Crown Prince of Ebele – 247th Trials Graduate – Husband of Atzi Moctezumo and Father to Zenza Nagi
- Chiamaka Nagi – Princess of Ebele – Younger sister to Chike Nagi and Zenza's paternal aunt

Sekhmeti:

- Rameses Sahra – Pharaoh of Sekhmeti – Father of Jamar Sahra
- Jamar Sahra – Crown Prince of Sekhmeti – 247th Trials Graduate

Seraphim:

- Howard P. Thames – Pontiflex Catalan of Seraphim – Religious leader of Seraphim and father to Donarick Thames
- Donarick J. Thames – Son of the pontiflex

Glossary Of Characters By Faction

- Archibald Llywelyn – General of Seraphim – Father of Oswald Llywelyn
- Oswald Llywelyn – Son of Archibald Llywelyn
- Montwyatte – Archibald's right-hand man

Aighneas:
- Morrigan "The Morrigan" Gewalt – President of Aighneas
- Rihannon Gewalt – Younger sister to The Morrigan
- Arturo Lionheart – 247th Trials Graduate – Student of The Morrigan
- Heather Ables – A student of The Morrigan

Hexen:
- Yggfret Bloodfang – The Goblin King
- Summer Helsdottir – Witch
- Xena – Vampyre
- Zero – Shifter
- Jessabelle – Witch

Stonehearst Asylum:
- Dr. Johannes Faust – Head Doctor
- Malcolm – Human+ Patient Handler
- Eugene Winnifred – Asylum Director
- Harriet Favreau – Asylum Head Nurse
- Atalia Vaishi – Asylum inmate who led a group of patients to summon Wren back from the dead.

Notable Weapons of Deus:
- Mångata – Wren's Ætherkalis
- Lacuna – Wren's Soul-Eating Athame
- Tsukuyomi – Kaito's Katana
- Amatsu – Kaito's Tanto
- Opochtli – Xipilli's Trident
- Agni – Chike's Blast Rifle – Currently in use by Zenza

ABOUT THE AUTHOR

LYRA R. SAENZ IS A WRITER OF SCIENCE Fiction/Fantasy. A romantic at heart with a love for supernatural horror, she believes that while happy endings don't come easily, they do come, even if it means excising your ex into a glass jar.

Born and raised in South Texas, Lyra is a multicultural, eyeliner-wielding member of the LGBTQ+ community, an animal-lover, and a cynic of all things political. She presently haunts the Houston area with her amazingly supportive partner and her feline-shaped void, Violet. Lyra grew up bouncing between her Chicano and Scandinavian heritages never feeling like she really fit in one world or the other.

Despite growing up on enchiladas and lefsa, she'll never turn down an offering of sushi or pho. And while her friends were getting boyfriends and girlfriends, she was too busy crushing on dreamy anime and manhwa characters to bother with real people. So with one foot on either side of the border and her head full of East-Asian pop culture, she started creating her own worlds.

A lover of all things witchy, paranormal, and ghostly with a side of Victorian-futurism, cyberpunk, and posthumanism, Lyra imagines worlds where the IT tech is a werewolf and the coffee machine has a fairy living inside it but the androids love to take walks down the forest trail and host the occasional bonfire. When she isn't lost somewhere between an inkwell and a notebook, she can be found acting as a throne for the real queen of the household -Her cat and her royal majesty demands snuggles constantly. Or sitting and listening to her partner play video games while she unsuccessfully knits and/or binges her latest international tv show.

https://www.bookwitchsaenz.com/

Facebook: BookWitch.Saenz

Twitter: BookWitch_Saenz

Instagram: BookWitch_Saenz

BookWitchSaenz@gmail.com

MORE BOOKS...

Prelude

Falsetto in the Woods

Ragtime Swing

Sonata

Song of the Sea

The Devil's Trill

Bercuese

To Heal a Songbird

Ghost March

Nocturne

4 Horsemen Publications
Romance

Ann Shepphird
The War Council

Emily Bunney
All or Nothing
All the Way
All Night Long
All She Needs
Having it All
All at Once
All Together
All for Her

Lynn Chantale
The Baker's Touch
Blind Secrets

Mimi Francis
Private Lives
Second Chances
Run Away Home
The Professor

Fantasy & Paranormal Romance

Beau Lake
The Beast Beside Me
The Beast Within Me
The Beast After Me
The Beast Like Me
An Eye for Emeralds
Swimming in Sapphires
Pining for Pearls

D. Lambert
To Walk into the Sands
Rydan
Northlander
Esparan
King
Traitor
His Last Name

J.M. Paquette
Klauden's Ring
Solyn's Body
The Inbetween
Hannah's Heart
Call Me Forth
Invite Me In

Valerie Willis
Cedric: The Demonic Knight
Romasanta: Father of Werewolves
The Oracle: Keeper of the
Gaea's Gate
Artemis: Eye of Gaea
King Incubus: A New Reign

V.C. Willis
Prince's Priest
Priest's Assassin

Cozy Mysteries

Ann Shepphird

Destination: Maui
Destination: Monterey

Horror, Thriller, & Suspense

Erika Lance

Jimmy
Illusions of Happiness
No Place for Happiness
I Hunt You

Young Adult Fantasy

Blaise Ramsay

Through The Black Mirror
The City of Nightmares
The Astral Tower
The Lost Book of the Old Blood
Shadow of the Dark Witch
Chamber of the Dead God

C.R. Rice

Denial
Anger
Bargaining
Depression
Acceptance
Broken Beginnings: Story of Thane
Shattered Start: Story of Sera
Sins of The Father: Story of Silas
Honorable Darkness: Story of
Hex and Snip
A Love Lost: Story of Radnar